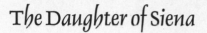

The Daughter of Siena

Also by Marina Fiorato

The Glassblower of Murano

The Botticelli Secret

The Daughter of Siena

MARINA FIORATO

St. Martin's Griffin
New York

THE DAUGHTER OF SIENA. Copyright © 2011 by Marina Fiorato. All rights reserved. Printed in the United States of America. For information, address St. Martin's Press, 175 Fifth Avenue, New York, N.Y. 10010.

www.stmartins.com

Library of Congress Cataloging-in-Publication Data

Fiorato, Marina.
    The daughter of Siena : a novel / Marina Fiorato.—1st ed.
      p. cm.
    ISBN 978-0-312-60432-5—ISBN 978-0-312-60958-0 (pbk.) 1. Palio di Siena (Festival)—Fiction. 2. Horse racing—Fiction. 3. Young women—Italy—Fiction. 4. Siena (Italy)—Fiction. 5. Italy—History—1559–1789—Fiction. I. Title.
  PR6106.I67D38 2011
  823'.92—dc22

2011003165

First published in Great Britain by John Murray (Publishers), an Hachette UK Company

First U.S. Edition: May 2011

10 9 8 7 6 5 4 3 2 1

To my sister Veronica and her husband Richard Brown
who know a thing or two about horses

The Daughter of Siena

Siena

1723

The Donkey

Two gentlemen of Siena stared down at a stinking corpse that had been flung over the wall at the Camollia gate.

'Is it a horse?' asked the younger, for the body was so decomposed it was hard to tell.

'No, it's a donkey,' answered his elder.

'Hmm.' The youth was thoughtful. 'Whatever can it mean?'

'Well,' said the other, who was pleased to be asked, and whose air of the greybeard who knew it all did not endear him to his friends, 'in 1230 the Florentines who besieged Siena used to throw the corpses of donkeys over the city walls. They hoped the carcasses would bring pestilence and plague.'

The youth pulled his neckerchief swiftly over his nose and mouth. 'Jesu. D'you think this one is diseased? It stinks enough.'

'*Dio*. It's not the olden days. Someone's ass died and they dumped it. No more, no less.'

His companion craned upwards and stroked the beard

that he one day wished to have. 'I don't know. Look; there's some blood and skin on the top of the gate. This fellow was thrown over. Should we tell someone?'

'Like who?'

'Well, I don't know. . . the duchess? The council, then? Or the Watch?'

The older man turned towards his young companion. He had never known the lad to question with him and felt justified in hardening his tone just a little.

'The Watch?' he scoffed. 'On the eve of the Palio? D'you not think they might have better things to worry about than a dead donkey?'

The boy hung his head. He supposed he was right. It was the Palio tomorrow and the whole city was a ferment of excitement, a ferment that sometimes bubbled over into violence. Nevertheless, he walked backwards for a little until he could no longer see the grisly heap. Intensely superstitious, like all Sienese, he could not help thinking that the donkey was an ill omen for the city. Uneasy little thoughts gathered round his head like the flies that rose from the corpse.

I

The Owlet

For her nineteenth birthday, Pia Tolomei, the most beautiful woman in Siena, was given a necklace and a husband.

Her name-day was spent sitting quietly in her chamber, a day like any other – the same, the same, the same. But then Pia's maid told her that her father wished to see her and she knew exactly what was coming. She'd been awaiting this moment since she was eleven.

She laid down her hoop of embroidery with a shaking hand and went down to the *piano nobile* at once. Her knees shook too as they carried her slight and upright form down the stair, but she had courage. She knew it was time to face what she had dreaded for years, for as long as she had been old enough to understand the expediencies of the marriage market.

For eight years Pia had expected, daily, to be parcelled up and handed in marriage to some young sprig of Sienese nobility. But fate had kept her free until now. Pia knew that her father would not marry her beyond her ward, the contrada of the Civetta, the Owlet. And here she had been fortunate, for the male heirs of the good Civetta families were few. A boy that she was betrothed to in the cradle had died of the water fever. Another had gone to the wars and married abroad. The only other heir she could think of had just turned fifteen. She had a notion her father had been waiting for this lad to reach his majority. She went downstairs now, fully expecting that she was about to be shackled to a child.

In the great chamber her father Salvatore Tolomei stood in a shaft of golden light streaming in through the windows. He had always had an instinct for the theatrical. He waited until she approached him and laid her cool kiss upon his cheek, before he pulled a glittering gold chain from his sleeve with a magician's flourish. He laid it in her palm where it curled like a little serpent and she saw that there was a roundel, or pendant, hanging from it.

'Look close,' Salvatore said.

Pia obeyed, humouring him, masking the impatience she felt rising within her. She saw a woman's head depicted on a gold disc, decapitated and floating.

'It is Queen Cleopatra herself,' whispered Salvatore with awe, 'on one of her own Egyptian coins. It is more than a thousand years old.'

His ample form seemed to swell even further with pride. Pia sighed inwardly. She had grown up being told, almost daily, that the ancestors of the Tolomei were Egyptian royalty, the Ptolemy. Salvatore Tolomei – and all the Civetta capitani before him – never stopped telling people of the famous Queen Cleopatra from whom he was directly descended.

Pia felt the great weight of her heritage pressing down on her and looked at the long-dead queen almost with pity. That her long, illustrious royal line should distil itself down into Pia, the Owlet, daughter and heir to the house of the Owls! Pia was queen of nothing but the Civetta contrada, sovereign of a quiet ward in the north of Siena, regent of a collection of ancient courtyards and empress of a company of shoemakers.

'And on the other side?'

Pia turned the coin over and saw a little owl in gold relief.

'Our own emblem, and hers; the emblem of Minerva, of Aphrodite, of Civetta.'

She looked up at her father, waiting for the meat of the matter. She knew he never gave without expectation of return.

'It is a gift for your name-day, but also a dowry,' said he. 'I have spoken with Faustino Caprimulgo of the Eagle contrada. His son, Vicenzo, will take you in marriage.'

Pia closed her hand tight around the coin until it bit. She felt a white-hot flame of anger thrill through her. She had not, of course, expected to choose her own husband, but she had hoped in her alliance with the Chigi boy that she could school him a little, to become the most that she could wish for in a husband; to treat her with kindness and leave her alone. How could her father do this? She had always, always done as Salvatore asked, and now her reward was to be a marriage to a man she not only knew to be reviled, but a man from another contrada. It was unheard of.

She knew Vicenzo by repute to be almost as villainous and cruel as his father, the notorious Faustino Caprimulgo. The Caprimulgo family, captains of the Eagle contrada, was one of the oldest in Siena, but the nobility of the antique family was not reflected in its behaviour. Their crimes were many – they were a flock of felons, a murder of Eagles. Pia was too well bred to seek out gossip but the stories had still reached her ears: the murders, the beatings, Vicenzo's numerous violations of Sienese women. Last year a girl had hanged herself from her family's ham-hook. She was barely out of school. 'With child,' Pia's maid had said. 'Another Eagle's hatchling.' Apparently Salvatore could overlook such behaviour in the light of an advantageous match.

'Father,' she said, 'I cannot. You know what they say of him – what happened to the Benedetto girl. And he is an Eagle. Since when did an Eagle and an Owlet couple?'

In her mind she saw these two birds mating to create a dreadful hybrid, a chimera, a griffon. Wrong, all wrong. Salvatore's face went still with anger and at the same instant she heard the scrape of a boot behind her.

He was here.

Pia turned slowly, a horrible chill creeping over her flesh, as Vicenzo Caprimulgo walked forth from the shadows.

A strange trick of light caught his nose and eyes first. A beak and two beads – like the stuffed birds in her father's hunting lodge. His thin mouth was curved in a slight smile.

'I am sorry, truly, that the match does not please you.' His voice was calm and measured, with only a whisper of threat. 'Your father and I have a very particular reason for this alliance between our two contrade. But I am sure I can. . .persuade you to think better of me, when you know me better.'

Pia opened her mouth to say that she had no wish to know him better, but she was too well bred to be insolent, and too afraid to speak her mind.

'It's something you can do at your leisure, for your father has agreed that we will marry on the morrow, after the Palio, which I intend to win.'

He came close and she could feel his breath on her cheek. She had never been this close to a man save her father.

'And I assure you, mistress, that there are certain arenas in which I can please you much better than a fifteen-year-old boy.'

The malice in his eyes was unmistakable. There was something else there too: a naked desire, which turned her bones to water. She shoved straight past him and back up the stairs to her chamber, her father's apologies raining in her ears. He was not apologizing to her, but to Vicenzo.

Alone in her chamber, Pia paced the floor, fists clenched, blood pounding in her head. Below she could hear the final preparations being made for the celebratory feast she had believed was for her own name-day. How could her life be overturned in this way?

Several times during the evening Salvatore sent servants to knock at her door. She ignored them: the celebrations would go on whether she was there or not. Despairing and frightened, she sat huddled in a chair as dusk fell, hungry and shivering, although it was not cold.

Eventually her father came himself and she could not refuse his bidding. She was to take a turn about the courtyard with Vicenzo, he said, to admire the sunset. The servants were all inside. It would be a chance for her to get to know her husband.

Pia did as she was commanded and walked Vicenzo to his horse as the sinking sun gilded the ancient stones. Still frozen by shock, she made no attempt to converse with him, and by the time they had crossed the courtyard his sallies and courtesies had turned to scorn and provocation. Numbly, she observed how the shadows of twilight closed around her. She took him, unspeaking, to the loggia where his horse was tied and waited silently for him to mount. Suddenly he lunged at her, spinning her behind the darkest pillar. His hungry lips mouthed at her neck and his greedy hands snatched at her breasts.

'Come,' he whispered viciously, 'the contracts are inked, you are nearly mine, so nearly.'

She fought him then, desperately crying out, although there was no one to hear, striking him about the face and chest. Her struggles only seemed to madden him more, and when he grabbed her by the hair and threw her through the half-door of the stable she thought she was lost. She smelled the warm straw and tasted the tang of blood where she'd bitten her cheek. But Vicenzo seemed to check himself.

'Stay pure, then, for one more night,' he spat, as he stood over her, 'for tomorrow I'll take you anyway.' He turned in the doorway. 'And never strike me again.'

Then he kicked her, repeatedly, not about her peerless face, but on her body, so the bruises would be hidden under her clothes.

When at last he was gone the shock hit her and she retched, great dry heaves, into the straw. In the warm dark she could hear the Civetta horses, snorting and shifting, curious.

She straightened up, aching, and walked directly out of the courtyard straight to the Civetta church across the piazza. She laid her hands on the heavy doors that she had passed through for years, for her christening, confirmation and shrift. Tonight she did not tenderly lift the latch but hurled the oak doors open so they slammed back against the pilasters, sending angry *echoes through the belly of the old church. She ran to the Lady Chapel and there her legs gave way, her knees cracking on the cold stone. She prayed and prayed, the pendant pressed hard between her palms. Not once did she look up at the images of the Christ or Mary; she was calling on far more ancient deities for help. She thought it more likely that the antique totem between her hands could help her. She prayed for something to happen, some calamity to release her from this match. When she opened her hands there was the imprint of Cleopatra on one palm and the owlet on the other.*

The Palio.

A year of planning, ten men, ten horses, three circuits of the piazza, and all of it over in one single moment.

No outsider could conceive of – let alone understand – what the Palio meant to the Sienese. That they ate it, breathed it, slept it. That they prayed to their saints for victory every day, the year round. That all their loyalties, their colours and their *contrade* proceeded from the Palio, as the web radiates from the spider. The concentric circles of their customs and society originated from this piazza and this day, and this smallest circle of all – the racetrack. Scattered with the dust of tufa stone hewn from the Tuscan hills, run by Sienese-born men on Sienese-bred horses, right under the ancient palaces and towers of the old city. The Palio was the centre; the Palio was Siena. To know this was to know all.

On the second day of July 1723, Siena was punishingly hot. But, despite the heat, the numbers assembled to catch a glimpse of the Palio di Provenzano seemed greater than ever. On other days the beauteous shell-shaped Piazza del Campo lay as serene and empty as a Saint Jacques scallop, but today it was crammed with a thousand Sienese, drumming their drums and waving their flags. Every other place in the city was empty: every street, every courtyard, every dwelling, church and ale-house. The courtrooms were deserted, the apothecaries closed. The bankers had put away their tables and the tailors had pulled down their blinds. At the hospital-church of Santa Maria Maddalena the sisters instructed the orderlies to carry their patients in litters to the piazza. Even the starlings gathered to watch the Palio in the hot blue circle of sky high over the track. They wheeled around the tower-tops, to gather in smoky clouds and break apart again, dissipating like ink in water, all the time screeching with excitement.

Everyone had their role on this day of days, from the greatest degree to the least. At the very top, on the bal-cony of the great Palazzo Pubblico, with its crenellations of terracotta teeth and tall clock tower, stood the govern-ess of the city. Duchess Violante Beatrix de' Medici, fifty and plain with it, presided over the race with great dignity and grace, as she had done for ten years now since the death of her husband.

Below her the *capitani*, the captains of the *contrade,* were in final clandestine counsel with their deputies. These were the greybeards, the chiefs of their families;

silver heads bent close as they discussed their final pacts and *partiti*. Their faces, weathered and lined, had seen it all, and they knew the city and her ways.

The *fantini*, the jockeys, dressed in silks of colour so bright that they stung the eye, were being given their *nerbi* whips, vicious lengths of stretched oxhide, which they would shortly use not only on their horses but on each other. These young men, the flower of Sienese youth, were alive with tension, their black eyes glittering, their muscles taut. Fights, both verbal and physical, broke out in little volcanic pockets along their lines. To a man they had abstained from the pleasures of their wives and lovers for weeks now, to prepare in body and mind for the race.

Ill-disguised betting syndicates signalled across the crowd in their secret ciphers, street sellers brought skins of wine or dried meats to those who had been in this square since sunrise, canny fan sellers sold paper fans in the *contrada* colours to their members. The Palio band repeated obsessively the solemn notes of the Palio anthem, a task they would not leave off now until tomorrow's dawn, each musician sure of his harmony and his counterpoint.

Even tiny children flew the bright flags of their *contrada*, trying to emulate their older brothers, those princes of swagger the *alfieri*, who, in the main parade, tossed their larger flags so high and so skilfully. The little orphan boy and water-carrier known as Zebra – so-called because he wore the black-and-white colours of the city, not of any *contrada*, showing allegiance to no one and everyone – trotted busily back and forth, bringing wooden goblets for the thirsty in exchange for coin, sure-footed of mission and purpose.

The horses too, mere dumb beasts, circled in readiness. Their bridles were bright with streamers, their manes woven with ribbons, their saddles hung with pennants. They were led in rein but knew that they would soon be loosed to race, and must win for the colours that they bore.

Pia of the Tolomei felt lowlier than all of these. As a betrothed woman she was not afforded the respect that she had known when she was a marriage prize – a renowned beauty to be bargained for and bartered over by the well-to-do families of the Civetta. She was now merely a spectator, required to cheer for her betrothed and nothing more. But Pia of the Tolomei had no intention of fulfilling that role. Yes, she was going to watch her betrothed ride in the Palio, but she would not be cheering for him. Pia of the Tolomei would be praying that during the course of it he would be killed.

For tonight she was to be wed to Vicenzo Caprimulgo in the basilica. For the last time she was wearing the red and black of the Civetta *contrada*. Her bruises were hidden under a girdle in the same Owlet colours around her handspan waist and her lustrous black hair was piled high under her hat. She was seated, as she had been for the last nineteen summers and thirty-eight Palios, on the elevated benches of the Owlet *contrada* next to her father. Mindful of this position, this upbringing and her aching ribs, Pia was trying not to cry, for by the next Palio, the

Palio dell'Assunta in August, Pia would be sitting across the square, as Vicenzo's wife, wearing the black-and-gold plumage of the Eagles. She would graduate up the order of birds of prey to the very top.

All about her she could feel the mounting excitement, almost palpable, like a current of air or a haze of heat, but she felt completely outside of it. Pia had been born in Siena and had scarcely been outside the city. Tuscany had a coast but she had never seen the sea. Yet despite her hermetic existence in her *contrada*, her nineteen years bound by the city walls, today for the first time she felt that she did not belong. By reason of her betrothal she was no longer an Owlet but was not yet an Eagle; she was an odd, vestigial, avian genus. An aberration.

In Siena every citizen was a product of their *contrada*. Their identity began with their ward and ended where the Dragon *contrada* became the She-Wolf, or the Unicorn became the Tower. Pia was familiar with the colours of each ward or *contrada* from the red-and-blue of the Panther to the yellow-and-green of the Caterpillar. And twice a year these divisions of geography and hue assumed an even greater significance.

In a few short hours the bitterness of loss would settle like a pall over the losing *contrada* and delirious joy would infect every soul in the winning ward. Vicenzo, she knew, would give anything to win today. In the horse draw, which took place some days before the race, he had drawn Berio, a big, handsome bay whispered to be the fastest horse in Tuscany, the horse that every *contrada* prayed to draw. As Vicenzo was reputed to be the fastest rider in the city, his chances were very good. And if he did win, thought Pia, how would his triumph manifest itself in their marriage chamber? Only this race, lasting three score and ten heartbeats, could prolong the life of her maidenhead. She shuddered.

Pia sat forward in an attempt to engage herself in the spectacle below. She watched as the horses and riders circled the track, following the Civetta colours out of habit, when her eye was caught by a lone horseman. He was walking his mount slowly, and with complete control, through the Bocca del Casato gate, the arch of the architrave framing him like a painted angel.

The horseman was a stranger to Pia. He was also the most beautiful living human she had ever seen. He had the olive skin of the region, a full mouth set in a stern and concentrated line but with the promise of softness. He had dark curling hair caught in the pigtail fashion of the day with a ribbon of the Torre colours of the Tower *contrada*. His eyes were dark and his features those of antique statuary – sculpted marble perfection. His form was well proportioned and muscular, his legs long and his hands gentle on the horse. But there was more too: he seemed noble. If nobility were to do with the new science of physiognomy rather than birth, reflected Pia, then he should be sitting on the palace balcony above her head, not the homely duchess.

Pia had escaped into books for the whole of her childhood and despite Vicenzo's violence yesterday she still believed in courtly love – perhaps now even more so. But she did not immediately cast the stranger in the role of all the Tristans, Lancelots and Rolands of whom she had read. She was too much of a realist to imagine that anyone high-born loved where they married.

She did, however, allow herself to wonder, just for a moment, how it would feel if she was betrothed to that unknown horseman and not Vicenzo. Better yet, if only he could ride for her as her champion, that courtly ideal of centuries ago, with none of the very real and physical threats that marriage promised. She would not have to touch him, nor even meet him. Touch, she now knew, was dangerous. To yearn at a blessed distance: that would be the thing. What would it be like, she wondered idly, to sit in her loge, watching that horseman ride for *her*, with perhaps some token of her favour hanging about his neck or twisted in his horse's mane?

When the unknown horseman dismounted with the other jockeys to pay the traditional tribute to the duchess, he stood next to Vicenzo. In an apt allegory for his *contrada* the horseman of the Torre towered over his rival from the Eagle ward. Vicenzo did not, Pia reflected, compare well. The *fantini*, the jockeys, lined up below Duchess Violante's balcony, each one eyeing her with matching insolence, in a pantomime of resistance to the Medici overlords that had been enacted for ten years now, ever since the duchess had come to the city.

All save one.

The unknown horseman alone of the pack slid his tricorne from his head and fixed his eyes to the ground with something akin to respect for the duchess's sex, if not for her rank. Pia's heart warmed a little, but chilled again when she turned her eyes on her betrothed. Vicenzo was peering up at the duchess with marked insolence. He had not removed his tricorne. How she *hated* him, Pia thought. This tiny thing, that he could not remove his hat for a lady – this elementary lack of good breeding – invited her contempt almost more than the outrages he had visited on her last night.

Next to Vicenzo stood his father. Faustino Caprimulgo, captain of the Eagle *contrada,* was tall and wiry, dark and swarthy of feature but with the whitest hair curled in a close cap to his head. His high cheekbones, cavernous cheeks and long, hooked nose made him resemble nothing so much as the eagle of his banner. Faustino always stood drawn up to his full height, an eagle in his eyrie, with the confidence that came from being the head of the oldest family in Siena. Despite the pomp and posturing of the Medici, all of Siena knew that in reality it was the Caprimulgi who ruled the city. They had ruled it in the days of the Nine – the ruling council of the old republic – and ruled it in all but name still. The son stood shoulder to shoulder with his father, fixing the duchess with the same hawklike stare, a merlin beside a falcon, a smaller, meaner version of the sire.

Pia watched as the war chariot of the Palio drew up alongside the palace, drawn by four milk-white oxen carrying the Palio itself – a vast black-and-white banner in the colours of the city, emblazoned with the figures of the Virgin and the pope. Attendants folded and handed the flag to last year's victor, Ghiberti Conto, captain of the Snail *contrada*, who knocked three times and was admitted to the palace doors. Moments later he appeared on the balcony next to the duchess and gave up the banner to her. The duchess took it with a nod – custodian for a few short moments before she would give it to this year's victor. Pia, without feeling the slightest disloyalty, reached for the coin of the Owlet where it hung around her neck and prayed that the winner would be the unknown horseman and not Vicenzo.

Pia sat forward and searched for the horseman in the Tower colours among the other jockeys below at the *canapi* starting ropes, all detachment gone. She saw the *fantini* whisper to each other from the sides of their mouths, last-minute threats or promises, as their bright silks whispered too. At this moment pacts were being made or broken as vast amounts of money changed hands. The other horses were circling and bumping shoulders; one reared and threw its rider – the green-and-white Oca colours of the Goose *contrada*, she noted, not he.

She realized that the stranger must have been drawn as the *di rincorsa* rider in the outside position at the ropes, and so it proved. He rode to the cord later than the others, but seemed to have no interest in the benefits of his good fortune. Usually the *di rincorsa* position was used to an unscrupulous jockey's advantage, to jostle rival *contrade* into a bad position at the start. But Pia saw him, seated absolutely still on his horse's bare back, speaking to no one, his eyes seeing far into the distance, making no attempt to jostle or harry. His stallion also stood unmoving amid the mêlée, the pair resembling in their stillness the bronzes of the mounted Cosimo the Great that she had seen on her one and only trip to Florence. Pia willed him to beat Vicenzo with a violence that surprised her, her eyes boring into his broad back, staring so hard at the blue-and-burgundy silks that they blurred.

There was the customary confusion at the start of the race. As the horses circled and reared, the *mossiere* or starter judge called false start after false start. Then finally, in a moment of almost unbearable tension, the horses lined up and stilled as if bade by an invisible command. The yells and screams of the crowd abated for one eerie, silent second, and the unaccustomed tongue of the great bell Sunto sounded in the Torre del Mangia above Pia's head. Silent from one Palio to the next, the bell's song bawled out above the city, to tell that the hour had come. All heads turned and all gazes swivelled up – for it was said that the *bandierino* weathervane on the Mangia Tower would turn in that last breath of wind to the quarter of the city that was to be favoured with victory. The bronze arrow quivered toward the duomo in the Eagle *contrada*, and the cheers from that ward almost drowned the last chimes of the bell. Pia swallowed, sickened at the omen. But the time for reflection was up. At the stroke of seven, Sunto stopped ringing and the little *mortaretto* firecracker cannon sounded at the starting rope; ten horses leaped forth from the *entrone*, and they were off.

It was impossible for anyone who had not been here, thought Pia, to know that blood-curdling roar of the crowd, to feel the thunder of the hooves shiver your very ribs, to smell the sweat and the straw in your nose and taste the tufa dust in your mouth. The horses went by in a whirlwind, their flanks gleaming and polished with sweat, their mouths flecked with foam, past the *palazzo*, thundering up the curve to the Bocca del Casato. She could see the Tower colours – her champion was ahead, nudging shoulder to shoulder with Vicenzo.

By the second lap Vicenzo had pulled clear by three, four horses and was past the deadly San Martino corner – a treacherous slope truncated by the sharp stone buttress of a sturdy *palazzo* – but there Vicenzo's horse was barged by the horse of the Panther party, while the Panther jockey's whip dealt Vicenzo a stinging swipe across the face. Taking advantage of this, the unknown horseman swept into the lead, while the heir to the Eagles was flung back in his saddle as his horse faltered and checked. Then, as if time had slowed, Vicenzo cartwheeled over the reins, crashed into the San Martino corner and fell in a heap. At the collective gasp of the crowd, the unknown horseman glanced back over his shoulder and, without a moment's pause, threw his legs over his horse's neck and vaulted off, landing on the dust and straw.

Pia leaned forward, her heart in her throat. For a horrible instant she thought that *she* had made this happen. She had wished that Vicenzo would be killed, but had not imagined it would look like this. From where she was sitting it looked as if Vicenzo had turned blackamoor on one whole side of his body – yet the dust of the track was white. Her own thudding pulses told her in an instant that this colour was blood. To the music of the screaming throng, the unknown horseman dodged the oncoming hooves and ran to help, picking up the crumpled man.

Vicenzo's head was at an angle that was never meant by nature, and his rescuer, doused in spraying blood, was desperately fumbling for the fractured artery. Locating the source of that dreadful fount of blood, he planted his hands firmly on Vicenzo's spurting throat. Both men were covered in gore and the dust of the track darkened beneath them like their shared shadow. As Pia looked on desperately she saw Vicenzo's bay horse Berio pass the little black-and-white *bandierino* flag that marked the finish line – prancing with glee at his victory, as if he knew that a horse could win the Palio *scosso* – without a rider.

For the second time that day the crowd was eerily silent. By now a knot of people in the Eagle colours had gathered around the fallen rider – Faustino's white head among them – joined soon by judges and marshals, an apothecary, a physician. At last the unknown horseman stood and shook his head.

Pia rose to her feet and willed herself to join that dreadful party. She stepped past her new relatives heading down to the track. Feeling, numbly, that it was somehow her duty to be with her dead betrothed, she made her way through the crowd. She was bumped and jostled and once thrown to the ground. Her brain felt slow and stupid, her limbs as heavy as if moving through dunes of sand.

She had spent nineteen years in a hothouse, a rare orchid untouched by human hand. She had been nurtured and raised and cherished as a marriage prize, and now the glass of the hothouse had been broken by her betrothal and she was exposed to the violence of the elements. As of today she lived in a physical world, a world of brutality. A world where yesterday her intended could push her down and violate her, a world where today strangers shoved her to the ground. At that moment she did not know which offence against her person was worse.

A fellow in the crowd – her father's ostler – recognized her and the red sea parted. She straightened and called upon her dignity, feeling a fraud as the people moved aside for her, knowing her for the fallen man's betrothed, anticipating and respecting a distress that she did not feel. She saw her father Salvatore on the fringe of people skirting the body. He did not reach out to her, but was deep in conference with Vicenzo's brother, a pale and strange creature – Nello, was it? As if in a dream she walked past them, right to the centre of the knot of folk, and saw her first corpse.

Pia gazed down on Vicenzo's body. She saw the broken flesh at the throat, the bone piercing through, the blood black on the dust and the foam-flecked mouth, open a little to the flies. Only yesterday that mouth had spoken in her ear with the whisper of threat, with a promise. Then, last night, he'd made good on that threat, fulfilled the promise. That mouth had fastened itself on hers, that mouth had breathed wine-stale breath into the hair at the back of her neck, as he had tried to force himself into her. Breathed and breathed until his hot gasps distilled into sour spittle and ran into her hair. Could it be true, wonderfully, terribly true, that it would never breathe again? It seemed impossible. Her forehead grew cold and her stomach lurched. Feeling as though she would faint she reached out to a solid shape for support.

It was the horse Berio. Victor and murderer. The fastest in Tuscany, the horse who'd made Vicenzo punch the air with joy when he'd drawn him in the lots. She buried her hands in Berio's black mane and lowered her clammy forehead on to the velvet bay of his neck. The horse stood under her hand, bemused, unsure; as if puzzled that no one was garlanding him with flowers, thrusting sweetmeats in his mouth. He looked curiously forlorn, shaking his head repeatedly as if bothered by a fly, looking down at Vicenzo's still body. Pia's eyes began to flood.

'Don't worry, don't worry. It wasn't your fault, it was mine,' she whispered. 'I willed it.'

As if comforted, the great bay stood still at her shoulder, whickering and nibbling the lobe of her ear. Pia, weighed down by her guilt, felt the great coil of her hair escaping in a cascade of hairpins as the horse nuzzled her; her black hair and his black mane mingled, tangled, became one. Her smart black-and-red hat slithered from her head to be trodden by Berio's great feet.

Through Berio's black mane she saw the Eagle Faustino stagger to his feet with his child in his arms. She saw the unknown horseman place a hand for an instant on the captain's shoulder, and Faustino turn to leave with his awful burden, followed by his *contrada*. The Eagles filed from the square silent as a wake, forgetting all about the banner that was theirs. Not for them the joyous victor's Te Deum in the basilica, nor a wedding; but a laying-out, a mourning and a burial. Pia felt Berio being taken from under her hand by a groom – her hair being disentangled from the long black mane by the ostler. It was as if anyone could touch her now.

As the sorry procession left, Pia felt a great burden lifted from her. She breathed out the death and the day; and relief, sweet and clean, rushed into her lungs. Abruptly freed from her contract, she did not know what to do. Her careful upbringing, all those lessons in the etiquette of her class, had not prepared her for this. Then she knew. She could go home. She turned to go back to her family, to the Civetta, to her hearth, but the barrel-like form of her father blocked her way. She reached out to Salvatore, feeling, now that she was touchable, that it was the day for a rare embrace.

Instead her father took her by the shoulders, turned her determinedly round and whispered fiercely in her nape, just exactly where Vicenzo had breathed into her. 'The Eagle still has an heir,' he hissed. 'There is a son yet living, so play your hand right.'

He propelled her, with a little push, firmly in the direction of the Eagle cortège. Her treacherous sinews gave way then, and her knees buckled, and she was caught by two men of Eagle colours. One, she knew, was Vicenzo's brother, Nello; the other, a cousin of the same blood. They grasped her by her upper arms and, in a semblance of support, marched her forth, her feet stumbling and her fancy boots dragging and scuffing in the dust. She was captive.

Pia struggled. She heard herself saying no, no, no,

repeatedly. The crowd, witnessing all, began to seethe and bubble like a cauldron with a muted hubbub of enquiry and answer, but all *contrade*, for once, were united in respect for the grief they saw before them. The poor dame couldn't accept that her betrothed was gone. She was swooning and babbling with grief. The Eagles would look after her.

In a desperate appeal Pia twisted her head round to seek the unknown horseman, but he did not mark her. Standing in the blood, as if the dark stain was now a shadow snipped from his heels, he was wiping his hands and face with his own scarf. The gore left the scarlet of his neckerchief unaltered. But everything else was changed.

As Pia was carried under the Bocca del Casato gate, the one through which the horseman had entered the arena, she felt a tug at her sleeve. Hopeful of salvation, she looked down and saw only the little water-carrier Zebra. He held something out to her in his hand, trotting to keep up with her. It was a black velvet pouch with the gold Medici arms stamped upon it, a purse of mourning alms from the duchess.

As her captors snatched the purse without a word of thanks, Pia looked back one last time, far over the heads of the multitude, to the palace balcony. She might have imagined it, but she thought the duchess had raised a hand to her – a gesture of greeting, sympathy, what? – before the shadow of the architrave swallowed her.

High above the piazza, Duchess Violante Beatrix de' Medici watched as the struggling girl disappeared from view. She rose, at last, to her feet. And the black-and-white Palio banner, unmarked, fell from her hand over the balustrade in a graceful fluttering arc, to rest in the blood and the dust.

2

The Tortoise

Duchess Violante Beatrix de' Medici was born in Bavaria, the home of the modern fairy tale. She did not hear her first story in the crook of her mother's arm, but in the schoolroom as a grammatical exercise. Soon after Violante's marriage contracts with the Medici were settled when she reached the age of twelve, her mother decided she should know a little of the language of her future home. Violante was duly set to learn an Italian folk tale called La lepre e la tartaruga:

One day a hare saw a tortoise walking slowly along and began to laugh and mock him. The hare challenged the tortoise to a race and the tortoise accepted. They agreed on a route and started off the race. The hare shot ahead and ran briskly for some time. Then, seeing that he was far ahead of the tortoise, he thought he'd sit under a tree for a while and relax before continuing the race. He sat under the tree and

*soon fell asleep. The tortoise, plodding on, overtook him and
won the race.*

Thus Violante's mother told her a fairy tale by proxy.

Violante Beatrix of Bavaria, widow of Ferdinando de'
Medici, princess of Tuscany and governess of Siena,
threw open the casement of her chamber. She had been
in the city for ten years and her chamber still did not feel
like her chamber, just as her palace did not feel like her
palace. In fact, the ducal palace where she now stood,
her grand and accustomed residence, was still known, by
every single Sienese, as the Palazzo Pubblico. The ancient
building only served to remind Violante how young the
Medici dukedom was; that Siena had ruled herself for
centuries before her, and would get along well enough
for centuries after. Nominally, she ruled here – she was
governess, duchess, regent. But her rule was a façade.

No one knew that she was still, at fifty, the same frightened little girl at her father's court who chilled inside
when her mother bade her play the dulcimer for their
guests. No one suspected that the daughter of Ferdinand
Maria, Elector of Bavaria, and Adelaida, princess of
Savoy, was shy in company, loved music more than conversation, and had a dread of public speaking that she
struggled to hide. No one understood that she had loved
Ferdinando de' Medici every single day, though he had
died without ever once loving her in return. And no one
guessed her most secret sorrow: that she mourned daily

for her stillborn twins, had lit a candle for their birthday for nineteen summers, and could have told you, if you'd asked, exactly how many years, months, days and hours old they would have been now, if they had lived. And, thanks to her failure to provide an heir for the grand dukes of Tuscany, the ailing, youthful dukedom might well die likc a sickly child. She was an aberration, a placeholder. The ancient city would wait her out.

Violante was not given to fancy or superstition, but could not help returning to a conference she had had the previous evening with her chief councillor, Francesco Maria Conti. The haughty statesman, whose sense of self-importance proceeded from being cousin to the pope himself, had come to her presence chamber with an unsettling piece of news. In his accustomed black coat and fingering his silver-topped cane, he had not quite met her eyes as he had told her that two men in the Porcupine *contrada* had found a dead ass cast over the Camollia gate. She had not understood the message until he told her, in his accustomed tones of contempt veiled in courtesy, that when the Florentines besieged Siena in the thirteenth century, they cast dead donkeys over the walls to bring disease and pestilence to the city. Baldly speaking, said Conti, the ass was a signal that Siena was about to fall. Violante had a chilling feeling that Vicenzo Caprimulgo's death was the beginning of something, perhaps the beginning of the end.

From her open window, Violante saw the servants of the *comune* clearing the piazza and scrubbing at the dark patch of blood at the San Martino corner. She moved her eyes determinedly away from the blood and concentrated on the things that had not changed. The starlings screeched, the evening air smelled fresh and cool, as the setting sun varnished the square below. She admired the golden palaces standing sentinel to the old day and the nine divisions of the great square, radiating out from the fountain to give it its scallop appearance. She remembered she had once seen a painting in one of Cosimo de' Medici's summer palaces, a painting of a woman of great beauty, with flowing red hair, rising naked from a great scallop shell floating on a blue sea, the kindly winds personified to blow her to shore on an azure wave.

Today, watching the Palio that had ended so horribly, Violante had seen a woman on the Eagle family benches: young and beautiful, with her dark hair piled high, her red-and-white gown pinched in at her tiny waist and her porcelain cheeks touched with a hint of pink on the cheekbones. Rising above the sea of flags and banners, she had seemed as calm and serene as the goddess herself. Seeing her so youthful and beautiful, the Venus of this scallop, Violante had felt a keen thrill of envy. But then, Violante had seen her leaning on the dead man's horse, and she had realized that the beauty was the dead man's betrothed, and further enquiry told her they'd been due to marry today. Her heart ached for the girl, and she felt the guilty aftertaste of her envy. She sent a purse to assuage her feelings. Violante knew the emptiness, the agony of loss, for she too had lost. *Ferdinando* – she had not meant to think of him tonight.

Violante pulled her head inside the palace, retreating inside her cool shell, hiding. She closed the window and her mind against the blood outside. She did not want to know. Her emotions were exhausted by the sudden remembrance of her dead husband and she had no compassion to spare. She walked across the room to her looking-glass, a full-length Parisian mirror; and even its dim antique reflection, so forgiving of a multitude of sins, offered her no comfort. She saw a middle-aged woman, not even a little handsome, even though she had the finest powdered wigs from Montmartre and wore a gown of lavender silk woven by the Huguenots of Spitalfields. She fingered the stuff of her skirt and saw, in the sunlight, that the age spots on her hands were beginning to freckle through the lead paste she had applied not one hour ago. The ugliness of her hands next to the beauteous mauve silk depressed her still further.

She wore purple, or one of that colour's close cousins, every day of her life, and all because of a chance remark from her now-dead husband. Ferdinando had once, in the days of courtship when he had still taken the trouble to be kind, told her that the colour was becoming to her; perhaps because the word *viola*, purple, was so close to her name Violante. It was an aside, a play on words, a thoughtless sally, and served to compliment his own linguistic acuity rather than her beauty. But it was one of the only times that he had paid her person or her name even the tiniest amount of attention. She clung to it, through the years of dismissal, of isolation, of casual or calculated cruelty in the face of his lovers. She held fast to that tiny comment and had dutifully worn violet, mauve, lavender or porphyry every day since, in the vain hope that he would, some day, notice her once again.

She clung to it, despite the fact that the jest Ferdinando should have made is that her name was closer kin to another word: *violare* – to break, to violate or even to rape; words that aptly described, in turn, his treatment of her spirit, their marriage and the one and only time they had lain together. And yet now that he was dead and she was free, Violante continued to wear violet.

She turned from the mirror, suddenly deathly tired. *Ferdinando*. Once she had started to think of him she could not stop. She did not call for her women but laid herself down on the coverlet just as she was, in her silly violet dress, and gave herself up to it. *Ferdinando*. Her remembrances of him flooded her. She was wallowing and she did not care. Tears sealed her eyes, and she slept at last.

∞

Pia was taken back to the house of the Eagles as the twilight thickened. The two kinsmen of Aquila had held her, firmly, in a bruising grip high on each of her arms. Their grasp was an insult, but she was becoming inured to this new, tactile, brutal world. She disengaged her mind from her body and began to think. She walked with them. She did not struggle now. She knew if she were to get out of this, it would be by stealth.

Why did her father, after years of hoping and waiting and negotiating with the best Civetta families, suddenly want to ally her with the Eagles, at all cost? It went against all sense, against the hundreds of years of tradition in which the *contrada* was everything: identity, family, locality. Could it really be true that, before Vicenzo's body was cold, her father was negotiating a marriage contract with the dead man's brother? She stole a sideways glance at the man who held her left arm. She could not remember seeing him before today and his looks suggested why he might have been hidden. He was a strange, freakish fellow, his features an indifferent copy of Vicenzo's, but it was his colouring that set him apart. His hair was as white as his father's, his skin as pale as whey, and his eyes, under their light lashes, pink.

As darkness fell Pia found herself in streets she did not recognize – but the design of the sconces holding the guttering flambeaux and the fluttering banners of black and gold told her she was in Eagle territory. A palace loomed out from the dark and she was half lifted over the threshold. Her consorts left her in a flagged stone hall, while they followed the menfolk and the body. A beefy maid approached, her waist bristling with a chatelaine of keys. She spoke in a Sienese dialect so thick that Pia could scarcely understand her, but she understood her nod to a nearby stairwell. She was to follow.

Instead, hardly knowing what she was doing, Pia turned and walked straight back out of the palace door. Once, she'd marched from her own house, to seek sanctuary from her betrothal. Now, she'd do anything to be back there, to be away from this dark *palazzo*, away from these alien streets: to be home. Two crossed pikes came together with a singing of metal song an inch from her nose. She turned to see the beefy maid smiling. She wagged a great finger in front of Pia's face, as close as the pikes had come and just as threatening. With her other forefinger she tinkled the ring of keys.

'Up you come, *amore*. Don't be frighted. Pretty frocks for 'un, above stairs.'

There was an obscenity in the kindness, the waving of the keys like a trinket. It was the temptation of the Devil: *come here, little girl. I've got some pretty dresses to show you, if you'll just follow me up the stair.* Pia had no choice.

The stair was dark and winding and damp. At the top of it was a chamber, tall-ceilinged, oddly shaped, with chapel-like windows, their panes still hot from the day, ruby-paned with the fire of the old sun. One oil lamp burned, its flame puny in the glory of the sunset.

There was a bed and a rug, a jug and a basin. Pia swallowed.

The maid, smiling still, clicked her tongue. 'Now there, *amore*. No blubberin'. Master says be sweetly faced for *domani*. Look there in the gardyrobe – be gowns and stuffs for ye.'

Pia opened the door of a great garderobe in the corner of a room. The action reminded her of home with a swift and stifling blow. Her mother, dead on Pia's child-bed, had lived on for her daughter only in the gowns she had left behind. Pia's father – whether from a rare flare of finer feeling, from grief, or from sheer forgetfulness – had never cleared the gowns away. As a child and then a woman, Pia had gone into her mother's garderobe every day, walking among the gowns – the velvets, the fustians, the samites – speaking to her, singing to her, playing games with her, hiding behind her skirts. Pia tried to conjure the woman she had never known, the woman who might have made her life different. Friendly gowns, they were: the crimson of good burgundy for feast days, the yellow of an egg's yolk, the green of the olive's leaf. A garde-corps too: a supple dress of tan leather for riding.

Here, in her new garderobe two gowns hung on hooks: one black, one white. Both were magnificent, stiff with jewels and embroidery, the richest things she had seen in this dour house, the first manifestation she had seen of the Eagles' great wealth.

'Black for tomorrow,' said the maid, 'white t'day after.'

She bustled to the door, knocking the oil lamp to the floor with her ample hips as she went. The flame hissed and died at once. The maid smiled and smiled. 'Now rest ye. Much to do *domani*.'

The door closed and a heartbeat later came the unmistakable turn of a key. To Pia, who had grown up with a morbid fear of being imprisoned, it was a dreadful sound. Perhaps it was because her famous ancestress, another Pia of the Tolomei, a woman who had been immortalized in Dante's *Purgatory*, had spent her last days shut in a tower. Perhaps it was because Pia had grown up in a city encircled by walls and had barely left it, not even to see the sea. Either way, she had to clench her fists to stem the wave of panic and stuff one of them in her mouth to stop herself from crying out.

Trying to be calm, Pia watched the day bleed to death outside her new chamber window. Alone except for the two gowns hanging in her wardrobe, their silks whispering a threat as they turned on their hooks. *Black for tomorrow, white the day after.*

3
The Eagle

The horseman of Siena had ridden under the eye of an eagle once before.

He was seven and was already obsessed with horses. He used to ride out at dawn, be gone for the day in the Tuscan hills, and come back at night to the Tower contrada for dinner, touched with sun, dropping in his saddle and covered in white tufa dust like a little ghost.

One morning he saw an incredible thing in those hills. As the sun rose, an eagle blotted out the light and dived like a stone, taking a lamb from a grazing flock in his great talons. With a giant beat of wings that stirred the boy's hair, he took off over the hills, disappearing over the pink and gold towers of the city with his bleating burden, like a Bible illustration. The boy was still staring, open-mouthed, when there was another flutter of wings from a nearby cypress. A smaller bird burst forth and, as if it had witnessed the capture of the lamb, landed on the back of the largest ram. There the foolish bird fluttered around with a whirr of wings, leaping and flapping and attempting to carry the ram off. Soon his claws became entangled in the ram's wool and he could not free himself.

Laughing at the spectacle, which had shifted from drama to comedy in one short moment, the little horseman slid from his saddle and ran to the ram. He arrived at the same time as the shepherd, who took his knife and cut the bird free from the greasy wool. Seeing the boy hovering close, he spread and cut the prime feathers, clipping the wings. He handed the bird to the little horseman, figuring, rightly, that the boy would not mind the black blood.

'He's yours,' said the shepherd, in thick Sienese. 'Take him home for a pet.'

Boy and bird regarded each other, the boy's eyes glittering with delight, the bird's button eyes holding an expression that was at the same time foolish and free. The boy stroked the small blue-black head with nail-bitten fingers.

'What kind of bird is he?' he called, for the shepherd had already headed back down the hill to his flock, shaking his head over the loss of the lamb. The fellow turned at the question and half his mouth smiled.

'To my certain knowledge he is a daw,' he replied. 'But he would like you to think him an eagle.'

The horseman of the Tower *contrada* had been so shaken by the events of the Palio that he slept in his father's stable with Taccola, the stallion he had ridden that day.

He could not explain, even to himself, why he would feel more comforted here than in the house and he would have been better off in his bed, for in the warm close straw, hooves galloped through his dreams and the parched bedding, which tickled his nose, merely served to remind him of the racetrack and the flood of blood that had soaked the dust. The sweet-smelling warmth of the horse's silky hide only brought back the events of a day he would rather forget. It was not the first time a man had died in his arms. But he had hoped that here, at home again after long years of absence, he would be spared such sights, such smells.

When he was shaken awake he felt relief as he recognized the little face before him. It was Zebra, dressed in his familiar black-and-white garb. The boy was well known as a go-between, carrying messages for coin, crossing, without limit, the *contrada* lines in a way that others could not. This errand, so early in the day, must have been worth much; it was barely light outside the stable door. The horseman sat and blew straw from his lips, rubbing the back of his neck.

'Zebra. What is it?'

Zebra spoke in the staccato rhythms of hoofbeats. 'The Eagle. He wants you. At his house. Before daybreak.'

'Me? Why?'

Zebra shrugged. He never needed details; his payment was reason enough.

The horseman knew well who the Eagle was. Faustino Caprimulgo, alone among all the captains, not only represented but had somehow *become* the emblem of his *contrada*. Perhaps it was the hawklike appearance; perhaps it was the ruthless predator's dispatch of those who crossed him. Perhaps it was that he could, from his own eyrie of the towers of his *palazzo*, see everything that passed in his city.

The horseman considered, his brain as slow as if stuffed with straw, as golden motes of dust drifted before his eyes in the first light of day. To refuse such a summons, even from the captain of a rival *contrada*, would be a direct insult. But to walk into the house of a man whose son had died under his hands seemed nothing but the greatest folly. What if Faustino wished to punish him for Vicenzo's death? What if he found him culpable in some way? Could the *capitano* think, as the horseman did himself (*now* he knew the terrible theme that had marched through his dream), that he could somehow have saved Vicenzo?

The horseman eyed his messenger. Zebra had been no more than seven when the horseman had left two years ago, which made him no more than nine now. The boy looked as if he had had little sleep. The night of the Palio, even a tragic one such as yesterday's, was his busiest night: missives from *fantini* or *capitani* to each other, payments to be made between syndicates, even messages between lovers of rival *contrade*. Zebra was dropping where he stood, his little beady eyes closing. The horseman hauled himself from his bed and pushed the boy down gently into the warm hollow of straw he had left. Zebra had barely bitten the coin the horseman proffered before he fell asleep, curled up like a babe. The horseman took the coin from the boy's mouth and placed it in the warm little palm, before he set out in the pre-dawn.

If he had ridden the race to the finish, he would have won and the Torre *contrada* would have been delirious with joy, still celebrating into the daylight, yet he didn't fear any repercussions, even though their hopes had been pinned to his colours and he had let them down in order to try to save a life. In fact the horseman didn't remember a time when he had ever been afraid. His earliest memories of life with his father were of being placed on horseback, even as a babe: huge towering beasts from whose broad slippery backs he fell with astonishing regularity. He had cried, but not been fearful to clamber back up next time a stallion came for shoeing. There had been no mother to pick him up, to cover him with kisses, so he had hardened under his father's watchful gaze. His mother was never a presence in their little house, for she was dead, or gone, before the child had begun to remember and his father never spoke of her.

The horseman's father, Domenico, was a man who loved horses more than he loved people. He was more than a blacksmith. As a farrier he would not only shoe the horses that came to him but he would care for their legs and feet, running his expert hands and eyes down their strong limbs with almost the same affection with which he touched or regarded his son. He would speak gently to the beasts so that even the most fearsome would stand still under the calming flow of words and gentle hands. He was well known as the man to visit for any equine ailments, from foot to fetlock.

His pride in his work would reach its peak every year at the Palio races of July and August. In fact, his demeanour changed with the seasons: in the summer, in the run-up to the races, he was happy, talkative, voluble and full of anticipation. In the winter he was withdrawn and morose, his mood black, his spirits depressed at the notion of so long to wait before his year reached its zenith. The day after the second Palio, the Palio dell'Assunta on the sixteenth day of August, was the worst, even if the Tower had been victorious.

Domenico loved his work, took pride in his horseshoes and, when it became clear that his son was a gifted rider, he began to take pride in the young horseman too. Domenico's greatest pride, though, was that he had once shod the horse of the Grand Duke Cosimo III de' Medici himself. He told, endlessly, the tale of the fabled day when he had been called to Florence to tend to the ducal stallion. This story reached its apogee when the old duke's own daughter-in-law, Violante Beatrix of Bavaria, had entered Siena in triumph as the city's new governess ten years ago. Then, as the duchess's sheen slowly faded and the old rhythms of the city reasserted themselves, the story lost some of its currency and was now rarely told. Only the closest companions would be taken aside and told about the time, back in '03, when the farrier of the Tower *contrada*, in a rare commission to Florence, had been chosen to shoe the horse of the grand duke.

The horseman trod quietly past his father's door, knowing that, even though the next Palio was little more than a month away, the old man would keep to his bed today, lying under a coverlet of depression. The horse-man did not fear, as he left his house behind, that he might never see his father again; he did not bid his beloved streets farewell, nor cross himself more fervently than usual before the church of his *contrada*. The great Piazza del Campo, yawning and vast in the dawn light, was empty save for the watchmen in their tricornes and the *comune*'s servants sweeping up the dust track. Although he turned his eyes from the dark shadow of the bloodstain that still remained at the San Martino corner, he was not afraid as he approached the Caprimulgos' ward. He was merely curious.

Curiosity had once made him seek a life outside the walls of the city and the quiet rhythms of his father's life. Curiosity had made him follow a band of cavalry on the long road south to Milazzo, fired with a sudden desire to keep the Spanish out of their peninsula. There he had joined the Austrian cavalry and, as the fastest rider, was given the pennant to carry. The first day of the second battle of Milazzo, he rode down into the valley first of all the horse, with all the exhilaration of ignorance. Above his head streamed the banner of the Hapsburgs, the great black eagle seeming to flap its wings in anticipation. Riccardo had had no idea of what was to come. That day, he had been just another daw who thought himself an eagle.

With an effort, he wrenched his mind back to the present. Today he was curious to know what the captain of the Eagles wanted with him. The wakeful starlings, in their hundreds, screeched and whirled above as they had done every day for millennia, restored to their noisy dominion once more. But the horseman read no sooth-sayer's message in the curve of their flight, no harbingers of death nor portents of evil. After Milazzo he had vowed never to be afraid again.

Riccardo's steps quickened down the steep rake of the piazza, then slowed again as he climbed the slope to the Eagle ward. The citizens of Siena were always going up a hill or down one: the city was a warren of houses and *palazzi* perched on vertiginous gradients in a town plan unchanged for centuries. Maps, yellowed at the edge for hundreds of years, still held true today. In fact, as the streets of the Eagle *contrada* closed around the horseman, and the tall and ancient houses gave respite from the rising sun, it was as if he had stepped back in time, to an earlier age. There was no one around to break the spell of old days; the alleys were silent. Above him, from every window, hung the banner of the Eagle, a black bird on a yellow ground, its beak in profile and talons outstretched to kill, like the standard he had once carried. Each flag hung still and straight from its pole like a hanged man and not a breath of breeze stirred.

Just as the horseman reached the fortified *palazzo* of the Caprimulgo family, the chapel bell tolled six. The great doors were open, and the horseman passed through. No one challenged him so he walked to the great hall of the house, the silence thick around him, settling after the fading bell like a pall, heavy and almost palpable. In the centre of the great chamber, at the very heart of the house, he saw a box, a young man lying in it, and an old man bending close. The old man's hair was white. The horseman stopped, waited.

At length, Faustino Caprimulgo raised his head a fraction. 'What is your name?'

The horseman's voice rang out like the bell. 'Riccardo. Riccardo Bruni.'

'Son of Domenico Bruni, the farrier of the Tower *contrada*?'

'Yes.'

Riccardo may have been fearless, but he was not without feeling. He had heard so many tales, since he was a boy, about the horrific crimes of this man. And yet today, Faustino was just a father grieving for his son, in the terrible distortion of nature that forced the old to bury the young.

'Come closer, Riccardo Bruni.'

The horseman took three steps forward; now he could see the boy in the box, the coffin resting on a trestle, which, had circumstances been different, would have been used for a feast. Vicenzo's eyes were closed, his jaw tied up with a bandage knotted around the top of his head. The blood had been washed from him, his neck straightened and the place where his spine had broken through his throat covered by the high collar of his yellow-and-black Eagle livery. His face was untouched, his aquiline nose unbroken.

'How old are you?'

'Near on twenty.'

Faustino nodded his silver head, once. 'The same as . . .' His face crumpled; he could not say his son's name.

Riccardo looked away, unable to gaze upon the ruin of this man's countenance. But Faustino spoke again.

'A terrible thing, for the sire to witness the death of the yearling. My house dies with him.'

Riccardo frowned slightly, for he had heard there was a younger son to carry the Aquila line – a sickly but wiry fellow, yet cast in the hawkish mould of his brother and father. He assumed that this boy had met his end in the time Riccardo had been away from the city.

The *capitano* turned from the coffin and fixed his yellow eyes upon Riccardo. *Here it comes*, he thought.

'When he bled and you held him, you pressed your hands to his neck.'

'I did.'

'To stop the blood.'

'Yes.'

Now Riccardo thought he knew where these questions tended. Could he have done more? Could he have saved the boy? But Faustino began to walk around him in a circle, a buyer purchasing horseflesh, considering.

'Have you seen service?'

'Why do you ask?' Careful, now.

'It is a soldier's trick, to compress the wound. To not let it bleed out.'

Riccardo knew now whom he was dealing with. Faustino was not a thug, but a clever man. Little wonder then that he ruled here and had done for so long.

'I served at Milazzo. I was in Sicily these past two years.'

'At Milazzo? You fought for the Austrians? Why?' Faustino stopped walking and turned, interested.

Riccardo met his raptor's eyes. 'I like to fight.'

The captain's expression told him that on another day he would have smiled. '*Do* you.' It was not a question. 'You were looking for a war.'

'Yes.'

'And you found one.'

'Ycs.'

There was a silence, long enough for Riccardo to reflect that this tragedy had truncated the usual processes of acquaintance. Having just met, they had nonetheless travelled, somehow, some distance to this place where he and Faustino completely understood each other.

'You are quite a rider.'

Riccardo, knowing that he was, did not gainsay the older man.

'If you had not leaped to save my son, you would have won the Palio.'

This was also true. Riccardo remained silent. There was a thoughtful pause and then, as if consciously changing tack, the captain brought his hands together with a clap that sounded hollow through the chamber.

'Today, I bury my son.'

It was said with a businesslike dispatch that belied the words. But there was a clue here to real feeling, which had come and gone across the captain's face moments before; still, he could not say the boy's name.

He continued, 'Tomorrow, in the evening, you will feast with us here. Although you are not of our *contrada*, I owe you a debt of honour.'

Riccardo's eyes widened. He had expected censure, perhaps punishment, and had walked to the Eagle's lair to meet it willingly. His life was cheap to him. Perhaps that was why he rode faster than any other, perhaps that was why he had walked into the house of Aquila without the quickening of a heartbeat: because at the heart of his courage was the fact that he really did not care if he died. Such courage is not true courage. True courage is when a man quakes with fear in the face of death, yet still risks his life for something he cares about. Riccardo Bruni did not know this yet, but he was to learn it soon.

'Here at sundown, tomorrow,' stated Faustino.

Riccardo did not accept nor refuse; nor, it seemed, was he expected to. Faustino was well used to being obeyed without question.

'Before you go,' said the captain, now almost conversationally casual, 'I have another dead man to show you.'

Faustino swiped aside a tapestry of the Eagle arms and passed through a dark door. As he trod smoothly down a steep turn of stone stairs, Riccardo, curious, followed. The tapestry, the stair, once again gave him the strong impression that he was entering the past, reverting to a time that respected brutality and shunned civilization. Once, in Milazzo, he and his troop had come upon a blackened village where no crickets chirped and no birds sang. He walked the streets with his fellow and realized that every soul was dead, put to the fire by the Spanish. Heavy wooden bars had been placed across each doorway to trap the villagers, the women and children too. He had felt the same prickling then, coming over the hill of parched grass and down into that damned village, as he felt now. With every step he knew he was about to witness a horror to which the boy in the box up above was but a prelude.

There was the glow of a guttering torch below and a sharp fierce odour of metal. Riccardo's eyes adjusted slowly and he became aware of what he saw, only seconds after he knew why his shoes were stuck to the floor. The beast before him was a man: the metallic smell was the well-remembered scent of blood.

A man lay face-up on an iron grid that resembled a rack. His body was horribly beaten and broken. This was retribution. Faustino, unmoved, reached over the horror to grasp a chunk of the unfortunate's hair and raise the head – so Riccardo could better see, better understand. Below the swellings of flesh and the bulgings of eyes and the breakings of teeth, he could just make out the features of the rider of the Panther *contrada*, limitless suffering writ there, his hair soaked with sweat of unbelievable pain. This was a man who had not known what he was dealing with when he swiped his whip across Vicenzo's face in the heat of the race, who had not known that, when he unhorsed Vicenzo at the San Martino corner, the stroke of the whip was the stroke of a pen upon his own death warrant. No fresco could ever re-create such suffering. Riccardo could not look in the Panther's still-open eyes, for to do so would be to look into the pit of hell itself.

He did not ask why he had been shown this man. He understood. '*This* is war,' he said, simply.

'Yes.'

Faustino's yellow eyes were calm and unrepentant. He had started a fire and he did not care. He had taken the life of another young man, the same age as his son, and he did not care. Another father would grieve and bury his child. And he did not care. There was no attendant torturer, no guard in the dim dungeon, no companion for the Panther's last moments, and Riccardo knew, in that instant, that Faustino had done this himself.

Suddenly unable to stay, Riccardo walked up the stone stair and out of the great doors into the day. The new light was already sinful, already tainted by what had passed. He sensed rather than saw the captain follow him and, when he turned in the sunlit street and paused to look back into the gloomy hall, he was in time to see Faustino return to his coffin-side vigil. But something had changed. Now two carpenters in Eagle colours lifted a coffin lid between them and waited for a nod from their *capitano*. Faustino craned to gaze his last upon his heir, then dipped his head. The heavy lid was lowered into place, causing a shadow to fall across legs, breast and finally the face of the young body: a shroud of perpetual darkness. Faustino's head stayed low, as if he could never raise it again. Unable to countenance a man who felt such agony of loss over one young man while he tortured another to death in his dungeons, Riccardo could remain there no longer. He turned to go without taking his leave, his footsteps on the stone punctuated by the hammering of the coffin nails.

As he walked away a scream followed him down the alleys from the coffin's side: 'Vicenzo!' Faustino could utter the name at last, this one final time. Head down, striding as fast as he could away from this house of death, Riccardo did not notice that someone in the upper windows was watching him go.

∞

Black for tomorrow.

Pia, her eyes shadowed from sleeplessness, dressed herself in the black gown as she'd been told. She eased the tight sleeves carefully to her shoulders, wincing as she noted five black fingermarks on each slim white upper arm. Pia looked at the marks dispassionately. Abuse seemed commonplace to her now. She peered, straining her head over each shoulder, trying to determine whether Nello or his cousin had hurt her more. Nello had it by a whisker – his bruising, on reflection, was more defined. She caught herself in the middle of this exercise and wondered if she was losing her wits.

The maid came to do her hair before the great window of her prison, smiling and talking all the time, friendly, garrulous and utterly malicious. Pia knew by the cruel pull of the sausage-like fingers on her hair that the spill of the oil lamp the previous night had been no accident.

From her eyrie she saw the horseman – the man she had noted yesterday, the fellow who had leaped to Vicenzo's aid – enter the house at the stroke of six. Why was he here, a man of the Torre? She leaned forward a fraction, as if to call out a warning, placing her outspread hand on the window. But the maid pulled her back by her ringlets, the poker around which she turned her hair threatening to singe her ear. Pia registered the warning. She watched her handprint vanish from the cool glass, leaving just five smoky fingerprints. They looked like the marks on her arms.

Half an hour later, when the maid had gone, the horseman emerged again, walking freely from the place as Pia had wished to do the previous night. This time Pia did not lean forward, nor place her hands against the window. Her mistrust of men, planted by her father, given libation by Vicenzo, was brought into full bloom by this man. Why had he jumped to save Vicenzo? How could he walk in and out of this place, a palace of a rival *contrada*, as if he were kin? Because he was complicit, in the pocket of the Eagles like her father, all of them boiling in the same stew. Pia placed her fingers into her own prints on the pane, carefully, precisely. Before she had got to the thumb, he was gone.

She ate the plain pastry that had been left on a tray and drank all the ewe's milk. She knew that she must stay strong, not get ill. Today there would be a laying-out and a burial, no more. She must remain strong, keep her wits. It was not the black-dress day she feared, it was the white.

She was summoned downstairs and covered her head, processing behind the black-clad family as the body was churched and interred in the Eagles' chapel across the square, in the Eagles' crypt. She stayed quiet and small, but was made to stand, ominously, between Vicenzo's white-haired father and white-haired brother. She mumbled the creed and kept her head bowed.

At the end of the mass she hung back in the church doorway, until the family had gone. When the last black figure had gone into the house, she lifted her heavy skirts and ran, flitting from shadow to shadow, deep dark slices of merciful shade in the bright new day, friendly shadows that would hide well a slim woman in a black dress. Her heart was bursting. One more street and she would be in the Dragon *contrada*. The Dragons were friends to the Owlets; they would shelter her. She almost laughed. She'd been right, so right to wait, to be docile, to seize her chance. One more courtyard and then she could laugh, laugh at her father's plans, laugh at the great fat maid, laugh at the white dress she'd never have to wear.

A shadow blocked her way. It was all right – shadows were her friends. But it was not all right.

'Now, my pet, you've lost your way and no mistake. But Nicoletta'll help you, have nay fear.'

The maid's grip on her upper arms deepened the bruising of yesterday.

∞

Riccardo had known for a long time that something was rotten at the heart of his beloved Siena. It was why he had left. Now he knew what ailed the city and he could give the pestilence a name.

Faustino Caprimulgo.

Riccardo walked the golden streets back to his father's house, thinking of the next day and the next night to come, of the invitation he could not refuse. He opened the door of the Torre stable: the boy Zebra was gone from his bed and the horse too. At daybreak his father would have led the stallion out, and walked him gently back to his owners in the Maremma.

Riccardo squatted and took a handful of the straw, cold now, letting it fall through his fingers. He said the horse's name: Taccola. Jackdaw. He remembered another time and place, when he was no older than Zebra, the day he had seen the eagle and the daw, the daw he had brought home and kept here in this very stable till it died. It seemed an innocent, golden time – before Milazzo, before this new war he was embroiled in – and with all his heart he wished himself back there. It was this, not anything else he had seen that morning, nor anything he would encounter the next night, that made him want to cry.

4

The Wave

'One more push, my lady.'
Violante was soaked with sweat, the contractions pulling her from the birthing bed till she was almost sitting upright. She thought she would die, had never known such pain. But she welcomed every spasm, embraced the agony, enjoyed it. For she knew she was doing her duty. All of Florence waited outside the palace and her contractions beat time with the jubilant bells of the duomo. A few more pains – for there could not be many more, surely? – and the longed-for Medici heir would be in the world. Her tiring maids pressed cool cloths to her forehead, but Violante pushed them away – she had never felt more confident in her role. This, this was what she had been born for. This was her moment.

She had worried and fretted all the way through her confinement, found new confidence to ask for the best physicians from Vienna and the best leechers from Rome. Her father-in-law

Cosimo de' Medici, galvanized from his usual torpor by the prospect of a Medici heir at last, had granted her every boon.

Even her husband Ferdinando had spoken to her, these last nine months, with something approaching kindness. She had counted the weeks anxiously, for she knew that Ferdinando's sister, that chilly countess Anna Maria Luisa, had miscarried six times, so many that the citizens had begun to whisper about the curse of the Medici, that a shadow was on the great house, that an heir would never come. Such talk did not assist Violante's spirits, but she had carried her precious burden for a full term. She would bear a son for Ferdinando, and he would love her at last; for that, if not for herself.

She was supremely confident, strong and sure for the first time. She was thirty, so no green girl, and old to be brought to childbed. But only now did she feel she had grown into her womanhood at last and knew, as she laboured, that this was what she had been born to do. Suddenly there was a rush of waters upon the coverlet, an easing of the terrible pain below, and the midwife held up a tiny bundle slick with blood, with a knotted blue rope connecting mother and son. Mother. Violante was a mother.

She tried this new and wonderful word on her dry tongue, saying it over and over like a prayer. The dame took out a knife curved like a sickle and cut the cord but it did not matter. Violante knew she was connected to her son for ever now. She thought she could not be happier, but she was wrong, for her womb gave another great lurch and soon the midwife held up a second child, the exact copy of the first. Twins. It was the greatest and happiest surprise of her life. Not one, but two boys.

She held out her arms to her sons in a gesture of command she had never used before. The midwife understood and gave her the children at once. In contravention of every birthing convention for a high-born lady, Violante laid them, sticky as they were, on her chest. It was the most perfect moment of her life. As one, they ceased to cry and opened their eyes, looking at her with tiny beady orbs the colour and size of capers. Wondering, she returned their gaze, looking from one to the other, knowing that if she spent the rest of her life doing just this, she would be supremely happy. Violante melted in their quiet gaze, her lips curling, blinking away tears, for nothing should dim her sight of them. She was perfectly happy for the first time since she had herself been born. She knew, in that moment, unquestioningly, that they loved her.

She held them, gently but firmly; would not have them taken from her and cleaned. Her maids were scandalized – the children must be doused and swaddled properly and given to the wet-nurse, but Violante did not care. She asked the women to lay a balmcloth over them and leave them be. And at length, exhausted after two days of difficult labour, her eyes began to close. Her sons' little heartbeats raced against her chest, their little mouths sought her nipples. She felt a tug as her breasts began to leak milk in her willingness to suckle the Medici heirs. She did not have to do a thing. She was a mother – her body knew what it had to do. The little princes fed. Violante, contented, slept.

She woke, cold, clean, in a white cotton nightshift and stiff clean sheets. Her sons were gone, but she knew that while she slept her women would have taken them, at last, to be cleaned, swaddled and dressed, to be given such rites as were fitting for the heirs to the grand duchy. She saw, in the dim twilight, a hunched shape of the midwife on the end of the bed. The shape was shuddering, as if the dame laughed. Violante could have laughed too, her heart bursting with joy.

'Where are the boys?' she asked.

The nurse turned around and Violante saw her face was silver in the twilight, shimmering with tears.

At that moment, she knew.

Violante began to shake her head, tried to sit, but could not. The midwife ran from the room, shivering with sobs, as another dark shape entered. A priest unknown to her. Violante knew what he would say before he uttered. His face was half in shadow – she could not see his lips, but heard the words well enough.

'They are gone, mistress.'

'No.' It was a whisper.

'They are with God, mistress.'

'No.' It was a cry.

'Only the righteous are taken into the arms of the Lord.'

'NO.' It was a shout. 'No no no no no!'

Now she had the strength to rise but still could not – and she knew they had foreseen this and had strapped her to the bed. She pulled at her bindings till the straps cut, raved and foamed and near pulled her arms from their sockets.

'Where are they? I want to see them. I want to see my sons!'

She could not believe the priest – she wanted, she needed to hold her babies again, knew that if she could just hold them to her breast they would open their little eyes once more and everything would be all right.

The priest took a step back. 'We buried them, mistress. With full honours. They lie in the family tomb.'

The family tomb. With all the other dead Medici.

She screamed then, and would not stop: animal, primal screams. Soon the room was full. Shady figures held her arms, a cloth was pressed to her nose, a leecher bled her thrashing arm above a china bowl, the blood pooled black in the twilight. She breathed in the sickly, heavy smell of laudanum.

She woke in the darkened room a few times over the next few days. Someone attended her at all times, always a dark figure sat upon the end of the bed. The nurse that had been sent to tend her, the one who had cried, the one in whose tears she had seen her sons' deaths written, was there constantly.

One time, when she woke, the nursemaid had turned into her husband. Ferdinando had left off, for once, his lustrous dark wig. He lifted his head and she saw that he, too, wept. Today he was not the heir to a dukedom, but an ordinary man. He turned away, as if he could not face her while he told her what he must.

'His name was Bambagia. A pricking-boy I met in Venice – you recall – when I went with Scarlatti in 1701?' He did not wait for a reply. 'He was nothing. A carnival plaything. He never removed his mask, even when we fucked.'

The brutal words did not penetrate her fog of grief. She was numb with pain. Why was he telling her this? He had had lovers for years – there was one who rarely left his side. She could not care about this further betrayal. All she cared about were her little boys, now lost to her.

'If he'd taken off his mask I would have seen – I never would have done it.' He dropped his head. 'He had syphilis. And now I do too. You might also.'

Syphilis. She knew of the creeping evil disease, flesh eating, the maggots of pestilence that buried themselves in the brain and drove one mad. To feel that now this curse may have been laid upon her, that she might be hirpling to her grave, made her glad. She wanted to die.

'Why are you telling me this?' They were the first words she had spoken since she had raved at the priest. Her voice was hoarse with screaming.

'Because the doctors tell me that syphilis causes stillbirth. I wanted you to know . . . I wanted to tell you . . . I didn't want you to think it was your fault. It was my fault. I wanted to tell you that I'm sorry.'

It was the first time he had ever apologized to her for all of his transgressions and it touched her not at all. None of it mattered now. She wanted to protest, to say that the twins had been alive, that they had cried, and fed, and looked her in the face. But the words would not come. She looked at him, this handsome florid man, this lover of music and art, this man the people loved as the 'good Medici', saviour of an ailing dukedom, and knew that he was doomed by disease. He had failed his father and his inheritance, and she could not pity him.

He moved to the head of the bed, sat gently beside her.

'They were baptized. My brother did all, for I could not.' His voice broke. 'They were named Cosimo and Gastone de' Medici.'

He held her hand for the first time since they had been hand-fasted in marriage, in the very duomo she could see from the casement. Only then did she begin to cry.

In the days that followed she was to learn that tears were infinite. She had thought that if she cried for days, weeks, months, eventually the well would run dry and she would begin *to heal. But no. Her tears, once they began to flow, seemed an unstoppable stream; a great wave, which, undammed, swelled to an amplitude fit to drown her.*

Violante always woke at the point in the dream when Ferdinando touched her hand. It was the last time he had touched her. Ferdinando, now gone too, had died lame, blind and raving from the syphilis. He was buried next to his sons. She envied him, wished she too was in that cold mausoleum in Florence, knew that if her remains mingled with her sons' little bones, she could warm them again.

So many ghosts. She wished they would leave her be.

Always she woke with tears running into her ears, her heart pounding, and her breasts – even though she was nearly fifty – still aching, the nipples still pinching with the milk reflex. She had had the same dream, year in, year out, for nearly twenty years. She sat up in her bed, wiping her eyes, blinking in the pre-dawn gloom. She breathed in and out, heavily, then lit an oil lamp to chase away the dream and the memories too.

At first, she had thought the killing grief would drive her mad. She had not known that the pain she had felt, as an unloved child and an unloved wife, could be more acute, that her loneliness could be any keener. With bitter irony, Gretchen, her own wet-nurse, whom she had called from her father's court in Bavaria to tend to the babies, arrived in Florence the day after the boys died.

Gretchen never left, for one look at her little mistress told her that the duchess needed her now more than ever. But in truth, Violante had never felt so alone. After she had failed in her duty, her father-in-law Cosimo never spoke to her nor looked at her again. Her sister-in-law Anna Maria Luisa could barely conceal her joy. Her babes had been taken away; she could not have borne it if Violante's sons had lived.

The only kindness in her life came from an unexpected quarter. Gian Gastone de' Medici, Ferdinando's younger brother, offered her a sympathy that seemed little to do with the fact that he was now the heir presumptive of the dukedom. Gian Gastone detested his own sister Anna Maria Luisa, and had shown her no sympathy or solicitude through her multiple miscarriages, also caused by the syphilis of a faithless husband, the Elector Palatine. But, for his sister-in-law Violante, nothing was too much. Gian Gastone took upon himself the baptism and funeral arrangements – so close, more cruelly close than nature intended. Such events, normally separated by a lifetime, were held apart by the span of a few mere hours. Not only did Gian Gastone visit Violante in person – though the slim, handsome libertine had much better claims on his time – he also sent remedies to her room: sweetmeats, tonics, iced fruit, and made sure that she had the care of his personal physicians. She had never forgotten Gian Gastone's kindness.

Violante also remembered one of those doctors telling her that she could wait a twelvemonth and try again for another child. She laughed in his face. It had been trouble

...ough to bring Ferdinando to bed with her once – that dreadful violent assault against love and nature – she knew he would not do it again. Cruellest of all, her breasts were engorged with milk, full and hard to the touch, mapped with blue veins, and leaking day and night. Months later, when she at last ventured out in the street in a litter, any babe crying in the square was enough to cause the vicious pinching in her nipples. Her treacherous breasts began to leak the milk that would never again nourish those tiny searching mouths that she had fed but once. Her heart ached for the lips that had mouthed at her flesh, for the twin pairs of eyes that had looked at her so calmly. The littlest eyes but filled with such *love*, love only for her, a love she had never been offered before or since.

Ferdinando never came near her again, and in time Violante knew that his confession on the birthing bed had come to naught; she was not infected with his malady. As the days and weeks crawled by in their relentless agony of loss, she realized, appalled, that she had no symptoms of syphilis, no blood in her waters, no imagined scars upon her face. The only scars that criss-crossed her flesh were the marks that had silvered her skin where her belly had distended with child. In her confinement she had refused to anoint them with oil of olives as her ladies had urged her, for she had been as proud of them as a veteran of his battle scars. Now they were as painful to her as the forty scourgings of Christ.

Her broken heart was caged in a healthy body. She was to be given no early release from this prison. She remained healthy and knew her sons would have been too. She never visited their graves in that huge marble mausoleum. Such a place had nothing to do with her twins, so warm and small and living; it had nothing to do with the moment they had shared, that one short moment of communion, of pure love given and received, with no thought or agenda. She marked every birthday, without fail, as the years went by, relived that first and last look they had shared, felt the sweet kiss of those tiny mouths at her breast.

When Violante saw Ferdinando die, slowly and terribly, she was glad. She knew that, in the moment she came face to face with his sons, she had ceased to love him, and in the moment he had confessed to her, their bond was inexorably broken. Three years later, when her father-in-law Grand Duke Cosimo offered her the governorship of Siena, she took it. She knew she was running away from Florence, but it was no use. The dream followed her here and would not let her go. When she entered the city gates as a new widow, the first thing she had seen was a statue of the city's emblem, a she-wolf suckling boy twins. In a dreadful irony the image was everywhere, ever present, even on the frescoed walls of her new home, the Palazza Pubblico. There was no escape.

Her rule had been a disaster. Her fragile hold on the city was slipping, and yesterday another son was lost, another heir doomed never to come to his inheritance. Vicenzo Caprimulgo had been taken. The age-old rivalries that had bubbled and seethed in this city for hundreds of years had surfaced. That foolish Panther had taken a life and she knew that Faustino would not let that rest.

Violante jumped from the bed and padded to the window, throwing open the casement as she had done the night before. The patch of blood at the San Martino corner was still there, despite the efforts of the *comune*'s servants. She could no longer take her eyes away from it. It looked as if the city had been bruised. Siena was bleeding internally, just below the skin.

She must take action.

She looked carefully at the nine divisions of the campo. The Nine. An idea began to bubble to the surface of her consciousness. She heard the bells of the mourning Eagle *palazzo* – the Caprimulgo house – telling the *contrada* it was six. Daybreak. It was time to act.

She cast about for a robe to throw around her shoulders. Without her corsets she was depressingly rotund: too many comfits and sweetmeats nibbled out of unhappiness. But this morning she had no time to think of her vanity. She ran her hands through her cropped greying hair. She was suddenly in too much of a hurry to call her waiting women and begin her lengthy dressing process, too impatient to wait for the placing and powdering of her heavy wig. Instead she grabbed the great black-and-white banner of the Palio, which had been brought to her room from the piazza where she had dropped it. She suspected her household did not really know what to do with it. Technically the Eagle *contrada* had won; even though their horse Berio had crossed the finish line with no rider, the victory still held. But she could understand why the Eagles had neglected to collect their banner – there was no triumph to be had in such a win. Violante wrapped the heavy silk around herself like a robe. She put on a simple lace cap and tied it under her chin, took her oil lamp and crept barefoot down the stairs to the centre of Siena – the very heart of the palace and the city itself. She opened the heavy doors and reached her destination.

The Hall of the Nine was built to celebrate the long-dead republican government, the nine Sienese men from the greatest families. It was the government that she had supposedly replaced, but it was also the government that still existed here in reality. She needed to look back to look forward, and in this place the very walls themselves would tell her what she must do. For here, adorning the walls, were the three wondrous frescoes by Ambrogio Lorenzetti – the *Allegory* and *Effects of Good and Bad Government*, each depicting a view of Siena and its countryside.

She had lived with these paintings for ten years, had held receptions, councils and colloquies here; she had looked at them ten thousand times but never truly *seen*. Now, in the faint dim of the dawn, she tracked her lamp around the walls, the flame throwing a warm disc of light upon the details. She examined every brushstroke at close quarters. She wanted to learn what she must do.

Violante looked to her left. In the representation of good government, the prosperous townspeople were trading and dancing in the streets. Beyond the city walls a lush countryside could be seen in which abundant golden crops were harvested. In the allegory of bad government, crime was rampant and diseased citizens roamed a crumbling city. The countryside without the walls was parched and bleak, suffering from the killing thirst of drought. Over all, a white-faced Devil with ivory horns presided, black-robed, with a dish of blood in his hands and a goat at his feet. His aquiline features reminded her of Faustino Caprimulgo. She shivered and could not meet the Devil's yellow cycs.

Violante took a few paces back to look at the two frescoes together and tried to think straight. The paintings showed the two faces of the city, the black and the white. Siena's very flag, the Balzana, was a slab of white atop a slab of black, each half equal to the other. But now under her rule it was as if the flag seemed inverted, that the black was riding in triumph. How could she transform it, how could she make the white half win, how could she emulate the stable republican government of the Nine that she saw depicted here? Who could defeat the Devil in his own dance hall? She shuddered and drew the silk of the Palio closer round her shoulders.

Violante shifted her lamp to the third painting. Here, flanked by the depictions of the black-and-white city, was a central panel. And here she found hope. Here, in the centre, where a grim-faced judge, like Christ, separated the saved from the damned, was inspiration. For here, Justice was depicted as a woman. She gestured to the scales of balance, held by the personification of Wisdom floating over her throne. It was the figure of Justice who decided whether to condemn or be merciful for, on her right, a convicted criminal was beheaded; on the left, gladdened figures received the rewards of reprieve.

Violante felt inspired. Could she be the figure of Justice, could she take the reins at last and unite this divided place?

Justice was not alone in her endeavours. At her feet, the personification of Virtue was also portrayed as a female figure, modelled on the Queen of Heaven. Mary, the patron saint of the city. Mary, the mother who had seen her son live and die too; Mary, to whom Violante had prayed throughout her pregnancy and her bereavement, that mortal woman who knew what it was to lose a son. Violante felt a kinship or a sisterhood, as if she, too, was not alone.

But then, as she let her eyes wander over the fresco again, she spotted something she had never seen before. Another female figure held what was clearly an hour-glass, two delicate curves of glass with the sand of time running between them. Violante knew she did not have much time. If she did not heal this city before the duke-dom ended with her, Siena would be ruined for ever.

The obstacles were great. In the fresco Mary passed out virtue among twenty-four faithfully rendered and recognizable images of prominent male citizens of Siena. The very men whose descendants now ridiculed her and made nonsense of her rule. She saw the faces that she knew: shuttered, circumspect, minding their own lucrative business. Families that had ruled this place from time out of mind: the Chigi, the Albani, the Piccolomini and, of course, the Caprimulgi.

Violante knew Faustino Caprimulgo had corrupted the city for over half a century; that he had crossed her time

and time again over sumptuary rights and trading monop-
olies; that he flouted tithes and taxes, and disregarded the
laws that were implemented to keep the citizens safe. He
murdered, he trafficked, he stole. But he could not do it
alone; there had to be complicity. He had allies, not only in
his own loyal *contrada* but, of necessity, in others too. He
had treaties and alliances. In each of the thirds or *terzi* of
the city, the *contrade*, each of the seventeen wards, were
operating in a complex web. In this intricate machin-
ery, the separate wheels of commerce and corruption,
from the tiny to the vast, functioned independently but
were all inextricably linked, like the cogs in the belly of
a watch. But however much she might know about the
surface of the city, she could not hope to know about its
fine workings.

She needed someone on the inside. A Sienese.

She toyed with the idea of asking her chief councillor,
Francesco Maria Conti, for help. He was entrenched in
the ruling party of the Giraffa *contrada* in the east of the
city, where he lived in palatial elegance. And it was he
who nominally helped her in her day-to-day government
of this city, he who presided over his fellows in the council chamber, the Sala del Concistore, next to this very
room. He should be the ideal candidate to unite city and
duchy, but Conti had never been completely able to hide
his contempt for her and Violante had never trusted him.
She did not know whether his dislike proceeded from her
sex, her Germanic origins as the Elector of Bavaria's
daughter, or her familial connections with the Medici.
She only knew that he disagreed with her in chamber at

every turn, that in foreign policy his advice was so biased to the papal position as to be virtually worthless, and that he hampered any lawgiving that she embarked upon. No, he would not do. But she thought she knew who would.

It was so light now that she did not need her lamp. She blew it out and, as she did so, the great doors opened.

'Madam?' An elderly waiting woman, her hair in a fat white plait, entered the hall. 'I was worried for you.'

Her accents were gentle and guttural, recalling for Violante Bavaria and home. This was the duchess's wet-nurse and oldest ally.

'Gretchen.' Violante's voice was excited. 'Find that orphan boy for me – Zebra. And, while he comes, writing materials.'

The old woman, who had opened her mouth to suggest her mistress should dress or take breakfast, registered this new tone in the duchess's voice, shut it again and disappeared.

Violante did not want to move from the place that had inspired her, so when her butler appeared she asked for a writing desk to be set in the window and took up her quill. Then she sat down and wrote to Gian Gastone de' Medici, her brother-in-law and the only man in her family whom she felt she could count upon as an ally, the only Medici ever to show her any kindness. To do what she planned she needed the support of the state.

She also needed the support of the city. She could see the city only as a stranger – for she was on the outside, something that had become abundantly clear yesterday at the Palio. She needed to move from within. But there was one man here who had shown courage without partiality: the unknown horseman, who had run towards danger, unafraid, to help a dying man, a man not of his own *contrada*. She sealed and directed her letter to Gian Gastone just as Gretchen came back into the great chamber with the boy Zebra. The old lady pulled off the lad's cap and pushed him forward with a little shove, but not without affection.

Violante thought the orphan looked tired and felt a sudden misgiving that she would add to his load. She had a stool drawn close and some bread and milk brought before she spoke. She watched him as he sopped the bread in the milk, eating hungrily. He could not be more than eight or nine.

'Zebra.'

She felt foolish, but did not know his given name. He looked at her with a completely open countenance, not noticeably shy or diffident, and he began to smile a lopsided smile. She realized she was still wearing the Palio banner around her shoulders, had a simple cap on her head, and bare feet. She must look quite a sight. But she smiled back, encouraged. Perhaps there was still some innocence in Siena.

'Do you know the horseman of the Tower *contrada*? Do you know who he is, where to find him?'

Zebra ducked his head in a nod, his mouth stuffed with bread and milk.

Violante was relieved. She had half expected the horseman to have left Siena by now.

'Go to him in my name, with this seal.' She passed him a small plaque bearing the Medici shield. A glance at her family arms gave her courage. 'Bid him come here to the palace at his earliest convenience.'

As Zebra bowed, she noted his black-and-white clothes, the same colours as the banner that she still held around her shoulders. She had a sudden notion. She folded the flag respectfully, warm from her body, and gave it to the boy.

'And on your way, take this to the Caprimulgo house.'

The boy looked up, startled.

'Put it in the hands of Faustino Caprimulgo and tell him . . .' She hardened her tone with the timbre of resolve. 'Tell him Violante Beatrix de' Medici, no—' She corrected herself. 'The governess of Siena sends him this, with her condolences.'

Black and white were the colours of the chessboard too. She had made her first move.

5

The Panther

The Panther, the young man who lay dead in the Eagle's dungeons, was once young and whole and happy, growing up in his father's house. His father, captain of the Panthers, was an apothecary who had amassed a small fortune and bought a fine new house in the Pantera *contrada* in the west of the city. The *capitano* decided to bring objects to his house that befitted his new class, filling it with paintings.

The young Panther had a favourite – a painting by the Sienese master Sassetta. He passed it every day in the parlour, where it hung over the armoire. It depicted a panther at bay, trapped in a deep pit, magnificent, sitting back on the bunched black muscles of his haunches, snarling with pin-sharp ivory teeth. On the lip of the pit were gathered a group of rustic shepherds, some pelting the beast with sticks and stones, some throwing him food. The young Panther was struck by the nobility of the beast: doomed to die, but still defiant. The boy was struck, too, by the attitude of the shepherds, good and bad, offering both death and life. He asked his father what the painting meant.

His father, looking down at his son and considering his tender age, told the tale simply. The panther had fallen into the pit by some mischance, he said. The shepherds discovered him and were sure he was going to die. Some tortured him for his last hours, but others chose to relieve his final moments with food.

'Did he die?' asked the boy.

'He did not,' answered the father. 'The food revived him, and he leaped from his trap and sought out the shepherds. He slaughtered the ones who had taunted him, but, seeing the good shepherds cowering, he reassured them, saying: "I remember those who sought my death with stones, and I remember those who gave me succour. Set aside your fears. I return as an enemy only to those who injured me."'

The boy seemed satisfied. There was plenty of time, his father thought, to apprise his son of the deeper meanings of the painting, of the Panthers' position in Siena, their relative relationships, their alliances with the Tower, their rivalry with the Eagles, the implications for trade and politics. Time enough for that.

He never got a chance.

∽

Riccardo Bruni woke convinced that the dying Panther was with him. He blinked enough times to convince himself that the stable was empty of any soul save his, and scratched his skin in the places where the straw had printed its shapes into his flesh. He closed his eyes and listened as the bells rang seven.

He opened them again to see Zebra ducking under the half-door and handing him the duchess's seal.

'You are summoned to the palace,' said the boy, eyes round.

Riccardo turned the seal over in his hands, saying nothing, studying the Medici cognizance of the circle of red balls on a gold shield. He imagined what it would be like to be part of a family so exalted that they had their own arms. He supposed the duchess wished to acknowledge his chivalry yesterday, although it had seemed a small enough gesture among the surly captains.

Uncharacteristically, he took a moment to consider his appearance. His stockings were less than white, his jerkin was covered in straw; one of his cuffs was missing a button, one of his shoes a buckle. Riccardo retied his hair and crammed his tricorne on his head. Sighing inwardly, he cuffed Zebra gently about the head, smiled to mitigate the offence and flipped him a *ruspo*, the coin spinning in the air.

'Am I to spend this day too doing your bidding? My pockets will be empty.'

He walked the short distance to the *palazzo*. He had lived under the shadow of its tower all his life, the tower that had numbered his hours and days as he grew up like the gnomon of a sundial. This was the very tower that gave his *contrada* its name, for it stood sentinel at the edge of his ward, yet he had never been within the palace. The curiosity that he had felt the day before, when summoned to Faustino, returned.

After giving his name at the great doors, Riccardo was shown into a vast chamber where paintings crawled over every inch of the walls – paintings of places he knew well, so cunningly rendered it was as if he looked through a window. There was the duomo, the Chigi palace, the Loggia del Papa. There was the Colle Malamerenda – the Hill of Bad Meals – just outside the city, where twenty people were killed in a brawl between the Salimbeni and Tolomei families when there were too few thrushes brought to a feast. Raised to think of nothing but horses, he picked out a great horseback procession and saw, among the noblemen, a noble lady riding astride, her robes falling either side of her horse's back, almost down to his hocks. As he stood, gazing at her unmoving figure, the double doors at the end of the hall opened.

The duchess was dressed from head to toe in violet, just as she had been yesterday. It was a strange colour for a woman of her years. But when Riccardo looked into her round caper-green eyes with their short stubby lashes, and at the array of wrinkles radiating from them as she smiled, he felt oddly comforted. He took in the wide sympathetic mouth, the soft jaw below, saw the ample bosom and waist that her corsets could not hide. She was not handsome and likely never had been, but there was something essentially motherly about her. It was not at all what he thought he would feel in the presence of a duchess.

Nor did he expect what she went on to say. In her gentle, Germanic accent she explained that the frescoes showed good and bad government, that she wanted to bring back the happy, peaceful times and end the needless rivalries between *contrade* that ended in deaths like Vicenzo's. She had seen him help the dying man during the race. She asked for his help.

His refusal was gentle and civil, but decided. It was not that he didn't agree with her. He did. She argued well, held her hands wide and told him that this place where he now stood, the Palazzo Pubblico, was and always had been the focus of the city – a civic, not a religious centre. She told him that the stony finger of the Torre del Mangia, which crowned the concave curve of the crenellations, was the highest tower in the land, that you could almost see it reaching into the sky with civic pride. Riccardo could see all this. But he had to refuse. She was an outsider. He didn't doubt that she loved her adopted city. But Faustino, monster that he was, was Sienese born and bred. The Caprimulgo countenance was there before him in the very frescoes that she had shown him. He couldn't take sides against a Sienese, against his own people.

'I am sorry, Madam.'

He bowed and took his leave before he could read the disappointment in her eyes.

∾

White for the day after.

Pia, having revealed herself as a bird that wished to fly, had had her wings clipped. She was not allowed any of Vicenzo's funeral wake-meats in the great hall. She had been locked in her chamber all day. She dared not look in the garderobe at the dress that terrified her so much, but she knew it was there. Sometimes, in a trick of the draught, the beaded skirts would slither on the wood, or the hanger would knock on the door.

She slept eventually, woke again, tried to recite her favourite verses or remember extracts of her favourite legends. It was not a cheering exercise. All her heroines – Guinevere, Iseult, or Cleopatra as conjured by William Shakespeare – made sorry ends. She determinedly tried not to recall her ancestor, the first Pia of the Tolomei, tragic heroine of Dante, who was freed from her tower only by her death at the hands of her jealous husband.

During the night that followed, Pia tried to find hope. She tried to believe that her father, Civetta to the bone, would not wed her to an unknown groom of another *contrada*. But as the dawn paled, she knew that all hope was gone. It was White Dress Day.

Perhaps she had misjudged Nello – perhaps the marks on her arm were an accident. Perhaps he was a kind man; perhaps someone who struggled under the affliction of such an appearance, under the daily shadow of an older, handsomer brother, would have developed a tender soul? At least *he* had not violated the twelve-year-old heiress of the Benedetti and led her to hang herself from a ham-hook.

Chin high, Pia opened the door of the garderobe at last and, shaking, took out the white dress. She silently suffered the indignity of being stripped and dressed by Nicoletta. The maid then began to dress her hair, clucking and smiling as if Pia were her own daughter, but pinning the pearls in a little too firmly so blood beaded on the girl's forehead, and scraping the diamond combs across her tender scalp. When Nicoletta held up a looking-glass at last, Pia gazed on a face of beauteous perfection, and a stranger looked back at her. In defiance, she pulled Cleopatra's coin from her bodice to hang outside the beautiful, terrible, dreaded white dress. It was the only thing left of Pia of the Tolomei.

Today's procession was a little different from yesterday's. This time they walked, not to the Eagles' church, but up the stony streets to the basilica, the bells bawling out across the towers. The formidable Nicoletta, in her best fustian, was Pia's bridesmaid, and behind her straggled a company of minstrels, actors and jugglers in bright motley. Tuneless trumpets and accordions anticipated the discord to come as they followed her up the Via del Capitano.

In the Piazza del Duomo, huddled in the sheltering shadow cast by the vast black-and-white building, a crowd gathered. All *contrade*, in their different colours, had come to witness this strange mixed marriage: an Owlet wed to an Eagle.

Inside, in the dimness of plainsong and frankincense, the families of the Civetta and the Aquila flanked the nave. Pia's father, standing at the altar, could spare her a nod, but not a smile, as he took her hand for the fasting. Salvatore had found himself a shaft of light to stand in, but he shared it with another – Nello Caprimulgo – her intended, turned to a wraith of light. His pale hair and skin glowed, he wore silks as white as her malign dress, but his red eyes were demonic. Pia's fantasy of a kindly man crumbled. Salvatore put her hand into Nello's, and the Eagles' heir grasped it as brutally as he had held her arm after the Palio. Those bruises were fading to yellow under the sleeve of her white dress, but there would be more.

Pia listened to the marriage mass as if it were happening to someone else. Unable to look at her groom, she slid her dry eyes east to the *facciatone*, the huge unfinished wall of the nave, begun in the days of the Nine and abandoned when they ran out of money. It was a monument to waste, built in stone. She herself was the human embodiment of waste. Nineteen years of promise, reared and schooled and protected as the daughter of the Civetta, ended here, unfinished, on the day of the white dress.

She began to panic. Trembling, she kept her lips tight for all the responses. And when it came to the vows, she refused to speak. A dreadful scene ensued, her father and Nicoletta cajoling, threatening, trying to prise her lips apart with fingers and nails, as the spittle ran down her chin, as if she were an animal.

Finally, Nello leaned close and whispered in her ear, his breath warming her as his brother's had. 'Vicenzo said you were frighted by the story of the Benedetto slut.'

She was so shocked, she stilled herself to listen. The girl had not been thirteen years old.

'I cannot besmirch his memory. It was I who hung her from the butcher's hook. We shared everything, you see, Vicenzo and I. Everything.'

Pia lurched backwards and searched his awful eyes for a jest. But he merely nodded.

'Ah yes, you understand me now, don't you? We could not have her blabbing, you see. But there is a time to stay silent, and a time to speak.'

After that Pia did as she was bidden. She let Nello put his ring upon her finger: an eagle bearing a bloody jewel in his mouth. She suffered his kiss, for the applauding congregation. She threw coins for the cheering crowds in the square. She even took her new husband's hand as they walked back to the Caprimulgo house.

She was given leave to return to her chamber to prepare for the feast, and there she collapsed. Her knees buckled and sobs racked her, shook her to the very core, frightening her with their violence. After a time she pressed her hands to her mouth, calming herself. She sought the looking-glass. If she appeared dishevelled at dinner she knew she would suffer for it. But Nicoletta had taken the mirror, perhaps in case her mistress smashed the glass and damaged herself with the shards. This gave Pia an idea.

Before she went to dinner, she took a pearl pin from her hair and drove it, again and again, into her wrist. She was not attempting to take her own life – she was both too brave and too cowardly for that – but she'd grown resourceful in the last few days. Holding her wrist away from her gown, she spread dark smears of blood on the lawn sheet where her hips would have rested last night, in an imitation of how her bedding looked at the appointed time each month.

The first time it had happened, when she had just turned thirteen, she'd thought she was dying, with no mother to tell her otherwise. Too well bred to swap such confidences with the maids, she'd prayed for four days while the bleeding lasted, until it had gone away, only to return the next month. Older now, Pia turned this curse into a blessing and she sopped the rest of the blood for good measure with a bandage ripped from her shift. When the bleeding had stopped, she placed the bandage and shift in the soiling chest for the laundress. She knew Nicoletta would see; she saw everything. Pray God it was enough to keep Nello from her bed.

She put the guilty pin, encrusted with blood, back in her hair, and lifted the latch of her chamber, wincing at the pain in her arm. Her prison was now her chamber. There were no longer any keys. She was wed, and could not escape the bars that enclosed her now. Not knowing what else to do, she went down to dinner, thinking that she knew what to expect.

∞

It was dusk, and Riccardo Bruni was attending, as he had been bidden, a sumptuous feast in the palace of the Eagles. He had thought it a wake for Vicenzo, but as he mounted the stairwell to the *piano nobile* he heard the tinkle of crystal and laughter, and when he entered the great salon, the dining table was crowded with candles and flowers, and fruit piled in pyramids like the great prisms of Egypt. The diners, in their snowy wigs and shining buckled shoes, wore clothes of such bright colours that mourning seemed out of the question. It looked more like a wedding.

To his right sat Faustino, an honour for Riccardo indeed. The *capitano* alone was wearing full mourning, a black suit and breeches, black shoes with square buckles and a white wig tied with a black ribbon.

Oppositc him sat Nello, the scarce remembered younger brother and now heir of the Eagle *contrada*: his features a bad copy of Vicenzo's as if a pupil had tried to imitate the work of a master. Riccardo knew now why this second son had been kept in the shadows. What man, let alone one of Faustino's sensibilities, would parade a son with skin leeched of colour like a corpse, eyes of a strange reddish-pink, and hair of pure white like his sire's?

And, next to Nello, the most beautiful woman Riccardo had ever seen.

Faustino, alert as ever, caught him looking and made the introduction.

'May I present Pia of the Caprimulgo, formerly Pia of the Tolomei, daughter of the Civetta *contrada*, and wife to my son Nello?'

Pia of the Tolomei.

She sent a tiny nod in his direction, an almost imperceptible raising and lowering of her perfect chin. Riccardo's condolences died on his lips; she had, in the space of a day, changed one husband for another. And yet congratulations did not seem appropriate either. She did not speak, and Riccardo, who could read humans with only a little less success than he could horses, knew that it was not grief that restrained her: she seemed hostile.

Chastened, he took his seat opposite her, assuming her hauteur to be a natural attitude for a married woman of note to take towards the son of a lowly farrier.

Riccardo ate little and said less, but he was an observant man and sensed the undercurrents of emotion as the sumptuous Sienese fare was paraded before him. Even at a time of mourning, the wealth of the *contrada* was on display for all to see. Each course was wonderful: hare *pappardelle*, *scottiglia* fried meats, and *ribollita* bean stew, followed by sweet *cavallucci* biscuits – sophisticated versions of the dishes that he ate every feast-day, dishes that were the scent and taste of home to him. Each delicacy was placed on a polished pewter dish, which he picked at dutifully with a two-pronged silver fork with a handle of elephant's tooth. But he had no appetite. His eyes kept straying, inexorably, to Pia. He felt an intense pleasure just being in the same room as such a woman; but at the same time he could not forget that dreadful meathouse below the *palazzo*'s foundations, where the dead son of the Panther *contrada* lay stretched out like a butchered swine.

Riccardo reached for the jug of Chianti at the same time as Faustino, and realized, as he did so, that the white-haired *capitano* was getting steadily drunk. The son Nello was conducting a self-important, increasingly one-sided conversation with his father about horses, designed, Riccardo suspected, to display his knowledge to him, not to his sire. Something strange underlay the young man's demeanour, not grief, nor resentment, but something else. Riccardo caught a flicker in Nello's eyes, no more than an instant in the candlelight, but it came to him in a jolt. Nello was *happy*.

Meanwhile, Pia, Nello's new wife, kept her eyes on her plate, crumbling bread between nervous fingers into little piles on the cloth. Below her snowy cuff, Riccardo noticed a series of cuts on her wrist. They looked fresh. To her left her father – Salvatore Tolomei, a round, smooth barrel of a man – was speaking to his deputies about grain quotas, ignoring his daughter and whatever troubled her.

The Civetta delegation had been invited because Salvatore had, against all tradition, allied his daughter to the Eagles. Riccardo was less certain why he himself was there. Faustino had thanked him that morning, so what more did the Eagles owe him? He wondered what they wanted of him. He was offered no clues throughout the dinner. Faustino's conversation never touched on the Palio and Vicenzo, nor even the hasty marriage of his widow, but only the city: homilies delivered with a pointing finger, a leaning shoulder and wine-soaked breath.

'Saint Bernardino,' he mumbled, 'our very own saint, said: "Leave your *contrade*, unite under my symbol and the banner of Christ." You can see it there on the duomo.' He waved uncertainly towards the window. 'That green medallion, spikes like sunrays. But they didn't even finish the duomo, didn't finish it, built one wall and let be.

'See,' Faustino went on, breathing heavily, jabbing his finger into Riccardo's shoulder, 'God never had a chance in this city. It is the *contrade* to the end.'

He struck Riccardo as a man who usually had a very tight grip on his person and his humours, but the events of the last day had been too much for him and had cracked his resolve. His son had been taken and somewhere in the fog of Faustino's drink-addled mind, he felt the need to grip on tight with his eagle's yellow talons to everything about him. Despite the horrors of that morning, Riccardo suddenly had to fight a wholly unwanted pang of sympathy for the man.

The *capitano* continued, his words blunted by drink, 'We say *no*. The Nine said *no*. The Nine said: "Unite in your *communities*. You shall each have your *own* symbol, your *own* church. You shall not show your *family* banners nor carve your arms and your mottoes into the stone of your lintels. You will be loyal to your *contrada*, for that is everything." And more. For if we have friends, if we have alliances, we can take this city back from the corrupt dukes and have it as she was under those noble fellows, our ancestors.'

Faustino was moved almost to tears. Riccardo reflected that he had heard the same sentiments from two mouths today: a good woman and an interloper, a bad man and a native. Faustino, eerily, almost seemed to follow his train of thought.

'Saint Bernardino,' he said. 'Aye, he knew what he was about. His own symbol, the name of Christ and the sunrays, is on the Palazzo Pubblico too. They didn't finish the cathedral. Not God's house. Left it uninhabitable. No, they finished the *palazzo*. The home of the Nine. The very place where that Medici bitch dwells.'

With this, Faustino turned back to his remaining son.

Riccardo, released from the gaze of these raptor's eyes, took a pull from his glass goblet and found the courage to set about amusing the lady of the house. She looked white and drawn – shattered by her loss, or her gain: he could not tell. Like him, she was an outsider in the house of Aquila, but unlike him she was its captive. She sat between the backs of her future husband and her father, ignored by both, useless now the alliance was secure, required only to stay quiet and produce an heir with the winter.

Riccardo pushed his beans around his plate, arranging them, placing them with his fork. He flicked his eyes up once to see her draw down her dark brows in a questioning look. With a flourish, he turned his plate around to face her, smiling at her, inviting her to look. He had made a white horse of beans, constructed artfully and exactly, with the arched neck and high tail of a stallion of Araby. The pale borlotti beans gleamed from the polished pewter, a steed crossing the face of the moon. She looked down at his plate, and he could have sworn that, on another day, she would have smiled back. Instead, her eyelids lifted and she looked him full in the face for the first time.

She was exquisite.

He knew – everybody knew – that the Tolomei were descended from Egyptian royalty. Salvatore Tolomei, and all the Civetta *capitani* before him, never stopped telling people of the Ptolemaic dynasty and the famous queen Cleopatra from whom he was directly descended.

But beyond that well-worn history Riccardo had known little of the Owlet, Salvatore's only child and heir. Before he had gone to fight in Milazzo, he had been vaguely aware of Pia as a silent dark girl with black plaits like ropes. She was little worth his notice then as he chased more obvious fare: older, blonder, knowing girls, girls from his *contrada*. Now Pia was a woman and the most beautiful he had ever seen.

Her skin was white as asses' milk with the tiniest bloom high on each cheek like the delicate pink of a spring blossom. She was the sum of thousands of years of Ptolemaic beauty; what was long-dead was now living, breathing, elemental. Her great eyes were so dark, so fathomless, as to defy the viewer to divine where the radius of the pupil began and ended. Above, the lids and lashes were described in one heartbreaking sweep, as if God had turned artist and taken a tiny brush along the top of her lashes, continuing the line at the edge of her eyes.

She wore no wig, no patches and powder as other ladies did. Her lustrous hair, blackest black varnished gold by the lamplight, was half piled high with a constellation of pearls and diamonds pinned into her inky locks, half down with ringlets left loose to fall over her milky bosom. Her throat was encircled by pearls that could not rival her skin, and one golden coin rested on a pendant between her perfect breasts. The waterfall of diamonds that adorned her bodice could not match the glitter of her eyes, nor could the white silk of her wedding gown match the glossy sheen of her hair.

She was Cleopatra brought to life, taken from her sarcophagus living and now beautiful, with full rose lips and blush cheeks. But she was sad, so sad, and when Nello leaned across, took his new wife's hand in his and squeezed it cruelly, Riccardo wanted to kill him.

He did not know whether Pia had loved the man who had bled to death in his arms yesterday, but he sensed she had no love at all for her new husband. Heedless of Nello's presence, Riccardo drank in Pia's beauty until it filled him up, and what remained of his small appetite departed. He felt that he must speak to her, say something, but his brain was a blank page. He looked down at the horse he had made on his plate and trotted out the only question that he could think of: 'Can you ride?'

His insides shrivelled as he spoke – what a way to interrogate this queen of a girl! She shook her head slightly, and her ringlets fell about her bosom, glimmering in the candlelight. He thought for a moment that she would not answer, but she said, 'No. I never learned.'

She said it as if such a pastime was beneath her and dropped her gaze, snubbing him. It seemed to Riccardo as if the whole table was listening, and he wondered if she drew glances wherever she went.

Faustino, well into his cups by now, leaned across. 'Perhaps you can teach her?' he said loudly, digging Riccardo in the ribs. 'Eh?' He turned to his remaining son. 'Eh, Nello?'

Nello's face was suddenly still with impotent anger – he could not gainsay his father, but his skin grew paler still and his pink eyes glowed with fury. There was no way to answer the captain without offending at least half the company, so Riccardo stayed silent. Pia dropped her amazing eyes, and the moment seemed to stretch out as thin and taut as the string of a harpsichord. It was broken only when Faustino began to rise unsteadily to his feet. As Riccardo awkwardly tried to help him, he realized that the *capitano* was going to address the company, and sat down again, balling his fists under the table with discomfort.

'There, outside the window,' began Faustino with a drunken rush, 'over the bridge and behind the *monasterio*, there's a hill humped like an old sow, do you see it? It's the Colle Malamerenda – ah yes, Salva' – this to the *capitano* of the Civetta – 'I know you see it, I know you know it.'

Pia's rotund father was looking straight at Faustino, his dark brows drawn together in a question, not sure where this tale tended.

'The Hill of Bad Meals. Your family, Salva, the Tolomei, had a feast there once to reconcile with the Salimbeni. Both houses came to table but here is the meat of the matter – or rather, the lack of it.' He laughed alone. 'There were not thrushes enough for the company. *Capite?* Not enough birds to eat.' The table was silent. 'And the families quarrelled again. And your family, Salva, killed one and twenty Salimbeni and so named the hill to be known ever since as the Hill of Bad Meals.'

He paused, nodding repeatedly, weaving where he stood.

'Now. Here we mourn the passing of my son, but we also unite our two *contrade* in marriage. Now we have a pact – our son and daughter joined in matrimony – the thrushes are plentiful, and there will be no bad blood between our two families. Welcome, all, to this strange meeting – a wake and a wedding all at once.'

He waved an expansive arm to encompass the assembled, nearly sweeping aside a candelabrum as he did so.

'Welcome, Pia.' He waved the other arm to his daughter-in-law. 'I regret that you changed one son for the other.' Riccardo held his breath and dared not look at Nello. 'But welcome, Pia, and your father likewise. Our alliances are well, and good for this house. Welcome to the Torre too.' Faustino's hand descended on Riccardo's shoulder like a blow. 'Here. This noble fellow from the Tower *contrada*, a good man. Riccardo. A good man. Didn't mind the hooves or the blood. Tried to save *him*.'

Riccardo felt the eyes of all upon him, but looked only at Pia. Yesterday, with her gaze trained on Vicenzo as he died, had she known then that she would be forced to change one brother for another, that her alliance would stand? Faustino broke in on Riccardo's thoughts, bringing his fist down on the table with a crash that made the plates and glasses jump and the candle flames leap high.

'But I won't let him go – his death won't be in vain. We will make our friends know us, make our enemies know us. Eagles, owls and thrushes, the whole grim order of raptors. We may hunt the little birds together. And if you are on the side of Aquila, if you are with the Eagles, there will always be thrushes enough.'

Faustino sank down heavily to an appalled silence. Riccardo could not look at Nello's face – his father's meaning had been abundantly clear: '*I regret that you changed one son for the other.*' He looked instead at Pia and read fear in her great eyes. She had registered the slight against her husband and Riccardo felt a sick twist in his gut, an unaccustomed pang of foreboding.

So *this* was fear.

He was not afraid for himself, but for her. He glanced sideways at the grim-faced Faustino. Something had just been announced, a gauntlet had been thrown down.

Into the silence Faustino's handclaps sounded like twin thunderbolts, as a quartet of pages advanced into the room. All were garbed in Eagle colours of yellow and black. The first pair bore a great confection from the kitchens; the second bore the Palio banner itself, folded into a neat triangle between them. The dish was set on the table to a collective intake of breath, and the flag set before Faustino with no fewer gasps. Riccardo fixed his eyes on the great platter placed directly before him – Faustino's pastry chefs had outdone themselves. The pudding was a wondrous and terrible thing: a great white sugar horse, prancing and arching on a celestial clouds of baked meringue. And on the horse's back Death himself rode, with his face hooded and his evil scythe curved above his head. Death's robe was not solidly black but pied in black and white like the Balzana flag of Siena. Unsteadily, Faustino reached forward, broke the end off the scythe and offered it to Riccardo. It was licorice, a strange enough sweetmeat for a funeral, but for a wedding the portents were disastrous.

Faustino took the Palio banner from the tablecloth and waved it under Riccardo's nose, stroking the folded fabric in his hand as if he held a hobbled dove.

'That barren bitch sent it me,' Faustino mumbled. 'The duchess. Sent it to me as condolence for my son.' He exhaled a long breath. 'It was a noble act. 'Tis such a shame.'

Riccardo's senses prickled. 'A shame?'

'By the Palio dell'Assunta she'll be gone. She's got till the sixteenth day of August. *Novus novem.*'

Riccardo wondered exactly how much Faustino had had to drink. Was the duchess in danger? That little Latin tag at the end – Riccardo was not much schooled but it was close enough to Tuscan to guess that it was something about 'nine' and 'new'. What was happening to him? Since when did he care about the fate of others? Why had his cold heart been touched twice today, by a young woman and an older one? And yesterday too, what had made him run back, through the flying hooves, to help Vicenzo? That gesture had brought him to this place tonight and to the *palazzo* and its chamber of horror earlier that day. It was better to have nothing to do with any of it. Riccardo got to his feet.

'Nello!' bawled Faustino.

His younger son stood to mirror Riccardo. Riccardo froze.

'Take him. Show him,' Faustino commanded and turned to his guest. 'Signor Bruni. Riccardo. Goodnight.'

Riccardo wondered if Faustino had thought better of allowing him to live. His back prickled as he left the room after Nello. He could sense Pia's eyes on him, but he dared not turn to look at her.

Riccardo and Nello walked down the panelled passages, an unlikely pairing. Riccardo knew Nello did not want him here, that he resented his reckless act of compassion for his older brother. But something was making him act with civility, something beyond his father's directive. Nello needed him for some reason.

'I hear it said that you will ride for the Tower next month in the Palio dell'Assunta?' Nello's gambit was a polite enquiry.

Riccardo was sure of it, but answered carefully, 'If they elect me.'

Nello nodded. 'You should know, then, that I am riding for the Eagles. And I will win.'

This was no challenge; Nello did not say it to provoke. It was said with complete confidence and more: satisfaction. Riccardo knew that his earlier instincts had been right – Nello was glad his brother was dead. He was now the Eagle's champion, something that, throughout his freakish childhood, he must always have longed to be. Riccardo made no reply, as he followed the pale figure down the stone stair, his feet stumbling only a little as he realized where they were headed.

The Panther was still there, his beaten flesh beginning to stink and stretch on his bones in the summer heat. Nello began to unbind the body. With an increasing feeling of unreality, Riccardo began to help and felt the slippery ropes come away in his hands, jellied gouts of blood gathering like blackberries at the Panther's wrists.

Nello laid out a long feed sack on the stony floor. Riccardo had no choice but to help Nello roll the body up in the sack. He took the legs as Nello took the head, but instead of turning up the stair again, Nello approached a blind wall with a stone eagle carved into it. As they moved closer, the torchlight carved deep shadows in the stony grooves, throwing the eagle's single eye into relief. Nello pressed his thumb to the eye and the wall sprang back, not with the stony grating of a long-closed tomb, but quick and silent and well used.

'Come on,' he said.

The dark door closed behind them on some hidden spring and they entered a stony tunnel with torches burning in sconces placed a man's length apart. This was one of the *bottini*, the underground network of aqueducts and sewers below the city that radiated out under the *contrade* to the hills. They carried the body carefully along the white stone walkways, skirting the green pools of stagnant water. Riccardo fixed his eyes on Nello ahead of him, his white hair gleaming in the torchlight.

Riccardo's misgivings were a cold stone in his stomach.

'Is he to be laid in some private mausoleum of the Panthers?' His voice sounded forth into the black beyond and returned to chase behind them, as if spirits rose to moan at them from their necropolis.

Nello's laugh, likewise, circled around the tunnels and back. 'He's to be laid in the most beautiful place in the world. None too private, though.'

The way was long and the grisly burden heavy but Riccardo did not mind if it meant the dead Panther would be given some small rite of passage. All the same, his arms were aching by the time Nello stopped and set down his end of the body on the walkway. Riccardo did likewise. Above them, a square of light, bleeding white, showed around the edges of a trapdoor. Nello stood tall and pushed, and with a grating of ancient stone a paving slid sideways to reveal a rectangle of sky pricked out with stars. Nello vaulted up until his head and shoulders were in the night air and looked around.

'Clear,' he said. 'Push him out.'

This was no easy task. In the end Riccardo, being the stronger, had to clamber into the fresh air to yank the body from below. He had expected to emerge into some clandestine cemetery outside the city, where the body could be disposed of in secret, thus minimizing any reprisals from the Panther *contrada*. He could not have been more wrong.

He was right in the centre of the deserted Piazza del Campo, and the paving from which they had emerged formed the lowest balustrade of the fountain. He and Nello dragged the body out, under the noses of the stone wolves who spouted water, silvered by moonlight, into the bowl of the fountain, as if they gathered to feast on the carrion. They rolled the Panther out like a ham from a cloth, like Cleopatra from her carpet. *Pia*, thought Riccardo. *She is part of this now.*

Nello dragged the body to the very centre of the piazza's shell. Riccardo helped him unwrap the body, but refused to help him place the arms wide in the position in which the Eagle *contrada* left all their dead – the knifed knave in the alleyway, the greedy prelate on his own altar. Everyone would know who had done this deed, and if the Aquila wanted to send a message, it was not Riccardo's message to send. The dreadful flesh gleamed pale in the moonlight, angelic, not aquiline; in the cruciform almost Christ-like. Sickened, Riccardo turned away from the Panther's ruined corpse and looked Nello in his eyes. In the moonlight he seemed almost normal – his white hair merely blond, his pink eyes darkened now to an amber hue. Hawk's eyes, like his father and dead brother.

'What now?' Riccardo asked.

'Now?' said Nello, all pretence abandoned. 'Now you go back where you belong.' With that he vaulted nimbly down into the tunnel again, pulling the opening closed behind him.

The sound of stone on stone alerted two officers of the Watch, who had turned a corner into the piazza. Their tricornes were sharks' fins in the moonlight, the barrels of their pistols gleaming.

Without hesitation Riccardo made straight for the Palazzo Pubblico for the second time that day, Saint Bernardino's medallion, IHS, the name of Christ in the sunrays, leading him there like the star of the nativity. His step quickened faster and faster as if it was the ghost of the Panther rather than the Watch who pursued him, and despite the lateness of the hour he hammered fit to wake the dead on the great doors. Sure that no one inside had heeded him, he turned back to face the square: he could not evade the Watch now. But as he looked at the vast moonlit space, he felt the doors open at his back. His last thought as he plunged into the palace was that Nello had been right. It was the most beautiful place in the world.

∞

Pia retired to her chamber as soon as she could, her head aching, reeling from the day she'd had to endure. The wedding feast had held a surprise for her, as if to taunt her further: the unknown horseman whom she had seen at the Palio, the one she had secretly named as her champion. The comparison between him and Nello was even more extreme than it had been between him and Vicenzo, but when she had watched the horseman leave the feast with her new husband, she'd known him for the Eagles' creature and she damned all three of them in the same breath. Them – and all the men on the earth, including her father: he could burn too. There was no point remonstrating with Salvatore – it was too late for that – but she had begged him at the feast to send on her books and her mother's clothes. He'd waved away her requests and turned from her to discuss grain quotas with the Eagle *capitani*. She suspected he had forgotten her words as soon as they were uttered.

She'd gone up to her chamber after the feast and sat there waiting as the moon rose, with a growing sense of dread. Her bedding had been changed, so Nicoletta would have told Nello that she was undergoing her woman's courses. She prayed it would be enough to keep him away, even on their wedding night.

But he came. She heard his step on the stair: dreaded, expected and lighter than Nicoletta's. When he entered the room, his hair was disarranged, his pink eyes glittering; he seemed excited. As he came towards her she saw something else glittering – something in his hand.

A pair of small horse shears.

Pia was sure she was going to die. She kept quite still, sitting on her bed, while he set about her. But instead of slicing her throat, he began grabbing great chunks of hair and shearing them off. Her beautiful locks fell about her in swags and hanks of blackness on the white coverlet. At first she held her hands over her scalp, trying to protect her hair, but when he sliced at her fingers too, as if he would cut them off, she moved her hands to cover her face instead. The blood from her fingertips seeped into her eyes but she did not care: anything was better than seeing the look on Nello's face as he chopped at her in a frenzy. She went limp, letting him fling her about and turn her as he would, thinking that only by letting him wear himself out would she survive. At last, his fury spent, he yanked her to her feet. He stood her in front of the window, turned into a looking-glass by the lamplight inside and the darkness without.

She regarded herself dispassionately – as strangely detached as she'd been the day he'd laid bruises on her arm. She looked quite different: her hair now about her ears and forehead, and her face smeared with her own blood. Behind her face Nello's floated, sated and gloating. She understood that she was lucky. With a wisdom well beyond her own innocence, she knew that if he had not cut her hair he would have raped her, even if she bled.

'There,' he hissed in triumph. 'Let's see if he'll smile at you now.'

When he'd gone Pia picked up the shears from the floor. She brushed her own hair from the blades and noticed, as if they belonged to someone else, that her hands were shaking terribly. She looked at her reflection in the window again and, consciously steadying her hands, tried to neaten her hair until the sides fell evenly and the black slab of her new fringe lay straight across her forehead. She saw that huge tears were swelling in her eyes and falling down her face unchecked. So she was to be punished for the actions of others as well as her own. While she cut, she damned the horseman again. Because he'd smiled at her and asked her a question, she'd paid a high price for his caprice. And yet his smile had been the one bright moment in a terrible day. He'd been the only man to address her, to question her, as if he cared about the answer.

Can you ride?

An idea began to form slowly in her numbed brain. If she *could* ride, far and fast, she could get away from Nello. There was no escape from this city, isolated in the hills, without a horse. She must order her thoughts. Think, *think*.

Pia stooped to tuck the shears into her laced boot. She would not be unarmed in the presence of her husband again. As she bent, Cleopatra's coin fell from her bosom and hit her smartly in the teeth, swinging, winking, on its chain. As she straightened up, Pia of the Tolomei caught a glimpse of her reflection in the window. The candle-light was just bright enough for her to see how much she resembled the long-dead queen.

6

The Forest

When Violante Beatrix de' Medici was a little girl, and used to gaze from the windows of her father's Bavarian castle, she did not see the expensive glazing, nor the fine leaden quarrel-panes, but looked past and through them to the forest. She loved the trees, the way they whispered reassuringly at night, the way they stretched out and closed around the castle like friendly arms reaching to embrace. When, on occasion, she could persuade her nurse to take her for a walk – a battle, for fresh air was not deemed to be healthy for the young princess – she loved the darkness, the deepness of the cover, even on sunny days. She felt safe in the forest, and more at home than she did in the airy, gilded rooms of the palace.

Walking further one day than she ever had, she met the woodsmen with their axes, hacking at the trunks, their blades biting white wounds into the wood, chips flying to land on the dark mossy ground like snow. She stopped in her tracks, and the woodsmen stopped too in her presence, pulling their caps from sweaty crowns, spitting the deer gristle that they chewed to the forest floor to lie with the sawdust. Violante turned and the tears spilled from her eyes. The nurse, trudging back to the palace in the princess's wake, tried to explain: trees had to be felled to make the chairs in her father's palace, the houses of the poor, even the books that she so loved to read. For that moment Violante didn't care. She wanted the forest to be left alone.

Six short years later, she was sitting in the great salon of her new home, the Palazzo Vecchio in Florence, holding the hand of her new groom. She had been married that day in Florence's great duomo, had endured three hours of interminable feasting, and was now listening to a musical recital. She could barely concentrate on the music for her stomach was churning with the unbearable and thrilling expectation of her own wedding night, when Ferdinando, the handsomest man she had ever laid eyes on, would take her to bed. To compound her misgivings, she smelled that smell that had once made her so unhappy — wick wood, newly cut and carved. She looked across the great chamber at the only new thing in this room of priceless antiques, the pianoforte.

Ferdinando credited himself with the invention of this instrument. In reality, he had been closeted for the last few months with the true inventor of the pianoforte. Bartolomeo Cristofori was a comely Paduan who had developed this strange hybrid from the harpsichord and the clavichord. It sat squat, newly carved and varnished, on four spindly legs. Violante had peeped beneath the lid, breathed in the sick smell of new wood, and gazed at the intricate arrangement within of strings and hammers. Shyly, she had struck a black key, then a white one, and listened to the resonant discord, a strange new note, thicker, cleaner and somehow more real than a harpsichord. She marvelled that something with such a beautiful exterior could be so complex on the inside.

Moved by a sudden association of ideas, she squeezed Ferdinando's hand, but he did not mark her. He was watching intently, sitting poker upright, as a boy rose from his chair and approached the instrument. As Bartolomeo Cristofori himself played the accompaniment, the boy began to sing a motet in the clear chiming tones of a castrato. He was a beautiful youth with the blond curls of an angel and a voice to match. Violante felt tears start in her eyes, both for the forest of her childhood and the beauty of the sound. She turned to her new husband, whom she knew by repute to be a connoisseur of music. Ferdinando looked happy for the first time that day.

Only one man at the recital knew that Ferdinando was enraptured by the singer – the famous countertenor Cecchino – not the song. This man knew Ferdinando very well, for he was Gian Gastone de' Medici, the groom's younger brother. He felt sorry for the little Bavarian bird, for to his certain knowledge Ferdinand had sodomized the castrato the night before in scenes of quite astonishing debauchery, even to a libertine such as he. Gian Gastone was an accomplished gamer as well as a dedicated homosexual, and he knew that Violante had been dealt a marked card. He sensed, as he listened, that this would not be the last time that Cecchino made the little bride cry; and he made a bet of his own, just for fun, that Ferdinando would not lay a finger on his wife, that night or any other.

Violante opened her eyes. Gretchen was leaning over her, shaking her shoulder, her long grey plait tickling her cheek. 'Madam, there's a young man to see you.'

Violante blinked, as her dream fled with the shadows outside the warm circle of Gretchen's lamp. The old woman said with emphasis: '*The* young man.'

So Violante ended the day where she had begun it – in the Hall of the Nine. Riccardo Bruni stood alone in the great chamber, twisting his tricorne in his hands. His eyes moved around the great paintings restlessly. He looked hunted. Gretchen had told her mistress on the way down the staircase that she had turned the Watch from the doors, as they had come in pursuit of him, but it looked as if it was more than the Constables of the Watch that the young man feared.

He spun round at her footstep, took a pace towards her, and for a moment she thought he might throw himself into her arms. Then: 'I'll help you.' It was all said in a rush. He stopped. She looked in his eyes. That a man so tall, so well-favoured and self-assured, could look so haunted roused her vestigial maternal instincts. He needed to be fed. A blanket, a fire and some broth.

'Gretchen,' she said, 'the kitchens.'

Moments later, Riccardo Bruni was seated before the golden mouth of the kitchen fire that the servants kept burning late into the night lest the duchess need anything. He had a blanket round his shoulders and a cup of broth in his hands. Gretchen hovered in the shadows outside the firelight, an unobtrusive chaperone. Violante sat opposite Riccardo, on the other side of the flames, watching him closely. The smell of new wood burning on the fire, summer sap hissing, brought its own memories and she felt a terrible sense of foreboding. The young horseman, though, looked better, and she felt she could now ask.

'Did something lead you to change your mind?'

'Faustino Caprimulgo . . . He . . . took a life.' Riccardo breathed out as he spoke. 'No. More than that. He beat a man to death.' He looked up. 'The Panther, the one who knocked Vicenzo from his horse.'

Violante shuddered, recalling the race and the way the hot-headed jockey of the Panthers had lashed out with his whip, not knowing that he struck the heir of the Eagles. She had expected reprisals from Faustino, but this? This was a shock.

'His name is Egidio Albani, son of Raffaello Albani, captain of the Panther *contrada*.' She had taken the trouble to find out and had sent a purse round to his house.

'I helped carry him. I had no choice. He is outside.'

Violante half rose. '*Here?*'

'In the square. He is laid out, for all to see, in the Eagles' cross. He is a message.'

She looked down, considering. She had heard reports many times over her ten years' rule of bodies found posed in that dreadful attitude. She spoke her first thought. 'He should have a Christian burial.' Her second thought surprised her. 'Did the Watch see?'

Riccardo shook his head. 'No. They followed me instead. There was no one else in the piazza. Nello . . . I'm telling this all wrong.' He brushed his hand across his forehead as if to wipe away the memory. 'Faustino's younger son, Nello, bid me help him carry the body. He left me to be found with it. It was a plan.'

'Of Faustino's?' Violante's eyes were gentle, her question sharp. She could see Riccardo thinking about the answer carefully, his face serious and golden in the firelight, his lashes casting spindly shadows on his cheek.

'I don't think so. He invited me to his son's passing feast . . . and Nello's wedding feast. I think he likes me.' The words sounded childish and pulled at her heart.

The question had nudged his remembrance. 'Faustino said something strange, though. At the end of the feast he showed me that you had sent him the Palio banner.'

Violante's skin began to prickle. Her gambit, had it worked? Had Faustino seen the honour in her gesture?

'He was grateful, but he said . . . he said that it was a shame that – forgive me – you would not be here to see the next Palio.'

Now Violante's flesh began to prickle with dread. The Palio dell'Assunta was a little over a month away. Her voice was a whisper. 'What did he mean? That I would be dead, or gone from Siena?'

Riccardo Bruni would not meet her eyes. 'I do not know. Only that you have a month of your rule left to you. Until the sixteenth day of August. He said something else too, just as I was leaving the feast . . . something about the number nine.'

'What did he say *exactly*?' Violante's voice was sharper than she had meant.

Riccardo furrowed his brow, struggling to remember. *'Noveschi novemi.* No. *Novus novem.'*

Violante sat up very straight. There had been nothing amiss with her schooling. *'Novus novem?* You're sure?'

He was. 'Yes.'

She looked at him and then at the flames, the burning, damned forest. Hot fire, hellfire.

The New Nine.

'He's rebuilding the Nine. He's going to take the city back.' She rose abruptly. 'Come with me.'

She took him, by the light of Gretchen's candle, to the map room. Every inch of the wall crawled with territories and cartographs, from the ancient to the modern. They stopped before a great plan of the city, gold in the candlelight, grey in the creeping dawn. The artist, unknown and long gone, had rendered the houses of the city both great and small, the civic buildings, the *contrade* with their churches and palaces, with the fine lines of his etching. All was complete and exact, and it looked to Violante like a plan of campaign, a battlefield. And crowning all, above the name of the city, two twin boys suckling at a she-wolf's teats – the town's very emblem: the she-wolf suckling the infants Romulus and Remus. According to legend, Siena had been founded by Senius, son of Remus. So both twins had founded great cities: Romulus created Rome, and Remus fathered a child to found Siena. Violante felt suddenly awake and alive. She paced and pointed as she spoke.

'Here are the walls of the citadel. Here are the three thirds or *tertieri* of the city. Terzo di Camollia, Terzo di

San Martino, and here, in the Terzo della Città, right in the heart of the city, sits Faustino, in the Eagle *contrada*. He needs eight conspirators to revive the Nine. Who are his allies? Not the Panther, that we know.'

'Civetta,' said the young man, abruptly. 'Salvatore Tolomei's daughter was married to Nello before Vicenzo was cold.'

Violante saw a light jump in his eyes. She recalled the young goddess she had seen at the Palio: betrothed, bereaved and now wed. Violante was too used to political alliance to find this strange.

'Very well. And we may now, firmly, place the Panthers in opposition. But who are the other seven? We must understand Faustino's alliances, his funding, his plan. How does the Palio connect to this? Why is that to be his endgame?' She was reminded, once again, of chess.

'Duchess,' Riccardo diffidently interrupted her flow, 'might we not, that is—' He gestured between the three of them, joining them in an ineffectual triumvirate. 'Might we not need . . . help?'

Violante turned suddenly. 'We do need allies. You are right. Here we are: an old lady, a middling one and a young man . . .' She paced about. 'But this very day I wrote to my brother-in-law, Gian Gastone de' Medici, to assist me in this matter. He is a good man, and jealous of his inheritance; he would not let such an important part of his duchy secede from him. Nor would he wish to inherit a rotten city.'

'You inherit the apple and the worm comes too,' put in Gretchen grimly.

Violante glanced out of the window. The city slept, but the dawn must be coming. 'Go home, Riccardo Bruni,' she said.

He looked straight at her, and she answered the question in his eyes.

'No. I am not giving up. But you are right. We need alliances. I shall think on it, and we will speak again.'

He bowed and went to leave by the great doors. 'Wait,' she called, 'it is better that you are not seen. Gretchen, lead Signor Bruni out through the kitchens.'

She watched him hesitate, and thought that he would thank her, but his thoughts were elsewhere. 'And Egidio? The Panther?'

She liked him for his question and opened her mouth to say that she would send her sergeant-at-arms to recover the Panther's body, that she would have him returned to his family directly with a pall for the funeral. But other words came.

'Signor Bruni. Riccardo.' She laid her fingertips on his arm. 'I promise you that by nightfall he will be in the ground. But for a few more hours he must lie where he is.'

∞

When Riccardo had gone, Violante wandered back to the map room and looked again at the *contrade* of the city, divided into thirds, the thirds of the city bounded by walls, and the she-wolf and her boy twins presiding over all. One twin suckled and one looked straight out of the etching at her.

She called for her riding cloak and set forth, alone, on a pilgrimage. In the grey light of dawn she passed through the silver city, a slip-shadow, hurrying east across the piazza. In the near-dark she could see a body lying in a cruciform shape by the fountain, but she averted her eyes and hurried past. She took the little streets to the Giraffa *contrada*, the ward of her chief councillor Francesco Maria Conti. She passed his *palazzo*, the hereditary seat of the Conti family, and wondered if Conti was watching her from behind his blank, black windows. She quickened her steps before her practical self assumed control once more. After all, Conti knew that she had come here. He knew why as well. Conti knew most things. She reached the Giraffa church of San Francesco, the plain, block frontage looming from the dark, laid her hand on the door and went within.

Inside, there were candles burning, and an acolyte sweeping in readiness for morning mass. She smiled at the boy who stared, round-eyed. Violante walked forwards, the familiar length of the nave, to the icon that hung above the altar. She paused to genuflect, crossed her bosom. Then, with no disrespect but merely friendly familiarity, she smiled at her friend, the Madonna del Latte.

Violante had first seen the painting when, as the new governess of the city, she had made it her business to visit every *contrada* and its attendant church. At mass, sitting in the prominent pews of the Conti family, she had laid eyes on the most wonderful representation of the Virgin she had ever seen. Violante had always been drawn to

Mary, a woman who had known what it was to love a son and lose him and mourn him. Here before her, Mary fed the infant Jesus, holding her breast to his mouth, while the infant suckled hungrily.

Before that mass and that day, Violante had been telling herself how well she was doing, throwing herself into her new position, learning about every family, every *contrada*, every trade and tradition of her new city. Then, looking at the Madonna feeding her son, both parties gazing only at each other, absorbed in this elemental bond, she had felt a physical pain in her breast. For the rest of the service she could neither speak nor sing.

Afterwards, dining with Francesco Maria Conti at his house, she had asked about the painting, as casually as she could. Conti, with the pride due to his *contrada*, told his new mistress that the painting was by the Sienese master Sassetta, and told her defensively that the panel could not be moved into the palace. She would never have desired such a thing, knowing that the painting gave her such pain; but over the coming weeks she had been drawn back again and again to the quiet church, to commune with the mother and child. Gradually, the panel had begun to give her peace, not pain, and she had begun to share her problems with the Madonna.

Today, in the grey dawn that would reveal the Panther's body to the city, she told Mary that Egidio Albani had been slain and laid out like her own son Christ. Under the almond eye of the icon, she suddenly felt a terrible misgiving. How could she let Egidio's mother find him like that, let the city talk of his torture, just to win allies against Faustino? Egidio was a boy of twenty. *Twenty,* Violante read in the Madonna's eyes. *The same age your twins would have been, had they lived.*

Violante ran from the church, hurrying in the grey, unpromising dawn light to the Piazza del Campo. She would instruct the Watch to gather up Egidio's body, to wash him and box him and take him home to his mother. But as she reached the great shell-shaped *campo* she stopped, abruptly. A small knot of people gathered next to the fountain, over the Panther's body.

She was too late.

7
The She-Wolf

The sorrowing sun was setting at the end of a battle-battered day in Milazzo when the young Riccardo Bruni was taken to be one of a scouting party in the hills. General Alvaraz y Leon, the notorious Spanish general, had been firing villages that had harboured the Austrians. Advance parties of Spanish had been rounding up villagers, ready for Alvarez y Leon's men to ride through with their firebrands.

In one village Riccardo's troop came upon a little church with a stone cross, in which all the citizens had been trapped within, save one. A young woman tugged at a vast tree trunk that had been cast across the door. 'I cannot move it by myself,' she gasped, 'and my son is within with his grandam. It is time for his feed.' Riccardo could hear the shouts from within, overlaid with the high, keening cry of a baby. The men began to dismount but Riccardo reached her first. The woman turned to him. 'Help me,' she begged.

She was fair, with the apricot skin of the South and pleading eyes as dark as pansies. As she grasped his arm in desperation, he could smell the sweet heat of her body. His eyes dropped from her gaze to where her breasts strained at the lacings of her bodice. What he saw there made him take a step back. A dark stain spread from each nipple into the open weave of the cambric. The thudding of his heart became the thudding of distant hooves: the captain laid his ear to the ground. 'Above a hundred horse,' he said, 'heading this way. Let's be gone.' He did not need to explain; they were only five men. Riccardo, his knees giving way with fear, allowed himself to be dragged away.

The woman screamed after them until they were almost out of sight and then turned back to the wooden trunk, clawing at it desperately. Riccardo rode with his eyes shut, as behind them Alvarez y Leon and his hundred horse swept into the village with their torches. He wished he could shut his ears too.

That night on the cold hill he did not feel the heat of the fire nor hear the songs the men sang to cheer themselves. He turned his back to the blaze and watched instead the little church burning merrily in the valley below, the cross silhouetted black against the flame.

In the morning they rode down the hill into an eerie blanket of silence. No birds sang. The church was charred rubble, with a hundred black skeletons within and one without, her hand outstretched to the door. 'Aye,' said the captain with grudging respect, kicking the skull of the single skeleton with his scuffed boot. 'The she-wolf will stay with her cub even as it burns.'

Riccardo threw up again and again into the ashes, and as he emptied his stomach on to the razed ground he vowed never to be afraid again.

Riccardo awoke in the hay of the Tower stable, with his father shaking him by the shoulder. The skeletons disappeared, insubstantial as smoke. Riccardo raised himself up to a sitting position. He looked on his father's stocky form and smiled, half relieved and half strangely sorry. It was morning, and outside an angry horse clopped and neighed on the cobbles. Domenico Bruni, squat and bearded, cocked his head to one side and smiled back at his son, his dolorous day in bed forgotten. He was back to work and, it seemed, happy about it.

'Give me a hand, Dawdle Bones,' he said, not without affection. His voice, unused for a whole day, was gruff. 'I've a mighty tricky fellow in for shoeing.'

Domenico thrust down his arm, to haul up his son. It was encircled with the leather bracelets of the farrier's trade and smelled, like Domenico's whole body, of horse. After his strange dream, after everything that had happened yesterday, Riccardo could not have imagined anything more comforting than his father's arm. He grasped it and rose to his feet, draping his own arm over his father's shoulders as they walked companionably to the street. The younger man, taller by a head, looked nothing like his father, but Domenico was the sum total of Riccardo's family, and family was all.

Riccardo followed him to the cobbles, where a black stallion danced and spun, its inky flanks shining wetly in the morning light. The song of the bells, the screech of the starlings, the smell of the fearful horse, all served to root him here. Of course he would not help the duchess. This was his *contrada,* the Torre, the Tower. These were his people. He was home.

The waiting beast bucked and skittered, his eyes full of fear, rolling to show the whites. The ubiquitous Zebra, on one of his many disparate missions around the city, was making a gallant attempt to hold the head-rein. His little tricorne hat lay on the ground where it had been knocked; his nose was bloody where the creature had raised its head too fast. Riccardo rapidly tossed the boy a rag.

'Stand clear,' he said.

Zebra did not need to be asked twice. Cheerfully enough, the boy went to sit on the mounting block to watch the drama, rolling the rag into two little nubbins, which he stuffed up his nose.

Riccardo eyed the plunging horse. He could tell at once that the animal was not naturally bad tempered – horses rarely were. There was usually something frightening them and with this one it was clear what it was. The horse could see the farrier's bench and his father's instruments: the paring knife, the rasp and the hoof pick. Riccardo walked forward, talking all the time, of anything, of everything, of nothing. He took the huge, heavy velvet head in his hands, felt the warm nap of horsehair under his hands, and the massive skull beneath the skin. Riccardo cupped his palms behind the creature's eyes, blinkering them, closing off the world, letting the creature see only forward. Only him.

'*Buongiorno*,' he said.

The horse calmed at once, snorted, nibbled his collar. Riccardo felt the breath, sweet with hay, on his cheek. He wanted to rest his head on the black silken cheek and close his eyes.

He needed to come to ground, to blinker his own view. He needed to block the unwelcome sights from his mind's eye: the events of last evening, his night in the palace, the map, the revelation of the Nine and, overlaying it all, the image of the Panther, decomposing, arms spread, in the Piazza. He thought of the duchess and her kind eyes, of how she had rescued him, of her concern that the Panther should be buried with all rites. But he also understood why she had to leave the body where it lay. He understood, but he was sick to his guts.

To help his father, that was the thing. To shrink the world into a circle, to the earthbound round that was the horse's shoe. To do something essentially Sienese, with a man who, like him, was also Sienese, born and bred here. To forget about the duchess and what he had promised her.

He thought, now and again through the morning, of the beauteous Pia, of her long luxuriant hair as black as this horse's cheek, of how it would look tumbled across a pillow. When he'd told the duchess they needed help, he'd thought of Pia, of how she'd looked at the feast, of how he'd seen her eyes as fearful as this yearling's. He'd thought of saying her name out loud to the duchess, claiming that Pia would help. She would like, he knew, to walk in peace, to raise her children – even if they were Nello's – without the threat of the blood eagle.

But he had stopped his tongue. He had seen Nello's freezing gaze when her smile had fallen upon Riccardo, and he did not want to compound Pia's troubles. Nello was a man who could talk of the Palio one instant, and the next drag a ruined body into the night, to grow warm with the dawn and reveal itself to the city stinking in the full glare of the sun. He whispered all this to the horse, into the warm twitching ear that flicked past his nose like a black feather. *Yes, I'm listening.*

Riccardo's morning pleased him – the simple rhythm of the hammer, the burning smell of the pared hoof. His father's familiar homilies fell from his lips on to the cobbles like horseshoe nails.

'No shoe, no horse.'

'A horse runs on one toe . . . 'Tis as if we walk on tiptoe or balance on a single finger.'

'The foot, the hoof is all.'

Riccardo smiled at his father, glad that the old man's spirits were lifting with the approach of the next Palio, in a little more than a month. Domenico talked on, expecting no reply, getting none. He talked of this horse, of others, of the trials run out in the nearby Maremma, of likely *fantini*, unlikely winners.

Zebra crept forward off his block, closer and closer, to watch the shoeing. In a city obsessed with horses, Domenico Bruni was a shaman or an alchemist, possessing knowledge that could heal a lame horse, or craft special shoes to correct an uneven stride. He could work magic, and on most days strangers would gather at the forge, to ask advice about feed, or tack, or bedding. Every day Zebra would hang around, helping and hindering all at once, hoping one day to know a fraction of what Domenico knew.

Like most men, Domenico was happy to talk of the subject he loved and, kindly man that he was, began to talk to Zebra, the boy's answers muffled by the rags up his nose. Riccardo, communing with the yearling, heard his father's gruff voice teaching the boy exactly the same things he'd been told as a child: the anatomy of a hoof, the topography, the little hills and valleys, the names and terms that were the longitudes and latitudes of his father's world. The sight of the old man and the little boy bent over a hoof took Riccardo back to his own education, the only schooling he had ever had. Zebra, rapt, was almost bent double, peering close, fascinated. Domenico was thrilled to have a pupil.

'The hoof is like a castle, or a citadel. On the outside there are very strong walls, and the hoof is the same. This dark layer on the very outside is the wall, it is hard and brittle. The walls are a protective shield for the softer hoof within; they are very tough, and gather the impact of the hoofbeats and spread it evenly.'

He moved his pick inwards to the concentric lines of the hoof.

'Here's the water line, just inside the walls, like a moat. It is very resistant – it carries the force of the strikes upon the ground and supports the outer wall.

'The white line is the inner layer of the wall. It's this yellowish ring, see? This is like the grass-filled motte of a castle. It is spongier so it wears faster than the hard walls and actually goes in a bit; see, it is a groove, and look – it has got sand and grit inside.

'When a horseshoe is applied, it is fixed to the wall. Nails are driven in, oblique to the walls. Watch me. You bang them in here through the outside edge of the white line and they come out at the wall's surface.'

Domenico grasped the foreleg firmly between his knees and began to hammer. Riccardo steadily kept up his stream of talk, crooning to the horse, gently pulling its ears. The horse stood stock-still.

'Does it hurt?' asked Zebra, as the hammer struck sparks from the iron shoe.

'Does it hurt to bite your fingernails?' countered Domenico. 'No. Not unless you bite them to the quick. 'Tis the same here. For that is all this hoof is – like a fingernail. If you drive the nails into the walls correctly a horse won't feel a thing.

'Now, inside the walls we have the thirds of the hoof. The frog is the dark island in the middle, like the bailey or the keep of the castle. It is this heart-shape – see? It is squashy and gives to the touch – it absorbs the shock of the hoof striking the ground. If the hoof is the fingernail, this is the fingertip.'

Domenico dropped the hoof with a clang, took Zebra's hand and pushed one of the child's little fleshy pads with his heavy hardened fingertip. Riccardo remembered how his father had taken his own hand at the same age and pressed their fingers together. Domenico bent again and took up the next hoof.

'And see – this is the sole. It is soft in shod horses because it never touches the ground. It is crumbly too, like ciabatta, and you can scratch it out with a hoofpick – see?'

He suited the action to the words and Zebra watched, fascinated, as the soft flesh crumbled away to the ground like the sand in an hourglass.

Domenico shifted around, to move his shadow from the heel of the hoof.

'And here is the final third – the castle gateway, at the back here. It is called the bars – like a portcullis. They are inward folds of the wall at the heel of the hoof. And above it all,' he finished, 'just like in a castle, there is a crown at the top: the coronet. This is the crown of the hoof.'

Domenico's gnarled finger circled the glossy hoof, indicating the coronet, his lesson done.

It was suddenly borne in upon Riccardo that his father's life was bounded in a horseshoe: the grand amphitheatre of the Piazza del Campo and the smaller, horned foot of the animals that raced there. His world was no greater than that. It struck him too, with the singing clarity of the hammer blow, that the hoof was the map he had seen that morning in the palace: Siena with her boundary walls and her regional thirds. For a moment the revelation seemed hugely significant, a key to unlock the future of the city. He did not know quite what to do with the concept, so he recounted all of it to the horse, which nodded sagely. Riccardo was jolted from his warm, golden Sienese reverie by his father's voice as the fourth foot was placed, ringing, on the floor.

'Now, that's enough schooling, Zebra. Get you to the fountain for me – fill this bucket.'

Riccardo was so drowsy that for a moment he did not register what his father had said. Slowly, the significance of the command penetrated. Domenico had sent Zebra for water from the Piazza del Campo, from the fountain where the Panther's carrion rotted as the sun rose high.

He dropped the horse's head and ran, not heeding his father's shout. Zebra was swift and as the great square opened out before him he saw the boy ahead of him, running to the well, under the shadow of the palace and the great tower, swinging his bucket. Before he could stop him, Zebra had pushed his way through the knot of people by the fountain. Riccardo slowed, defeated. He was too late. He looked up as a black cloud of starlings passed overhead. As the boy's scream pierced the air, they checked and turned as one, changing direction back to the tower. Riccardo ran to the boy's side, dropped to his knees and turned Zebra's head into his shoulder, away from the terrible sight. The constables were here now and a physician whose presence was twelve hours too late. Zebra vomited, suddenly, and Riccardo held the back of his clammy little neck over a drain. He doused his own kerchief in the fountain and wiped the boy's forehead and mouth. Zebra's lips were soft, his skin tender. He did not deserve this.

Riccardo realized that all of this morning had been a dream. A dream of Siena not as it was, but as it could be.

As he stood the boy wrapped his arms round his leg, tight, not letting go. Riccardo gently loosened Zebra's grip. He kneeled again and looked into the boy's face, a face that would never again see a world that had no evil in it. The face of innocence lost.

Enough.

'Zebra, do you want to stop this? Do you want us all to live in peace?'

An old woman, a middling one and a young man, the duchess had said. To that, add, *a boy*. Useless, she might say, but Zebra could go anywhere, was tolerated by all, questioned by none. Zebra nodded and Riccardo knew he was done with holding his tongue.

'Then help me. Find out when Pia of the Tolomei takes her shrift in the Aquila church.'

8

The Goose

Pia lifted the little bottle that Nello had handed her to the
dying light of the pantry window and read the white
apothecary's label. 'Mullein': she spelled out the writing
inscribed in a neatly inked hand. 'Birch bark, myrrh, indigo,
mulberry, rock alum, black sulphur.' Above the black characters was a tiny picture of a white goose with an orange beak and
a black bead of an eye, and, above him, the green-and-white
pennant of the Oca, the Goose contrada.

Pia looked down at her husband, sitting, shirtless; his white
hairless flesh and scooped chest luminous in the sunset. 'What
is this?'

Nello took the ribbon from his white hair and shook it free.
'Dye,' he said briefly. 'I did not ask you to question me. I told
you to apply the pigment. Begin.'

He dipped his head over the sinkhole of the stone basin. Pia
could see the bones of his spine protruding from his pearly skin.

She did not know what he intended by dyeing his hair – perhaps he was, at last, tired of his strange colouring; perhaps he had some shred of vanity in his barren soul and wanted to resemble normality in time for the Palio dell'Assunta in August when every eye in the city would be upon him. Whatever his reasons she would not argue. Not after last night.

Wordlessly, she poured water over Nello's head to wet the hair as directed on the bottle. The water was cold and she had the satisfaction of seeing him flinch. It seemed wrong that his hair was longer than hers. She applied the inky mixture to his scalp, rubbing it in, reluctant even to touch his flesh, until all the white was subsumed under the pitch-dark pigment. The harsh mixture stung her palms as she rinsed the excess away from his head, the black swirling away like a long inky serpent. She imagined the mixture draining and spreading into the bottini aqueducts far below the city, poisoning the waters just as Nello had poisoned this house.

When all was done, she wrapped his head in a cloth, the hair now as dark as her own shorn locks. Nello flung from the pantry without a word of thanks. Pia tried to rinse her palms, washing them over and over again in the stained basin, even applying a tough little pig-bristle brush until her flesh felt raw. But no amount of scrubbing helped: they remained as black as sin.

As the bells tolled three times, Pia of the Tolomei stepped out into the Eagle *contrada* from her new palace. She had pulled a lace veil high over her head. She might have worn a wig, as older ladies did, but the wounds in her scalp hurt too much, so she covered her shame, assuming that she was now hideous to behold. In this she was quite wrong. Her hair, neatened with the shears, swung in a shining black bell. Her face, under the little cuts and scratches, was still perfection, her extraordinary eyes still undefeated. With her lustrous hair short, the resemblance to Cleopatra was even stronger. In his misguided attempt to blight Pia's beauty, Nello had given it new potency.

Pia, knowing none of this, quickened her step. She was a little late for shrift. She went without erring through the now-familiar streets. It gave her no pleasure that she had changed one *contrada* for another and now knew the ways of the Eagle by rote. Back in the Civetta *contrada* there was a quiet little square called the Piazza Tolomei. She'd always felt safe there; now she wondered if she would ever see it again.

Pia heard Nicoletta, her constant millstone, puffing behind her in the heat and was glad she was in discomfort. For the past two days Pia had taken to going to shrift. The maid could not come with her into the confessional so Pia was able to talk to the priest uninterrupted, or just to sit in peace. Her faith had been shaken by what had befallen her of late. She had no great wish to talk to God and placed more faith in the little heathen coin around her neck, but the chance to escape from her life – even for a quarter of an hour – was too tempting to miss.

She thought of the first Pia, languishing in Dante's *Purgatorio*, and envied her the comfortable limbo the poet had constructed, where boredom and sameness and regret were the only ills that could befall her. For this Pia, the purgatory in which she lived was never free from fear. First Nello had shorn her hair, then he had forced her to dye his – her hands were still stained black – and every night she had to contend with the very real fear that he would come to her bed and claim what was his as her husband. At least, as she knew from Faustino's instruction to the cook, her husband and his father would be away from home tonight at some convocation in the duomo. At least tonight she would be spared.

The *contrada* was sleepy as the sun reached its height. Most of the Aquileia would be asleep at this time. Pia skirted some children playing on the warm cobbles. Three days ago she would have smiled at them. Three days ago she would have dreamed of what her own children would look like. Now their little limbs and glossy curls hurt her too much and she avoided them as if they were curs. Pia dodged a bucket of slops flung from a doorway, but the filthy water doused Nicoletta, cheering Pia considerably. The maid, cursing, set about the perpetrator's shoulders with her fan, chasing the goodwife back inside.

There was a minor commotion going on outside the church. A little boy in black and white was engaging an elderly priest in a conversation about the Devil. The boy had seen him, he insisted, in the Piazza del Campo. The Devil was lying in a cross like Jesus but was hideously ugly and covered in blood. The boy pulled at the old priest's robes. *Come and see, come and see, come and see!* Pia recognized the boy – it was Zebra: messenger, water-carrier and the boy who had given her the duchess's purse of alms. Pia was surprised. She had always thought him a level-headed boy. And yet she still crossed herself. She had never before believed in the Devil; now she knew she was married to him.

As Zebra pulled the priest around the corner, Pia slipped inside the church on silent feet. It was dark now, and cold. As her skin cooled she quickened her steps up the nave, leaving Nicoletta puffing in the back pews. Pia seated herself in the blessed, walnut-scented dimness. She drew the curtain, dark red as arterial blood, across the box. It fell almost to the floor, but was not quite long enough to cover the toes of her silver slippers. It was enough, though. She was alone at last.

She heard the priest climb into the confessional box and the creak as he sat. Someone had blown out the candle on his side of the grille, so Pia could not see him, but like everyone else in this city he smelled of horses. His step was lighter than the usual priest; he must be new: a younger man. What would he say when he heard her guilty secret?

She began to speak as he took his seat, the familiar patter of the confessional, rehearsed, familiar.

'Bless me, Father, for I have sinned. It has been one day since my last confession.' She paused. 'The truth is, Father, I prayed for someone to die, and they did. I killed a man.'

'No, you didn't.'

She leaned forward, abruptly. 'What?' she hissed.

'If you mean Vicenzo, the guilt for that lies elsewhere.

It was the Panther who whipped his face and made him fall. You can set that burden down. But you may take up another, if only you will.'

It was the horseman.

Pia had an ear for accents. This man's Sienese was not as broad as Nicoletta's, but he had the same slightly long A. He pronounced the word 'can' just as he had in 'Can you ride?', the question that had set her mind to work.

She was suddenly angry, and with relief felt her rage rush and rise in her. She'd been so afraid, it felt good to feel this.

'Then try this for a confessional,' she spat. 'I have angered my husband. He found me disobedient and he punished me.'

'How did he punish you?' It was a whisper.

'He cut off my hair. Look at what he did.'

Pia pulled down her veil with a swish of lace on hair. She heard a creak as the horseman craned forward. Her candle was lit, his was not; she knew he could see clearly the dark tresses chopped close and dense around her head, curling around her chin, the shorter chunks sitting choppily on her forehead.

'Can *you* pay the penance for these locks, the tax on that one smile bestowed and unreturned, on the one question asked and answered? Leave me alone.'

The voice came again, angry too, but not at her.

'I will. Forgive me. I should not have come.'

'Why *did* you come? What have you to ask me?' She did not even know his name. 'Who are you?'

'My name is Riccardo Bruni.'

Bruni. Out in the Tuscan Maremma, halfway to the coast she had never seen, there was a castle where the first Pia, Dante's Pia, had been imprisoned. According to legend, there was a bridge near by called Pia's bridge. It crossed the river Bruni. It seemed too much of a coincidence. Was fate leading her to trust him? The omen bought him a moment longer.

'What do you want of me?'

'I came to you to ask you for help. Our duchess, the governess of Siena, wants to move against the Eagle *contrada*. But having seen you like this, I cannot ask.'

'Why?'

Signor Bruni hesitated. 'If your husband did this for a look, what would he do if you betrayed him? I cannot ask you.'

'My life is over anyway,' Pia said. 'I am languishing in purgatory.' She pressed her fingers to the grille so hard that tiny bumps of flesh bulged through the filigree. She quoted the words of Dante's Pia: 'Ah, when you return to the world, remember me, the one who is Pia.'

The words were a farewell. She heard him rise and begin to draw back the curtain. She suddenly could not bear the thought of being left alone in her personal limbo, waiting for more outrages to be visited upon her.

'Don't go.'

It was her own voice now, modern, insistent. This man, the duchess: could they help her? She needed to know more.

'Are you not my husband's creature?'

'I am no such thing. But I must give you a warning, before I go. The Panther was a man called Egidio Albani. He whipped Vicenzo's face in the Palio and he paid for it with his life. Your father-in-law beat him to death, in your own house, and last night I carried the guts to the piazza with your husband, to be spread out as a message.'

Pia grew cold with horror. While she sat in misery in her chamber, while Nello was visiting his petty abuses upon her, a greater atrocity had already taken place in the cellars. The horseman had taken a risk in telling her this, making an assumption about the sort of person she was. And he'd been right. Now that she knew this, she could not retreat.

'Now I know about the Panther, about what they did, about what Nello had you do, you have me, don't you? I know what kind of man he is, he and his father. You'd better tell me the rest.'

She heard him sit again. 'Faustino Caprimulgo plans to rebuild the Nine, to make Siena a republic again, to take the city back from the Medici duchy. The duchess asked me to help her, and at first I refused, but after last night I agreed. Here is her seal.'

Pia peered at the gold Medici arms painted on the plaque that he pressed against the grille. They matched the purse she had been given when Vicenzo died. Mistrust crept back.

'Anyone may carry these arms,' she said scornfully. 'I have them myself.' But she relented as the seal was drawn back again into the dark beyond the grille. 'The duchess is a good woman, by repute. Learned too.' She paused for a moment to marshal her thoughts. 'If I am to believe you, who else stands with her in this alliance?'

'She has writ to her brother-in-law, heir to the grand duchy.'

It sounded plausible. 'And on the other side, my father-in-law Faustino, and. . . who?'

Signor Bruni said carefully, 'There must be eight more, to rebuild the council of Nine. We think that he also has your father in harness.'

Her father, Salvatore, in an alliance with the Eagle to rebuild the Nine. She knew it at once to be absolutely true. It all fitted.

She said slowly, 'Have you heard of the Priory of Siena?'

When the horseman said nothing, Pia continued, 'The priory of Siena was a council of lawgivers, august citizens of the city, greybeards from all *contrade*. The priory originated and gathered in Owlet territory. My father, as the *capitano* of the Civettini, holds the ancient title of prior.'

She felt no compunction in revealing all this – her father clearly felt no loyalty to their *contrada* any more, so why should she?

The voice in the dark was tentative. 'You think his title places him above such alliances?'

'No. I think quite the reverse. My father is the prior. To have the sanction of the priory is to confer a certain legality on Faustino's actions. He would not act without my father. I am sure he is involved. You saw them last night – it's the entire reason for my marriage.' She spoke as realization came to her. 'First to one brother, then the other . . .' She finished in a whisper and had almost forgotten Signor Bruni was there, when his voice came again.

'In his cups, Faustino told me that by the next Palio the duchess would not be here. That is in a little more than a month. The Palio dell'Assunta, on the sixteenth day of August, is the conclusion of the plan, the day they intend to take the city. We don't know why or how. But before then the nine conspirators will meet. I must be there when they do.' Riccardo took a breath. 'Do you know of any such meetings?'

It was the moment. She must decide if she was for the Civetta and Aquila or the duchess and this man. She did not hesitate.

'Faustino told his kitchens he would not be at home to dine tonight.'

'*Where is he going?*'

At this, Pia stopped, unable to take this final step. Was this whole discourse a trick devised by Nello to test her loyalty to her new *contrada*? She did not even know if the Panther was really dead – but her instinct told her she could trust this man.She opened her mouth to tell Signor Bruni about the duomo, but it was too late.

Footsteps sounded in the nave. Pia opened the curtains of the confessional to see the priest returning. He seemed visibly shaken. In the distance, she could hear Zebra still keening about the Devil. It was loud enough to warn Signor Bruni. And then Pia knew that the horseman had not lied. As the priest came closer, she could hear him muttering about the Panther, beaten and laid out in the piazza, and watched as he fell to his knees in prayer.

At once the horseman was gone. The flurry of his borrowed priest's robes created enough wind to extinguish her candle as he swept from the box in a swirl of acrid silver smoke. He dropped back into the shadows and Pia prayed that Nicoletta had not seen or heard him leave. In the silence that followed, she heard a gentle snoring from the back of the church, and realized her corpulent maid was no more pious than she.

The priest of the Aquila climbed into the box, huffing a little, and fumbling in his gown for his tinderbox. As he struck a light he apologized to Pia in unctuous tones.

'Forgive me, Signora Caprimulgo. A dreadful sight in the square, a man dead and laid out, and a little parishioner afeared. And here you sit, patiently in the dark . . .'

As she listened to the priest go on and on, Pia went over in her mind all that Signor Bruni had told her. So it was true about the Panther's body. But what of the rest? She wanted to trust him, but could not; not yet. But there was a way to trick him out into the light.

Her voice rang out, clear as a bell, speaking not to the priest but to the horseman, hiding in the shadows. She would give him more than a clue: she would offer a safeguard, the meaning of which was couched in legend like the riddle of some Grecian oracle. She would test him, try him and find him true.

'But Father, I see by night, like Minerva.'

∞

Riccardo went back to the Palazzo Popolo, dispirited, as the day cooled a little and the city woke from siesta. As instructed, he entered the cool marble loggia of the Cappella di Piazza and began to climb the Torre del Mangia, the palace's great tower. The duchess had deemed it unwise for them to meet again in the palace itself. To run there for sanctuary once was one thing, but to be admitted with regularity would be a sign to the watchful. Violante suggested they should meet instead at the top of the Torre del Mangia. At the bottom, she would post her most faithful sergeant who would not allow anyone in or out while the duchess was in conference two hundred feet above. Riccardo was to enter through the street entrance of the Cappella and Violante herself would come from the palace entrance to the tower through the library, when alerted by her sergeant that Riccardo was by. With walls eleven feet thick, no room for two-way traffic on the stairs and an echoing organ pipe of a stairwell that gave ample warning of any approach, the *torre* was the perfect place for a clandestine meeting.

As Riccardo climbed, with each turn of the stair he thought on what Pia had said, going over and over their short conference. It was quite a climb; no wonder the *torre* was named 'tower of the eater' after its first guardian, Giovanni di Balduccio, who spent all his wages on food – he had clearly needed fuel to make the climb so many times a day. Riccardo's stomach growled and he was reminded suddenly that he had not eaten since the feast last night, and not much had passed his lips then. He began to feel dizzy and a cold sweat soaked his skin, but then, in a burst of sunlight and a gust of air, he was at the top. The view of the golden city, spread out beneath him, took his breath away, the *campo* seen from above reminding him sharply of his musings on the hoof that morning, a world away.

He was so captivated by the glory laid out below that it was a good minute before he noticed the duchess. She was in her customary purple and looked much grander in her gown and wig than she had in her nightgown the night before, somehow less approachable. He bowed, suddenly shy, and she smiled.

'How went it?'

Violante was only partly successful in keeping the urgency out of her voice. As she waited for Riccardo to climb the stairs, she had been thinking of little else but the *campo*, the next Palio and the few short weeks it seemed she had left to her.

Riccardo nodded as if in answer to her question.

'She confirmed that there is a plot.'

Violante swallowed visibly. Riccardo went on to recount his conversation with Pia in fine detail, including the fact that Nello had cut off her hair. Violante was shocked: not so much at the blighting of a beauty but that a man could be so jealous of his wife. She had spent her marriage being ignored and was sure that if she had taken a lover Ferdinando would have been no more than relieved. But she had not, for she had made her choice when she wed and given her heart with her hand. She wondered briefly what it would have been like to be possessed, guarded, adored, as she had never been. But she wondered, too, for the first time in her life, if beauty were perhaps as much of a curse as her own plainness. Riccardo spoke again, breaking into her musings.

'She thinks her father is connected as the prior of the Sienese, that his involvement would give lawful sanction to the plot by reviving the ancient priory. I asked her when and where they meet, but we were interrupted. I think, though, that she was trying to tell me something . . .' Riccardo tried to order his thoughts. 'We spoke for some moments, then the priest returned. We'd blown out the candles in the confessional to cover my escape in darkness. He struck his tinderbox and apologized to her and she replied, "I see by night, Father, like Minerva."'

Violante thought for a moment. '"I see at night" is a Civetta saying – the motto of the Owlet *contrada*.'

'But she did not just say she saw at night, but that she saw at night like Minerva. Who is Minerva?'

'Menrva was a Tuscan goddess represented as an owl.' Suddenly the connection seemed significant, but Violante could not make the leap. 'She was wise, and her name means memory. The Romans called her Minerva.' *Minerva*. Something nagged at her own memory, tugged at it like a child tugs her mother's skirts. She tried another tack. 'What do owls do?'

'Fly.'

'But silently.'

'They see all around.'

'And they see at night.'

'Yes. We are back at the starting line.'

They caught each other's eye and smiled ruefully.

'Perhaps she means, then, that the Nine always meet at night.'

'She did say they meet tonight.'

Violante sighed gustily. 'We are circling the course again. Let us consider the facts for clues. She is Pia of the Tolomei, yes? Married to Nello Caprimulgo.'

He nodded.

'Unusual, to marry out of the *contrada*. But perhaps not in this context – they are building alliances.'

'That was her opinion too.' Riccardo brooded on the crime that was Pia's marriage.

'Pia Tolomei,' mused Violante, 'of the Civetta *contrada*. Named for her ancestor?'

'I suppose.'

'You've heard of the first Pia Tolomei?' she asked gently.

Riccardo did not wish to seem ignorant. The duchess, whom he'd dismissed as a well-meaning, kindly woman, was also clearly possessed of a formidable mind. Perhaps she'd spent many years being lonely, many years alone in great palaces and great courts; perhaps books were her solace. Pia had said she was a learned woman. Perhaps Pia had coded a message to him in some reference that he may not have known but which she'd known he would relay to the duchess? Something pertaining to her ancestor, the first Pia?

'Heard of her, yes. I don't know the story, though. Except she was a tragic figure.'

'Indeed. Pia of the Tolomei lived here in Siena in the thirteenth century. She is mentioned in Dante.' The duchess said the name as if he should know who Dante was. 'She was a great beauty but was imprisoned by her jealous husband, in the tower of the Castel di Pietra out in the Maremma, because he suspected her of taking a lover.'

Riccardo felt the duchess's eyes upon him. 'What happened?'

'Her husband killed her.'

Riccardo's skin chilled despite the heat of the day. 'Strange, then – with such a heritage – that Pia's parents named her so.'

'Indeed. A cautionary tale perhaps. History has a way of repeating herself.' She looked sideways at him and knew she was right.

'She said something of her own situation,' admitted Riccardo, 'that struck me as strange. She said: "Ah, when you return to the world, remember me, the one who is Pia."' He may not have had book learning, but his memory was excellent.

'She was quoting.' Violante stood a little straighter. 'It is from Dante; the story of the first Pia. The poet met her in purgatory.'

'She said that too!' broke in Riccardo. 'She said she was languishing in purgatory. The Palio freed her from one husband, and she was wed to his brother before the day was old: a man she detests, a man who . . .' He could not go on.

Violante leaned on the balustrade. She thought about Pia, who was as trapped by her status as she herself had been, but without love to sweeten the pill. She had loved Ferdinando and would not have flown her cage even if the door had been opened for her. Riccardo came to stand beside her and stared down at the city.

'She wants to help us.'

She turned to him then, squinting against the sun, sensing something in his tone. 'But you do not wish to let her?'

'No. Nello cut her hair just for smiling at me. If she acts against her family she would face not just his wrath but the weight of the law.'

Violante nodded. If a person betrayed their *contrada* they could, under Sienese law as old as this tower, be put to death.

She sighed and looked out again at her city, innocent and beautiful in the day. She was full of misgiving. It was clear the boy was infatuated with Pia, and she both envied and pitied him for this, but it would do him no good – and would put the girl in great danger. She thought of Ferdinando, of how much she had wanted him and how little he had wanted her.

Her eyes fell on the duomo. Ferdinando had once told her that the towers of this palace and the dome of the duomo were exactly of a height, demonstrating, he said, that the state was as powerful in this city as the Church. Faithless and long-dead, what would he have said to the threat that faced her now?

The duomo.

She straightened up abruptly, serious.

'The duomo.' She had spoken aloud without knowing it.

Riccardo was confused. 'What of it?'

'It was built on the site of an ancient temple. The temple of Minerva.' They looked at each other.

'Tonight, the duomo.' Riccardo breathed. 'That's where the new Nine will meet. And it is within the Eagle *contrada* to boot. But what hour?'

Now the duchess smiled properly. 'Of course. Nine of the clock.'

∞

The sun was setting as Riccardo Bruni crossed the Piazza del Duomo. He had kept his priestly garb and pulled the cowl close over his head. Stooped over to conceal his height, he hoped he would pass for one of the vast number of pilgrims who visited Siena on their way to Compostela or Canterbury. The great cathedral, striped in black and white marble, was gold and onyx in the dying sun. The starlings screeched as they sought their rest, black clouds in the golden sky.

Riccardo reflected that his father, now, would be slicing his bread and sausage and pouring a cup of wine. The duchess would be dining alone in her lonely palace at a long polished table, while a hundred silent servants revolved around her needs. And Pia Caprimulgo of the Aquila *contrada*? What would she be doing? Would she be playing the harp or dulcimer? Plying her needle? Or submitting to the rough attentions of her dreaded husband Nello? Riccardo's throat tightened. He plunged through the great doors of the cathedral and the duomo swallowed him whole.

Mass was over and the huge, cavernous space was darkening, slashed here are there by the vivid strikes of coloured light from the stained glass: twilight split into a rainbow by a prism. Where the light fell, nameless wonders sprang from the dark: frescoes of the damned, mosaics of the saved, priceless reliquaries holding the fragments of broken saints. Riccardo had been here for high mass, among the jostling, bright crowds, a hundred, a thousand times in his life. Pressed against his neighbours in the sweat and heat, he had always found it an awesome and godly place. But at night the place was vast, dark and forbidding. Tonight, it seemed that God had left his house and leased his domicile to the Devil. The thought, and the old stones, chilled him. Ghostly shapes moved silently about – a sacristan, a priest, an old lady with a broom. The dust of her sweepings rose to Riccardo's nose, there to mingle with the incense of the censer, lately swung through the faithful, belching the white smoke of sanctity.

Riccardo sank to his knees, but his lips did not move in prayer. His litany was a trinity of words that were all the same: *where, where, where*? The duomo was huge, with numerous chapels, vestries and votive niches. He must find a place that would allow him to overhear the Nine's conference, and for this he must find the place where they would meet.

He walked about in the light of the devotional candles, the wavering banks of tiny golden flames making a shimmering whole. He walked the length of the nave, drawn to the greatest mosaic of all – the She-Wolf. He gazed down at the grey beast, suckling her babes beneath his scuffed shoes, and the wolf, wonderfully rendered in tiny nuggets of silver and pewter glass, seemed to look back at him with the eyes of a beast who owns the city and everything in it, a beast who can count on the utter and unquestioning loyalty of her twins.

The duchess had said Minerva was a Roman goddess, that this cathedral was built upon a Roman temple. Beyond that, his own ignorance frustrated him. Could there be some tunnel, some way down into the depths of the cathedral, where the ancient stones of a Roman temple lay? He patted his feet along the mosaic, the nuggets of priceless glass winking at him knowingly in the candlelight. There was no telltale join, no cavity, no ring to raise a secret trapdoor. Riccardo cursed himself for his boyish notions. The She-Wolf looked on him balefully.

Riccardo spun on his toes and walked back up the nave to the Chigi chapel, a beautiful place ringed with ancient green columns and with a golden rood screen. If the She-Wolf did not hold the secret, then he must return to the Owlet – the Chigi were Civetta, to a man, and this was their foundation. He revolved around in the glorious little space. This was a possible meeting place, but it was open to the greater cathedral; a clandestine conference would demand a closed space. Very well: back to the symbol of Minerva.

He moved swiftly now, looking for an owl somewhere, anywhere. In the stones of the pilasters, in the glass of the mosaics, in the paint frescoes. He was becoming increasingly frustrated. He heard the great bells above chime the three-quarters – he had but a quarter of one hour before the meeting was to commence. Suddenly the whole notion, the Nine, the coded message, Minerva, seemed far-fetched. A bubble of mirth rose in his throat, but just as it seemed about to burst forth and betray him as a simpleton or a lunatic, he felt a presence at his elbow and turned to greet the priest. He did not recognize him and felt relief. The fellow was young and eager, he must have come here in the last year or so.

He sketched a pilgrim's blessing. '*Pax vobiscum*, Father,' he murmured and the fellow replied in kind, nodded, regarding him with benevolence.

'Here are many wonders,' he remarked.

Riccardo agreed.

'Have you seen the Chigi chapel?'

Riccardo relaxed a little. The young priest was proud of his new church and wanted to show it off. Such instruction could be useful.

'There are many wonders here indeed,' he agreed. 'Is it true this place is built upon a Roman temple?'

'Indeed, so it is said: the temple of Minerva.'

Riccardo nodded, his face shaded by the cowl. 'Meet it is when our God can enshrine himself over the gods of ignorant pagans.'

The priest nodded solemnly. 'True, true, it is a common practice to commandeer a site where the faithful already gather – borrowing worship, I believe it is called. In Rome, too, there is a church named Sopra Minerva – on top of Minerva. A papal church, the very church of our own Francesco Todeschini Piccolomini.'

That name was certainly familiar, but Riccardo feigned ignorance. 'Piccolomini?

'Ah, you are not from Siena. Many years ago one of the

Piccolomini family of the Civetta *contrada* rose to preferment with the Vatican and became Pope Pius III. His own library is in this very place – there at the north of the nave. The Piccolomini Library.'

The Piccolomini Library. Riccardo's heart gathered pace. 'Is it possible to see inside the library?'

The priest hesitated and Riccardo's instincts began to prickle. From childhood he had had what his father called a *sensa sesto* – a sixth sense: the same sense, his father asserted, that allowed him to talk to horses and have them understand him. A sense that would always tell him when something was amiss.

As a child he had once tugged his father's coat insistently in the square outside, pulling them both clear as a stone detached itself from the duomo, falling and falling through the starlings and the sky, to land in the very spot they had been standing. Many times since he had done the same: turning to avoid the slice of a sword in battle, stamping out a lick of flame in a haybale, or pulling a child from the path of a carriage. Always, always, the portent was preceded by a pricking in his thumbs and at the base of his neck where he tied his hair. Riccardo felt it now.

In that split second of hesitation he knew that the priest wanted him to leave, that he did not want him to see the library.

All Riccardo's doubts vanished. The Nine were meeting, they were meeting tonight, and they were meeting in the Piccolomini Library. In the foundation of the most important Civetta who ever lived, a pope, no less. A man, moreover, who had a connection with Minerva.

'I regret, my son, that the library is closed to visitors,' said the priest smoothly, his face now shuttered too. 'Is there anything else I may show you before you continue upon your way?'

Riccardo shook his head, made his farewells and moved toward the great doors and the outside. But in the portico he looked about him and squeezed his length into the blackest shadow of one of the columns, nose to nose with a painted apostle who looked back at him with almond eyes. At length he heard the great doors grind closed and his world turned black. Riccardo counted a hundred heartbeats and emerged, creeping back into the vast dark space on silent feet. The candles for the dead burned still, lighting his way back up the nave to the forbidden door of the library. His hand shook as he took the handle: dreading it was locked, dreading it was open. The handle turned and he was inside. The candles were lit here too and a wondrous cycle of frescoes leaped from the walls at him, their glories reaching up into the dark. Everywhere was the same man in his scarlet robes and hat, in progress, in Siena, in conclave, in Rome: Francesco Todeschini Piccolomini. The portraits were so vivid that it took Riccardo a couple of moments to realize with relief that he was alone in the room.

Before he left, the priest had left just eight ornate chairs in a neat circle. Riccardo did not have time to wonder why there were only eight: under the watchful eyes of Francesco Todeschini Piccolomini, Civettini, cardinal and pope, he cast frantic eyes around the room for a hiding place. He struck upon the two great windows at the north end of the library with their two thick twin tapestries shutting out the night. One sweep of a hand would find him out at once, but it would have to do. In the dusty space he breathed steadily and tried to slow his heart. He had barely got his breath when he heard the strike of nine and the handle of the door. He tried to count footsteps, lost count, and heard the scrape of the eight chairs, murmured greetings and then silence.

'Well, Faustino, you have my sympathy and the sympathy of all. But if you'll forgive the indelicacy, we have now lost, in your son, an important part of our plan.'

Riccardo did not recognize the voice that broke the silence – aged, cultured, measured; it was not the voice of Salvatore Tolomei, Pia's father.

Then Faustino's voice. Slow and rumbling like a growl. 'My son cannot be replaced. But his place in our design can, and will, be filled by another.'

'So you mentioned at your house.' This was Salvatore. 'But can he ride as well as Vicenzo? There was no one in Siena to match your son on horseback, and his skill was the key to all.'

'Salva, I loved my eldest more than life, so you will know what it costs me to say this – Nello rides every bit as well as his brother, and better. Vicenzo was his better in all things, except this.'

'And the horse?'

'I will pair him with the best that there is.'

'But the best there is Berio, that tall fast bay,' put in another voice, troubled. 'And it is forbidden for the Eagles to draw him again, as Vicenzo rode him in July.

It's forbidden for a *contrada* to ride the same horse twice in a year.'

'I'm aware of the rules.' Faustino again, testy. 'But there is not a problem; I have found another horse, just as fast.' Now his voice held a smile in it, as if amused by a private jest.

'And how will Nello take all of this?'

'To be given a new horse, the best that money can buy? Well, I should imagine. In Siena that's better than being given a new bride, be she never so beautiful. Eh, Salva?'

Riccardo waited for Pia's father to rush to his daughter's defence. He waited in vain.

'And you'll train him?'

Faustino again. 'I will. He is to run in the Maremma – well away from the city. We have a castle there, the Castel di Pietra.'

Riccardo attempted to collect his thoughts. First, Nello was not present. Two, he was to take over his brother's place, not only in his marriage bed, but in whatever plan the Nine had for the coming Palio. Riccardo had not known that Nello was a rider of such skill, but imagined his childhood: growing up with his strange appearance, undersized and overlooked. He could not equal Vicenzo in any other arena of life, but Riccardo could imagine Nello riding and riding, every day, desperate to better his brother at this, essentially Sienese, skill.

'Are all the other horses taken care of?'

'That's up to you, *capitani*. We will bring them in through known traders. Boli, from Arezzo, supplies the San Martino fair.'

'And the horses of the other *contrade*? Our enemies, the ones not present tonight?' A new voice this time, younger.

'Simpleton, they will not run, they will not be drawn. It's very easy. Ten run. Nine for the Nine, and one other. I have elected that one should be from the Tower. Nine nobbled, and one clear winner.'

'And what of the Tower boy? He's a fine rider. What if he doesn't lose to Nello?'

Riccardo's flesh crept – it was as if they had torn back the tapestry and seen him.

'He'll lose.' Faustino spoke with utter certainty.

There was a clamour of questions, all at once.

'How is that to be achieved?'

'His horse will be handicapped?'

'He owns his own?'

'Not yet. But he will, that will not be a difficulty.'

'He is yours, this boy? Your creature?'

'Yes. I had him carry the carcass of the Panther. He knows the price. He knows who I am.'

This innocent word covered so much. Riccardo did indeed 'know' Faustino. He knew him in the sense that society would have it, and he knew him through and through, the workings of his predator's mind. Riccardo knew that Faustino could carve a man up on the rack, then have his son and a stranger carry him out like a platter of meat.

'And besides, I have contrived a distraction for him. He will not be a problem.'

'Faustino.' Another voice, gravelly and hesitant.

'Gabriele?'

'Why don't you just get rid of him. You know.'

There was a silence. Riccardo's throat tightened as his flesh crawled with dread.

'Because,' Faustino's voice was almost a whisper, 'because, he was the only one – *the only one in this city* – who tried to save my *son*. Not even his own kin went to his aid.'

There was an awful silence, broken eventually by the first authoritative voice. 'And Domenico?'

Riccardo strained his ears through the dull, thick cloth. Was his father in danger?

'There's no doubt he knows horseflesh – he will know the true quality of the beast I feed into his stable. But Domenico is a Torre. First, second and last. If his son has a new horse, what is that to him? He knows nothing of our plan.'

'And the next step?'

'The Unicorn next. I will move tomorrow and report to the next meeting: nine days from now, at nine of the clock, in the—'

'Don't say it! Even here we may be overheard!'

Riccardo's blood thrummed in his ears.

'Father Pietro prepared the place, emptied the church. He is my cousin's nephew, an Eagle to the bone. And Nello is without, guarding the door. No one will pass his rapier.'

'Still, we must be sure.' Salvatore again, blustering and peevish.

'Sure of what? The starlings in the eaves? The altarboy behind the curtain?'

Riccardo nearly left his skin as a hand caught at the cloth before his face – he could see the rough folds, caught in an unseen grip. He crammed every inch of his flesh further and further back into the window till his ribs and the cross-ribs were as one. If the toes of his boots could be seen, he was dead. But the cloth relaxed and fell to its full length. Riccardo breathed again, but almost swallowed his own heart as a blade came swinging through the curtain to strike a spark on the stone, inches from his left arm. The blade vanished again and he heard it punching through the tapestry covering the neighbouring window. Amid the universal censure of the other voices, Salvatore Tolomei could be heard above all, spitting with rage.

'What are you doing? You can't draw in the house of God! Do you want to bring ill luck to our enterprise?'

'He's right,' said a new voice, rough and straightforward. 'You shouldn't even be carrying a blade. I care not for the house of God, but it's what we agreed.'

'I've a right to wear a blade,' prickled the unknown voice, 'a unique right, for we are the governors, and we were given the right, thanks to the valour of our *contrada* at—'

'The battle of Montaperti against the Florentines,' finished Faustino. 'We know. You've bored us all with the story. But if you take my point,' he emphasized the word, 'we must all act as brothers in this. No blades in future.'

'You're one to talk,' scoffed the unknown voice. 'It's your hot head and your blade that has taken this enterprise backward. No, no, Gabi, don't try to stop me.' The voice shouted down a mediator. 'He beat up Raffaello Albani's son, left him in the square like carrion. He will not touch the Tower boy, but he lost us the house of the Panther – they'll never join us now. And you've opened us up to reprisals—'

He got no further. Riccardo heard Faustino's furious snarl.

'Beat up his son? *His* son? What about my son? What about *my* son? He bled out in the square too, and only the Tower boy held his throat to stem the flow.'

There was an appalled silence. Riccardo imagined the Eagle had flown across the room to wrap his talons round the speaker's throat. For some moments he could hear only Faustino's heavy breath. When the new voice spoke again, it was in calmer, measured tones.

'Salva, you wanted me to make sure. I *made* sure. And since when has a Sienese needed God? We are a city. The *contrada* is our God.'

Salvatore fretted still. 'And those are priceless tapestries! My family tapestries, brought back from—'

'Yes, yes, brought back from Rome by your illustrious papal Pannochieschi pisspot.'

Riccardo, knowing Salvatore might inspect the damage, shrank behind the tapestry and felt the sweat trickling down the small of his back. A clean hole from the sword strike now let the candlelight through, and golden dust motes danced in the soft beam. Beyond the cloth there was a strained silence, a silence that told Riccardo no one would gainsay Faustino Caprimulgo when they recalled what he had done to the Panther.

When Salvatore spoke again it was in a tight, small voice dripping with resentment. 'I mean to say, Fausto. Look to yourself, that's all. Look to yourself.'

They would do well to get to the end of their objective with any sort of accord, Riccardo thought. The alliance of the Nine was already shaky, so shaky there was surely a way to cleave them apart.

The elderly voice again, learned, assured. 'All right, gentlemen. When we meet again it will be in – how shall I put it? – let us say in the church of the Once and Future King. Apt, don't you think, Faustino? It could pertain to you and Nello.'

'The Once and Future King,' repeated Faustino, his voice heavy with irony. 'I like it. You, Ranuccio, undertake to bring the Giraffa there? The Giraffa *contrada* hold the mechanism for the horse draw. If we do not fix the draw, then the race is out of our hands.'

Ranuccio. Riccardo quickly calculated he was listening to the voice of Ranuccio Odeschalchi, *capitano* of the Bruco *contrada*, the Caterpillars. The Caterpillars were historical allies of the Giraffa.

'The Giraffa are a certainty,' Ranuccio agreed. 'I am sure of our man. In the affair of the donkey he did not miss a step. He cannot come to this meeting because it is crucial he is not suspected. He is adamant, though, that we will take the city. Not only by way of the draw, but by reason that the Giraffa are the only imperial *contrada*, and will give us the sanction of the ancient law. Then we will have three nobles, one imperial. And a prior.'

Riccardo could picture Salvatore, prior of Siena, mollified by this salve to his pride. Then there was movement, the ring of bells and the scrape of a chair as one man stood. It was Faustino.

'Gentlemen, before then we will place the horses and begin our training. I will ready the Unicorn, for all depends on the Unicorn. Ranuccio, make sure of the Giraffa, they must have all ready for the draw. The ninth of the Nine. Until the next meeting, we will maintain our old rivalries, maintain the semblance of discord.'

'And Romulus?' asked the learned voice.

'He will contact me before we meet next.'

'And will he come to our gathering?' Salvatore was all eagerness.

'That depends on the Giraffa. Now leave at intervals,' commanded Faustino, 'different doors, remember.'

Riccardo could hear the footsteps recede and, accompanying one of them, the scrape of a scabbard. Sword and Faustino stopped at the door.

'Faustino. This boy of yours. I don't need to tell you. He must win.'

'He will.'

Riccardo Bruni forced himself to stay where he was for another quarter of the bells, his head spinning. So – Nello was to win the Palio dell'Assunta in August. He and the other eight of the Nine were to lose it. This much he knew, but there were many unanswered questions. Who else had been in the room? Who had carried the forbidden sword and pierced the tapestries? What did the Unicorn contrada have to do with this? Where was the church of the Once and Future King? How could the

Giraffa fix the draw of the horses? And who or what was Romulus?

As the bells rang again he crept from his hiding place. The door opened under his hand and he raced down the dark nave and into the night. As soon as he reached the safety of the *campo* his legs buckled under him. His knees hit the still-warm stones and for a few moments he could not rise again.

This time, he did pray.

9

The Unicorn

Violante's father had had a cabinet of curiosities in his palace in Bavaria. On rainy afternoons when she was freed from the schoolroom, Violante used to wander into the small panelled chamber and look at her father's collection of wonders. The item that drew her again and again was a single spike of horn, suspended in a glass case, bone white and turned like a chair leg, sharpened to a wicked point. This, said the tiny card leaning against it, was a unicorn's horn. Violante pressed the pads of her little fingers to the glass, leaving a collection of smoky prints, which she knew would anger her father. But she wanted to get close to it, to touch it.

She learned, as she grew, that only a virgin could capture these fabled creatures; and although she would never tell, she used to look for them on her daily walks in the forest, turning quickly in the hope of catching the creatures unawares, convinced she could see a flash of white disappearing between the trees. *She continued in this secret quest even when she was old enough to understand what a virgin was. She never saw a unicorn but used to seek them out in art, and dream that she could catch one and have it lay its heavy head in her lap, in the attitudes she saw in tapestries and Books of Hours.*

As a newly married woman, delighted by the library in Ferdinando's Florentine palace, she sought the creatures out in books. She read, once, to Ferdinando, shyly, a passage from the writings of Marco Polo, fascinated that the traveller had seen a unicorn at first-hand. Ferdinando laughed at her.

'He is describing a rhinoceros, an ugly horned brute from the Africas. Unicorns do not exist.'

Violante closed the book and put it down as if it burned her. 'They do,' she said quietly. It was the first time she had dared to gainsay him. Ferdinando came closer to her and took her chin in his hand. She could not meet his scornful, beautiful eyes.

'Well,' he said, 'if they do, you may still capture one yet, my little maid.'

He left her then, feeling the imprint of his hand, feeling the full meaning of the words. She was, a month after marriage, still intact.

'The Once and Future King,' Violante repeated. 'The Once and Future King.'

She walked along the shelves of her library, trailing her long fingers along the spines of the books with love. She looked at the age spots on her hands and at the beautiful books with their jewel-coloured leather, tooled and chased with gold. She would die and rot but these things would remain for all time.

She had embraced literature and music when she had married Ferdinando, adopting his loves as her own, and when it became clear he had no love for her, these things had abided with her and been her comfort and joy. Living in the cold winter of Ferdinando's disregard, she had nonetheless enjoyed the company and courtesy of his circle, including the composers Scarlatti and Vivaldi, whose names would live for ever in their works. Ferdinando's books were her inheritance; she had brought them all to Siena and lined this room with them. She had escaped into those tales, casting herself as the tragic Iseult or the feckless Guinevere, women whom she could never have been, women who could once have captured a unicorn.

Now, she sought, with her ageing fingers, the solution to a puzzle, the echo of a chime that Riccardo had sent ringing in her head, the phrase that he had brought to her from the cathedral: *the Once and Future King*. It had fluttered around her head, intangible, and come to roost here like a dove in its cote. She sought it among the stacks.

Riccardo sat, wondering at the room in which he had found himself. There were more books here than he had ever seen all together in his life. They had met, as before, at the top of the Torre del Mangia, and Riccardo had given his account of the meeting he had witnessed, ending with the cryptic direction for the next meeting place in nine days' time: at the church of the Once and Future King. The duchess had led Riccardo through the inner door joining the tower to the palace. Gretchen, wearing her night-time plait, had joined them there, giving Riccardo a curt, but not unfriendly, nod of greeting.

'Gretchen,' said the duchess, 'go and find Zebra. Direct him here and come back yourself.'

So there were four of them in this unlikely alliance to save the city, a council of war comprised of the least war-like people that could be imagined. At length, Violante took down a book, bound in green leather, thick and heavy as a keystone. 'Here,' she said. 'The Once and Future King.'

She placed the book carefully on the dark wood table around which they were seated. Riccardo tried to make out the letters, but they were not in any language that he knew. LE M-O-R-T-E D'-A-R-T-H-U-R.

He raised his head. 'What is it?'

'*The Death of Arthur* by Sir Thomas Malory, an English writer.'

'Who is Arthur?'

'Was. Arthur Pendragon, ancient king of the Britons.'

'What is he to do with Siena?'

'I do not know, but that was what he was called: the Once and Future King.'

Violante leafed through the volume as she talked, the printed pages rustling under her hands.

'He was the son of a great tyrant called Uther Pendragon. Arthur plucked his legendary sword Excalibur from a stone, when no other man could draw it. He was king of a great court known as Camelot where his knights met around a round table. He had a beautiful wife called

Guinevere, who betrayed him with his first knight, a fellow called Lancelot.'

Violante looked at Riccardo carefully under her sandy lashes. She wanted to warn him of the perils of an attachment to a married woman.

'And at the end of his life, he gave his sword back to a lady in a lake.'

Riccardo shook his head. It all seemed nonsensical. He grasped the one element that made sense to him. 'In the duomo, one of the conspirators carried a sword, even in the church, and said it was his right, something to do with a battle.'

Violante sat down opposite him. 'The battle of Montaperti. The man with the sword must be an Oca, a Goose. At the battle of Montaperti the Goose *contrada* fought so valiantly against the Florentines they were given the right to wear swords at any time. They were given the title "governors" of Siena.' She appreciated the irony of the title. 'Orsa Lombardi is the captain of the Geese. The swordsman must be him.'

'Then perhaps,' said Riccardo tentatively, 'they may all meet in the church of the Goose *contrada*? In nine days' time? For is not a governor a sort of king?'

The duchess was not convinced. 'We will think on this later. Let us ask Zebra what he knows of these horses of which the Nine spoke.'

Violante could not remember the last time she had had a proper conversation with a man. With Conti, her chief councillor, she discussed the dry business of state, and at formal dinners she uttered the small nothings and niceties expected between the high-born at leisure. But not since she had been with her brother-in-law, Gian Gastone, in Florence, when she was lately married to a man who did not love her, and he was to be married to a woman he did not love, had she discussed something real. He had taken her to the Boboli Gardens and they had talked, with great candour, about the nature of love. Today, once again, she had been forced to think. It felt good. Her dull brain was beginning to wake up.

The door opened and Zebra was ushered in by Gretchen, yawning, scratching, his hair standing up like a palomino's mane. He had clearly been pulled from a bed of straw somewhere. The city was Zebra's home and he had a different stable every night – it was a credit to Gretchen that she had tracked him down so swiftly.

'Our *own* stables, madam, if you please,' said the old lady, her mouth set in a hard line.

Zebra grinned sleepily.

'Never mind,' said Violante. 'Sit down. Will you take something?'

Zebra's eyes snapped open. 'I liked that bread and milk from the other day.'

Violante nodded to Gretchen, who vanished. The duchess leaned forward in her chair until her corsets bit. 'Zebra, when does the next horse fair come to town?'

'Wednesday fortnight, *'donna*.'

'Too late,' said Riccardo, pacing behind the boy. 'The Nine are meeting again in nine days' time . . . They said they were placing horses in their stables before then. One for Nello, and one for "the boy from the Tower" – me.

Their plan, as we understand it, is to feed ten horses into the city, secretly. Nine are to be *asini.*'

'*Asini?*' questioned Violante.

'Asses. Donkeys. Slow and stupid,' supplied Zebra.

Violante recalled suddenly the tale of the rotting donkey that had been cast, a week ago, over the Camollia gate. 'Go on,' she said.

'Only one horse, Nello's, will be a runner. They intend to fix the horse draw, with the help of someone from the Giraffa *contrada,* so that only the New Nine, and my own *contrada* of the Tower, shall run in the Palio dell'Assunta on the sixteenth day of August. By the laws of our city only ten can run – those will be the ten. Those ten will run and Nello will win.'

Zebra had a child's capacity to cleave straight to the point. 'Well, the traders can bring horses to order. Outside traders and the *capitani* can visit other cities.'

'What do you know of this man they mentioned – Boli from Arezzo – who supplies the San Martino fair? Is he corrupt?'

Zebra's eyes were round as coins. 'No, '*donna.* Straight as a Roman road.'

'That does not signify. The trader may not have been told what they are for. He may have been merely told to bring nine duds and one runner.'

'I'll tell you this, though,' Zebra broke in, 'Nello's horse will have to be a star. 'Tis all very well being a good runner, but to *win?*' He turned to Riccardo, two men discussing horses. 'You've run it, you've seen the San Martino corner. You'd have to be a class horse.'

'Like Berio?'

'Like Berio, but, as one of the conspirators said, Vicenzo rode Berio in the July Palio. It's forbidden for a *contrada* to ride the same horse again. And yet I have never seen a better mount than Berio.'

'They are taking as few chances as they may.' Violante broke into their discourse. 'But I still don't see how that will let them take the city.'

'Bets,' said Riccardo briefly.

'Bets?' questioned the duchess.

The horseman nodded. 'Yes. The Nine will create a betting syndicate. An enormous amount of money changes hands at each Palio, but this time none of the other *contrade* will know that the race will be fixed. The Nine will make enough on one race to finance the coup and unseat your rule.'

Violante swallowed.

'But even this is not all,' said Riccardo gently. 'There is more – the talk of Romulus.'

'Zebra, have you ever heard anyone being called Romulus?' questioned Violante.

'Never, *'donna*, only the wolf's child.'

'Romulus and Remus. Twin symbols of Siena. They are known by all – there are statues everywhere,' said Gretchen, speaking for the first time.

Violante breathed out. 'Very well. Let us leave that aside for now. Let us set down what we know so far. Who are the dancers in this quadrille?'

There was silence.

'Who was at the meeting?' Violante persisted.

'Faustino,' answered Riccardo. 'Salvatore.'

'Let us be methodical.' She took up her quill and paper. 'Faustino Caprimulgo of the Aquila. Salvatore Tolomei of the Civetta.'

'Ranuccio Odeschalchi of the Bruco, the Caterpillar *contrada*, was named,' added Riccardo, 'and then there was the fellow with the sword.'

'Orsa Lombardi, of the Oca, the Goose.'

'Ah yes. We surmised they may well be central to this, as the governors of the city, the sword carriers.' Violante wrote it all down. 'What else do we know of the Goose *contrada*?'

'They are dyers by trade,' put in Riccardo. 'They dye the very Palio banner that the victor will win. They can change white to black.'

'That's right,' agreed the duchess. 'They built the *bottini*, the secret waterways below the city, to carry away the corrosive dye.'

Riccardo was reminded abruptly of the last and only time he had been down in the *bottini*, carrying the carcass that began all this. Before he could speak, the door opened to reveal a maid with the gruel. Zebra fell to it hungrily.

'And there was another name,' said Riccardo once the door had closed, 'Gabriele. He tried to persuade Faustino to kill me. And when Salvatore and Faustino started to squabble, Salvatore said; "No, no, Gabi, don't try to stop me."'

Zebra didn't wait to empty his mouth. 'Gabriele Zondadari, captain of the Wave – the Onda *contrada*.'

Violante frowned. 'Why them?'

All eyes turned to her.

'Well – why? They are a poor, insignificant *contrada*.'

'Sea coast,' said Riccardo. 'They defend the coast beyond the Maremma. They control what comes in and out of the city – including the horses.'

There was a loaded silence, broken by the duchess.

'Well, then. To recapitulate: Aquila, Civetta, Oca, Bruco, Onda. The Tower, through you, Signor Bruni, is their ally too, whether they know it or not. I suspect that the Panther *contrada* was set to be one of the Nine before the events of the Palio, and your actions that day, Signor Bruni, gave them a substitute. They also seek the alliance with Giraffa. And the mysterious Romulus. And we missed one out.'

'Who?'

She was not likely to forget. 'Unicorn. Leocorno.'

'Romulus and the Unicorn were named as the key to all,' recalled Riccardo, 'but were not represented there.'

'Perhaps they will speak at the next colloquy,' mused the duchess, 'and we will discover their purpose then.'

'Provided we may attend,' put in Riccardo. 'We must discover, first, where it is to be held.'

∞

When Pia was summoned to see Faustino Caprimulgo, she felt much more afraid than she had – could it be only a week ago? – when Salvatore had called her down on her name-day. The breadth of Nicoletta's smiles augmented her fear. The maid was always happiest when some misfortune befell her mistress. When she'd first seen Pia's hair she had positively beamed.

A certain fatigue now accompanied the fear. Four days had passed since her marriage, and although she bloodied her sheets every night, she could not rely on this ruse for much longer. In truth, she no longer believed that her deception alone kept Nello from claiming her. In her wildest imaginings she dreamed he might be physically incapable, but then dismissed this, remembering the fate of the little Benedetti heiress. It must be something else. As she followed Nicoletta's bulk down the stairs, she wondered, wearily, what else could happen to her.

When she entered her father-in law's salon she was pleasantly surprised. In her imagination she had transmuted him into a beast. But the man who greeted her sat at a desk, his white hair clean and cropped, his suit of clothes neat and brushed, his hose white and his buckles shining. He even smiled and rose from his chair as she entered. She looked about her. The room was pleasant: the leather smell of the desk-roll, the quills and inks ranked in shining pots upon it, the papers and scrolls neatly stacked, a wooden globe standing on the blotter to remind of a world outside Siena. She considered the wooden world for a moment. She had never seen any of those countries, not even the painted blue sea in which they floated. In the sunlight coming through the windows, her own peninsula and Europe were in the light. In the dark shadow, the Africas and Indies and the rest.

She could almost be in the *studiolo* of a civilized man. The sole anomaly was the great wooden shelves empty of books. She missed her own books only a little less than she missed her mother's gowns, for even Salvatore had known that a gentleman kept a library. It was this that gave Faustino away. He was no gentleman, and when she looked above the smile to the hooked, beak-like nose and the cold amber eyes, she knew him for what he was: a savage, who had beaten a man to death in his cellars. A wild man, little better than those who lived in the shadowed half of the globe, the half she could not see.

She stepped forward, chin high and defensive. Her newly sharpened instincts told her that he needed something. Her cooperation. And, ground down by fear, she knew that she would grant what he asked. Her courage rubbed away to reveal the transference of colours: she was yellow on the inside, as yellow as Faustino's eyes, as yellow as the Eagles' banner. A coward.

And yet when he asked the question she could not have been more surprised. 'My dear. Would you like to learn to ride?'

Her mouth must have dropped open, her eyes must have widened. It was the bastard son of the question she had been asked days before, by the horseman, at dinner.

He turned, hands behind his back, to the window, where the towers of the city pierced the lowering sun. 'It is an accomplishment suitable for a married woman. And it must be dull for one so young to be here alone.'

Pia discounted at least half of this. Why would Faustino care about her state of mind? She watched him carefully as he turned back to her, and she knew he had reached the meat of the matter.

'I had a notion that young Signor Bruni could teach you. When we broke that jest at dinner, it led me to thinking, and I have thought on it much since. I think it would divert you, and it would help you to understand your husband's great passion.'

Pia dropped her eyes and curtseyed. 'As you wish.'

Faustino pressed his long hands together. 'Good. Good. I will make the arrangements.' Now his eyes smiled along with his thin mouth. 'One more thing, though – you will find a new dress in your garderobe.' He was carefully off-hand. 'Put it on, would you? You will dine with Nello and me tonight.' He bestowed this rare privilege lightly.

'Of course.'

'Good girl, good girl. Nicoletta will see to your . . . hair and jewels.' Even he had the grace to drop his eyes from her strangely shorn head. 'Nicoletta!' he bawled, opening the door. He moved surprisingly quickly.

Pia was struck by a sudden notion. She had to act fast, before the maid came. 'Sir, speaking of clothing . . . My mother had a garde-corps for riding, in her garderobe at my father's house. If you would be good enough to have it fetched, it would do very well for me to wear at my instruction.'

'Eh? What's that?' Faustino seemed amazed that she would open her mouth and address him. 'Oh, yes, yes, of course. I will see it done. 'Tis a good notion.'

It was agreed in an offhand fashion, but Pia had the idea that Faustino's promises were worth more than her father's. In thinking him a savage she had done him a dis-service. A fierce native intelligence overlaid the brutality, and he had a completeness, a detail to his thinking. This boon he'd asked of her must be part of a bigger, infinitely complex plan, and he would be able to keep all these spheres suspended in the air, like the coloured balls of the juggler who had followed her to her wedding. And now, she too had another sphere to cast into the air. She made her tone as offhand as his and spoke quickly as she heard her maid's heavy tread approaching from the floor above.

'And your servants may as well fetch her other dresses too, with your permission, of course. She had several good gowns that would not shame your house, and I could wear them, to save your further generosity.'

He nodded, his amber eyes flaring with pleasure at the bride he had bought for his son, crediting her with courage, pleased with her parsimony. Then, just as Nicoletta came heaving into the room, his eyes flickered to something outside the window.

Following his gaze, Pia saw a large fellow in the greasy leathers of a horse dealer, leading two horses into the courtyard below. One horse was white, the other black, an embodiment of the city in horseflesh.

'Ah, Boli is here, good. Excuse me, my dear.'

The interview was over.

As she followed Nicoletta back up the stair, Pia's smile was almost as wide as her maid's. She was beginning to learn how the game was played.

∞

Riccardo worked quietly and conscientiously alongside his father all day, waiting for the horse that Faustino was to give him. Nothing happened. The bees buzzed lazily around the flowers that broke through the cobbles' cracks.

At siesta Domenico went indoors, to shelter from the shimmering heat. Riccardo lay in the straw of the stable, but he could not rest. He tried to persuade himself that Faustino had changed his mind, that he had misunderstood the Aquila captain. Even if he was to be given a gift of horseflesh, it would have to be a nag, a mule so poor that it could not threaten Nello's win.

He and Domenico resumed their work until the starlings circled to their rest and the sky clotted with darkness. Then, only then, did the clop of hooves herald the approach of a horse, led, in a head-collar, by Zebra. As the horse approached, Riccardo met Zebra's clear eyes and the boy gave the tiniest nod. It was from Faustino. And it was lovely.

Domenico dropped his pick on the cobbles. The horse was fantastically beautiful, so white it was hard to look at the sunlight sheen on the flanks. The beast had a long head, with a noble arched profile. His jaw was deep, his ears small, but his eyes large and expressive, his nostrils flared. The neck was sturdy, yet arched, above withers that were low, muscular and broad. The horse stood perfectly still, the tail, high and well set, twitching a little, catching Zebra at the edge of his eye, the only indication that he was not a statue.

Domenico gave a long, low whistle and approached to run his hands down the horse's delicate legs, checking the shoes one by one.

'Brand new,' he said. 'I could not have shod him better myself.' He slapped the horse with a friendly pat on the flank, and it did not shift. 'And what a looker.'

'I've never seen a prettier white,' said Riccardo.

'A prettier *grey*,' corrected his father. 'Look closely at the feet and points. There's some grey hair there. He was born a grey. In fact . . .' He approached the horse carefully from the side and felt the left cheek gently, finding what he sought as the stallion stood still and let him. Domenico dropped his hand and backed away, astonished.

Riccardo saw the look on his face. 'What is it?'

'Feel his cheek,' said his father.

Riccardo approached, talking softly, and the horse looked at him calmly from one liquid eye. Riccardo moved his fingers gently over the bunched muscle and the soft hair. His fingers traced a little scar, a line that turned a corner and became another line.

'It's an L.' He looked at his father, wide-eyed.

Zebra caught the exchange. 'What? What does that mean?'

'He's a Lipizzaner,' breathed Domenico, awestruck.

Riccardo, remembering well the stories that his father used to tell him in the place of fairy tales, said, 'He's from the Spanish Riding School. They're bred at a stud at Lipizza in the Hapsburg lands. A rare and incredible breed. Horse royalty. They're born black and turn white,' he went on, thinking suddenly of Siena's flag. 'And they're all branded, with an L on the left cheek.'

'Can I feel?'

Riccardo lifted the boy, feeling his warmth and solid weight as the little bitten fingers sought the brand. From behind them, Domenico clapped his hands with excitement.

'*Dio*, *Dio*, I've never touched one before, never seen a finer horse since I shoed the Duke Cosimo's horse in 1703. But even his was a Neapolitan, not a Lipizzaner. Jesu. That he should come to my stables! And yet his shoes are new and his coat is strapped to silk. Why have you brought him to me, Zebra? Whose is he?'

Riccardo gave Zebra a squeeze before he put him down. *It's all right,* the quick hug meant. *You can tell him.*

'He's Riccardo's,' answered the boy. 'A gift from Faustino Caprimulgo – for the service he did to his dying son.'

Domenico's black brows shot into his hair. He shook his head. 'Well, son. You have a powerful friend there. Such a horse is as rare as chickens' teeth, and not cheap either. That you should own a Lipizzaner! My son!'

It was not clear whether he was prouder of the horse or the horseman, and he clapped each on the shoulder in turn, chuckling to himself.

Riccardo watched the noble creature standing stock-still and could not help but be affected by his father's spirits. But he felt slightly sick too, knowing now, with the coming of this gift, that he had some place in a grand design. He was confused, however. This prince among horses did not look like an *asino* – he looked like a runner. The stallion had a wide, deep chest, broad croup and muscular shoulder. The legs were well muscled and strong, with broad joints and well-defined tendons. The feet were small, but tough, the newly shod hooves sparking on the cobbles. Riccardo could not fathom what Faustino meant by giving him a horse of such quality, but in spite of all that he could not help a childish bubble of joy swelling in his chest. He had never owned his own mount before and this beast, as beautiful as the moon, was *his*. He began, despite himself, to smile.

The horse was already saddled in fine leather with stirrups that jingled and shone.

'Well,' Domenico said, 'I'll give you a leg-up. We could lead him to the block, but he looks steady enough – I don't think he'll move if you mount him blind. You must go and thank Faustino at once.'

'In truth?'

'Of course. Did you not hear me say he is a powerful man? You did him a service, he thanks you with this incredible piece of horseflesh, now you must thank him in turn. 'Tis the way of things. Why do you linger?'

Riccardo could not, of course, explain his reluctance. And in any case it would be the natural thing to do.

'And do not forget that my business comes from all quarters – we cannot afford to offend him and his.'

Riccardo realized then, with a sunburst of joy, that he had been given licence to see Pia again. He put his foot in his father's clasped hands, sprang on to the horse's back and gathered the reins. A moment later he found himself sitting on the cobbles, winded, wondering how he got there. He tried again, this time with Zebra holding the leading rein and his father holding the head-collar. He did better this time; he stayed on for perhaps three heartbeats before the horse brought up his head and his hard skull crunched into Riccardo's chin. Riccardo, once again on the ground, tasted the metal of blood in his mouth. He had bitten his tongue. He looked ruefully at the horse and he could have sworn that the horse eyed him back with a touch of amusement. He did not dance about or pull at his captors, nor did he rear or baulk. When he was let be he stood still. But he simply would not have a rider on his back.

Riccardo tried to mount half a dozen times, Domenico thrice. Zebra was not allowed to try. In the end the three men, a young man, an old one and a boy, stood in a semicircle around the beautiful, intractable beast. Domenico chuckled; Riccardo found it hard to see the humour in the situation. He could not win a race on a horse he could not even ride.

He tried, at last, the method that had never failed – he stood before the horse, took the heavy white head in his hands, and began to whisper to it, holding his hands either side of the eyes, like blinkers, as he had done a hundred times before. He noticed, as he spoke, a healed bump of scar tissue, gathered into a star where a wound had healed, in the dead centre of the horse's forehead. The stallion seemed to listen calmly to the words, even blew pleasurably. Riccardo tried to mount one more time. Zebra and Domenico watched with bated breath. Riccardo sailed elegantly over their heads to the ground.

Domenico rubbed his white stubble, making a scratching sound. 'Well, 'Cardo, there's a bit of a way to go with this one. Better go to Aquila on foot, else it'll be nightfall.' He clicked his tongue twice and walked the horse around Riccardo where he sat. 'I'll settle this awkward bugger.'

Riccardo, beaten for today, watched the beautiful horse retreat through the half-door into the dark. He could swear it looked back at him and blew a little snort of mirth. Chastened, he hauled Zebra along with him and took some comfort in the small hand closing round his.

They walked unchallenged through the Eagle *contrada* at dusk, and when the palace of the Eagles loomed out of the dark, Riccardo left Zebra safely outside and was shown to the great salon upstairs.

∞

Pia could barely believe her own reflection when Nicoletta held up the looking-glass. The maid had spent so long on her toilette she had heard the bells ring four times. The dress Faustino had bought her was woven of cloth of gold, and the lace bodice stiff with filigree, which gave Nicoletta ample opportunity to scratch Pia's flesh. The stifling gilt stomacher gave the maid further chances to hurt her as she laced the stays so tight that Pia's face flushed.

Nicoletta polished the blunt hair with a silk scarf and painted Pia's eyelids with a single stripe of gold across the lid, poking her eyes till they watered. The maid then clasped a hundred gold chains around her neck, strangling and choking wherever she could, pinching her nape with the clasps and covering Cleopatra's coin completely. But nothing this bullying servant could do would subsume the power of the queen.

For when Pia saw herself in the glass she knew she had never looked so alluring. She knew she was being prepared for something and swept down the stairs, borrowing some of the queen's power from across the centuries. Only the notion that tonight – the night of the gold dress – might be the night Nello claimed her made her stumble.

The dining solar looked different when not dressed for a feast. Only two figures were there, at either end of the long table. She took her place halfway between them. When the food was served it was simple fare: a quiet supper of wine and snails and polenta, which made her garb seem even more extraordinary. Pia ate silently while the men conversed, ignoring her. She felt certain that she'd been primped and called to table as part of some shadowy design, but neither man seemed to take any notice of her; Faustino's earlier friendliness had evaporated. Only when the men were drinking their Marsala at the end of the meal did her part in this play become clear.

'Signor Bruni,' a servant announced. And he was in the room.

It all happened so fast and so unexpectedly that Pia took a gulp of her wine and felt the heat in her chest and head. At the head of the table, Faustino greeted Signor Bruni with his raptor's grin. The horseman caught sight of her and his mouth fell open, but it was his reaction to Nello that took her notice.

Over the last few weeks Pia had become used to keeping her ears open and her mouth shut. She'd honed her considerable intelligence to fill in the blanks with information. She watched Signor Bruni stumble and pale before her husband, and then watched as he collected himself with relief. Of course – it was the first time he had seen Nello with his hair coloured this rough black, dyed by her hands. Perhaps with the pale skin and pink eyes that no artifice could alter, he resembled the dead Vicenzo as he'd bled to death into the sand of the Palio's track.

In the presence of the horseman, Nello seemed as poisoned and resentful as ever. Pia's senses prickled again – why should Nello fear and resent him? Could he, likewise, see the ghost of Vicenzo standing before him, someone dark and tall and well favoured? Was he still haunted by the phantom of his brother? Pia turned her back on him and watched Signor Bruni sketch a shallow bow to Faustino, with the careless elegance that seemed bred into his bones.

'Signor, I am more grateful than I can say for the gift you have given me.'

Faustino waved his hand, almost bashfully. 'Well. Well. Ridden him yet?'

'Ah, I . . . that is . . . we need to get better acquainted.'

A narrow crescent of Faustino's teeth gleamed in the dim. 'Then I wish you the joy of him. He is not a bad horse.' The smile spread, as if he was laughing at him.

Faustino did not seem disposed to continue the conversation, so Signor Bruni bowed, turned and, not looking at Pia, walked to the door.

Pia was puzzled. So Faustino had given Signor Bruni a horse? Was it one of the ones she had seen led to the house earlier, the black or the white? Was it a belated gift for the service the horseman had rendered Vicenzo? It made no sense. His hand was at the door when Faustino called him back.

'I thought of a name for him.'

The horseman looked confused.

'The horse, dear fellow. I call him Leocorno. The Unicorn. By reason of his colour, of course. But also he has a scar on his nose like the stump of a horn.'

Pia sensed a joke to which she was not party.

'Of course, the animal is yours,' said Faustino, waving his hand in dismissal. 'You may call him what you will.'

'No, no,' said Signor Bruni, clearly not wishing to give offence. ''Tis a fine name. I will keep it. And thank you. Again.'

Faustino looked at him piercingly, as if making up his mind. 'If you would thank me,' he said, 'there is one more thing you can do for me.'

Pia waited, while her flesh crept. Here it was – the reason she'd been primped and polished.

'At the feast here, you may remember, we broke a little jest that you might teach my daughter-in-law to ride.'

Signor Bruni looked at Pia, and she dropped her eyes, suddenly ashamed of this charade.

'Well, it turns out that she is minded to learn,' Faustino continued smoothly, 'and her father and I agree that it is becoming for a lady of Siena to know horseflesh. I would like you to teach her. An hour or two a day, just until the

Palio. My son is a little preoccupied: with his training, you know.'

Signor Bruni looked at Nello, who also dropped his pink eyes beneath his newly black fringe.

'I would pay you, of course,' Faustino continued.

Pia understood now – she'd been decorated to tempt the horseman, so that he could not say no. He looked wary, and she felt mortified that Faustino had been so obvious. He was Pandarus to her Cressida and her cheeks burned.

Signor Bruni was blustering. 'Of course,' he stuttered. 'It would be an honour. That is . . .'

'Well?'

Signor Bruni straightened his shoulders. 'That is, if her husband, if Signor Nello, gives me leave.'

Once again Pia marvelled at his honour and propriety. Her sentiments warmed her innards along with the wine. With this one request he had turned her from whore back to wife, had placed the entire affair above board by asking her husband's permission.

Nello rose from his chair and Pia clenched her fists as he headed towards Signor Bruni. He could ruin everything now. Ruin her chance to learn to ride, far and fast, ruin her opportunity to help Signor Bruni and the duchess, ruin the longed-for chance to have some honourable company or, indeed, any company that was not Nello or Nicoletta. Pia steeled herself for the answer, but she knew Nello for an obedient son, and knew he would not gainsay his father. It felt pleasing to regard him with scorn instead of fear.

Nello walked up to Signor Bruni, and when she noted the difference in their heights she no longer feared that her husband would hit him. The two men were so close that she could hardly hear what he said. 'You have my blessing,' came the answer. 'I have more important matters to attend to.'

The hatred in his strange eyes belied the words, and his white hand gathered the cloth at Signor Bruni's throat.

'But *don't*,' he spat, 'put my *wife* on your *horse*.'

'*Nello*,' warned Faustino, low-voiced and threatening, as if his son had said too much; but Nello was past and out the door, and Pia heard him clattering down the stairs. By the time she turned back, Faustino's urbane mask was in place once more, and any anger at his son concealed. He smiled again, the smile she knew so well, the one that did not reach his eyes. 'There,' he said, looking from one to the other. 'You see? It's all agreed. Tomorrow, here, in the courtyard, at, shall we say, nine of the clock?'

As Riccardo bowed, then left, she knew. Faustino *was* a pander. She was to distract Signor Bruni, to keep him from his training. She was to be a bauble to dandle in from of him, dressed up and painted like a jade in cloth of gold. Faustino had seen the horseman fall for her, hard, at the feast of her wedding day. Faustino would occupy Signor Bruni with Pia, so he could not train for the Palio. This scheme would leave Nello free to train as much as he liked. Meantime, the lessons would foster Nello's hatred for Signor Bruni until it reached such a pitch he would go to any lengths to beat him in the race.

As soon as she could go, Pia swept from the room with as much dignity as she could muster, trying to contain her fury. She, a married woman, had been dangled in front of this man, this riding teacher. But even her fury could not douse the tiny warmth just under her heart that had nothing to do with the wine: it was the small hot coal of pleasure that someone could still find her attractive.

Once in her room, Pia felt oddly deflated. She was just about to lie down upon her bed – alone once again, she thanked God – when she noticed one of the doors to the garderobe was hanging slightly ajar. There was a chance, just a chance . . . She opened the doors upon a miracle.

Faustino had been as good as his word and despite his many transgressions she blessed him. She ran her hands over the dresses. There they all were – the crimson, yellow, green, and the garde-corps for riding, of supple tan leather, the skirts divided in two. She went inside and buried her face in them, rubbing the fabric on her skin, breathing them in. She would have slept in there if she could.

Her mother was home.

∞

'Was she there?'

Zebra's question, delivered from the depths of a shadow, startled Riccardo as he left the house of Aquila.

He lifted his finger to his lips and shook his head. He kneeled so that his eyes were on a level with the boy's. 'Zebra, do you know anyone in the Aquila kitchens?'

'Of course! Caterina, the kitchen maid.'

'Go in and beg for some food and find out when Nello goes to the Eagles' castle in the Maremma.'

Zebra disappeared through the gate. As he waited for him, Riccardo thought of his new horse, Leocorno. Unicorn, Faustino had said, by reason of the white coat and the scar like the bump of a horn.

Zebra emerged from the kitchen with a pancake and a smile. '*He* goes to the Castel di Pietra tomorrow, early, to begin his training,' his head jerked in the direction of the stables, 'with his new horse.' The boy's words were heavy with significance.

'His new horse?' Riccardo decided quickly. 'Let's have a look then.'

Zebra's eyes widened a little, but without question he led Riccardo to an inner courtyard through a door in the loggia. They trod softly over the cobbles and opened the half-door to the Eagles' stables. Riccardo noticed the fresh straw and sparkling tack, the new wooden beams, and thought of his father's humble workplace. A hurricane lamp burned in a sconce with a soft glow. Riccardo unhooked it and moved inside, smelling the home smell of horse and hay. A dark flank gleamed from the shadows and Riccardo walked round Nello's new horse: a big beast, pure black, heavy in the shoulder, fairly fidgeting with nervous vigour and quivering with power. Riccardo was not worried for himself – he had already begun the stream of soft talk that would gentle the beast – but he pulled Zebra round to the horse's head. If this was a race winner, he would likely be skittish and temperamental, and he did not want Zebra to catch a hoof to the skull. The horse rolled his eyes at Riccardo, showing the whites, snuffling and shaking its head. Riccardo ran his hands down the horse's legs.

'Do you know him?' asked Zebra.

'No, I don't recognize him,' Riccardo murmured, low voiced. 'Strong fellow and ready to run. Not handsome, though.'

Zebra scratched his chin in a gesture he had caught from older men. 'Faces don't win races,' he said in Sienese, a local saying as old as it was true.

Riccardo smiled. 'Indeed. Indeed.' He frowned suddenly. 'Zebra.'

'What?'

'His coat is rough. He needs some condition on him. He's sickening. And smell.' Riccardo sniffed the air, and Zebra did likewise. Overlaying the hay and horse there was a faint, chemical tang in the air, like an apothecary's shop.

'Perhaps they're giving him physick.'

'Yes, But there's something . . . something . . .'

He looked at the horse again. Something troubled him. He would like to see this jittery horse run, as that was the only true test, but Nello was set to train in the Maremma – out of the city's eye.

'Zebra,' Riccardo said, 'how about a night in the Eagles' nest? Are you up to it?'

Zebra shrugged. 'One bed of straw is as good as another. And they know me well here.'

Riccardo looked at the boy, all ruffled brown hair and clear green eyes, a sprinkling of freckles across the snub nose. He felt a rush of affection, a sudden misgiving about leaving him here.

'You're sure?'

The boy nodded, his eyes drooping.

It must be past midnight. *Let him rest.*

'Very well, then. Stay, and sleep, and, in the morning, offer to help with the horse. I want to know how he goes, with Nello on his back.'

'And you?'

'I'll be back in the morning.' Happiness swelled in his throat. 'To teach Pia to ride.'

Zebra's tiredness did not blunt his beady intelligence. He shot Riccardo a look from under his brows. Riccardo was chastened, and as he crept from the courtyard he reflected that if a child of nine could read his feelings that easily, he had better learn to guard them more carefully.

∞

Pia could see Signor Bruni from her windows, leading a white horse into the courtyard of the palace of the Eagles just before the bells struck nine.

Had she been less nervous she might have asked herself why he was not riding his prize. But while Nicoletta arranged her hair with her usual tweaks and snatches, Pia was busy smoothing down her garb. Her mother's riding garde-corps fitted her like a glove, the smooth, supple, embroidered leather close at the bodice and flaring into an enormous divided skirt designed to part around the horse's neck. It felt strange that she was now the same size as her mother had been when she died. But it heartened her that she too had been a rider, that she would be learning a pastime that her mother had enjoyed, as the scuffs and stains on the strange garment clearly showed.

As she arranged her clothes Pia watched Signor Bruni down in the courtyard do likewise. He twitched at his garments, pulled up his riding boots and straightened the silken kerchief, dyed in the burgundy and blue of the Tower, at his neck. As he smoothed his dark curls into the velvet ribbon at his nape, Pia found herself noting his beauty, while at the same time consciously rejecting it. The fellow was here to teach her to ride. She wanted his skill and that was all.

Signor Bruni's looks had not passed Nicoletta by, either. The maid kept up a constant stream of chatter. 'By San Bernardino, he's a handsome-looking fellow, that ostler. No wonder the master . . .' The maid broke off, catching her lip between snaggle teeth. 'At any rate, ye're done. Away with ye.'

Pia turned to go and then stopped at the door. 'Aren't you coming?'

Nicoletta shook her head, jowls wobbling. Her smiles today were small. 'Master said ye've to shift for ye'self.' She lifted her chins. 'I'm needed in the house.' She comforted herself by cramming down the small smart tricorne, with a feather in the side, too firmly on Pia's tender head.

Pia's spirits rose as she descended the stairs, but she was thoughtful.

Did Faustino imagine that, left unchaperoned, she would dishonour his son? She had already decided, as much for her own sense of dignity as for the benefit of Faustino's spies, that she would act towards Signor Bruni with the utmost correctness and decorum.

In the shady courtyard, she greeted Signor Bruni.

'Signora Caprimulgo.' He bowed.

Pia could not get used to the name. 'Signor Bruni.'

'Please, signora, call me Riccardo.'

It was very properly said, but she had her own reasons for preferring his family name – the river Bruni of the legends, the river that Pia's bridge crossed.

She could see his eyes travelling over her garde-corps with approval – a trifle old-fashioned, but it would serve. A beautiful white horse stood obediently in the shadows next to the little dappled palfrey that had been brought for her. This must be the horse that had been led to the house by that pirate – Boli? – with his black counterpart, the horse Faustino and the horseman had discussed last night, a gift from the Eagles to Signor Bruni. The horse that Nello had said she must not ride.

The windows all around the wide courtyard seemed to be watching them like glassy eyes. Her tutor did not smile and nor did she. She could see that he, too, had his eyes on the windows all around. He too had clearly decided that their time together was dangerous and had imposed a little distance between them. In the church of the Owlet, protected by the grille of the confessional between them, they had talked intimately. Now they were to be in each other's presence daily, their acquaintance must begin again on a new footing. Pia had decided that she should affect the demeanour befitting to her rank. Signor Bruni was her riding teacher and the son of a farrier. But in subsuming all her instincts in the rigidity of class, she knew she would also have to conceal her burning curiosity about the mysterious white horse, about the duchess, about the coup of the Nine. But then she was extremely practised at hiding her feelings.

'You said you'd never ridden before, signora.' Signor Bruni seemed to forget himself in his curiosity. 'Why did you never learn?'

'Riding in Siena is a very male province,' she replied stiffly. It was not his place to question her. 'Have you not noticed?'

Signor Bruni shrugged, making even this offhand gesture seem elegant. 'I have no women in my family,' he said. 'I never knew my mother. It's just my father and me.'

Pia's *froideur* melted. He too had grown up without a mother. 'My mother was accomplished.'

'She rides?'

'Before she died, yes, I never knew her.' She paused, just long enough for him to realize that they shared the kinship of the motherless. She rushed into the silence. 'This is her gown that I wear.'

'Then it is in the blood. I am sure she will guide you.' His smile came again. He could scarcely have said anything kinder or more comforting to Pia, than if he had researched his utterance for a fortnight.

Pia glanced up at the windows once more. Although it seemed that they were not observed, she kept to this safe thread of discourse. Talk of the Nine and the duchess must wait – but she had to talk. Her seclusion, her unhappiness, her fear, overcame her intentions and her breeding. She had, for perhaps the first time in her life, a sympathetic ear.

'I was never allowed to ride. Unless I walked, I have spent my life in a carriage, a litter, a sedan chair.' She glanced at him under her lashes. 'You see, I am the only heir of the Tolomei. My mother died in childbed. My father treated me like glass.' Her voice was brittle with bitterness. 'I was his marriage prize, and he did not want to damage his investment.'

His green eyes were kind. 'And now?' he asked gently, with the air of one who already knows the answer.

'Now it does not matter,' she said. 'I am wed. The deal is done, the contracts drawn up. I can now damage myself as much as I like.'

They had reached their mounts. Pia, remembering Nello's warning, did not reach out to the white stallion, but patted the palfrey on her dappled neck.

'You are not afraid of horses?' He seemed delighted.

Pia, recalling the Palio, when she had taken Berio's leading rein and let him nibble her ear, shook her head.

'And you wish to learn? This is not against your will?'

Pia opened her eyes very wide. 'I want to. Very much.' She bent as close to him as she dared. 'Signor Bruni, I need to learn to ride *far* and *fast*.'

She looked into the very depths of his eyes, eyes as green as capers, and met his unwavering gaze. She thought he understood her. 'Very well. Then let's begin.'

He led the little palfrey into the sun, bits jingling, mane tossing. The little mare had spirit, and Pia looked on with curiosity as Signor Bruni spoke calmly in its velvet ear awhile. He pushed and stilled the horse with his body and hands and then turned to Pia and looked her up and down.

'Ready?'

Swiftly he bent and laced his hands together for her.

'Put your left foot in the stirrup – just the toe, that's right.' Pia did as she was bid. 'Then your other foot in my hands. Then hop twice and jump. That's it, hop, hop, jump, and fling your leg over. That's it!'

Pia sat on the palfrey, feeling the unfamiliar saddle under her. She fitted her boot into the other stirrup – no mean feat, as the metal arch just would not stay still – and nearly fell. The insecurity of the seat, her height above the ground on horseback, surprised her. If the beast took a single step she was sure she would fall. The palfrey shifted her weight and Pia lurched, clutching at the pale mane with both hands.

'Don't worry,' he said a smile in his voice. 'Let go of the mane.'

'Then how do I hold on?'

'With your knees.'

Pia squeezed the beast with her legs and sat a little straighter. Better. Signor Bruni picked up the slack reins and showed her how to hold them – correcting her fingers with his over and over again. She marvelled at his patience.

'Three fingers over each, let the reins lie over your thumbs, and the little fingers to control. The reins guide the horse and these littlest fingers,' he touched each white digit in turn, 'will tell your horse what you want it to do. You're talking, with these fingers, to the horse's mouth. That's how you tell it what you want, and it will tell you too. You'll begin to feel each other, all the way down the reins. If you're doing it right, these fingers will pain you tomorrow as though they've been crushed in a vice.'

He clipped a longer strap on to the complicated apparatus at the horse's mouth.

'A leading rein,' he said. 'Today we will be at ease. Just sit on the beast, learn to feel her rhythms and hold on with your knees. Head up, heels down. Find your seat. That is all we will be doing at first.'

Nervously, she watched him, so tall and confident, pay out the rein till he stood in the centre of the courtyard. He clicked his tongue sharply twice and the horse began to amble slowly round in a wide circle. At first, even this leisurely walk had Pia feeling that she would surely tumble. But at length, she found her seat, just as he had said: sitting straighter, holding the reins correctly, heels down in the stirrups as Signor Bruni shouted, 'Good, good.'

Pia began to enjoy herself, living in the present moment, here in this wonderful courtyard, surrounded by hundreds of years of history and the towers of the city beyond, and the hot blue square of sky above. Seated on a horse made her feel as if she belonged in Siena as never before: as if she had kinship to all the thousands of riders before and after.

When the sun was high – too soon – Signor Bruni slowed the horse to a standstill and offered his hand to help her down. It was a perfectly proper chivalric gesture, and as she felt the warmth of the firm fingers she felt absurdly like crying. It was the first time that someone had touched her with kindness since she had left her father's house. Frogmarched, jostled, bullied by her maid, shorn by her husband. This hand was different, strong, gentle, kind. This hand said: *let me help you, let me guide you down, lest you hurt yourself. I wouldn't want you to hurt yourself.* This touch felt so good that she left her hand in his a fraction longer than propriety allowed, even when her two feet were safely on the ground. But the touch was different now. He had turned over the palm, looking at the black stain. 'What . . .?'

She snatched her hand away, glancing up at the windows that were like eyes.

He dropped his hands to his sides. 'Nello's hair,' he said, not a question, but a statement.

She did not need to nod. He was looking at her again, searchingly, kindly. She had a feeling that he had divined the tenor of their marriage, the terror: what he'd done to her hair, what she'd done to his. This strange grooming of coupled birds. She dropped her eyes and would not meet his. She thought if she endured his level green gaze for a moment longer she would not have the strength to go back in the house. She turned and walked back across the courtyard, faster than she'd meant.

'Wait,' he called after her. 'There's something you should know.'

She ran.

As she climbed her stair she heard a whisper. 'Mistress.'

A little black-and-white figure materialized in her sun-blinded vision. Zebra.

'Signor Bruni instructs me to tell you that your husband has gone into the Maremma to train. The servants tell me he will be there for a fortnight at least.'

He smiled at her, the second, lovely, uncomplicated smile she had received today.

'He thought you would like to know.'

Pia nodded, dazed, and clumped up the stair. She was heavy with the riding robe and with tiredness. But her chamber seemed light and airy, and as she fell back on the bed, measuring her full length, she registered what the boy had said and felt herself lighten with relief.

Nello had gone, and Signor Bruni had wanted her to know it.

She no longer had to hide; she no longer had to bloody the bed. Nello wanted to win the Palio more than he wanted her. He wanted to claim her when he was a victor, just as Vicenzo had planned. He had only three weeks to prepare for the race but they were to be married for the rest of their lives. She could not even worry about this life sentence today. For fourteen blessed days she could sleep soundly at night, not fear the lift of the latch.

The thought brought home to her, suddenly, how tired she was, how the fear had wearied her, and the lifting of that fear had made her drowsy. She did not have the energy to get up and remove her mother's riding garb. Let it be her coverlet: it only brought her closer. But as she drifted off to sleep the smell of the horse on the leather recalled not her mother, but *him*.

IO

The Dragon

Pia Tolomei, realizing that her life became more and more unhappy with each passing day, knew exactly what to blame for her situation: her beauty. Her beauty made others stare in the street. Her beauty made men desire her, women dislike her, and her husband hate her. Her beauty made her a bargaining chip in a marriage settlement she did not want. Her beauty made Nello hack off her hair for talking to a stranger at dinner.

From the age of ten, twelve, as the sunburst of her beauty was rising to its zenith, she was forbidden to take any but the gentlest exercise. The physicality of her life as a child, the vigour of playing with her friends and running through the shady arches and squares, all this was denied her. It dawned upon her one day that she had not felt the thumping of her own heart for years; she never felt short of breath, even after a vigorous measure, or a steep flight of stairs. She spent her life being still, *silent, decorous. She wondered if her heart had shrivelled within her and died.*

She was encouraged instead to take up the pursuits of well-born young ladies, drawing, music, languages, and her only solace, reading. Because she was named after a tragic heroine, because she was living the life of a tragic heroine, she sought in books a mirror for her sadness. She was aware of the new thinking, the new sciences, the enlightenment of the world; but she devoured instead legends and tales of old, because she herself was preserved in the amber of a bygone age.

A particular tale came back to her now, from the Morte d'Arthur, of a lady who had a curse laid upon her for being too beautiful. Trapped night and day, suspended naked in the scalding breath of a dragon, she was finally saved by a knight called Lancelot who slew the dragon and set her free.

Pia Tolomei was a clever young woman and a brave one, but even she was given to flights of fancy. She had been planning her escape from the moment her father had given her Cleopatra's coin, but sometimes she just wanted to be rescued by someone else.

And now she thought she might have found her Lancelot.

'There – Siena.' Signor Bruni spread his arms wide, like a showman, as if he had conjured the city, revealing the vista below.

Pia sat on her little palfrey, with Signor Bruni holding the leading rein. From her high seat she marvelled at the scene – in the morning sun she saw her city as she had never seen it before. A silvery mist lay low in the valleys and far, far away the low red roofs and the tall towers were gilded with the morning sun. Starlings wheeled around the Torre del Mangia, and the squat striped duomo crouched above the city like a sleeping tiger. Pia's mouth dropped open and she just gazed.

She'd had a dozen lessons, and fallen a dozen times. She'd made no fuss, she had not cried: she'd simply clambered back on. Pia was now accustomed to pain and the management of those sensations, and had driven herself onward. On the second morning her thigh muscles were screaming with every step, her fingers and forearms throbbing, her back aching, as her body woke up to the muscles it did not know it had. By the third morning she'd begun to show aptitude; she was beginning to sit easily, beginning to feel the horse through her hands. She knew she was a good pupil, but her only fault was that she wanted to go faster, learn more. Far and fast, was her litany. Far and fast.

For the first two days in the courtyard, Signor Bruni had taught her to ride without reins, to hold on with her knees and control the palfrey with the merest pressure of her legs. But soon she wanted to go further, faster, swifter. She was driven by the clandestine agenda that she would not yet share with him. He'd bent to her will; she could now trot a little, he'd taught her to rise and fall with the exacting rhythm of the horse's steps, yet by sheer determination she'd mastered the basics of this most difficult of speeds in one session. And, since the courtyard of the Eagles' palace was a little small to canter,

Signor Bruni had taken Pia out into the hills where he used to ride as a boy, to show her his favourite western aspect of the city.

His stallion, ever at his shoulder, trotted behind them, seemingly quite happy to be in Signor Bruni's company. But Pia wondered why he never mounted the horse, and wondered too at the relationship between Signor Bruni and his benefactor. Ever mindful of propriety, Pia knew that Signor Bruni had asked Faustino's permission to take his tuition outside the city walls and that Faustino had given his consent. If she was right about her father-in-law's motive to give his son a spur to beat the Tower horseman in the Palio, Faustino would give them any licence to become as close and as free as they liked.

They'd made their way through Siena, Pia riding and Signor Bruni leading his horse, the shadows still cool in the early morning. As they left the Eagle *contrada* Pia began to feel much more at her ease. It was good to ride through the streets of her city on horseback – the pastime and the place seemed as one. As they went down the hill into the close overhanging palaces of the Forest *contrada*, Signor Bruni corrected her seat. In the winding alleyways between the dye shops of the Goose *contrada* he reminded her to keep her heels down, and through the archways of the Dragon *contrada* he told her to relax her hands on the reins.

At last, on the outskirts of the Porcupine *contrada*, they reached the Camollia gate. There they passed the place where the bones and skin of a dead donkey had been cast over the walls a week ago by a person unknown. The Porcupine citizens had left it to rot where it fell, too afraid of the omen that the city would fall to lay their hands on the corpse. Pia and Signor Bruni both crossed themselves against the omen, but they travelled through the gates untroubled by such portents on this golden day. Once the shadow of the architrave had passed over Pia's dusky head, she began to smile.

Signor Bruni was to teach Pia to canter, and she listened carefully to his instruction as he assured her that the smooth gait of the horse when cantering was much easier to sit than the trot. Pia gathered her reins with a new confidence. She could already see fine muscles begin to appear in her slim arms, muscles that would tell a trained eye that someone could ride. She knew her legs were changing shape too, and that she had new strength in her limbs. The muscles she was developing were riders' muscles – Sienese muscles.

Her new attire formed a large part of Pia's happiness. She had spent every day since she was twelve being laced into heavy chemises and gowns and corsets, forcing her tiny waist into smaller and smaller breathless circles. Her clothes had suppressed her as much as her position, as much as her menfolk. Now, in her mother's riding dress, she was beginning to breathe. Her mother had taken her outside the circle of her stays and Signor Bruni had taken her outside the circle of Siena's walls. Under these benign influences she could feel, just for a day, that she was free.

'You should name her.' Signor Bruni broke in on her thoughts.

She turned and looked down, regal, questioning.

'The horse. You've had her for a week. What should she be called?'

She considered. She felt like a queen sitting on her palfrey. For that moment, they were there as one, woman and horse, and for that moment the city was perfect: beautiful, ideal and distant, suspended in the mist like Camelot. For that moment, she belonged in that kingdom; she and her horse both fitted.

'Guinevere,' she said, and watched Signor Bruni shiver as if their thoughts had marched together and they were both in the world of Arthur. 'What is it? Does my choice not please you?'

He sighed, shook his head. 'No, it is a good name. But it reminds me of what I have to tell.'

Pia's eyes widened as she listened to the incredible account. The duchess and horseman had deciphered the clue that she had dropped at shrift, and Signor Bruni had been there at the duomo to hear the first colloquy of the Nine.

'They are planning for Nello to be the victor, and for the Nine to be enriched through betting syndicates. Time is marching, the Palio approaches, and before that, the next meeting of the Nine, wherever that may be, is due to take place in two days' time, at the church of the Once and Future King – Arthur. So now you can see why his queen's name made me jump. And then, *then*, Romulus, whoever he is, will come to be the puppet master of the whole affair.' He looked at Pia, his eyes narrowed against the rising sun. 'Have you seen Nello ride?'

Pia shook her head, her rook-black hair swinging about her ears. 'Never. His brother's skill was well known, but as you know Nello rides in secret, far out in the salt marshes of the Maremma. I know, though, that he spent his life in Vicenzo's shadow.'

She could see that a piece of the puzzle had suddenly found its right place in Signor Bruni's mind. 'Is that why he had you dye his hair? Your hands . . . Is he . . .' He could clearly not easily articulate the strange perversity that had occurred to him. '*Becoming* Vicenzo?'

'Perhaps.' Pia did not want to remember that night of the dyeing, even at this distance. 'He once told me they shared everything.' She thought of the little heiress on the ham-hook and shivered. 'He wants to live his life in Vicenzo's hue. He wants Vicenzo's pigments, his riding skills, his wife,' she looked down, 'and his victory. Vicenzo won the Palio, even after death: Berio came in *scosso* without a rider. Now Nello must win it, too.' She looked directly at him with her olive-dark gaze. 'It is not a commonplace rivalry. It is more that he loved his brother too much, wanted to consume him, to *be* him. He is driven by love of a dead rival – and now,' she hesitated, 'and now . . .'

'The hatred of a living one.'

She was silent.

'That's what we're doing here, isn't it? That's why Faustino gives us these freedoms? He's fostering Nello's hatred, nurturing it like an incubus, to ensure his son's victory.'

Pia had not known he saw so much. Her silence was all the confirmation he needed.

'And yet, you are here. You agreed to the lessons.' He was almost accusing, almost as if she were a true Eagle after all, one of them.

Pia turned her near-black Tolomei eyes on him. 'Agreed to them? I *wanted* them.'

'Why?'

Now, with this ally and with her city laid out behind her, she could tell what she had to tell. 'I needed to learn to ride.' She breathed out the relief of admission. 'I need to ride away from Nello.'

'Far and fast?'

She smiled the ghost of a smile. 'Far and fast.'

'Even though Nello's hatred of me might help him to win?'

She did not answer him directly. 'It is a little risky,' said Pia. 'To bet a city on a horse race.'

Signor Bruni shrugged. 'They are fixing the runners. I am considered, rightly or wrongly, to be the only rival to Nello's skill. And so I have been given a horse that cannot win. I have not ridden him yet, let alone trained him, and now the Palio is only a week away.'

He sat down and began to pitch stones into the valley, where the morning mist swallowed them. The black curls ruffled across his face in the breeze, obscuring his profile. It was hard to see his eyes.

'But there is something else too. There has to be. You are right, no one would bet a city on a horse race. This Romulus that they spoke of has some part to play. The Palio is but one part of the design, a distraction.' He turned to her, appealing. 'Do you know where they will meet? Do you know the whereabouts of Arthur's church?'

Pia slid from her mount with a new confidence. 'I have read the *Morte d'Arthur*, the very book of which the duchess spoke. I have a well-thumbed copy in my father's library. There are many, many churches and chapels throughout, and hermitages, and shrines. Mostly in ancient Britain. But without the book in front of me . . .' She shook her head. 'Neither Faustino nor Nello say anything to me. I heard of their first meeting through a chance remark made to the cook. But in the house of Aquila, all is secret. They hush their tongues when I am in the room.'

Signor Bruni cast another stone into the valley. 'Well, listen when you can. They may drop something else.'

Pia looked at the white horse, standing still, head high. 'Leocorno. The Unicorn. He's well named.' White as snow, framed by the fairytale view. 'What's wrong with him? Why won't he let you ride him?'

'I don't know. I was hoping you might. I just know that Faustino gave him to me. He does not want me to win, so he gave me a horse that would lose.'

Pia went to Leocorno, reached out a gentle hand to stroke the white nose. 'All I can tell you is that they bought this horse from Boli, the horse trader from Arezzo, and this much you knew already. He came to the stables the same day as the big black beast for Nello. He's friendly,' she said with surprise, as the horse nudged at her hand. She knew of the legends: that a maid might befriend a unicorn and she was, yet, a maid. Abused, pummelled and bullied, yes, but as yet untouched in that way. Leocorno knew her for what she was.

'Friendly enough when no one's trying to ride him, yes.'

Pia ran her finger over the scar between Leocorno's ears. 'Poor thing,' she said. 'He's been hurt. Battle scars.'

Signor Bruni stood abruptly and walked over to Pia and Leocorno. She started, as if she had angered him, but he ignored her.

'*Battle scars*,' he repeated softly. 'Battle scars.'

Then, louder and more abruptly, he said, 'Keep talking to him, right in front, where he can see you.'

Pia slid her eyes sideways to Signor Bruni, who was treading gently behind Leocorno. 'What is it?'

'Battle,' he said. 'You were right. He's been in a battle.'

'Where?'

'I don't know. There are always wars. I was in one myself.' The tone of his voice told Pia that there were secrets that Signor Bruni kept too. 'Keep talking to him.'

He moved behind the horse's left ear and clicked his fingers smartly, while Pia talked away, of nothing, of everything.

Nothing. Leocorno did not even twitch his ear. Signor Bruni trod softly around the hindquarters and clicked again, just behind the other ear. Nothing.

'Move to the side this time,' said Signor Bruni quietly, 'and keep talking where he can see you.'

Pia did as she was bid, watching while Signor Bruni hunted around for a dry stick and approached Leocorno from behind again. This time he snapped the stick behind the stallion's ears, with a crack so loud the echo sounded around the hills. Leocorno shot forward, powering through the tufts of coarse grass, kicking up tufa dust like little clouds around his flying hooves as they spat up stones.

Pia whistled softly between her teeth – something she had never been allowcd to do. 'Hc's fast.'

She looked at Signor Bruni. His eyes were narrowed, watching the horse. He nodded, clearly excited, as he saw, for the first time, Leocorno's incredible turn of speed.

'Will he come back?' asked Pia.

Signor Bruni shrugged, clearly thinking the same thing. 'I don't know.'

Within a few heartbeats Leocorno was a tiny dot, resolving again as he turned in a dust storm and trotted back, the incomparable city hanging in the mist behind him like the backdrop of a stage. Truly, thought Pia, he suited his name today: a unicorn before this fabled land-scape. He shambled to a walk as he stopped, shaking his head, blowing reproof at Signor Bruni.

Signor Bruni took his head in his hands and kissed his white nose, hard. 'Bless you, bless you, my dear, *dear* Leocorno. I did not know that you were deaf. What was it? A cannon?' He turned to Pia. 'A fellow in my troop lost his hearing that way too. Blown up and landed in a tree. Couldn't hear a thing unless you bellowed at him. Don't fret, *caro mio*,' this to Leocorno. 'We'll make all things right now.'

Pia, watching, remembered the way Signor Bruni had spoken to her when she had first fallen off her palfrey and felt a powerful pang of longing. She watched the gentle hands and heard the gentle tones as Signor Bruni calmed the jittery horse, and she knew that the gentleness that he displayed, not just his strength and skill, was a significant part of what drew her to him. No one had ever bothered to be gentle with her in her life.

She approached the horseman and his horse, drawn to him, to be next to him. 'Now what?'

Signor Bruni carried on stroking Leocorno. 'I don't know. It explains why he won't have a man on his back – he thinks he's going into battle. I think he was a war-horse. He may have belonged to a general or even a king – he's a true-bred Lipizzaner with a brand. Perhaps the mount of a Spanish hussar at Milazzo – we might have been on the same campaign.' He pulled Leocorno's ears affectionately and chuckled helplessly. 'How can I whisper a horse that cannot hear? My one skill is useless.'

Pia considered. 'I think he would let you ride him if only he could hear you. Why don't you *shout* to him? I'll hold the head-collar while you try.'

Signor Bruni looked dubious, but Pia nodded and smiled. Clearly feeling foolish, Signor Bruni began to bellow in Leocorno's ears, cupping his hands around his mouth, his voice echoing around the hills. The horse flicked its white ears forward and listened. Pia began to smile. Gently, Signor Bruni slipped his foot into the stirrup, still yelling, and vaulted smoothly into the saddle, gathering the reins. Leocorno twitched slightly and swished his tail. Pia and Signor Bruni exchanged a look, and Signor Bruni steeled himself for a buck. But it never came. Signor Bruni lowered his voice gradually until he was silent. He was still in the saddle. He regarded Pia in quiet triumph.

Even with her limited experience of horseflesh she could tell that Leocorno was powerful, quivering with energy. He had the breadth of muscle stock beneath his pearly skin that spelled a winner. Very, very carefully, Signor Bruni turned Leocorno's head towards the city, the Torre del Mangia and its golden crown, the needle of a compass. He squeezed his heels into the white belly and Leocorno, with no hesitation whatsoever, raised his head and ears and took off as if winged, rushing lightly through the warm day, smoothly racing, running, his hooves scarcely touching the ground.

Pia watched with pride as they receded into the distance, becoming a dot, a speck. She was not afraid to be alone. Only one idea occupied her mind at this moment: that Faustino had made a mistake. This horse was incredible. On this horse Signor Bruni could destroy all Faustino's plans in the single moment it took to run the Palio. She saw the horseman rein Leocorno to turn and come back for her, as she knew they would, and a second idea began to form, resolve, become a certainty.

On this horse he could beat Nello.

∞

Violante's dream of the twins woke her again in the early morning. She walked to the window and as she watched the sun rise over the *campo* she began to think about the Nine and the missing *contrada*. Were there eight present in the duomo that night because they had not elected a ninth? Or because they wished to petition the Giraffa to join?

She looked down at the San Martino corner, where Faustino had lost his son, Vicenzo's blood returning to the city, seeping through the stones. And there too, by the Fonte Gaia, was the dark stain of another body – Egidio, a boy transformed to a blood eagle. She placed her palm on the window, thinking hard, then turned and rang the bell for Gretchen, her handprint melting from the glass. She thought she had found another ally.

Violante sent for Zebra to bring Signor Bruni to her but the boy told her that Riccardo had gone into the west with Pia. Long after the boy had left, Violante sat still with a hand pressed to her heart. Riccardo was riding straight into the jaws of the wolf. Pia was married and to a vicious creature who had already punished the girl for receiving a mere smile from Riccardo. Beyond this, Violante could not condone the entanglement of a married woman – she, who had suffered for so many years through Ferdinand's infidelity. She gave herself a little shake. Such musings were not helpful. If Riccardo was gone from Siena, she would go on the mission herself.

Surrounded by her tiring women, Violante stood holding her arms wide as she was corseted and petticoated, and her heavy gown and mantua were lifted on. Her wig was placed and powdered, her stays tightened. She called for her jewels, which Gretchen brought to her lady's table. The duchess unrolled a swag of black velvet and the jewels slithered and glittered on to the wood. Today she needed all her warpaint and finery. Unguents and ointments were rubbed into her sagging skin, her face was whitened with lead paste and a little patch applied high to her cheek. She looked in the glass afterwards and saw the same face looking out from all that finery. No artifice in the world could make her beautiful, but she looked grand, important, imposing. Only the eyes gave her away.

She called for her litter, and her footmen, in their Medici livery, then changed her mind. She called instead for Gretchen, an old riding hood and a leather half-mask. She would go alone, with no retinue – her title, and her appearance, should be enough.

She sent a runner ahead so Egidio's father would expect her, and then Gretchen and she set out into the west of the city. It was just early enough for the heat not to have risen from the stones and the shadows were still cool enough for the heavy cloak not to be a punishment. At the doors of the house of the Panther, Violante sent Gretchen inside and waited to be admitted, knowing that she would not be refused. She turned around in the little courtyard, gazing at the wonderful court of tall, blank-walled *palazzi* surrounding her, with a bright hot arc of blue above, studded with the omnipresent starlings, just beginning to rise on the warm currents of the early-morning air.

The door opened and Violante entered a dark hall-way. She waited, as she was bidden by the maid, outside a panelled door and spent a few moments looking at a painting of a panther at bay. Violante was then ushered into the presence chamber of Raffaello Albani. As soon as she shed her cloak and swept into the room, she knew she had no need of her finery. Albani was a broken man.

He sat, in a single chair in a room empty apart from a few candlesticks and some paintings. He wore a simple black coat and black breeches, a white stock and silver buckles the only flash of light on his person, for there was no wig on his bald head. He raised hangdog eyes to her and she knew then that he had not slept since his son had been beaten to death and laid out in the *campo* for all to see. She did not even have time to offer her condolences before he began to speak.

'He was within his rights, you know. It is allowed, you know, to use the whip on another jockey. He did not mean to kill the son of the Eagles. He was a good boy, Duchess, such a good boy. And for the Eagle to beat him as he did, take him and . . .' He could not go on. 'I thank you for your purse.'

From that moment she knew him for a decent man. To suffer under the weight of such grief, and yet to thank her for the alms she had sent, showed her a dignity and grace that she had not expected. She had met him before: the last time, in fact, on the day of the Palio when the *capitani* and *fantini* had come to pay homage to her. Then she had barely noticed him, nor his son Egidio, until he was dead and laid out like the Christ. She remembered a tall patrician man in a suit of clothes befitting a successful apothecary: elegant and aspiring. Now, she looked upon a ruined man.

She bustled forward in her heavy dress and sank down in a puff of silk and petticoat rings, clasping his hand where it held the chair hard, all decorum forgotten. In his reddened eyes she read the raw pain she knew well: the loss of a child. But for the first time, looking into those defeated eyes, she asked herself whether there might not be a more terrible loss than the one she had known. If she had grieved so much for her tiny babies, how much more terrible was it to lose a boy who had been on this earth for twenty summers, who had grown up around your table, who could converse and love and have opinions?

Tears started to her eyes, not tears of self-pity, but for this man's sorrow. Flustered, he tried to rise, but Violante held his hand tight.

'I want these deaths to stop. There is a way to do it, but it will take great bravery, and it will require that you dissemble and tolerate the society of the one who took your son. But if you can do this, we can bring him down utterly. Will you hear me?'

As he shook his head, his own tears spilled. 'No. I will finish him, but I will finish him in my own way and my own time. There will be no legality in it, no quarter. I cannot, cannot be in his presence, he who was with my son when he died. I should have been with him. Me.'

He turned away to a painting on the wall. It showed a panther in a pit, at bay, snarling at his captors.

She had lost him and knew there was no more to be said.

On Sunday, Pia spent the whole of mass praying that Signor Bruni would beat Nello in the Palio. It pleased her to be in the Aquila church, praying for the downfall of the house.

She emerged from the Eagles' church with the omnipresent Nicoletta at her heels, but mistress and maid had gone no more than three steps when Pia felt a tug on her sleeve. She turned to find Zebra, just as she had when he had given her the duchess's purse and when he had passed to her the news of Nello's absence. Recognizing that he brought her only good things, this time she smiled.

'Well?' Nicoletta snapped.

'Begging your pardon, mum. The mistress left her prayer book.'

He handed Pia a parcel wrapped in a stole. It was intercepted by Nicoletta who unwrapped it to reveal a prayer book, bound in black buckram, tooled in gold. Grudgingly, she handed it to Pia. Pia had never seen it before and opened her mouth to say as much, when she met the boy's hazel eyes, heavy with meaning. She thanked him and walked on. Nicoletta, the banker, gave Zebra the tiniest tin coin she could find in her purse.

Back in her room Pia opened the book, expecting to find a message – perhaps from Riccardo – and her heart quickened. But she got a surprise: there was a second cover underneath the first.

Le Morte d'Arthur by Sir Thomas Malory.

And it was not just any copy, but her own, with the

little owl of the Civetta on the flyleaf of the quarto. She hugged it to her.

He had done this for her. She was no longer alone.

∞

'Signor Faustino, she is improving so much that I wondered if we might have your leave to ride outside the walls again today.'

Faustino, framed by the windows of his great hall, steepled his long white hands and regarded Riccardo with his raptor's eyes. 'She's coming on well, you say?'

'Yes, sir. She's cantering well now. If we have your leave to go into the country, we might try a gallop.'

'Hm.' Faustino touched his fingertips to his thin lips. 'And how is your Unicorn?'

Riccardo made a quick calculation: if he maintained that he still could not mount the stallion, Faustino might conclude that there was no need for him to fill his time with Pia. If he revealed that he could now ride the horse, Faustino might want him to spend more time with Pia and less on practising for the Palio.

'Well, too – I'm schooling him now, and he's got quite a turn of speed.'

Faustino's black eyebrows shot up into his white hair. 'In truth? Well. Well. If you draw him in the Palio, we shall see. It's all about what happens on the day, and that, my dear Riccardo, is in the hands of chance.'

He's not as worried as he should be, thought Riccardo, and wondered why.

'I think, then, as to that other matter, it would be well

for you to take young Pia out of the city again.' The amber eyes flicked upwards, suddenly aflame. 'Why don't you take her into the Maremma? There are some fine gallops in the salt marshes, near our castle.'

Riccardo gave a brief bow and left the hall. He ran out into the stableyard like a child.

The presence of an actual child in Zebra, holding his mount, sobered him a little.

'Zebra,' he said, 'could you ask around about this horse, Leocorno? Try to get hold of Boli, or someone who knows him, and find a little about his history?'

Zebra looked doubtful. Riccardo sighed. 'There's coin in it.'

Zebra's grin spread from ear to ear. He handed over the reins with a courtly 'signor', and ran. Shouting the comforting words needed to precede each mount, Riccardo vaulted up on to Leocorno.

∞

The *Morte d'Arthur* transformed the lonely hours Pia spent in her room, and even her troubled nights were now filled with dreams of knights and faithless ladies and adventure. She was careful to keep the book's existence a secret from Nicoletta, knowing the maid would make sure some accident befell it.

Nicoletta continued to exert her malign and bullying presence. Each night she would extinguish the light as she left Pia to sleep, pinching at the candle as assiduously as any mother putting her babe to sleep. But one night at dinner, Pia had spied a tinderbox, squat and silver, sitting on the great oak sideboard. She had swept it, unseen, into her skirts. On the nights when she read into the small hours, she made sure that the heavy drapes were closed without the tiniest gap so no chink of light could give her away.

Riccardo had given her a world between two covers. In her desire to reciprocate his kindness, she scoured the pages for references to Arthur's churches, but there were many mentioned in the volume and she would have returned to her next riding lesson with nothing to report, had she not chanced, on her way back from shrift, to be waiting outside the apothecary's shop for Nicoletta.

The maid, in her usual inversion of their roles, had insisted that they go home by the Strada Romana. The hospital-church of Santa Maria Maddalena had a fine apothecary shop there, where she would buy a salve for her bunions. Pia, waiting, knew better this time than to run. She did, though, cross the street to find shade in the loggia of a tall palace. The palace of San Galgano.

She fiddled absent-mindedly with one of the many horse-stays set into the exterior wall, lifting the heavy iron ring and letting it drop back against the stone with a clang. Lift drop, lift drop, lift drop. Only on her third go did she notice the design of the thing. It was a sword, buried in stone, with a little man's head growing out of the hilt where a jewel might sit. She stepped back into the sun and looked up to the second-storey loggia. The *piano nobile* was placed on a level with the church opposite, to compensate for the fact that the church stood on a slight hill. And outside the elegant, double-arched window were a number of friezes of the saint who gave the palace its name.

Pia had heard of Saint Galgano and his relics, which lay dry-boned and silent somewhere in the hospital-church across the street. In one relief, he was doing great deeds as a knight. In another, he was taking a great sword out of a stone.

Pia looked about. She saw two moneylenders setting up their tables in the shade of the palace, piling their coins on their *banco* benches. They must live locally, for their strongboxes would not stand to be carried far. She greeted them, quickly, one eye on the apothecary's door for the returning Nicoletta.

'Why the sword, do you know?'

The men were puzzled.

'Beg pardon, miss?' said the first.

Pia repeated, 'Why is there a sword on the horse-stays, on the friezes?'

'Ah,' said the second, pinching his spectacles on to his nose like a schoolteacher. 'Because our blessed San Galgano buried a sword in the stone, in the round church of Montesiepi, above the abbey of San Galgano.'

Pia thanked them and crossed the street just as Nicoletta emerged from the apothecary's. For once, her smile was almost as wide as her maid's.

∞

The next day Pia called Nicoletta to her chamber. She sat hunched on her bed, and as the maid loomed over her she clutched her pelvis.

'Nicoletta, I know you have a good care of me and look after me as if I were your own. Indeed, I know you have a care of me like one of your own kin. And perhaps you will not be surprised then that I come to you, now that I am in great pain.'

Nicoletta, clearly delighted to hear it, sat heavily beside her mistress on the bed, causing Pia to steady herself lest she roll into her bulk.

'Well, my pet, tell Nicolctta all. Is it your women's courses? For I have noted, sure, that you have been bleeding wondrous heavy.'

Pia gripped her stomach harder and made herself speak in gasping, groaning tones. 'It is. The pain is most severe, and the bleeding comes and goes more than once in the month. I thought perhaps . . . I know you go to that hospital-church we passed the other day – Santa Maria Maddelena, was it? And that if *you* seek solace there, the sisters must be very learned for I know you have a great knowledge of medicine.'

Nicoletta simpered at the compliment. 'That is true. I do go there sometimes, for they have the best physick, mayhap because they have some blessed relics in their holy house.'

Pia was careful to keep her eyes low so Nicoletta could not see them flare. 'Of San Galgano?'

''Tis so. And it is true there are sisters who do have the knowledge you speak of, of female troubles and such. But if you're sufferin' in your women's parts, 'twill pass soon enough. With the wax of the moon the cramps will go. Might get worse for a little, afore it gets better.' This prospect stretched her smile even further.

Pia flicked her a look, and sighed.

'Well, perhaps you're right. I must bear it as well as I can. But in truth, I have been worrying that this malaise may prevent me from carrying a child, and you must know that my dearest wish is to do my duty.'

She rose slowly and limped, doubled-up, to the window, all the time watching her maid keenly in the glass.

'But you are right; and there is no need for my father-in-law to know of it, lest it get worse and then, perhaps, I must ask him to call for his physician. But do not fret, my dear Nicoletta. There will be no need for him to know that you did not see the necessity to act early . . .'

Nicoletta's smile snapped back small. 'Well . . . I might have cause to step that way this week, for my poor foot will need a fresh poultice. Perhaps I'll mention it to the sister hospitaller, have her send some novice along.'

Pia grasped the windowsill in genuine relief. 'Oh dear, dear Nicoletta! I knew I could rely on you.'

∞

Nicoletta was as good as her grudging word. The very next morning a nun from Santa Maria Maddalena was shown into Pia's chamber. She was wearing the black habit and the characteristic white wimple of the hospital sisters, the starched snowy linen of the headdress reaching skywards like gull's wings.

When Pia saw the nun's face her heart sank, for Nicoletta had grasped back some points in their game by supplying a novice no older than Pia herself. Had Pia really been suffering, this slip of a nun would have been of trifling help, but she was more concerned that the girl would know little of the real matter on which she sought enlightenment. But when the nun sat on the bed as she was invited, Pia was encouraged. Although her eyes were sad, her expression serious, the young nun's face was intelligent and her discourse was lively. She took just a moment to introduce herself as Sister Concetta, before she launched into detailed questions about Pia's last bleeding, the colour, duration and amount of her flux. Pia held up a hand.

'Sister, I won't lie to you. By the grace of God, my health is good. But this city needs physick. I need you to tell me as much as you can of your patron saint and the foundation of San Galgano. Now, you can walk from this room this moment and tell my father-in-law what I have asked you. But I beg that you will not, as lives may be saved if you tell me what I need to know.'

She watched the nun's eyes search her face and travel over her head, to her temples and ears where the scratches from Nello's shears were barely healed. The novice's next utterance was completely unexpected.

'What happened to your hair?'

Pia, having undertaken to tell the truth, did not hesitate. 'My husband cut it off.'

'Why?'

'A man smiled at me.'

The nun nodded, her eyes suddenly the sheen of glass. She reached up and unbound her headdress. Under the white wimple was a bald, livid scalp: a desert of burned, healed flesh, stretched taut and webbed with scar tissue.

Pia stared.

'Aye,' said Sister Concetta, 'my husband did not use the shears but the firebrand.' She tied her headdress on again, and placed her hands, with great dignity, in her lap. 'Now, what would you like me to tell you?'

∞

The Castel di Pietra rose out of the day like a jagged tooth.

Pia did not know what she had expected of the Eagles' stronghold – perhaps a modern house or a summer palace, with all the attendant creature comforts. But this place was like a castle of legend – murky, medieval, pricked out with arrow slits.

She and Signor Bruni had ridden out for the best part of the morning. Pia had galloped once, far and fast, just as she'd wanted, the wind in her hair, the salty air splintering past her face. Whatever else happened to her, Signor Bruni had given her a great gift: she would always love riding, now and for ever. She was committed and, for the first time, she felt truly Sienese. Signor Bruni had given her so much without ever asking for anything back or acting with anything less than absolute propriety. And because he had behaved this way, because of all the men in her life he had asked nothing of her, today she had something to bestow on him. Two somethings.

But the time had to be right, and the place. They were nearly there.

They had been in full flow, racing together, Signor Bruni tempering Leocorno's extraordinary speed so that they could be shoulder to shoulder, until the Castel di Pietra had risen from the friendly horizon like a pirate's ship and stopped her in her tracks. The sun was high, and the Eagles' castle offered a welcome shadow, but neither rider was eager to get any closer. An evil miasma seemed to rise from the place, shimmering in the heat haze, like a cloud of hornets from their nest.

At length Pia kicked Guinevere to ride up to the stone edifice, taking the palfrey right under the cool shadow of the curtain wall. As she touched the walls of the ancient place they crumbled under her fingers, the stone black and crystalline, like muscovado sugar. They looked up to the windows. The building was so ancient that even to see glass in the leads was a surprise. Silently, they circled the entire fortress. There was a huge heavy door studded with iron, and a small sliding panel set within. Pia urged Guinevere to climb the incline behind the castle, and Signor Bruni followed, curious. But Pia had not yet found what she was looking for, so went on, unspeaking, pushing through a dark thicket of thistle and mandrake. At the western corner stood the dark finger of a single tower. Pia stopped.

'It was here,' she said. 'Here that the first Pia of the Tolomei was imprisoned, for dishonouring her husband. Here she died.'

Signor Bruni watched her, wary. She bent her ear to the wall of the tower, as if she could hear screams across the centuries. She had thought the first Pia was a literary cipher. Now, here, before this dank stronghold, she knew Pia was real, her imprisonment no less dire, her death no less painful because she'd been immortalized in Dante.

The first Pia was a living, breathing woman who had been murdered by her husband, and in the very same castle that had passed down, hand-to-hand, through the Sienese signori, until the deeds rested in the hands of Faustino Caprimulgo.

The citadel and its portents terrified Pia. She pulled Guinevere's reins and backed the palfrey away. 'Not me,' she said, almost to herself. 'It will not be me.'

Signor Bruni sought to reassure her. 'Of course it will not,' he said. 'Times are different now.'

Pia turned Guinevere away from the tower, as if she had not heard him, but she had registered the kindness once again and knew what she was about to do was right.

'If the castle is here,' she said, again to herself, 'then *this* way must be . . .' She trailed off as she rode away. Out of the portentous shadow of the castle Pia suddenly felt sure. Her heart thumped against her ribs. 'Come on,' she said. 'I know of a special place.'

Signor Bruni followed her willingly as she led him through a thick overhang of trees into the forest behind the castle. Pia was blinded by the sudden blackness after the burning day, but it seemed as if she did indeed see in the dark like Minerva. Behind her, Leocorno slipped on the tussocks of marshgrass and samphire but Guinevere, guided by her rider, placed her feet neatly; Signor Bruni was the pupil now, Pia the master. She turned in the dark closeness of the forest and laughed at him, the first time she'd laughed in weeks. She rode on fast, as she'd always wanted, pushing herself, wanting to tire her muscles and quicken her breath.

At last Pia could feel Guinevere tending down a slope and heard the run and rush of water. They were at a stream, arched across by a beautiful stone bridge, as old as the castle above. Pia slid from her horse and knotted Guinevere's reins to a low branch. Signor Bruni slid from Leocorno's back and dropped the reins, while the horse bent his head to crop the salty grass.

Pia led Signor Bruni over the bridge and at the height of the arch she stopped and leaned on the parapet, looking down into the dappled rushing torrent.

'I wanted you to see this place,' she said. 'It is called Pia's bridge. Her bridge. The first Pia, the one in Dante. She was held prisoner in this castle, the castle Faustino owns. When I was a child my father told me all about this place. He showed me the castle, the bridge. He wanted to make me afraid, keep me obedient. But he told me something else, which never had a meaning for me until I met you.' She pointed down, almost shyly. 'This is the river *Bruni*. *Your* river. Do you see? Do you know now why I started at your name, when you told it me in the confessional? This place is where you and I meet.'

He looked at the river, at the bridge, at her. His beautiful face was serious. 'Why did you bring me here?'

It was time. 'I wanted to give you two things. Firstly, because of your kindness, I received the book of Arthur. In return, I know where the Nine will meet in two days' time.'

He looked surprised, as if he'd expected her to say something else.

'I read the book from cover to cover, searching for all the references to churches or chapels. There are many, as you can imagine. But it was not the many references to churches that were significant. Do you remember you spoke of the duchess's conclusions? She mentioned King Arthur's *sword*, and that the Goose *contrada* alone have the right to wear their swords at all times. The duchess suggested the Nine would perhaps meet in the church of the Oca *contrada*. In this she was quite wrong, but she was quite right to centre her deductions on the sword.'

'Excalibur?'

'Yes. But it is not Excalibur itself, but rather the *location* of it that is the clue.'

Signor Bruni was struggling to remember the fate of Arthur's sword. He looked down at the water rushing below. 'In the lake?'

Pia smiled. 'No – in the stone. Remember, Excalibur was found in the stone, and none but Arthur could draw it out?'

She turned to look at him.

'They will meet at the hermitage at Montesiepi in the hills above the city, just above the abbey of San Galgano. They will want to meet away from the city, if they have this exalted visitor. It is the perfect place. A ruin, in a dense forest, remote, yet but a few hours' ride from the city.'

'Why are you so sure?'

'Because of the legend of San Galgano. When Galgano renounced his old life he plunged his sword into the stone of what was to become his hermitage. It is still there, a little round church was built around it, and to this day no one has been able to take it out.'

'Truly? There's a sword in a stone here in these hills?'

'Yes. And not only that. Many think it is *the* sword, the very same sword, Excalibur. That it was recovered from Britain and brought across the map by a succession of godly knights over the centuries, the last of these was—'

'San Galgano,' he finished.

'To rest here, in these hills.'

'So when the captain of the Goose *contrada* broke jest about the Once and Future King, he played upon a double meaning – Arthur and Galgano.'

'Triple meaning. Nello too.' Her husband's name all but choked her. 'The king to come.'

'Then there it is,' Signor Bruni concluded. 'Two days' time – at the round church of Montesiepi above the abbey of San Galgano. And that is where Romulus will reveal himself.'

She smiled again, as if smiling was a habit that formed more strongly with each hour she spent away from her *contrada*. She felt proud that she had helped him link together two legends, a little local knowledge and some wrought-iron horse tethers on an Eagle's palace. Perhaps Minerva had assisted her after all. She touched the owl token around her neck.

But he was clever too. 'And what was the second thing?'

She drew a breath. 'This.'

She took his hand and carried it to her chest, where she pressed it against her pendant, her breastbone, her heart. And then she kissed him, taking his face in her hands and pressing her mouth to his. She reeled as the fire burned in her veins but he held her, crushing her slim frame, pushing his hands into that thick, blunt hair: the hair of an Egyptian queen. The hardness of his stubble, the softness of his mouth, the hardness of his teeth, the softness of his tongue, all were part of the rushing of her pulses above and the rushing of the waters below. The torrent was so great she did not hear the rustling in the bushes, or see the glinting pink eyes of the watcher in the shadows.

In the end she had to pull away, for she did not trust herself. Weakened, she held on to the parapet but the horseman took her by the shoulders and turned her round, almost roughly.

'Let me lie with you,' he said urgently. 'Now, here.'

Pia looked deep in his eyes, and saw there joy and pain and yearning all at once. She had not known that you could not give one kiss, alone, of itself. She had wanted to thank him for his kindness – no, more: she had wanted him to know how she had come to feel about him. As the Palio approached, there were not many days left to them. But she had succeeded in making things worse. She had been an innocent, a fool. She did not have the wisdom of Minerva; she did not have even the wisdom of a schoolgirl. But how could she have known? She had never before felt the fire that he had lit in her, that she had lit in him.

She understood now and was sorry for the pain she had visited on him. A kiss was not an end in itself. It was the start of something. But having begun, she could not continue. He knew, even before she spoke the words.

'I would dishonour him in a heartbeat.' Gently, she took his hands from her shoulders. 'But I won't dishonour you, or myself.'

'I'm glad to hear it.'

Like a player hearing his cue, Nello Caprimulgo stepped from the trees on the castle side of the river. The lovers sprang apart. Nello walked to them, and took Pia hard and possessively by the arm.

'Signor Bruni,' he hissed, 'I thank you for your *tuition* of my wife. My lord father told me you might be riding here today. I will take over from here. Your lessons are done.'

Nello turned and led his wife back over the bridge, his fingers like a vice on her upper arm, bruising her in the places he'd hurt the day they met. Pia dared to turn once and shoot an agonized glance over her shoulder at the horseman, who stood frozen and horrified, straining her eyes to burn an image of him into her brain.

Once they reached the thicket, Nello bundled her on to his huge black horse and sprang up behind her. Without a word he kicked the horse and it thundered through the trees, the branches whipping at her face. She had expected him to take her back to the city but he headed in the opposite direction. He jumped the stallion over an ancient retaining wall, far too high for a beast carrying one rider, let alone two, and the horse knocked his left hock painfully on the topstones. Then Pia knew where Nello was taking her, and that by nightfall she would be locked in the tower she had feared so much, destined to relive the fate of her long-dead ancestor.

∞

Violante watched the sunset from the palace. Darkness had fallen completely when Gretchen came to her and told her that the view from the *torre* was particularly beautiful this evening. Violante nodded and entered the tower through the library door. She began to climb, higher and higher, until she saw Riccardo waiting for her at the dark summit, looking, in the arc of bright moonlight, ever more like the avenging angel. Relief washed over her that he was here, living, not yet struck dead by Nello's sword or pistol, but as she regarded him more closely, she could see a strange look in his eyes.

'Did Pia tell you anything?' she asked without preamble.

'Yes.'

She could not read his expression. It was as if joy and despair had combined. 'And?'

'The Nine meet at San Galgano. There is a sword thrust into the stone there – it is the root of Orsa's sally about King Arthur.'

'San Galgano,' she breathed. 'I have heard of it. But it is ruined, no?'

'The abbey is, yes. But there is a hermitage there, a round church where the sword is buried. The Nine meet there tomorrow, at nine o'clock.' He seemed almost indifferent.

'Well done,' said Violante warmly. She recounted her failure to recruit Egidio's father, yet under the bright

moon, huge in its midsummer waxing, she still felt optimistic, despite the fat clouds gathering and scudding
across its friendly face.

Riccardo said nothing. And then he looked her in the
eye. 'She kissed me.'

'Oh, Riccardo.' The very thing Violante had dreaded
had come to pass.

He turned his back to the city. 'Nello saw us. He's
taken her to the Eagles' castle.'

Riccardo did not hear her sigh as it was expelled and
snatched by the wind, nor hear the whisper of her purple
skirts as she turned away to look over the city, to hide
from him the dismay in her face. He could not tell her the
rest – that they'd been fools, that Faustino had given
them leave to ride into the Maremma, that they'd ridden
straight into a trap, giddy as children, only for Nello to
spring the mechanism and catch them red-handed.

He asked, suddenly needing to know: 'Lancelot,
Guinevere, Arthur: what happened to them all? Pia reads,
you know; she has read the legends too.'

Violante hesitated for a moment, not wanting to tell
him. Then she touched his scarlet shoulder, so softly he
hardly felt it. 'Come,' she said. 'I'll tell you.'

The duchess led the horseman from the tower down the
stair into the library. She sat him down, took out the book
and sat beside him. Then Violante Beatrix de' Medici, who
had never had the chance to read to her own child, began
to read from the *Morte d'Arthur*, translating as she went.

'*And when matins and the first mass was done, there was
seen in the churchyard, against the high altar, a great stone*

four square, like unto a marble stone; and in midst thereof was like an anvil of steel a foot on high, and therein stuck a fair sword naked by the point, and letters there were written in gold about the sword that said thus: – Whoso pulleth out this sword of this stone and anvil, is rightwise king . . .'

Riccardo heard her without a sound. At length she could see, from her eye's corner, his dark curls sink lower and lower. The boy had ridden to the Maremma and back, and courted a married woman in between. Violante stopped her reading and watched as the heavy head sank to his crossed forearms, there to rest. He was asleep. She watched him for a moment, regarding his angel's face at peace, the flare of the nostrils, the generous curve of the parted lips. Then she crept to the door and called softly for Gretchen to bring a coverlet. She laid the fur around Riccardo's shoulders and left him be.

II

The Giraffe

At the top of a high tower in his palazzo in the Giraffa contrada, *someone else had his head in a book. Francesco Maria Conti, cousin to the pope himself and Violante's chief councillor, was engaged in doing something rather less than statesmanlike. He was poring over his scientific journals, journals by scientific luminaries such as Newton and Galileo. Luckily he was already interested in such things; gravitation, weight ratios, the behaviour of the spheres, magnetism and the interaction of materials were his pet hobbies. Today he was using these lofty theories to lowly ends: he was finding out how to cheat. His task was both simple and fiendishly complicated – he was attempting to rig the horse draw.*

The ten horses and riders for the Palios of Siena were chosen by the falling of black-and-white balls through a wooden mechanism. The weight and diameter of all the balls, with the riders chalked or written on them, were usually exactly the same. This time they must be different. He had to match certain riders to certain horses or else all was lost. Francesco Maria Conti was not worried, though. He was a confident and accomplished man. He also had a certain advantage. He had a prototype. His cousin, Pope Innocent XIII, had sent a runner from Rome with a velvet bag; within was a collection of balls with which the conclave voted for their college of cardinals. At the last election Pope Innocent, formerly known as the more common-or-garden Michelangelo Conti, had had these election balls made and specifically weighted in order to keep out the cardinals of his hated rival faction, the Farnese, to whom the Conti had lost vital papal states in the recent Wars of Succession. It had worked; the Farnese were a spent force. For now at least.

Francesco Maria Conti shook the little balls on to the table and lined up his callipers, paints, polishes and wood-shaving tools. He readied a pile of small lead musket balls for the crucible. He lit his burner but before he began to melt the lead, he used the flame to burn the note that had come with the velvet bag. He read the words as the flame darkened, then consumed them.

'Cousin, I will send one of my trusted cardinals to your colloquy Friday next, at nine of the clock. He will be bearing my ring. M.C.'

When the note was ash Francesco Maria Conti fixed his glasses to his nose and dropped the musket balls into the crucible. While he waited for the lead to blister and bubble, he decided to look through the fine brass and wood telescope that protruded from the window of his high tower atop the Giraffa palazzo. The scope itself, which had once belonged to Galileo, poked out of the high casement, giving the tower, in the twilight, the silhouette of a giraffe.

Conti was pleased by the symmetry of ideas and remembered a tale he had once heard of the giraffe that Lorenzo de' Medici once procured from the sultan of Egypt, in return for Medici alliance against the Ottomans. The giraffe was an immediate sensation when it arrived in Florence but shortly after its arrival its head became stuck in the beams of its stable and it broke its neck and died. Francesco Maria Conti, despite his scientific pretensions, held the deep-seated belief in omens shared by all Sienese. For this reason he had arranged for a donkey to be cast over the Camollia gate. And for this reason, he smiled when he remembered the story of the Medici giraffe. He hoped it was a harbinger of the family's doom.

❧

On her first evening in the castle of the Eagles in the Maremma, Pia of the Tolomei felt confident enough to go down to the stables to visit Guinevere.

That she was not, it seemed, to be a prisoner had much to do with her father-in-law, who had arrived in time for dinner. That fate that she had most feared – to be locked in a dripping cell with no light nor company but the spectre of death like the first Pia – was not to be hers.

In fact Faustino seemed almost pleased with her; she had played her part admirably and he was very satisfied with the way the day had gone. He seemed not at all put out that Pia knew he had engineered for Nello to catch her with Signor Bruni, and his benign smile seemed to be protecting her from Nello's wrath. Her husband ate nothing, the corrosive hatred in his belly clearly allowing no appetite nor room for food. He drank, though, heavily and in silence.

She was not even afraid in her father-in-law's company, merely sorry. She was not sorry for the kiss, for if she was never kissed like that again, it had been worth it. But she was so sorry that they had been foolish enough to dance to Faustino's tune, and even sorrier that her lessons with Signor Bruni were now over. They could take her tutor away, but they could not erase what he had taught her – she could now ride, far and fast. But she did need a mount if she was to escape as she had planned. Nello, she noted, was not to be sharing her chamber for now, and she suspected that she had been right about him: that he would not do so until after the Palio was safely won. He would keep whatever malign essences lived within his body – his anger, his lusts – locked up inside him to pour into the Titans' race.

Almost as heartening was the fact that Nicoletta had been left in Siena. This was fortunate, for she would never have been able to escape under her maid's beady eye. And escape was now her only option: after the Palio, she must be gone, or be claimed by Nello.

Before this week, she would have felt no sorrow at the prospect of running away. Then, there had been nothing in the city that she would miss. Now, there was. And yet to stay would be hopeless too. That kiss could not be a beginning, so it must be an end. And so, taking a hurricane lamp, Pia trod quietly down to the stables.

As she lifted the latch she saw Guinevere's dappled hindquarters almost at once in the warm circle of light.

She laid her hands on the little horse and was rewarded with a whinny of recognition. She hung the lamp on a curled iron hook and moved to the palfrey's head. She stroked and kissed the horse tenderly, wrapping her arms around the pretty head, resting her cheek on the warm, silky neck. Guinevere seemed so warm and solid and reassuring, and also the nearest thing in this world to Signor Bruni.

A shuffle and a snort from the next stall alerted her to the fact that Guinevere had company. In the next four stalls were four well-matched, handsome greys, calmly munching on oats. Four horses, the same size, eating oats to fatten them for a journey, thought Pia, who had learned more about horses in a fortnight with Signor Bruni than she would have done in a lifetime of common schooling. *Carriage horses.*

She turned around, holding the torch high. There, looming out of the dark corner, was the Eagles' carriage, lacquered and well sprung, with the Eagles' flag painted on the door in yellow and black. Pia knew that Faustino had readied his coach and four for the trip to San Galgano and the hermitage of Montesiepi the next night. Her father-in-law suffered from gout and rarely rode.

Another whinny of recognition came from behind her and she turned again to the stalls. There, shifting his weight and swishing his ragged tail, with the nervous energy of a winner, was Nello's black stallion. She looked at the sheer size of him, a good few hands taller than Guinevere, and took a step back. But his eye was kind and he blew at her in a friendly enough fashion. She took heart and approached quietly, putting her hand to his neck. A fragment of memory came and went in the blink of an eye as he breathed on her neck and nibbled her ear. Encouraged, she bent to look at the leg he had hurt as he jumped the wall. She chattered all the time, reassuring him, hoping he was not hurt. She ran her hand down the stallion's injured limb as she had seen Signor Bruni do. She need not have worried: the horses in the household of Aquila were treated better than the humans; the wound was properly dressed with a poultice strapped to it neatly and firmly. Nello, she knew, would regret this injury that the horse, his great Palio hope, had sustained when he had collected his faithless wife. She was sure he would blame her for it. And punish her too? She shivered.

'You'll be all right, boy,' she said. 'But what about me?'

∞

Riccardo Bruni was edgy and impatient and could find no peace. Each morning, before the sun got hot and high, he took Leocorno out into the Maremma and, with the grasses whispering underhoof and the salt breeze in his nostrils, rode over the salt marshes. Sometimes he got as close to Pia's prison as he dared. Sometimes he imagined he saw her dark head at the casement. But he was always too far away to be sure. Once, he saw Nello in the distance, like a child's lead soldier on the horizon, racing like shot fired from a pistol. Riccardo swallowed. Nello looked as if he could not be beaten.

In the city, sweltering under the shimmering haze of high summer, the heat lay like a blanket on the old stones. Children skipped from shadow to shadow to save their unshod feet. Riccardo helped his father when he could but, as the Palio neared and Domenico's spirits soared, Riccardo found the older man's increased chatter unbearable. He sought out the duchess, the one person he could talk to about Pia.

He climbed the Torre del Mangia, closer to the sun but into the breeze and out of the oven of hot stone, and from thence she would take him to the cool of the library, where there was the smell of books, the muffled silence of the volumes piled high on each wall, and a cool respite from the searing heat of the day. She would read to him, always from the *Morte d'Arthur*, translating as she went. Sometimes Riccardo would think, in awe, of the quiet intelligence that must be required to read one language and speak another. Mostly, he would just listen, with his head resting on his arms on the map-table as round as the one in Camelot, sometimes listening to the tales she told, sometimes hearing no words but just the calm rhythm of her speech. Violante's words soothed him, and he let them run over his head like a cooling brook. Sometimes he closed his eyes. Sometimes he even slept.

∞

Violante de' Medici did not care why Riccardo came to her; she found balm in his company. Under her eye in the library, he seemed younger to her. She could not believe now that he had ridden like a boyar, leaped from his horse in vain to save Vicenzo and put himself in Faustino's sights. Today he represented a welcome distraction from the inexorable approach of that fateful meeting at San Galgano, and then the Palio, and then – what? He had taken to coming every day, and she had taken to expecting him, and knew how much she would miss him if he stopped.

But these quiet sessions had another purpose too. Violante could see that Riccardo was dangerously drawn to Pia and was suffering the agonies of her absence. So the readings had an ulterior motive. She was reading him a cautionary tale, a private sermon of a boy who would become a mighty and jealous king, who would smite a favoured knight for stealing his queen.

Riccardo's dark head, resting on his arms, was still; Violante could not be sure if he slept or no. She smiled. It did not matter. She suspected he did not sleep much, rising early to train his new mount and twisting on his pallet at night, eating out his heart for his lady.

'*So when he came to the churchyard, Sir Arthur alighted and tied his horse to the stile, and so he went to the tent, and found no knights there, for they were at the jousting. And so he handled the sword by the handles, and lightly and fiercely pulled it out of the stone, and took his horse and rode his way until he came to his brother Sir Kay, and delivered him the sword . . .*'

The doors flew open and a breathless Gretchen entered. Riccardo's head rose – then he *had* heard – and he made to get up. Gretchen held up a hand.

'Stay. Your Grace, we have had an odd delivery. Will you come?'

Violante followed Gretchen down the stairs, Riccardo behind them at a distance. In the cool courtyard by the trade entrance to the palace, the gates were open and a carter was unpacking his load: brooms, perhaps a hundred or more, collecting like a spiky bonfire in the centre of the court. Gretchen began to berate the carter at once.

'Have you cloth for ears? Did I not say that we have no need of these brooms? And if we did, we would buy them single soldiers, not in battalions!'

The carter, who had the measure of Gretchen, nonetheless took off his cap when he saw Violante and sketched a bow.

'Madam, I was given orders to bring them here as a gift for you. I was told you was in need of them.' He screwed up his face, remembering. 'For the reason that you was cleaning up the city.'

Violante's heart speeded up as her skin chilled. 'Who told you this?' Faustino? Would he have the gall? 'Begin at the beginning.'

'Well, I was going up the hill to Montepulciano to take the brooms to market. They are the finest, madam, besom and gorse, with a olive-wood handle, you won't get better this side of Florence.'

Mistress and servant exchanged a look. 'Never mind your merchandise,' snapped Gretchen. 'Get to the burden of the tale.'

'Anyway I was whipping the mule up the hill, and this great gold coach near on run us down. The driver stopped and a great fat fellow leaned out and chucked me a purse. He bought the whole lot of the brooms and told me to turn around and bring 'em to you, miss. Er, madam.' The carter flicked his eyes to Violante, then dropped his gaze to the ground.

Violante was puzzled. She knew no portly gentleman, nor one who would send such a gift. She tired, abruptly, of the whole business.

'Then take them away again,' she said testily. 'You have your coin. Remove your brooms and take them to market. Sell them again, I give you leave.'

The carter shifted his weight from one foot to the other, but did not move.

'Well . . . that's tricky, madam.'

Violante assumed her best air of *froideur*. 'Why? I am governess here. My word is the law.'

The carter did not quite meet her eyes. 'Yes, madam. 'Tis just that—'

'Yes?'

'Well, he said to bring them here ahead of him, he said he was coming here himself. He said he was the heir to the dukedom.'

Violante and Gretchen exchanged another glance.

'Gian Gastone,' they said, as one.

12

The Vale of the Ram

Gian Gastone de' Medici, only surviving son of Grand Duke Cosimo de' Medici and heir to the grand duchy of Tuscany, was more than a little surprised to receive a letter from his sister-in-law Violante, the only woman he had ever liked.

Gian Gastone's dislike of the female sex did not proceed from a single event but from years of neglect. A lonely boy in a great palace, ignored by his family as the second son of the house, he began to develop what was to become a lifelong preference for the company of those below stairs – to be blunt, the lowlife. So it was the servants who told Gian Gastone that when his mother Marguerite was pregnant with him, she had tried to starve herself in the hope she would miscarry, and that when Gian Gastone was born against all odds, Marguerite had refused to nurse him, convincing everyone at court that she was dying of cancer of the breast. They told him, too, that when

Gian Gastone was four, and just beginning to register that he did, in fact, have a mother, she had disappeared to France, never to return. Abandoned by Marguerite, Gian Gastone took a great liking to his personal squire, a boy of his own age called Giuliano Dami: a tall, pale, beautiful youth with strange purple eyes the colour of grapes. From Dami he learned the major lesson of his life. The squire took his young master's virginity and taught him what pleasures could be due to men without recourse to the female form. Dami quickly identified his lover's appetite for idle talk and accordingly honed his natural ability to fish for gossip, trawling the great household for the silvery flitting fishes of scandal, filleting them and serving them to his master. It suited Dami to separate Gian Gastone even further from his family, to isolate him, to bring him closer under his own influence. Dami was a young man of great ambition, who had no intention of remaining a body squire to a minor Medici for the rest of his days.

Gian Gastone's sister Anna Maria Luisa was the second woman to fail him. Anna Maria Luisa mistook haughteur for noblesse and Gian Gastone could not, however hard he racked his considerable brains, ever remember having seen his sister smile. After years of indifference to him, it was she who had delivered Gian Gastone the harshest blow of all and had precipitated the event that would allow her brother's hatred of women to blossom into full-blown bloom. For it was his sister who had persuaded their father that Gian Gastone should take a wife and had in fact proposed the very woman who now tortured his existence: Franziska of Saxe-Lauenburg, the wealthy widow of Count Palatine Philip of Neuberg. Franziska's chief accomplishment seemed to be that her overbearing behaviour had driven her husband to drink himself to death in three short years.

Meek, as he was, under his father's eye, Gian Gastone obediently married and headed into dreary exile in Bavaria through the same Bohemian forests that had been such a comfort to Violante. His spirits sank permanently on his arrival at Franziska's ramshackle wooden castle of Ploskovice, where his new wife proceeded to torture him with her peevish moods.

Mother, sister, wife: all had played their part in turning Gian Gastone against the female sex. And that is how Violante Beatrix de' Medici, his brother's wife and widow, had – fairly easily, it must be said – climbed to the top of his order of women. He had met her only three times, but her kindness and sweet nature recommended her; and besides, he owed her more than she could ever know. Gian Gastone called for Dami, his constant companion, and waved Violante's letter at him.

Giuliano Dami was his salvation. In Dami he had found the companion, brother and soulmate he had never had. Dami understood the extent of his gluttony and helped Gian Gastone to understand the seemingly limitless depths of his own sexual depravity. Dami was not stupid enough to be jealous or to expect Gian Gastone to be his exclusive lover; he quickly saw the advantages of being a pander – of boys, of food, of alcohol, of whatever his master desired. This proceeded not just from a healthy slice of self-interest but also from a genuine affection for his handsome and increasingly rotund young master. With his soft sibilant voice, Dami would whisper in his master's ears a constant stream of almost hypnotic reassurance: that one day Gian Gastone would be the grand duke, a fate that became more and more likely with each misfortune that befell his master's

siblings. And now that the duchy was threatened with insurrec-
tion in Tuscany, Gian Gastone realized that his sister-in-law's
letter was a document of passage. Even his bullying wife could
not gainsay an expedition at such a time.

'Dami,' he said, 'pack my trunks. We're going to Siena.'

Dami bowed, smoothly and obediently, and just quickly
enough to hide the look of horror in his strange purple eyes.

Gian Gastone's golden carriage, with the Medici cognizance on the doors, sped through Siena's Piazza del
Campo. Pigeons and starlings rose before the wheels,
dodging certain death, and women and children fled
from the carriage's path. Violante and Gretchen stood
back as the great gold coach crammed through the gateway of the Palazzo Popolo. The team of six bays, frothing
at the mouth, eyes rolling, dug in their hooves, slipping
on the greasy pavings, sending the ridiculous bonfire of
brooms flying. The carter's unfortunate mule, which in
one day had been to Montepulciano and back, now
seemed doomed to die beneath the hooves of his more
exalted brethren. Riccardo calmed the cowering creature,
then caught the reins of the bolting team, stopping the
coach and speaking softly into the ears of one, then
another, till all half-dozen stood still as stone.

Violante, Gretchen, Riccardo and the carter watched,
spellbound, as four young fellows swarmed down from
the roof and racks of the coach, wrenched open the door
with its insignia and began, in a practised way, to prise the

occupant of the carriage loose from his confines. Giuliano Dami, whom Violante recalled as Gian Gastone's constant shadow, sprang down from the other door of the carriage, bowed to her most correctly and went to help his master retain as much dignity in his descent as he could. Violante felt a chill pass through her. She had never liked Dami, and the glance of his purple eyes, and the sibilance of his speech, awakened a painful memory in her.

In little under a minute, dishevelled, jugbitten and enormously obese, the heir of Tuscany stood before his open-mouthed sister-in-law. As if waking from a dream, Violante stepped forward and kissed Gian Gastone on both his sweating cheeks. She could not believe that this was the same person as the handsome slim scholar who had helped her most kindly when she had suffered her shattering loss, who had arranged for her twins to be laid to rest when she had been crippled by grief. This service he had rendered her had bound her forever in his debt, and for this reason she proceeded, as she had done all her life, to take refuge in etiquette and good form. She did not, in manner or look, rebuke her brother-in-law for descending upon her without notice. Instead she reminded herself that she had written to him, she had bidden him come.

She said, as warmly as she could, 'Greetings, my lord. I rejoice to see you here. Your father and sister are well? And your lady wife?'

Gian Gastone found this question slightly awkward. The truth was that he had broken his journey in Florence with the express intention of killing his father. During his overnight stay he had contrived to behave so badly that his father had had a severe seizure from which he was not expected to recover.

Gian Gastone and Dami had arranged an orgy in his father's chamber in the Palazzo Vecchio, and contrived that his father would walk in from evensong in time to catch his son and heir being importuned by his constant coterie of pretty Tuscan boys, the *ruspanti*. The acts taking place there, played out in Cosimo's own bed for greater effect, were debauched enough to give Cosimo – who was as overweight as his son but considerably more advanced in years – a major stroke on the spot.

Gian Gastone had left his father babbling and dribbling on the very same four-poster he'd sullied with his antics, and after a solicitous word with the doctor, who had assured him that his father could not live much longer, he allowed himself a little smile. His sister Anna Maria Luisa, passing him in the doorway of their father's death chamber, caught him at it, but nevertheless extended to her estranged brother a long white hand of friendship. Gian Gastone not only refused her hand but cemented his schism with his one remaining sibling by hissing at her, once, like a cat.

Now, Gian Gastone looked at his sister-in-law, his hooded Medici eyes almost closed against the Sienese light. He was surprised to discover what Riccardo Bruni could already have told him: that there was a certain balm to Violante's presence. But however sympathetic she was, he could not, in all conscience, tell her what had really passed in Florence.

He contented himself with saying: 'My father is knocking at death's door; would that my wife were too.'

Violante exchanged another glance with Gretchen and saw from the corner of her eye Riccardo tuck down his chin to hide a smile. The slight movement of his head was his undoing; although, in fairness, a man of his physical charms would never have enjoyed many moments' grace before he caught the eye of Gian Gastone de' Medici.

'Did that amuse you, my pretty popelot?' Gian Gastone called across his sister-in-law with ringing, friendly tones.

Riccardo, fully intending to remain in the background until he could quietly slope away, unwarily lifted his eyes to the velvet-clad mastodon before him.

Gian Gastone was shot through with green fire and Cupid's bolt all at once. He did not really understand why his sister-in-law had dragged him to Siena, although he appreciated it. It would not be politic to be standing over his father at the very moment he expired, but neither would it be prudent to be far away in his Bohemian sinkhole of a castle when Cosimo died, lest there be a vacuum of power to be filled by a greedy neighbour or, worse, his sister Anna Maria Luisa.

Siena was a wise choice, just near and far enough. Gian Gastone could trespass on the hospitality of his favourite kin, help his sister-in-law with her little local difficulties and protect his Tuscan dominions. And the compensations, as he could see as his greedy eyes raked over her young ostler, were stupendous. If he had had the energy

Gian Gastone would have walked all the way around Riccardo. But he contented himself to gawp where he stood.

Violante, filled with a familiar foreboding, stepped forward. 'Thank you, Riccardo, you may go now.'

With a speed that belied his great weight Gian Gastone shot out a flabby hand and grabbed Riccardo's arm.

'No, no, *Riccardo*, you may not. Stay a while.'

The hand beringed with jewels dug into the flesh, then rose and hovered upon Riccardo's cheek. Riccardo jerked away as if stung, contempt in his eyes. Violante held her breath, but Gian Gastone merely laughed.

'Spirit. I like him. Well, well, Violante, you sly old mare. And they say there is nothing to do in the country. I can see the local colour is amazing.'

For a moment everyone was still and silent. Even the horses stood, heads down in the heat, waiting. Above the courtyard the starlings slashed across the high blue, and screeched to break the spell.

Gian Gastone looked around him, gratified by the discomfort he had wrought, and rubbed his hands. 'Let's go in,' he said with dispatch.

In that short moment the balance of power had transferred to him, and he was enjoying the sensation of outranking Violante, however benignly he felt towards her. He felt as though he were already grand duke.

'Sister, call your cooks and minstrels. Let's celebrate our reunion. And you, *Riccardo*,' he caressed the name, 'will be our guest of honour.'

Riccardo and Violante exchanged horrified glances.

'*Ruspanti*,' Gian Gastone called to his boys, 'bring my litter. Why are you all roosting around like woodcocks? Let's be inside, let's feast – I'm so famished my stomach thinks my throat's been cut.'

There was nothing for it but to follow.

∞

An hour later, Violante was in the Hall of the Nine, beneath those extraordinary frescoes of good and bad government, in her best violet silk. She was sitting at the right hand of her brother-in-law who, as heir to the dukedom, had taken her place at the head of the table. To his left, in the place normally taken by Giuliano Dami, sat Riccardo Bruni, looking as if he wished he were anywhere else in the world.

Gian Gastone ate and drank continually, his fingers and chin dripping with grease, his cup forever filled, forever empty again. Violante herself choked down a little bread and could not eat more. The only balm to her feelings was the quartet of musicians she had brought from the cathedral at short notice, playing Scarlatti on their viols and violoncellos. She had even had Ferdinando's beloved piano brought up from the Hall, and found a harpsichord player to tackle this new and unfamiliar instrument. She did not want Gian Gastone to find the society in Siena wanting. She was, in the face of an outsider, fiercely proud of her city.

While he was gorging, her brother-in-law did not speak, but she knew that between courses they must converse and she did not know what to say. Although she had written to Gian Gastone and bidden him come, now he was here Violante could not comprehend how his presence would aid their cause. Now he was here, she wished him as far away from her, from the city, from Riccardo, as possible. She didn't know what to do. Should she lay the problem at Gian Gastone's feet, let him deal with the Nine and walk away from it all? Or should she say nothing and proceed with their plan for Riccardo to go to the round church of San Galgano and hear the Nine's final plans?

Violante suddenly felt an enormous balloon of regret swelling in her chest. She experienced an overwhelming affection for her little group – Zebra, Gretchen, Pia, Riccardo and she herself, a ridiculous, premature nostalgia for their odd little band of brothers and sisters out to save the city. She looked at Gian Gastone, so bloated and decadent, so changed from the young, slim idealist she had known. Her instincts were to keep the plot from him. Yet her abiding memory of her brother-in-law was that he was fiendishly clever, endlessly observant and that Dami and his *ruspanti* had their eyes everywhere. She crumbled her bread thoughtlessly on the table, torn, sure that her thoughts must be as clear to her brother-in-law as the workings in a glass clock. She was surprised, then, by his opening gambit.

'See,' Gian Gastone's wine-soaked breath warmed her ear, 'how your toy enjoys the music.' He waved his great paw in Riccardo's direction. 'He drinks it in like a horse at a trough.'

Violante glanced at Riccardo. She could see that he had, as she had, found refuge in the Scarlatti. She realized, with a shock of recognition, that she had known another, once, who had listened to music in that way, as if he heard every single note, every individual thread of melody woven together in a tapestry of sound.

'He taps his fingers and moves his eyes,' continued Gian Gastone in her ear. 'See, he is following the counterpoint. Put a fiddle or a clavier in his hands and he would be accomplished. He is not such a peasant – you have chosen well for your paramour.'

He could not be permitted to go on like that.

'Really, brother, I hardly know the fellow. He is an ostler, the son of a farrier. You were lucky he happened by to stop your coach. I assure you, he is naught to me – truth be told, I think it a strange caprice of yours to invite him to so high a table.'

Violante noted the ever-present Dami listening closely to her words and darting his violet glance at Riccardo. She bit her lip at the irony of what she'd uttered. Gian Gastone's insinuations revolted her. True, she wished to look after Riccardo, to nurture him: she knew that some might say she was filling an empty cradle with a substitute for what she had lost, but she had never thought of him in the way that her brother-in-law suggested.

'You assure me, do you? Then you will not mind if I fish in his sweet pond?'

Without waiting for a reply, Gian Gastone turned to Riccardo, pressing meats and dainties upon him. Violante could not hear what Riccardo said and felt once again, with an uncomfortable trick of memory, that she had been here before: looking on while a young and beautiful man was importuned by a Medici sodomite. But she did not fear for Riccardo's heart. She knew it was bound and sequestered in Pia Tolomei's white hands.

Before long Gian Gastone had turned back to her again. 'Do you think Ferdinando ever loved you?'

Violante started. Her thoughts flew to the one and only time she and her husband had lain together. Ferdinando had made her wear a man's wig and had leaned her over the footboard of the bed, turning her face away, leaving her shift to cover her breasts. She had known, even then – for she was not so green – that he wished to hide all that was female from his sight. Worse than the bestial, painful, hideous act was the expression on his face when she cast a desperate, pleading glance over her shoulder. It frightened her that she did not know the person who did this to her. There was no love nor desire, no communion; she was being violated by a stranger. *Violare*. And worse: she saw in that moment that his eyes were closed. He did not wish to see her. And it was this that hurt most of all. Ferdinando was fulfilling his obligations, but did not want any piece of her. This terrible little episode had marked the moment she had known, finally, that he had never loved her and never would. Violante had never admitted the truth, even to herself. Now, fortified by the new friends she had made, numbed by the distance from Ferdinando, she was able to answer Gian Gastone's question truthfully.

'No.'

Gian Gastone picked at his teeth. 'Neither do I,' he said. 'My father loved my mother once; she detested him and wanted him dead. I, in turn, detest my wife and would not shed a single tear for her. My sister Anna Maria Luisa, like yourself, married a syphilitic husband who could not give her living children. All he left her when he rotted was the Elector's army: a regiment of lead soldiers to play with but no war to wage. One can quite see why the people talk about a Medici curse. No, we have not one happy marriage among us.'

Violante considered these bold, stark truths. It was the moment for honesty. 'I loved your brother, though.'

For a moment the hooded eyes softened. 'I know that too. Ferdinando was a fool. And yet, there was a strange morality to what happened to him. He took lovers: Cecchino, in particular, of course.'

Violante froze. No one had ever dared to name Ferdinando's amour to her face.

'And it was that weakness, in particular, which gave him the malady of which he died. He was punished, in the end, for not loving you.'

Violante considered. She had last seen Cecchino in Florence's duomo at Ferdinando's funeral. The singer was wearing the same wig, perfumed and powdered, that Ferdinando had made her wear in their wedding bed. At the funeral the castrato's face had been a ruin of tears. She could not pity Cecchino, even though she was able to acknowledge that *their* union had been the true marriage in Ferdinando's life.

Nevertheless, her heart had become hardened against that sin of sodomy, the sin that had given her husband syphilis, the syphilis that had taken her sons. Of all the sins in the calendar, this one seemed particularly Tuscan. Saint Bernardino of Siena himself had railed against it from the pulpit, and in her own country homosexuals were known as *Florenzen* – Florentines. This sickness of the duchy shamed her, and her personal experiences added to political infamy to make her determined to cleanse her province. When she had fled to Siena, she had outlawed sodomy in the city and made sure that those who shared in the practice faced the harshest punishments of the law. Under her rule the Sienese spat at sodomites in the street.

Violante lifted her eyes to Gian Gastone and recognized a new, complicit candour between them. She felt, for a moment, brave.

'And what is to be your punishment for the same sin?' She steeled herself for his anger, but Gian Gastone's thoughts chimed, eerily, with hers.

'I am childless. The dukedom dies with me. And yet, I have had a long and happy marriage of a different kind. We allow each other our freedoms, we speak the truth to each other and we are the closest of companions.'

Gian Gastone turned to Dami and smiled, raising his hand to touch the hollows of his lover's throat. Dami smiled back, and yet Violante could not look in those strange eyes, winded suddenly by a complicated pain. Dami was Gian Gastone's Cecchino, but as Gian Gastone caressed Dami's neck she realized that they did not trouble to hide their love, nor conduct their affairs with discretion. At least Ferdinando had always practised his amours in a clandestine fashion. He had afforded her that much dignity. She recalled, almost word for word, the statutes she had accordingly written against homosexuality in Siena, bitterness in every clause, pain in every line. Her brother-in-law would have to be very careful here.

As the next trencher of food was placed before Gian Gastone, Violante recognized with an enormous weariness that he was only just beginning his feasting and drinking. She heartily wished herself abed. She dare do no more than glance at Riccardo, who, his head in the music, was eating nothing. There was no way she could speak to him, nor even send him a signal or message. Equally, she could not tell her brother-in-law of the city's ills tonight: the company was too loud and he was too drunk. She rose and excused herself, but not soon enough to miss Gian Gastone, full at last, vomiting copiously on the table, then removing his wig to wipe up the stinking mess. She fled.

∞

Riccardo glanced at the fabulous feast before him and heartily wished himself at home at his father's table, sharing a hard loaf and a cup of wine. He wondered, as he did at every moment, what Pia was doing now. He had no interest in the wonderful fare of Violante's kitchens, unlike the monster beside him who was conveying all before him into his gluttonous maw. Riccardo could not look upon him, this soon-to-be duke, this *noble* man. How could his country, his city, belong, one day soon, to this creature?

Riccardo stole a look at the gorging face, with its disgustingly full lips and hooded eyes, its multitude of chins. None of this would matter if the face was kindly or the eyes mild, but it had taken Riccardo very little time to identify Gian Gastone for what he was: a child, a wilful, dangerous child, with precocious intelligence and an iron will, a child who was absolutely used to getting his own way in the world, a child who had been taught that nothing was beyond his reach.

The household of beautiful young men who revolved around him like satellite planets around the sun were smooth and silky and silent, and utterly untrustworthy. Once or twice Riccardo caught them regarding him jealously. He could have set their minds at ease; he had no interest in Gian Gastone's breed of bedsport, no matter what size of remuneration the purse held. He had no intention of becoming the catamite to this walrus.

Riccardo felt a pang for Violante, abruptly deposed from her rank. He knew that the duchess had invited her brother-in-law here to help them to stem Faustino's climb to power, but he could feel nothing but boiling resentment against this interloper. Riccardo tightened his fist on his trencher knife. If he swiped the blade sideways into the flesh of Gian Gastone's throat, would he bleed like a pig at slaughter? He relaxed his fingers and put the knife down.

'Hungry, my pet?' Gian Gastone leaned in, crushing Riccardo's shoulder.

Riccardo flinched imperceptibly. 'No, my lord.'

'You must call me "Your Grace".' What do you think of our sister the duchess?'

There was so much that was wrong with this question that Riccardo took a moment to answer. 'She is a truly good woman.'

'You like the music?'

This was easier. 'I do, Your Grace.'

'Would it surprise you to know that my brother, the duchess's late husband, helped to invent the piano?'

'Nothing would surprise me today, Your Grace.'

Gian Gastone smiled abruptly. 'Yes, indeed. He gave his patronage – and his cock, too, but that's another story – to a fellow called Bartolomeo Cristofori, a pretty young harpsichord builder from Padua. They invented, together, the oval spinet and the *spinettone*, so that my brother could play counterpoint for him out of bed as well as in it. And from those two instruments they developed the piano, with the black and white keys: the fine sounds and airs of which you are enjoying tonight.'

Riccardo turned to him with a look of haughty contempt, but was unnerved to find it met by the astonished gaze of Gian Gastone. Something had even made him put his fork down.

'For a moment – no, never mind . . .' The duke resumed eating again, turning to Dami and dropping Riccardo mid-sentence.

Relieved to be dismissed, Riccardo rose from the table and ran down the stone stairs, gulping the fresh air of the courtyard as he went, almost weeping with relief to be out of there, to be away from this life of decadence, of nobility. The palace was no haven to him now, as it had been only that afternoon in the library. In that moment he thought he would never go back. He suddenly wanted his father.

He left, as he always did, through the kitchens, out into the air, and the friendly familiar streets of the Torre *contrada* swallowed him. As ever, he was careful not to be followed. But he was not careful enough.

∞

Giuliano Dami, on silent feet, followed Riccardo on business of his own. He trod from shadow to shadow to the Torre *contrada*, and watched Riccardo disappear through the half-door of a stable, and heard the soft whicker that greeted him. Giuliano peered in the neighbouring house; here an old man sat at a table, nursing a cup and a pipe of tobacco. He stared at the old man for a long moment and, suddenly making up his mind, lifted the latch. The old man looked up, expecting his son. His lined lids lifted, the whites showed about his eyes when they lighted on Dami, and he uttered one word.

'You!'

13
The Snail

After a troubling interview with Riccardo's father, Giuliano Dami wandered back through the Tower contrada. He knew he should hurry back to his master before he was missed, but he had a lot on his mind and he had always enjoyed cities at night. The looming palace against the star-studded night was alluring, the night warm and there was a scent of hyacinth on the breeze. All of his senses conspired against him and he dawdled. If someone had asked him why he dawdled, he might have said that thinking slowed him up.

Someone did ask him.

Footsteps followed. And a voice came out of the dark. 'Why do you walk so slowly?'

Dami turned. He must be out of practice, for he had one of the sharpest pairs of ears in Tuscany, attuned to everything from below-stairs gossip and returning wives to angry creditors. He walked, without changing his leisurely pace, back to his *questioner. The moonlight showed a youth of piercing beauty: ash-blond hair, pearly skin with barely the fuzz of an emerging beard, velvet-dark eyes and full lips. Dami let his eyes wander over the young man, his night-purple eyes heavy with meaning.*

'Why do I walk so slowly?' He smiled lazily. 'Perhaps I am a snail. What do you think?' He let one long finger stroke the young man's cheek. Slowly, slowly. 'And you? Perhaps you are a snail also? For it must be said that you, too, were walking very slowly.'

The young man smiled, his full lips parting to show excellent teeth. Slowly, slowly, he took Dami's finger between his lips and sucked. Dami had his answer. On the way back to the palace, the two of them walked a great deal more quickly than before.

Violante woke from her usual dream of the twins with a feeling of trepidation. Gradually the events of yesterday resolved themselves. The arrival of Gian Gastone; the return of Dami into her life, a man she hated and feared with equal measure without quite knowing why. The disastrous feast, which brought back so many ill memories. And today, Riccardo would begin the long ride to San Galgano, for she could still not decide whether to lay the whole business before her brother-in-law.

She lay for a long, long while, staring up at the folds and festoons of the drapes of her bed. A swallow flew into the room through the open window. The bird perched on her bedpost, cocking its little head at her, staring at her with twin black beads. Before she could reach for it, the bird flew away again, directly out of the window, with unwavering direction and resolve. Mocking her.

Violante threw back the coverlet and rang for Gretchen. She dressed, breakfasted and met with her council – presided over with smooth, insolent dispatch by Francesco Maria Conti – before she climbed the stairs to Gian Gastone's chamber. She had seen the state he was in by the end of the night and knew that he had carried on carousing after the feast, for she had heard laughter and music, as well as other sounds she had not cared to analyse, issuing from his chamber until the early hours. So she waited as long as she could before approaching him this morning. Violante had never drunk more than a goblet of wine at a sitting, even in the depths of her miserable marriage. She had no idea how such excesses would affect the constitution the following day.

But as she entered the chamber when bidden, she was pleasantly surprised by Gian Gastone's appearance. He was up, dressed in sober clothes, with his whiskers shaven and his wig combed and arranged. His feet were plunged into a silver basin from which rose the scent of lavender and she thought that, for the first time, he looked faintly regal. His demeanour and the friendly smile he bestowed upon her made up her mind. As she looked past him along the swallow's path, to her city, his city, she began her tale.

She had, it seemed, to become used to expecting the unexpected. Gian Gastone seemed excited by the task, galvanized out of his usual torpor by opposition. He rejected all notions of appealing to his father for help, for arms and armies.

'Florence is not defended,' he said. 'The payroll of the garrison shows most of the infantry are over seventy, with not a mouthful of teeth between them. It no longer has a standing army. The only infantry and cavalry billeted here are my sister's army from the Palatinate.'

Gian Gastone's lip curled and Violante could not tell which her brother-in-law liked less: the notion of Florence's geriatric army, or the presence of his detested sister's troops.

'I will deal with this problem, dear sister, myself,' he announced, closing that particular discussion. 'You will enjoy my protection and these treacherous captains will know what it is to be faced with a Medici.'

Violante attempted to furnish her brother-in-law with the details of what was already known, what was suspected, but he would have none of it, waving away her assistance with a massive hand. He merely asked, 'When are these nine fellows to meet next?'

Violante hesitated. 'Tonight, at the hour of nine. At the round church of Montesiepi above the abbey of San Galgano outside the city. My . . . man, from the Tower *contrada*, is to be there and hear their council.'

Gian Gastone appeared not to recall the name, if, indeed, he had ever known it. 'The pretty one?'

Her contradiction died on her lips. 'Yes.'

'Very good,' said Gian Gastone, 'leave it with me, dear sister-in-law.'

There was nothing for it but to quit the room. As Violante closed the great doors behind her, she could feel herself shrinking. She stood outside, swallowing. She had not expected to be removed from the affair so completely. For the last ten years she had ruled the city. For the last twenty days she had fought for it to remain in Medici hands. She knew now what a pair of crutches these two aims had been. Now that both had been taken from her, how would she live?

∞

Pia knew that it was time.

Both Nello and Faustino would be going to San Galgano that evening. When they had safely left in the carriage, she must saddle Guinevere and ride, far and fast, away from here, away from Siena. She had no plan; she just knew she had to choose a path and follow it, go somewhere, anywhere, and begin again.

She had no gold save Cleopatra's pendant. If she could get away, south, maybe, she could sell it for a little money. Maybe Palma, Messina, or Capri: places that she had never visited but had heard of, sybaritic, sun-soaked places whose exotic names she used to repeat in her girlhood chamber like poetry. Perhaps she could enter a great household as a servant. In her naivety Pia did not ask herself how easy it would be for someone raised in privilege to serve others. Anything would be better than what she could expect as Nello's wife.

She spent the day in a ferment of nervous expectation and curious reluctance. She was not quite self-aware enough to admit that, in some small part of her, she did not want to go. To ride from Tuscany would mean that she would never again see Riccardo Bruni, never laugh with him, or ride with him, or share a forbidden kiss with him. But she schooled herself harshly whenever her thoughts wandered to him and the time they had shared, for in Siena she was Nello's wife. She could not be with Riccardo anyway; it would be an added torture to have him under her eye every day.

In the afternoon she wandered, listlessly, about the castle, and from one draughty arrow slit saw the ostler leading his team of four greys into the courtyard, strapping them into their tracings, ready for the carriage. Pia calculated – it was about an hour's drive from here to San Galgano. A servant, armed with a bucket and brush, was covering over the Eagle arms with pitch paint. The sun was lowering, and the Nine were due to meet at nine of the clock. They would be off soon and she would be free to go. She felt again that odd foreboding at the pit of her stomach, but still she headed down to the stables to give Guinevere oats for the journey.

In the warm, low buildings she found comfort in the smell of hay and horse. As she fed and petted her palfrey, she gave a handful of oats to Nello's black stallion too, checking his bandaged leg, batting away his great head when he tried, as he always did, to nibble her ear. She fiddled with Guinevere's tack, making sure that everything was ready and in place, thankful now that Signor Bruni had insisted that she learn the name of every bit and every strap, and that she learn to saddle and bridle her own mount over and over again. Riding, he'd say, was a *whole* experience, and you should know everything about your mount. When she'd suggested, surprised, that the servants should tack up her horse, he'd been short with her. *Signor Bruni*. How long would it take her to stop thinking of him?

Footsteps sounded, voices spoke and got louder. Pia, bidden by some nameless instinct, ducked down in Guinevere's stall. A moment later she recognised the voices as those of Nello and Faustino. They were dressed for their carriage ride in boots and hooded cloaks. Pia might have stood then, for she was entirely innocent, visiting her horse. And yet she did not, for as soon as she was able to hear her menfolk's discourse she knew she'd be in danger.

'. . . troops,' said Nello, 'and a thousand men? 'Tis a little in excess, surely?'

Faustino's voice then. 'We want to be sure. And Romulus will have the men of all the Nine's *contrade* at his disposal too.'

'And these troops, they will be armed?'

'Of course. Pikes and muskets. We're deposing a duchess. It's a coup, Nello, not a carnival.'

Pia could hear Nello scuffing his feet like a sulky child. 'I still don't really see why he's helping us.'

'The duchess is childless, and so is that great fat sot of a brother-in-law of hers, lately arrived from Florence. And so is his sister Anna Maria Luisa. When they all die – and they are all advancing in years – there will be an absence of power in Tuscany.'

'So?'

Faustino sighed. 'Take a look at this water bucket.'

Pia jumped at the clang of metal as the *capitano* kicked the pail with his foot.

'If you fill it to the brim, and leave it out in the rain, what happens?'

Nello's voice, slow. 'It stays full.'

'It remains unchanged, exactly. But if you leave an empty bucket in the rain, what then?'

'The rain fills it.'

'Exactly. Tuscany is soon to be an empty bucket. And the rains are coming.'

'But why is Romulus helping the Nine fill it?'

'Because we are better than the alternative.'

'Which is?'

'Don Carlos of Spain, a foreigner and, moreover, the son of Elizabeth Farnese. The Farnese family are Romulus's hated rivals. If the Don becomes grand duke, the Farnese will regain the ascendancy. So Romulus will help us rebuild Siena as a republic and get rid of the duchess for us.'

Then Nello's voice again, grim. 'I care not what happens to the duchess, so long as the race is run. Three score and ten beats of the heart, that's all it takes – seventy heartbeats to victory. And nothing, nothing, should be allowed to interrupt it.'

Pia's skin chilled; she buried her face in her arm to stop herself breathing loudly and could see bumps raised on her skin like a plucked goose.

Faustino spoke, conciliatory. 'Of course. That shall all

be made very clear. And do not forget that we need to win the race to win the betting, so it's as important to the Nine as to you.'

Nello again. 'You say that the heir to the duchy has arrived from Florence. Will he not threaten our enterprise?'

'Not a bit,' assured Faustino. 'He can barely walk unaided, let alone act against us. All his arrival signifies is that we have *two* Medici lobsters in the pot. Besides, if Signor Gian Gastone interferes, I have laid down assurances to deal with him.'

Then, the scrape of a boot as the driver and footman approached, and the talk was ended. Pia heard the doors close and the rumble of wheels as the carriage rolled into the courtyard to be harnessed to the waiting team of greys. Her heart thudded as she sat, still in the prickling hay, until she heard the smart hooves of the greys move down the drive and out of earshot. Then she took her face out of the hot crook of her arm.

She did not even have to consider. She did not think of the great house in Capri where she would never now be a servant, or the danger she was riding into. In her heart she now knew she had the excuse she needed to abandon her plan. It was her moral obligation, she reasoned, and she could save the city and perhaps the duchess's life. But none of these motives was uppermost. She just wanted to see Signor Bruni again.

She tacked Guinevere up with practised shaking fingers, led her to the courtyard and mounted easily. She pulled her riding hood over her head and was away, the winds in her face, turning Guinevere's head to the hills and the abbey of San Galgano.

∞

Pia reached the abbey just before sunset. She had ridden out of the castle and had taken the road south-west to Grosetto. But then she picked her way over the hill tracks, as the crow might fly, to beat the carriage. By sundown she had reached Montesiepi. As the great abbey loomed above her, any fears that she would miss the place were dismissed in a breath of relief. As she rode through the lush close forest, the sun through the green leaves dappled Guinevere's flank, passing across her coat like a shoal of fishes.

The abbey itself was a vast place of stone, on a scale Pia had not expected. She began to feel disquiet. The church was as big as the duomo, and ruined too, with piles of stone and broken arches puncturing the blue sky. Pia vaulted from Guinevere's back, lowered the reins to tie them, and the palfrey dipped her head and began to snatch gratefully at the grass. Her sides gleamed with sweat and her mouth was rimed with froth. Pia patted her gratefully; she'd been faithful, and fast, on this difficult journey.

Knowing that time was short Pia trod carefully through the ruined door and looked about her. The ancient abbey was open to the sky, a perfect rectangle of blue framed and captured in stone. At the apex of the cruciform nave a single roundel regarded her like an unwinking blue eye. North. The round church of the hermitage should be through this gaping door and a little up the hill.

Pia hurried though the cloisters, peopled now by ghosts, expecting the echo of a snatch of plainsong, or the tread of a long-dead monastic foot. But the huge and cavernous space was unnaturally silent. Faith had left this place long ago, and now it was the dominion of an older god. The forest was closing in on the abbey from all sides. Even this great monolith would soon be consumed. Through each gaping window – robbed of its treasure, those jewels of glass – now a mass of foliage was the only colour to be seen. Hardy shoots had begun to ease through the old stones, working them loose like aged teeth. Pia felt as if she was in the wrong century.

She felt a hand on her shoulder and her bones dissolved into water. She turned, expecting Nello or a hand stained from the scriptorium, a ghostly face shadowed by a cowl, fearing the latter less. A cloaked figure greeted her but the face within was that of Riccardo Bruni.

He kissed her a hundred, a thousand times, as the old abbey and the forest creatures looked on. He was so overcome to see her that he made no comment on the utter folly that had brought her here, to him, to danger. But when they at last broke apart, he gripped her shoulder urgently.

'How did you come here?'

She smiled and said, 'I rode. Far and fast, just as you taught me. Guinevere is tethered in the tree cover.'

'And Nello?'

'He follows with Faustino. They come by road, by carriage, so are slower – I left after and arrived before, by taking the fields and hills. But they will be following hard upon. And we are not yet in the right place.' She took his hand. 'Come. I have much to tell you on the way.'

He took her hand and did not let it go as they walked through the vast abandoned place, the stones gilded with the dying light. Through the north transept they entered the world of the forest, and the cries of strange things huddled them together. Pia whispered what she had learned of Romulus and the grave danger the duchess was in. She told the tale almost with reluctance, because for just that moment she wanted Signor Bruni – *Riccardo* – to turn in his footsteps, bundle her on to Leocorno and take her away, now and for ever. But she was his bride only in this fantasy, in this forest. In her world, the laws of Siena bound her.

Pia quickened her footsteps and soon they came upon a little church at the crest of the hill, as small and round as the abbey was vast and square. They hesitated at the lip of the forest, mindful that they were about to leave their cover.

Raising one finger to his lips, Riccardo left Pia briefly to tread carefully all round the place, checking the terrain. When he returned, he took her shoulders.

'You should go back,' he said, 'before you are discovered.'

Pia said nothing, but slowly shook her head, her dark eyes never leaving his face. So he drew her with him out of the forest and into the little church. It was as round inside as the temple of a Roman or the chapel of a Templar. In the gloom of the lapida they could just make out a jagged piece of rock protruding from the tiled floor with a black cross-shape above – the hilt of a sword thrust into the stone: the sword of San Galgano, or perhaps of Arthur himself. The sword of a disillusioned soldier or a man who would be king. Riccardo regarded it for a moment. On another day he would have laid a hand on the thing just to test the legend, but time was short.

'Let us conceal ourselves here.' He pointed to a series of dark wood pews. 'They will have to proceed through here to reach the chapel beyond.'

Pia lay down close behind the darkest pews and without a moment of awkwardness or hesitation Riccardo lay down beside her, opened his arms and she huddled into the curve of his chest. Feeling the length of her body pressed against his for the first time, she had to remind himself of the sanctity of the place. She raised her thoughts and eyes to heaven and in the dimness she could just make out the perfect dome of the rotunda, decorated in one long, perfectly described spiral, like the shell of a snail, turning ever inwards, constructed of white stone alternating with red brick. As the horseman held Pia close to him she followed the snail-spiral with narrowed eyes. Time crawled slowly, and she would have had it crawl slower still. It was enough to have him hold her and look at the spiral. She knew that if she met his eyes she would be lost.

It seemed hours later when the glow of torches lit the gloom. Pia's heart beat fast and painfully. Riccardo held a finger to his lips and beckoned as they edged silently to the end of the pew. Nine torches processed forth and became a circle, each illuminating the cowled figure that held it. Once again Pia felt the echo of a monastic past, but here the echoes were not of sacred music and the footfall of a sandal, but the dark devilry of a black mass. For a moment she feared that the cowls held nothing within, just the gaping blackness of a demonic form.

As ever, Faustino was the first to speak.

'Well,' he said. 'The hour has come, and Romulus will be with us presently to plan the attack. But first, our own civic business. Is all in place for the Palio?'

'Yes. I have constructed the mechanism to determine the horse draw, aided by Romulus himself. Once that has proceeded successfully, the horses will be allotted as planned,' said another voice.

'And our syndicates?'

'The betting will take place in blocks. We have formed syndicates in each of our *contrade*, and each merchant and noble, down to the humblest baker and water-carrier, has given me their tithe.'

'And then?'

'They trust us, as their captains, to lay the money on their own *fantino*. But I shall lay the money on Nello as agreed, and our *contrada* will be the winners too even though he will triumph.'

'The losses shall be met by the other *contrade* who are unaware of our enterprise.'

'Thus the Nine will be enriched and exalted, and the others impoverished, soon to disappear.'

Pia met Riccardo's eyes. The betting would beggar half of the city.

'And what of Romulus?'

'His part in the bargain will be told soon enough. He will join us here shortly,' said the voice of the one who had spoken of the horse draw. 'In essentials he will move during the race, while the entire city is crammed into the piazza.'

'I hear a carriage . . . it must be him!' A younger, more nasal voice now; Pia's body stiffened involuntarily. Nello – not among the Nine's number, but lurking in the shadows outside the circle.

Pia lifted her head a fraction. There was indeed a rumble of carriage wheels. A carriage great and noble and heavy, of such bearing that Pia felt the vibration deep within her chest.

The Nine stood silently as they awaited the arrival of their master conspirator. Pia edged forward and craned around the pew. Each man in the church was still, their torches guttering and wavering slightly, breaking the circle. Pia held Riccardo tight, waiting too.

Outside, there was the sound of a horse whinnying and then the creak of someone descending from the carriage and moving on slow, shuffling footsteps across the stone flags of the lapida. The company turned as one as an enormous figure shuffled into the circle of torchlight. Pia heard Riccardo give a tiny gasp.

'Who is it?' she breathed.

'Gian Gastone de' Medici.'

Pia frowned. Could she have been mistaken in what she'd overhead in the castle stable? Was the duchess's brother-in-law somehow embroiled in this plot? Faustino had seemed to fear him, had placed safeguards against his interference.

An elderly voice spoke up uncertainly. 'Romulus?'

Swift as a knife-strike, Faustino spoke. 'Shut your stupid mouth, Orsa. You are mistaken. This is the old duke's heir, the fat sot from Florence.'

'Careful, signor,' Gian Gastone's voice was dangerous. 'You speak to the Medici.'

Pia watched the Nine carefully. She could see that they knew not whether to stay or make a run for it. Faustino had no such fears. He raised his head half an inch and prepared to face the situation, tempering the contempt in his tone just a fraction.

'My lord, how may we help you?'

'I'm here to help *you*.'

'How did you know we would be here?'

Gian Gastone waved a massive paw, his shadow cutting through the torchlight. 'We know all of your secrets. Moreover, there is one here who listens to all your council, wherever you meet, and who is loyal to me. This might surprise you, but you are labouring, I'm afraid, under a serious misapprehension.'

Pia's flesh crawled. She knew Gian Gastone spoke of Riccardo, that he knew he was hidden somewhere in the church, that he was enjoying this cat-and-mouse game. She prayed he would not utter the horseman's name, that he would take the opportunity to imply to Faustino that one of the Nine themselves was a turncoat.

'That is not possible,' Faustino said decidedly, then after a pause his tone changed. 'What leads you to think this? Perhaps you could share your wisdom with your faithful subjects.'

Pia registered Faustino's change of tone. He was keeping Gian Gastone talking, keeping him inside the church. There was something outside that Faustino did not wish the heir of Tuscany to see. She put her mouth to Riccardo's ear.

'Time wasting.'

He nodded and breathed, '*Stay here.*' She felt the chill of his body leaving her, the chill of being alone.

The chill of foreboding.

∞

Riccardo crept from his hiding place into the darkness, clinging to the shadow in the chapel. Once outside, he stole past the Medici coach, which loomed out of the dark in the glimmering greeny half-light of the forest. There seemed nothing amiss. He stilled the horses with a trailing hand and crept down the path on silent feet. He climbed an overhanging tree and settled in the leaves, controlling his breathing, prepared to wait.

His wait was not a long one. A covered carriage pulled quietly up the hill, a rival in size to the Medici carriage, drawn by six matchless bays. The driver halted the horses at the sight of the Medici coach. He jumped down to examine the Medici arms on the door, then walked back to the carriage and spent some little time in conference with its occupant. The coachman's tricorne obscured the face of the passenger, but a white glove bearing two rings grasped the carriage door agitatedly. The driver mounted his box again and clicked his tongue to turn the horses around on the wide path, away and down the hill again in the moonlight, their hooves dulled by leaf mould. The carriage turning to a child's toy, a speck, then nothing.

The meeting may have been aborted, but Riccardo was wiser than before. He had seen the insignia on the coach, a design that matched the ring that lay upon the glove. The crossed keys of Saint Peter.

∞

Inside the round church, Pia sensed that Gian Gastone really did not know what to do. Having made his dramatic entrance, he seemed to have run out of bluster.

'Count yourselves warned,' he said, 'by the Medici. Now I could,' he went on, 'have my regiments, who are even now hard by, take your names and your lands and your balls. But I'll be clement, this time, so long as you undertake to disperse and make no more mention of this Nine nonsense.'

Pia understood perfectly that Gian Gastone had no regiments approaching. Having lived with her father's dramatic posturing all her life, she knew Gian Gastone had drastically overplayed his hand. She edged to the pew's end and watched as the duke began to back from the church, challenging the conspirators.

'So now, what do you say?'

The Nine, in a silent malevolent circle, watched him, none of them making an answer, the only movement coming from their guttering torches. Pia knew they could overcome this interloper and his footmen in a fight, but something restrained them and in some ways their silence and their immobility was even more threatening.

Gian Gastone retreated, still making grand pronouncements, but they sounded increasingly hollow. He delivered his parting shot on the threshold. 'And don't forget that one of yours is my creature! The eyes of the Medici are everywhere.'

As Pia heard the rumble of the Medici carriage speeding away, she realized the danger she was in. But even when Faustino cried, 'Search this place!' she did not feel fearful. There was nowhere to run; her capture was inevitable. She lay there, beneath the pew, waiting, looking up at the concentric circles on the round roof, following the path of the spiral as the Nine closed in ever-decreasing circles around her. And when the torches finally lit up her hiding place, and as she looked up into her husband's cruel face, her only hope was that Riccardo might have got away.

∞

Riccardo was nearly floored by the Medici carriage rolling past him.

With sudden foreboding, he ran on silent feet to the door of the hermitage, but the tableau he saw there stopped him in his tracks. Pia, who had been in his arms so recently, was now in the arms of Nello, who held her not tenderly, but with a knife to her throat. Riccardo looked at its wicked, keen blade. If he revealed himself Pia would die before he reached her, and he would give himself away into the bargain. If he did not, Nello would punish her, with nameless, hideous abuses that he could not bear to speculate upon. Then, unbidden, he thought of Violante and knew that he owed something to her, to finish what he'd begun.

Sick at heart, hating himself, he hid as the Nine rode past.

14

The Caterpillar

Acaterpillar was crawling very slowly in a beautiful garden when he was met by a lively ant.

'Out of the way,' said the ant, 'and don't block the path of your superiors. It is beneath my quality to talk to such a mean creature as you.'

The caterpillar, unmoved, went upon his way, coiled himself into a silken cocoon and emerged the next morning as a beautiful butterfly. He flew into the air and spied the ant scuttling below on the ground. The ant was taken aback.

'Proud creature,' called the butterfly, 'there is none so mean that he may not, one day, be exalted above those who thought themselves his better.'

'Wake up, madam! Wake up!'

Violante opened her eyes to find Gretchen standing in her nightgown in a circle of candlelight, her old hands shaking so much that tallow dripped on the coverlet. The chamber was still dark, and below she could hear a loud banging and voices shouting.

'It is the horseman. Come quickly!'

Violante flung back the coverlet. 'On the tower?'

'No, madam, at the doors – hammering fit to knock them in.'

Violante leaped to her feet and grabbed a shawl. 'What's the hour?'

Gretchen, already hurrying away, answered the question over her shoulder. 'Barely sun-up, madam.'

The duchess followed her servant down the stairs to the main entrance where her guards were struggling to hold an impassioned Riccardo Bruni behind a cross of pikes.

'Let him pass!' she commanded.

As he came closer she could see the violet shadows beneath his eyes and knew that he had not slept. Something had gone badly amiss.

Riccardo pushed past Violante and mounted the great stair to the *piano nobile*, taking them three at a time. She followed at his heels, waving away the guards as they followed. Riccardo flung open every door he found until he came to Gian Gastone's presence chamber. There he found his quarry, snoring in the solar. Dami, dressed and immaculate, and playing solitaire at a side table, waiting for his master to awaken, was flipping over the cards with his long white fingers.

Riccardo strode to the bed, ripped back the covers and grabbed an ample handful of Gian Gastone's nightshirt. It was no mean feat to drag the heir of Tuscany's bulk to a sitting position, but Riccardo did it, and with one hand too.

Dazed, Gian Gastone opened his eyes, snorted once and focused his gaze on Riccardo. At the same time Dami leaped to his feet and the card table tipped, spilling the cards on to the floor.

'What,' asked Riccardo of Gian Gastone, 'did you do?' He spat out every word, his tone barely below a shout.

'What the—' began Gian Gastone. He got no further.

'I'll tell you what you did.'

Riccardo's heart and head were on fire and his anger was compounded by an unbearable feeling of guilt: if he had not left Pia alone, she might still have been safe. He had put the city above Pia, and would not do it again. He blamed himself very much indeed. In his passion he lost all coherence, all the arguments that had been marching through his head as he had ridden back through the night from San Galgano.

'You as good as told Faustino Caprimulgo last night that you had a spy in the church. Pia was discovered there and now he will think she is the Judas in his own family, a traitor to the *contrada*. Never mind what the law may say; now, *now*, Nello will visit such retribution upon her that I cannot, I cannot—' He broke off, balling his fists with frustration.

Gian Gastone held up both of his vast hands. 'Wait . . . wait. I don't know who any of these people are.'

Standing in the doorway, Violante covered her eyes with her hands. So Gian Gastone had barrelled into the clandestine meeting. With his ego and hubris, he would bring their whole secret scheme down. She took her hands away.

'Faustino Tolomei is the captain of the Eagle *contrada*. Pia Tolomei is wed to his son, Nello.'

'And you, *you* . . .' Riccardo advanced on Gian Gastone again, but was halted by the tone of the duke's voice.

'Do not put your hands on Tuscany again,' he said quietly. 'You are lucky I do not have you whipped and thrown from these doors. You are fortunate that I will even question with you. For it is beneath my quality to talk to such a mean creature as you.'

Riccardo dropped his hands to his sides in a gesture of hopelessness. Violante looked from him to her brother-in-law, and Gian Gastone, missing nothing, caught her anxiety.

'But, since you *are* the fortunate favourite of my dear sister-in-law, and because you are so pretty, I will forgive your transgressions.' He sniffed. 'If it means so much to you I can tell the Eagles' captain that it was nothing to do with the silly little bird.'

Riccardo snorted with derision. 'You won't get the chance.' With this, he turned on his heels and started down the stairs.

Violante followed him out of the room, pulling at his sleeve.

Riccardo rounded on her, all respect and rank forgot. 'How could you tell him?'

Violante spread her hands hopelessly. 'I thought he was the help we needed. I wrote to him, the day we first met. I never heard from him. Then he arrived, out of the ether.'

'And you *told* him? We had the matter in hand. All of us together.'

She could have wept. 'A little boy, an old lady, a middle-aged one and you? You said it yourself!'

'And yet we could have stopped them. And now Pia is discovered. She's under lock and key, she may be put to *death* under our laws – *your* laws! And now I am gone too.'

Violante did not move until she had heard his feet recede all the way down the steps and out of the palace. Then she moved to the window and watched his back depart through the crowd gathering to watch the horse draw. The Palio was in less than a week, but now it seemed not to matter anyway. Their scheming was at an end.

She pressed her hands to the place below her ribs where the stays of her corset bit. Lest the pain might kill her dead upon the spot, she transformed it, with a conscious effort, into blind fury at her brother.

So it had come to this. Pia was, at last, a prisoner.

Not in a tower like the first Pia, but back in Siena, in a dank cellar, deep underneath the Eagles' palace. Nello had dragged her down there himself, as if he would not entrust anyone else with the task. She had fought him then, and laid open his cheek with her nails. But he had shoved her into her cell regardless.

It was a stone room, with a studded door on one wall and a stone relief of the Eagle on the other. The eagle seemed to be watching her with its stone eye. She would not go near it.

There was one torch in a sconce, but it gave little comfort, throwing stretched and hideous shadows long upon the floor, shadows that could hide nameless terrors. But reality was worse than imagination; there were bloodstains on the stone floor that the scattering of rushes could not hide. She put her hand to them and rubbed the rusty bloom between her fingertips. The Panther's blood. Egidio Albani, beaten to death on this very spot. Egidio Albani, who had begun this whole coil with a stroke of a whip across Vicenzo's face. But her charge was different. Medici spy. A grievous charge, enough to hang her.

She must be publicly tried, but this would not save her from the summary justice of the Eagles who had tried and condemned and executed a man in this very room. The evidence was black and white; by now Nicoletta would have found the *Morte d'Arthur*, and it would take Faustino little time to divine that it was the book that had given her the clue to the meeting place of the Nine. She could not enjoy the irony that Thomas Malory had written it while himself in prison in the Tower of London, nor that his heroine Queen Guinevere had been imprisoned for betraying her husband.

She wondered if they would feed and water her, but countless hours passed before she heard the scrape of the lock and the grating of the opening door. Her heart leaped and raced with fear, but the huge bulk of Nicoletta filled the doorway, carrying a tray. Her smiles were enormous.

'Well, my pet. 'Tis a sorry chamber you've descended to and no mistaking. But you've Nicoletta to look after ye.'

She banged down the pewter platter, spilling the jug of water, dousing the bread and wetting Egidio's bloodstains, to make them red once more.

'Santa Maria, but it's dark in here. And you'll not have heard the news about the *contrada*.' The maid spoke conversationally, as if they were in a parlour, not a cell. 'They're talking about the Padovani heiress who turns thirteen this week – Eagle family, vintners, and the little mistress fair stuffed with coin.' Nicoletta leaned into the cramped room, looking over both fat shoulders before whispering conspiratorially, as if they shared a confidence: 'Mortal good match that'd be, for some lucky Eagle feller.' The maid's piggy eyes shone like beads in the dim and her smile stretched further.

So, Pia thought, her replacement had already been found.

Having delivered her message, Nicoletta turned to the door and spied the torch. 'Mercy! What a poor little light they've given ye! 'Tis hardly worth having.' She spat on her meaty hand and doused the light, the torch hissing in matching malice as the door closed again.

Plunged into the dark, Pia remembered how she had once told Riccardo Bruni that she could see in the dark, like the owlet, like Minerva. Why did everything bring her back to him? He was lost to her now, and she was blinded and afraid; shorn, in this blackness, of the little power she had ever had.

She had to feel for her bread and could not be sure, as she chewed it, that it had not been sopped in Egidio's blood.

She digested her meal and Nicoletta's news together. Nello would remarry when she was dead. They would keep her alive until the race was won, she thought, for even Salvatore would baulk at the murder of his daughter and Salvatore, the prior of the Civetta, was crucial to the Nine. But after that?

In the dark she began to talk to Egidio Albani, the only other person who'd felt what she felt now.

∞

On the evening of the horse draw, Violante decided to challenge her brother-in-law. She entered Gian Gastone's chamber without knocking and came across him as he was being assisted into his clothes by Dami. She did not turn her back to shield her eyes from the sight.

'Why?' she said, abruptly and without preamble.

'But, sister, you *asked* me for help.' He seemed genuinely puzzled.

She shook her head. She could not deny the truth of what he said.

Gian Gastone flicked at his cravat with irritation, and Dami, with the ease of long practice, untied it and began again.

'My dear sister, that man – Faustino is it? – is a thug. He exists in another century. He needed to be faced down. Now he has met with the Medici there will be no further trouble, you may be sure of it. By the end of our meeting he seemed quite amenable. You asked me for help. I helped. There is an end on it.'

Violante did not believe a word of it. But she thought she understood him.

Gian Gastone had anticipated his dukedom. She knew he had been mouldering in his wife's castle, unloved and with nothing to think on but the dukedom that was not yet his. She had conferred power upon him and he had jumped at the chance to rule, but he had done so wrong-headedly. He had given away any advantage they had; he had lost their chance to discover the identity of Romulus; they knew nothing more save that a coup was planned for the day of the Palio, not where or how this was to be achieved.

The only point upon which she could be glad was that Riccardo's name was kept out of the affair; and unless his boldness in striding in and out of the palace that morning had been observed, Faustino and the Nine were ignorant of his part in the plot to save the city for the Medici. However, in the process of preserving his own secrecy, Pia's presence in the hermit's church – however she'd come to be there – had been revealed. Riccardo had neatly summed up her fate: Faustino thought he had a traitor in the family and could quite possibly act against Pia with the support of the law; or leave it to the vengeful Nello to punish his treacherous wife without it.

Violante went to the window to look down into the milling square. In seven days, the Palio would be run once more. In seven days, her own fate would be sealed. And in seven days – for surely Faustino would stay his hand until the race was safely won – Pia of the Tolomei would be dead.

Then it came to her. She knew how she could save Pia from imprisonment and condemnation. The ancient city statutes stated that on the day of each Palio the governor of Siena could free one prisoner in the city – just one – from incarceration, no matter what their crime. If she read Pia's name at the finish of the race, the girl would have the city's protection from her husband and his father.

Violante turned from the window. She must see Riccardo. She would have Gretchen send for Zebra at once.

'Sister?' Gian Gastone broke in on her reverie.

Violante focused on her errant brother-in-law once again. Dami had dressed him in his finest, with a snow-white wig and a black coat and breeches of silk. 'Where are you going?' she asked, with a chill of foreboding.

'Dami instructs me that there is a quaint local event taking place today. Somewhat to do with drawing lots – no – horses to be ridden in the little race that they have here in a week or so. I thought that it would be good for us to appear for the people. A united front.'

Violante saw the sense in this and followed him as he led the way, not up the stairs to the balcony, but down the steps, heading for the great doors. Before she could question the wisdom of mingling with the populace in this way, Gian Gastone had shuffled off into the piazza. Violante hurried after him, hoping that in the mêlée she might get a chance to see Riccardo, but she was steered by Gian Gastone's men to a sort of loge they had constructed, set a little above the gathering crowd. The guards began to applaud loudly until some sections of the crowd joined in, but only the citizens nearest to the loge gave any notice to the Medici contingent. The rest were too busy taking note of the real business of the day.

∽

Riccardo skulked in the dark heart of the crowd, fidgeting, craning to see the gathering of the *contrade*. He could see his own *contrada*, bristling with the burgundy-and-blue flags of the Tower, featuring, in the centre, an elephant carrying a tower on his back. Domenico was there, too, holding his flag high, casting his eyes about for his son.

Riccardo narrowed his eyes. The elephant on his father's banner was carrying the city and he experienced a great fellow feeling for the creature. He, too, had the stones of the city pressing down on his shoulders, the weight of his duty pressing down upon him. His heart had shrivelled to a bean, but he knew where his duty lay. He began to push though the populace to his father.

Domenico was more than usually nervous. In the strange rhythms of his year, he had reached almost the zenith of his excitement. His son was about to ride in the second Palio of the year, and today, the day of the horse draw, was crucially important to his success.

Domenico had never told Riccardo how much he had suffered when his son had, not one month ago, given up his chance to win the Palio, in order to try to save another man's life. Alongside the fierce pride he felt in his son's humanity, he had to cope, too, with his own shame that he would rather Riccardo had ridden past Vicenzo's broken body and let him die, than have leaped from his horse to save him. It was so, *so* important that Riccardo should win this time, more so because of the strange and wholly unwelcome visitor Domenico had received in their house two nights before.

With sudden urgency he raised his head, straining to see Riccardo beyond the knot of the ten selected horses. He'd been amazed when Riccardo's Leocorno had been chosen by the *comune* – such a stubborn creature, but Riccardo said he was fast, and horse and master had fitted together well. Leocorno had been duly collected from his stables this morning. Ideally, of course, the Torre *contrada* would draw the fabled Berio, that fastest of horses, but Domenico could not see last month's winner among the group of ten eligible mounts. Suddenly Riccardo was at his side and Domenico, steeped in relief, clasped his son to his shoulder as if he would never let go.

Riccardo started in surprise at this unaccustomed affection. His father could not keep still, and the whites showed around his eyes. If Riccardo had not been so preoccupied with the events of last night, he might have wondered why his father was so pent up. But Riccardo could not bring himself to be interested in the proceedings. For one thing, he knew that the draw had, somehow, been fixed by the Nine and that Leocorno would be drawn for him and the Tower. For another, he cared only for Pia's fate. He had said no more than a cursory farewell to Leocorno this morning, the horse flicking his ear once as he passed. He knew he did not need to take long leave of a horse that he suspected would be back in the Torre stable that very night.

Riccardo had dispatched Zebra that morning to the house of the Eagles, to try to find out what he could about Pia's whereabouts. Zebra reported that the whole family were back in the city and had risen late. Faustino and Nello had taken breakfast in the *piano nobile*, but Pia was nowhere to be seen. Then Zebra, hanging around the kitchens for a biscuit, had seen the fat maid Nicoletta place a water jug and a loaf on a pewter tray, and disappear down the stairs.

Riccardo had shivered at this piece of news. He knew that Pia, as a traitor to her family and, worse, to her *contrada*, had been imprisoned with the full support of the law. He suspected she was being kept in the underground cellar where he had seen the dead Panther: cold, windowless and still stained with Egidio's blood. Knowing what he did of Pia's courage and resolve, he thought she would keep his secret at whatever cost to herself.

He glanced across to the Aquila party. Faustino, grinning, urbane and well rested, was looking confident of the day's proceedings. The horse draw was performed by Francesco Maria Conti, a smooth fellow in a black suit of clothes, carrying a silver cane and sporting a white half-periwig. Conti was a resident of the Giraffa *contrada* but considered to be neutral by reason of his being the chief of the Sienese council under Violante. Riccardo knew different. The moment Conti spoke, Riccardo recognized the voice from last night's meeting; he was the cowled figure who had spoken about the fixed mechanism for the horse draw, and the one who knew the most about Romulus.

Brooding over this, Riccardo listened dispassionately as ten jockeys were called out, coupled with horses. He barely even listened to his own name, teamed, unsurprisingly, with Leocorno. He hardly felt the conciliatory clasp of his father's arm or the cheers of his fellows, who knew that the handsome Lipizzaner stallion was incredibly fast. He missed the strange fact that Berio, last month's victor and the best horse in Tuscany, was not called, was not assigned to anyone. Instead, he was busy looking at Nello, who had been drawn with Cervio, his fine black stallion. Nello, pale beneath his strange black mop of hair, had two stripes of blood on his face, long scratches where a struggling woman's nails had laid his cheek open.

Riccardo wanted to push his way though the crowds and lay open Nello's other cheek to match, to march him back to his house and force him to unlock his Pia from her cell. He might have thrown everything away, along with his life, had the crowd not parted at that moment, trapping him. Municipal guards, in tight formation, approached on order. Riccardo stood stock-still, waiting for hands to fall on his arms, but the guards passed him by and advanced on the ducal loge. They came to a halt before his vast nemesis, Gian Gastone.

As Riccardo craned forward to hear what would be said, the heir of Tuscany's lower jaw fell into his many chins, leaving him gaping like a fish as he turned to his companion on the dais.

The square had gone completely quiet; not even a starling sang. The captain of the guard called: 'Giuliano Dami, you are arrested on charges of sodomy, in accordance with the duchess's own laws.'

In the company of the guards was a young blond man, with velvet eyes and full lips, pointing his finger to identify his seducer. It was Fabio Caprimulgo, Faustino's nephew.

Riccardo looked at Violante, who sat with her mouth as wide open as her brother-in-law's.

'How dare you—' Gian Gastone started to bluster, but Dami had been chained and dragged across the square towards the *comune*'s jail before he could get his words out.

Riccardo looked across at Faustino. So *this* was how he had chosen to deal with Gian Gastone; this was the 'insurance' that Pia had said Faustino had laid down against interference from the duchy's heir. If Faustino could deal with the Medici so ruthlessly, what chance did Pia have?

Had Riccardo spared even a moment to look at his father, he might have been astonished at the expression on the old man's face as he watched Dami being dragged across the square to jail. It was relief, naked relief.

15

The Porcupine

In 1559, Cosimo the Great, the first and finest Cosimo de' Medici to rule Florence, turned his greedy eyes toward Siena. He besieged the helpless city for fifteen long months. The Sienese were on their knees, diseased, starving, and reduced to eating the rats that had been too slow to leave their sinking ship.

Cosimo sent an outrider to invite the Sienese to surrender. The outrider was admitted into the city at the Camollia gate, in the contrada of the Porcupine. In less than an hour the Nine sent the outrider back to Cosimo, dead, bound and flung over his horse's back. When his companions tried to lift the corpse from the stallion, they could not take hold of the body, for the fellow was absolutely bristling with arrows. They could, however, read the piece of parchment tied to one of the shafts.

'You sent us a white flag. We send you a porcupine.'

Thus the Nine sent their message to the Medici: that they would not accept an overlord, now or ever.

Without Dami, Gian Gastone collapsed. He roared and cried, ripped down tapestries, broke furniture and sent every servant in the palace running to the apothecary's in the Panther *contrada*, at all hours of the day and night, for any and every kind of physick that would mend his broken heart.

How clever Faustino had been, thought Violante. He could not attack Gian Gastone directly but he could attack his beloved. By revealing himself at the round church, by getting in the Nine's way, Gian Gastone had opened himself up to Faustino's cunning vengeance and there was nothing she could do. Violante's own guards had acted according to the laws of morality she herself had tightened – she had even personally written several decrees against sodomy. Dami had been caught in a lobster pot of Violante's own making.

She had not imagined that she would have the city thrust back into her care so soon. Even more worryingly, Gian Gastone showed no interest in providing the assistance he had promised. He could think of nothing but Dami. He sent to the jailhouse with missives every hour. At first he sent authoritative letters, dictated to Violante's scribe, then impassioned pleadings scrawled in his own hand and sealed with his own ring, all demanding Dami's release. These were returned by terrified messengers who informed the duke apparent that Dami was to be indicted on the incontrovertible evidence of a reliable witness.

Violante felt a mixture of guilt and gladness as she faced her brother's wrath. She was glad Dami had gone from her sight; she felt he was a malign presence, and her world had lightened without him. But even Violante could not have wished for what followed. The decrees she had written against sodomy made the act, if proven, punishable by death. When it became clear that Fabio Caprimulgo had been singing like a lark to the judiciary, things began to look very grim for Dami indeed. Judgment was passed in open court, presided over by none other than Francesco Maria Conti, in the presence of a weeping Gian Gastone and with a silent, white Dami staring at his impotent master with pleading purple eyes. He was to be hanged in a week.

Gian Gastone locked himself in the library. He stayed there, either staring from the window with eyes of glass, or poring through the city's statutes, desperately trying to find a legal loophole. He could, he discovered, institute a change in the law – easily done for, as the Tuscan saying went, a Sienese statute may last a day – but it would not be ratified in time to save Dami, and he had no philanthropic interest in saving sodomites in the future. No one mattered but Dami.

But Violante knew that she held Dami's life in her hands. If Gian Gastone discovered the statute she intended to employ to release Pia Tolomei, if he knew that she had the power to free Dami, he would petition, bully and plead day and night. She could not take the risk. She waited until her brother-in-law, exhausted by tears, had fallen into a snoring sleep in his chamber, then took a candle to the law library, where the city's statutes slept in their ranks of stacked rolls until called upon. It was the work of a moment to locate the statute roll that she'd written in her own hand. Without ceremony she broke the waxen Medici seal on the document roll and slid the parchment from the slim cylinder. Placing the scratchy paper firmly in her bodice, she snuffed the candle and let herself out of the dark library unseen. As she mounted the stair to her chamber she reflected on how small a thing it was, this law, a little screw of paper that could save a woman from the gallows.

As the day of the Palio drew closer, Gian Gastone sent to the jail every day, requesting to see Dami. Although he had not discovered any statute that might permit Dami's release, he had learned that a condemned prisoner could receive one visitor of his choice before his sentence was carried out. He sent repeatedly to the jail, to tell Dami that he could request to see his love. Once he was there, in the cell, Gian Gastone was sure he could carry Dami out of there with the force of his name and figure alone. Every day he awaited the answer from Dami, but when it came, the instruction was wholly unexpected. Dami asked not to see his lover and master, but the Duchess Violante.

Gian Gastone seemed both mortally wounded and insistent that she should go. Violante had no wish to listen to the pleadings of a man she feared, but at the appointed time she crossed the piazza to the jail, with Gretchen in tow. At the gates the obsequious governor met her. She knew, of course, he informed her silkily, that Sienese law stated that she must enter the cell alone?

The place was cold and dank. The jailer set a stool for her on the damp rushes. She sat and waited, Dami's purple eyes glinting at her from the dark. The rest of him was an obscure, hunched shadow. His stare gave her a shiver, and recalled to her the darkest days of her life. She uttered a single word: 'Well?'

'They are going to kill me,' said the shadow, in the sibilant accents that had always chilled her flesh.

'I know.'

'Set me free.'

Here in this dark place, with no light, they could be themselves. There was no dissembling, no wigs, costumes, or patches.

'Why should I?'

The harshness of her own voice, echoing back to her from the dripping walls, surprised her. The echo died and she waited for the answer. She could not have dreamed of what he would say.

'Because I have never been righteous.' He leaned forward to give weight to this odd statement, so she could see the meaningful glint of his purple eyes. 'Only the righteous are taken into the arms of the Lord.'

Then she knew. She was back twenty years, lying on her childbed, listening to the words of another shadow. An unknown priest. The purple eyes, the sibilant accents, the fragment of scripture. She could not breathe.

'Set me free,' said Giuliano Dami, 'and I will give you back your child.'

∞

Domenico Bruni was concerned about his son. There were only seven days to the Palio and he did not seem to want to work his horse, nor even care for him. It was Domenico himself who curried Leocorno's silky white coat and who picked and cleaned his hooves. He could not ride him because the stallion would let only Riccardo on his back, and so he was getting little exercise. Riccardo would not even ride Leocorno in the horse trials, ridden by the *contrade* jockeys and their appointed horses, around the track in the great Piazza del Campo. It was as if he didn't care.

Since the visit of the stranger a month ago, Domenico had lived in fear. Now he clung to that which was dearest to him, as if he might, at any day, lose Riccardo. Now, with Dami in jail, his fears were different. He felt that Riccardo was lost to him already.

The sole person Riccardo wanted to see was Zebra, who came to the Tower *contrada* with daily reports of Pia. The horseman could not live with himself, could not bear to be inside his own skin, nor the kiss of the sun, nor the sound of the starlings. Everything hurt him: every sound was too loud, every sight too bright for his eyes. He slept long hours in the stable, and only a consuming desire to stay alive to see Pia once more kept him from running to Faustino's palace and tearing down the doors.

∞

It was Zebra who made the suggestion. On the second night of this malaise, he tapped Riccardo on the shoulder. Riccardo woke to see the familiar hazel eyes of his young friend.

'Go and see her,' said the boy.

'How?'

'How did you get the Panther out of there? You could get back in.'

In the velvet night, on the eve of the Palio, Riccardo crossed the piazza to the Fonte Gaia. He lifted the well-remembered paving and plunged into the *bottini* tunnels beneath the city. He walked the earthen ways by the glassy-green pools until his fingers found the outline of the stone door through which he had carried Egidio Albani those many weeks ago. At the end of the subterranean passageways he came to the stone door and pushed it, knowing that if there was a guard within, he was ending his own life, too. But he did not care. It was over anyway.

∞

By the time he came to her, Pia couldn't believe it was him.

Afraid and alone in the dank darkness, her mind had become so confused that when the wall with the eagle on it began to move she thought she was dreaming. In her reverie, Lancelot had come to save her from the dragon's breath. When a figure had come through the wall she almost greeted him with the knight's name.

But he took her in his arms at once. And then she was afraid of waking as he kissed her, hard and silently, feeling that she could spend the rest of her life in this fetid and bloodied place if she could just spend it in his arms. She felt his fingers numbering her ribs, knew she was so thin now that her Eagle wedding ring nearly slipped off into his hair. Soon it would not matter.

He took her arm to lead her out of the door and she suddenly knew it was not a dream. It was Riccardo and he was going to get her out of here. But she shook her head.

'Sit,' she said.

'But we must go.'

'Where? *Think*, Riccardo. We would have to run for ever.' She took his hand in her cold fingers, warming them, and looked in his eyes. 'And what kind of city would we leave behind? One run by Faustino? And what would happen to the duchess, who has to be got out of the way, and the Padovani heiress aged thirteen who is stuffed with coin? You *have* to ride the Palio. You have to beat them that way. They will not act against me before then. I am to be in the crowd. They cannot afford to anger my father before the design is complete.'

'And after that?'

She dropped her great eyes. 'Take this,' she said, unhooking Cleopatra's owlet pendant from around her neck. 'Take it as a pledge of my faith, and ride as my champion.' She'd once dreamed of having a handsome champion – how skewed and strange that dream had become.

'Pia.' He took her hands, clasping Cleopatra's coin within, hard, hurting her. 'What is to happen?'

She would not look at him. 'I will be condemned to die, by law, after the Palio. Nello will marry again – his bride is already chosen. They made a mistake with me, but they still need my father for a few days more.'

She took a breath – now she could finish it, the quotation she'd begun the day she'd been with him in the confessional, complete the prophecy.

'*Ah, when you have returned to the world, and rested from the long journey, remember me, the one who is Pia; Siena made me, Maremma undid me: he knows it, the one who first encircled my finger with his jewel, when he married me.*'

Riccardo looked at the ring on her finger and the owl in his hands, at the golden eyes that winked at him conspiratorially in the torchlight. She could see he was fearful, so fearful for her that he could not bear it.

'I cannot do it. You don't know me. I am a craven coward. I am responsible for many deaths, because I was afraid.'

Faltering, Riccardo choked out a dreadful story: of a church in Milazzo, of a young mother and a burning building. Pia listened with horror and pity, not only for those innocents, but also for him and these spectres that he had carried with him for so long.

Now she understood. She took his face in both hands.

'You were a child yourself,' she said. 'And if you'd stayed, you would have died that day and not lived to see this. You tried to save Vicenzo and now you have a chance to save more lives. Take it.'

He looked in her eyes and nodded once. She forced herself to speak again.

'And now I must ask you something much harder, and beside this, to win the race is nothing.'

'What is it?'

She uttered the most terrible sentence she'd ever had to say. 'You must leave me here. Promise.'

∾

'You have to get me out of here. Promise.'

Violante's heart was thudding in her ears, so hard that she could barely hear Dami. 'Tell me.'

'You'll free me?'

And she forgot Pia. 'Yes.'

Dami let out a long breath, and began to tell a story that was twenty years old. He had never repeated it to anyone else, not even Gian Gastone, and even now he knew he could not tell the worst of it, lest this woman kill him dead right here with her own hands. He would tell the light, not the shadow, the white, not the black.

∾

For Giuliano Dami had committed the worst and the best acts of his life twenty years ago. When, on Gian Gastone's orders, he had dressed as a priest to take Violante's twins from her and murder them, he had thought he was equal to the task. He had directed that Violante should be drugged before the abduction and when he entered the birthing chamber he could see that it had been a wise precaution. Even in sleep, she had an arm around each tiny babe as each suckled away at a full, blue-veined breast. Violante's face, as she slumbered under the heavy coverlet of laudanum, was a picture of serenity and happiness. But Dami felt no misgivings as he took each child from the breast, both dribbling a little warm milk from their mouths as they released Violante's nipples with tiny twin pops. Even this did not touch Dami's heart. He took the keening babes in his black robes to the next chamber.

There, in that dark room, he consigned his soul to hell, only to have it redeemed. He had never killed a child before, but thought it would be no great matter, for a babe so newly born could be easily dispatched and sent back to the void with only a momentary glimpse of the world he was never meant to inhabit. He laid one boy on the bed and held the other in his arms, in a horrible imitative pantomime of the way Violante had cradled the babes. He considered clasping his hand around the little folds of its neck, but found it difficult to get purchase on a throat so small. He cast about for a pillow to smother the child, but they had all been taken next door in the service of the new mother. In the end he pushed his forefinger down into the tiny mouth.

What happened next gave him a glimpse of the abyss down which he was to fall, for the babe, having been taken from its mother's teat, closed its warm wet lips around Dami's finger and began to suckle. Dami felt a shock of tenderness through his body, a dread so sharp that he reacted violently, forcing the finger further and further in, until the baby began to thrash around and then, at last, stop.

The other boy lay calmly on the bed, watching murder done. He followed Dami with caper-green eyes as he laid his dead brother on the bed next to him. As the purple eyes met the open gaze, Dami knew he would rather die himself than commit such an act again. And so, Giuliano Dami's damned soul flew from the closing jaws of hell just as the flames and demons snatched at his heels. He had killed one of the twins as he had been ordered by his master and lover. The other, he would save.

He wrapped both children, the dead and the live together, and took them down the back stair unobserved. By the banks of the Arno he took the living babe from the cloth, replaced him with three great stones and wrapped the bundle again. He heaved the other tiny body into the river, turning away before he even heard the splash. Then he picked up the living child and headed back to the *palazzo*.

By the great gates he found a fellow untying his horse. He knew the man slightly, a master farrier from Siena, known as the best in all Tuscany, come to tend to the duke's favourite horse. The man was on his way home, he said, and would ride from the city tonight, likely never to return. Siena was not far away, but it was far enough. Dami gave the child to the man to take away from Florence, telling him that he was to raise the child as his own on the grand duke's orders. He could see that the fellow was softened by the baby's eyes and the minute hand that reached up from the swaddling cloths. But the deciding factor was the purse that Dami proffered. It was almost as heavy as the child itself.

His soul by turns heavy and light, Dami went straight to his master, who was sitting, waiting patiently in a chamber as dark as the one where he had done murder.

'It is done,' he said. 'You are now the heir to Tuscany.'

Gian Gastone nodded once, and Dami turned from him, loving him a little less than he had done before. Only when he closed the door behind him did Dami begin to shake.

And so Domenico Bruni, crippled by grief at the loss of his young wife, but buoyed by his commission to Grand Duke Cosimo III of Tuscany, unknowingly took the Medici princeling home to Siena.

∞

Giuliano Dami, now facing his own death, did not want to take a chance on whether or not his act of murder or his act of salvation would weigh more heavily in the scales on Judgment Day. He just knew that he had a card to play, and he played it to save his own sorry skin.

He had feared Violante because he had wronged her so much, and she was nothing but a source of terror to him. How Satan himself must have laughed that she now held his life in her hands. Dami did not, of course, tell Violante the whole story. Even *in extremis* he was clever enough to know that if he confessed to the murder of one of her twins, she would never release him.

He diluted the tale thus: one of the twins had died, and been cast into the Arno; the other was to be murdered on the orders of Gian Gastone. He, Dami, had saved the child by giving it to Domenico Bruni. He realized he would be burning his bridges with his master, but could see no other way out of the noose.

Violante, shattered, sat for a long, long moment in silence, the chill of the jail freezing her hands and feet, her heart burning with the sun and shade of joy and loss. Joy that she had a son, and what a son! A man she already loved, with a love to which she could now give free rein. She felt again the aching loss of the boy who had died, whose little bones lay bleached at the bottom of the Arno, with three stones for his bedfellows, one for each hour he had lived. She felt loss, too, that she had missed twenty years of her living son's life, his first smile, his first tooth, his first communion. But then joy again that she had been given this gift of a truly good, a truly brave, a truly caring young man. She could take no credit for his manners or his bearing. She might have attributed his gifts to heredity, for Ferdinando had once been the finest of young men, Gian Gastone, too. But both had given their love to boys and men, and reduced their wives to misery; and one had stooped to infanticide to clear his path to the dukedom. What inheritance was that?

Violante stumbled from the dark cell into the blinding sunlight, pausing only to tell the jailer that Dami should spend one more night in prayer and penance and would be freed on the morrow with the dispensation of the Palio.

As Violante crossed the square, Gretchen had to hold her up. Violante was grateful for Gretchen's support and silence. She could not have recounted the tale, for she could barely make sense of her own thoughts. She only knew, as she entered her own dark door, that she had finally realized why Riccardo had always seemed so familiar, why she had recognized him on the first day they met, why she had warmed to him at first sight. He had recalled to her mind the young Ferdinando, his father. And the final joy and loss was felt as she passed the Torre del Mangia. For she might have found her son, but he had gone, angered, from her sight.

Violante could not face Gian Gastone yet. She knew he would be waiting in her presence chamber, pacing, awaiting the outcome of the interview with Dami. She wondered if he would still want Dami free if he knew what he had confessed to her. With a strength she had not known she possessed, she determined to conceal what she knew. She would use Dami as a bargaining counter in this chess game between herself and her brother-in-law.

She sent Gretchen to find Zebra, and when the boy arrived she took his hand and looked at the nine-year-old's bitten nails. What she would have given to have known Riccardo at this age. She smiled especially sweetly at Zebra today and asked him gently if he knew where Riccardo Bruni might be.

'As for today, Duchess, I do not know,' he replied, 'for he rode Leocorno out of the gates this morning, early. He's training hard, mistress.'

Zebra did not say that it was Riccardo's visit to Pia that had changed him, inspiring him to ride again, to win, to kiss his abandoned horse's white nose and ask for forgiveness. Zebra had seen it all, at daybreak, as Riccardo vaulted on to Leocorno's back and rode him into the hills, the westward way that they always took, to see the western aspect of the city. There, the boy knew, they would ride circuit after circuit, against the backdrop of Siena, training to win. Zebra said nothing of all this; for much as he liked the kindly duchess, he kept his information to be parcelled up for coin. He squinted up at her plain, troubled face and relented.

'But I can tell you for sure where he will be tomorrow morning.'

'Where?'

'Why, in the church of the Torre. At the blessing of his horse.'

Of course. On the morning of the Palio, each *contrada* blessed their horse in their own church. The Palio was to be run tomorrow. Violante forced herself to focus on the implications of this. Riccardo Bruni, *her son*, the finest rider in the city, was to ride in the Palio for the Torre party. The woman he loved was imprisoned by the Eagle's captain, whose son Nello was destined to win the Palio. Riccardo, the only rider with the skill to threaten the plan, had been given a horse by Faustino, a horse bred to lose the race. Nello was going to win and fulfil the expectations of a betting syndicate who would then bankroll the Nine. Siena, her city, would be taken from her. No, she thought with a shock, *Riccardo*'s city would be taken from him. The peasant that Gian Gastone had pronounced below his notice now outranked him. Violante had, at last, fulfilled her destiny. Tuscany had an heir.

Violante had a moment of sudden clarity. If Riccardo could win the Palio, the Nine would be beggared, and her son would still have a city. And according to Zebra, he was trying, and training, desperately to win. As for the threat of Romulus, whoever he was, and whatever higher power that threatened the city: well, Gian Gastone would have to step in. She must treat with this murderer. He had to atone for his crimes.

The duchess went upstairs to her presence chamber and turned the handle. Gian Gastone was there, waiting, and turned to her. She looked into his fat anxious face, the concealment of her revulsion the hardest dissembling she had ever done. He, and he alone, was responsible for the twenty lost years with Riccardo. She went to the ivory box below her window and drew out the statute that she'd hidden there. She handed it to her brother-in-law.

'I will free Dami.'

His face collapsed in relief.

'*If,*' she said, 'you will write to your sister Anna Maria Luisa. We need an armed force in the city; she has the Palatinate army billeted at Florence. You have little time.' She knew how he hated his sister, who had married him to a wife he detested and exiled him from his beloved Florence, but she did not care.

'Then send me a scribe, dear sister.' He was wheedling now.

'In your *own* hand, with your own seal.' She thought better of it. 'In fact, take off your signet ring and packet it up with the letter.'

Gian Gastone, his chins quivering with emotion, twisted the Medici ring on his sausage-like finger. 'But, sister, I am not sure it will come off.'

Violante planted both hands on the writing table and leaned in to him. 'It will,' she said, barely recognizing the strength of her own voice, 'even if we have to cut it off.'

∞

Letter in hand, Violante headed to the courtyard to seek out her fastest galloper. As she passed through the Hall of the Nine she saw again, staring out from the fresco of good government, the lady who held the hourglass, the sands of time running through her fingers. Violante quickened her steps. She must be swift; the Palio was tomorrow and Florence was a good few hours' ride away.

In the shadowy courtyard, where she had first greeted her brother-in-law, she called for her ostler. She commanded the old fellow, an ancient of the Dragon *contrada,* to find the fastest horse in the city to take an urgent missive to Florence. What about the horse Berio, she asked in a rush of inspiration, the big bay who had won the July Palio? The star horse had been missing from this month's horse draw, so was not needed for tomorrow's race. But the old ostler told her that after the July Palio, Berio had disappeared and had not been seen since.

Crestfallen, Violante gave her orders and climbed the stairs to her chamber. She gazed from her windows at the Torre *contrada.* Already the citizens of the Torre were decorating the streets with flags and streamers in the blue and burgundy of their colours. Somewhere, somewhere down there, Riccardo lived with a man who was not his father. She had been right to conceal Dami's confession from Gian Gastone. If Riccardo's existence was revealed, his life would not be worth a straw. Word had come from Florence that the old Grand Duke Cosimo was still in a deep malaise, his end expected at any day. Gian Gastone was within touching distance of his rule.

Violante grasped the windowsill until her knuckles were white. She wanted to scream, and cry, and laugh, and tear at her skin, and run down to the Torre *contrada*, to wait in the stable, if need be, for Riccardo and Leocorno to come home. Even after she retired to her bed, she could not sleep, her flesh burning, her heart racing, knowing that tomorrow she would meet her son.

That night, for the first time in twenty years, she did not have the dream of the twins. She thought of them, though, wakeful and wondering. She went over and over her short acquaintance with the boys. She remembered so vividly the differences between them: the twin who suckled strongly, the gentler quieter baby who held back. Which one was Riccardo? She recalled well that the babies had been given names, in the bogus christening–funeral stage-managed by Gian Gastone: empty names for empty caskets. She remembered Ferdinando sitting on the birthbed–deathbed, telling her what the boys had been named.

As the dawn, at last, crept across the sky, she wondered which twin she was about to meet – Gastone or Cosimo. She could not countenance that her son would share a name with his would-be murderer, so she decided, then and there, that Cosimo de' Medici had lived. The auguries were good; Cosimo would bring back the glory days of the Medici, the days of the first Cosimo the Great, who'd ruled Florence through her golden age.

Violante squeezed her eyes tight shut, daring sleep to come. She hoped Riccardo Bruni had slept the night well, for what she would tell him this day would change his world and his future, and all the days in the life of Cosimo Ferdinando de' Medici.

∞

At six in the morning on the day of the Palio, Riccardo Bruni was already up, currying and grooming Leocorno until the white horse shone. Today the stallion was to be blessed in the Tower church and later he was to run the race of his life.

Riccardo ran his hand under his own tight collar. The sun beat on his head and heat rose from the stones. He was dressed in his *fantino* regalia, in the burgundy and blue of the Torre *contrade*, with the kerchief of the elephant and castle around his neck. Whatever else happened today, he would at least see Pia again. He was jangling with nerves and fidgeted with Leocorno's tack, fiddling unnecessarily, repeating little tasks over again. Leocorno, in sympathy, twitched his ear and lifted and replaced his hooves. It was a relief to both of them when Zebra appeared in the yard.

'You're early,' muttered Riccardo ungraciously, for he had agreed to let Zebra help to lead the horse to the Torre church for the blessing. For this day only, Zebra found his partiality for Riccardo and the Tower *contrada* difficult to conceal. Zebra looked about him.

'Inside,' he said briefly.

Riccardo, curious, dropped Leocorno's head rein and followed Zebra into the cool, hay-scented dark of the stable. Leocorno nosily hooked his head over the half-door to listen to their council.

Zebra vaulted up on to a haybale and licked his lips. 'I was down at the horse fair at Asciano yesterday and I talked to Boli, you know, the horse dealer?'

Riccardo flapped his hands impatiently. 'I know who he is. Had he heard of Leocorno?'

'Heard of him?' The boy gave a pony's snort. 'He sold him to Faustino. Apparently all the traders know of him and no one will touch him. Boli got him at a card game with the other dealers.'

Riccardo was intrigued. 'He won him at cards?'

Zebra shook his head slowly. 'He lost his hand and had to take him.'

Riccardo looked at Leocorno's beautiful head hanging over the half-door, blowing and snorting as if he wished to join in the conversation.

'Why?'

Zebra lowered his voice as if the horse could understand them. 'Because he's a murderer. Killed three people in the last six months.'

Riccardo's eyes widened with shock. 'Are you sure?'

This time Zebra nodded. 'Sure. Boli told me himself. *Ah yes, the Unicorn*, he said. He crossed himself every time he said his name.'

Riccardo cleared his throat, then lowered his voice too. 'How did he kill them?'

'Threw two of 'em. Crushed another against a wall.'

'But why? He's a good bloodline, surely? You can see that just by looking at him.' Riccardo gazed across at the stallion's noble profile in the half-dark.

'None better,' agreed Zebra, looking too. 'Pure-bred Lipizzan, from Styria by way of the Spanish Riding School, just as your dad said. Schooled for the Spanish army as an officer's mount and became a general's horse an' all. But they say he was in a battle and it turned him funny in the head. Practically stood on a cannon, which turned him deaf. Threw his general off – fellow called Alvarez y Leon – killed him. After that he wouldn't have anyone else on his back.'

Alvarez y Leon. Riccardo went cold. He remembered the general, with his marauding Spaniards and their fire-brands. So Leocorno had been at Milazzo, just like him, had seen what he had seen.

'And then?'

'Boli kept him for a bit. He'd sell him, then the horse would kill his rider, and the family would give him back – didn't want the horse around to remind them, didn't even want the money back. Word got round that he was possessed by the Devil.' Now it was Zebra's turn to cross himself.

Riccardo, looking into Leocorno's liquid eye, didn't think it was the Devil who was in the horse. He'd been in a war, and knew that it was not demons but man who created that particular earthbound hell, but he said nothing.

Zebra went on, 'Boli sold him three times and there were three deaths. Boli thought it was Christmastide – that the horse was a real moneyspinner – he could sell him over and over. Then the last family, of the fellow that got crushed against a wall, got a bit upset and told Boli he should have the horse destroyed. But by then, Boli had another buyer.'

'Faustino Caprimulgo?'

'Faustino Caprimulgo.'

'So he does want to kill me,' Riccardo said.

Zebra shrugged his narrow shoulders. 'I'm not so sure. I just think he knows you can't win on him. You can't race a horse you can't ride.'

'But I can ride him. I *have* ridden him.'

'I might be wrong. But I tell you what I'd do,' Zebra said with a wisdom beyond his years. 'I'd get to the church before anyone and tether him to the altar so he sees only you. And after, I'd wait until everyone goes before you lead him out. And I wouldn't put him through the rest of the horse trials today either.' For the final trials took place on the very day of the Palio. 'I'm just not sure how he'll take to a crowd.'

Riccardo nodded. He rose and went to the horse, stroking the stallion's white nose. Leocorno whickered with pleasure.

Zebra, catching sight of the scar on the horse's forehead, stood too, reluctantly.

'And there's something else. This scar.' He ran his small fingers over the little star of raised tissue. 'I asked Boli why they named him Unicorn. He said he used to have a Lipizzan name – Neopolitano something – but they called him Unicorn because of something that happened on the last day of the battle.'

Riccardo, still stroking, waited.

'He took a bayonet to the forehead. Went clean through the skull. Apparently he was running around the cavalry lines with this great thing sticking out of his head, with everyone laughing at him and calling him a unicorn. But he was so mad by then, and dangerous with it, no one dared pull it out. He killed a sapper that tried, kicked him in the head; the boy had a perfect horseshoe on his face. No one would go near him after that. Finally they caught him and a *medico* yanked out the bayonet. But a bit of the blade stayed in there. That's what caused the bump – the skin healed over the fragment of blade. Boli reckons that's why he's so crazy – sees ghosts and everything.' Zebra looked sideways at Riccardo. 'Boli also reckons the blade'll work its way in and kill him in the end.'

Riccardo started at Zebra, stricken, and back at the horse. For a moment he couldn't speak. He stroked the horse a little harder and pulled the white ears. He was now even more determined to win: not for the duchess, but for the Unicorn. Trying to keep his voice steady, he said, 'Come on, anyway. We'd better get going if we're to be first into church. And Zebra, get you to the church of Aquila, to see how Pia does.'

He had no need to articulate to Zebra the world of meaning that that one word *anyway* covered. But as he and Zebra led Leocorno from the Tower's stableyard,

Riccardo had the distinct feeling that his world was being turned upside down, bit by bit.

He didn't know that the process had only just begun.

∞

Across the city to the west, Pia of the Tolomei was sitting in the church of the Eagles. Allowed out from her cell for appearances' sake, she had been bullied and bathed and dressed by Nicoletta. She sat in a gown of black and yellow, the colours of the Eagle, for the Palio. She reflected that last month she had had her final outing in the Civetta colours. This would be her last outing in the plumage of the Eagles. She sat on her hard pew regarding the world through a veil of black lace, a hooded falcon.

The church door opened from within and she could see Nello framed by the daylight in the doorway, leading his big black stallion. Latecomers eased past him touching his yellow-and-black sleeve for luck, the children with eyes as round and bright as coins as they goggled at him. Pia could see his lips tighten a little in an unaccustomed smile: a vestigial smear of a thing, communicating not warmth but pride. She thought he was happy. He had got what he wanted: he was in his brother's place – he had recognition, which he would transform later in the day to adulation.

Nello led his horse into the incense-laden velvet dark, the horse's new shoes clopping on the marble. As the doors closed behind him, Pia's eyes adjusted in the light of a thousand candles, and looked round at the pews packed with yellow and black. Cheers and stamping drummed in her ears, an audible shock after her days spent in a dank cell. At the altar Nello handed the head-collar to the priest and sat in the front pew next to Pia. She felt his thigh, hard from riding, lying along hers and steeled herself not to ease away.

Pia listened to the prayers in an agony of impatience. She wanted the race to begin, could not countenance the hours between now and seven this night, could not wait that long to see Riccardo again. She had barely slept last night, curled in the corner of her cell. Come what may, she would at least set eyes on Riccardo today and she was in a ferment until then.

Now, in the church, she sat just beyond a rough black flank as Nello's horse stood, stock-still and patient, wait-ing for his blessing as if he knew the form. Idly she fixed her eyes on the stallion's hindquarters, waiting, like the rest of the congregation, for the horse to defecate – a sign of good luck. Her eyes wandered down the left hock, just above the cannon bone, to check the wound that the horse had received when he'd jumped the castle wall. When she'd gone to the stables to pet her palfrey, the stal-lion had been gentle with her and let her stroke his rough flank. She craned forward. The wound had healed well and the hair was beginning to grow back. Pia peered closer and for a moment her breathing stopped.

The hair, growing back over the white scar, was a copper colour beside the rough black.

The horse was a bay.

Her heart began to thud and images gathered in her head like roosting starlings. Nello, his white hair dyed black by her own hand. The little bottle of pigment from the Goose *contrada*, the ward of the city that was the province of the dyers' guild. The horse's rough black coat, brittle under the hand and never gaining any condition, no matter how much he was curried and groomed. The mane and tail chopped about and hacked bluntly to make the horse appear different.

As if in a dream, Pia stood as the priest blessed the horse and took one velvet ear to cup to her mouth as she had seen Riccardo do. The hair tickled her lips.

'Berio?'

Tuscany's fastest horse answered with a low whicker, tossed his head once and began to nibble the lobe of Pia's ear, just as he had greeted her when she had gentled him at the deadly San Martino corner, last month when Vicenzo had crumpled and died. Then, she had placed a hand on the white star on Berio's forehead. And there it was, once a white star, now dark grey: the white hair – lighter than the bay coat – that the rough black dye could not quite cover.

Nello shot her a glance. She took her hand away.

'For luck,' she said, and smiled her best, dimpled smile.

He nodded once, shortly, and turned to lead the horse into the day, dodging the showers of holy water shaken over them from the myrtle branches held by the congregation. Attempting to gather together her fragments of shattered thought, Pia could almost feel the collective will of the people of the Eagle *contrada*. She looked at Nello to see how this was affecting him. He seemed satisfied, but ultimately unmoved. A more devout man, in this holy place, might have felt the weight of expectation that Christ felt when, under the breeze of a thousand waving palms, he entered Jerusalem. But Nello was no Messiah, thought Pia, and this was no donkey.

This was Berio.

Pia scanned the crowd for the little black-and-white figure that she sought. She spied the pied messenger and collared him, hurriedly, before her jailer could emerge from the church.

'Please, tell Signor Bruni that Nello's horse is Berio.'

The boy's eyes widened. She flapped her hands impatiently.

'*Berio*. Go!'

Zebra trotted back in the direction of the Tower, as Nicoletta's grip closed on her arm.

∞

In the Tower *contrada*, Violante waited for Riccardo outside the church of the Torre. She was the only silent and still figure in the jubilant crowd. She waited for the blessing to be over, anxious to tell Riccardo what she must. For some reason he'd kept his horse inside until the crowd had dispersed, instead of leading the *contrada* out as tradition dictated. Riccardo saw her there, and something in her eyes must have spoken to him, for he gave the reins of his white horse to Domenico at once. She then led him back into the empty church, and sat him down in the front pew beneath the altar. It felt like the right place. She thought of the hours and days she had spent before the figure of the Madonna del Latte, and closed her eyes.

'In the name of Mary, Mother of God,' she said, 'I swear that what I am about to tell you is the truth.'

He sat still and silent till she had finished, twisting his kerchief over and over in his hands. Only once did he raise his eyes to hers, when she told of the twin brother, Gastone, who had died at birth. When she had done he was silent.

'You are my mother?'

It was as if, for a moment, he was once again that little boy whose childhood she had missed. She had to bite her lip before she could answer.

'Yes.'

'And my father? My . . . real father?'

She cast about to say something good about Ferdinando. The man she had loved so much, hated so much. She pleated her violet skirt between her fingers: the colour she still wore for him.

'He was a great man, a man of letters and of music.'

She could see doubt written in his face and she wanted, so much, to hold him in her arms. Instead, she said gently: 'Do you know what this means? You are the heir to the duchy, and when Cosimo de' Medici, your grandfather, dies, you will be the duke of Tuscany.'

'But what of Pia, of the Palio?'

'You must ride, or you will not have a city to inherit. And Pia will be there at the Palio, I am sure of it.'

'And after? You could free her if I do this thing, I know

you could. You have it in your gift to free one prisoner after the Palio.' He was pleading now.

She could have wept. She had given her word to a worthless man, an abductor and murderer, and must leave an innocent girl to rot. She spoke carefully, for she did not want to lie.

'I cannot free her, for I have promised freedom to the man that gave you back to me: Dami, Gian Gastone's creature.' She could barely say his name. 'But as duke, *you* will have the power to help her.'

He was silent.

'We must keep your identity secret for now. You are not safe from . . . your uncle Gian Gastone,' the words were strange on her tongue, 'as you are the bar to his inheritance of the duchy. He tried to remove you once; he will do so again.'

He stood abruptly, turned here and there, and sat down again. He did not know where to put himself. He had lost Pia, Leocorno was dying, but he'd been given his mother back and a dukedom to boot. He shook his head.

He wished more than anything that he could turn back the calendar six weeks, to the day before the last Palio. To unsee what he had seen: Vicenzo, Egidio, Nello. But then, he did not want to lose some of the things he had found: Pia, his horse, his . . . mother. He looked at her now where she sat, a good, kind, plain woman.

'I cannot,' he said. 'I do not want any of it. I cannot be a *duke*.' The idea was laughable, but he had never felt less like laughing. 'I cannot even ride any more. Forgive me.'

He turned and ran from her, tears stinging his eyes.

∞

In the daylight he took the path to his father's house, his father who was not his father. His father was a duke, Ferdinando de' Medici, cultured, handsome, a man of letters and music. He thought of Domenico, squat and strong, a peasant who knew nothing of music but much of horses. A man who had loved him in his way, schooled him in his way, and given him the only language he had needed to learn, the only tongue that was understood in this city: horses.

He quickened his step, needing to be home, feeling that he owed Domenico that at least. He did not know how many more homecomings were left to him.

∞

Violante of Bavaria rose and followed her son from the church. She ached for the twin that was lost, but even more for the twin that was found.

As if in a dream she walked back to the palace. She did not know what to think. If Riccardo did not ride, then the Nine would take his heritage. But would he ever be reconciled with the idea of his inheritance anyway?

She stopped outside the palace, where the servants of the *comune*, preparing the terrain of the square for that evening, scattered their sand and sawdust at a respectful distance around her feet. She looked up at the roundel on the walls: IHS, a reminder of her faith. And below that, a pagan symbol: the she-wolf suckling the twins, one feeding and one looking out, as they always did, as her own had done. In the legend, Romulus had founded Rome and died; Remus lived to father a son Senius, who founded Siena.

But Romulus was not dead. He was alive, and coming for her city. Romulus was the puppetmaster of the Nine.

She woke from her dream, her mind shifting from the personal to the political. *Romulus*. She began to walk, faster this time, and with purpose. Here was another statue and another.

Back in the palace, having walked some miles and counted twelve statues, she took a map of the city from the map chest and began to mark the locations of the dozen statues. They were at key strategic points about the city – thoroughfares, city gates; they surrounded the heart of Siena, the citadel and palace, and cut it off. She wondered that she had not seen it before. Did Romulus intend to use these locations somehow?

Avoiding her brother-in-law for the rest of the day, Violante watched the remaining horse trials from the palace windows but did not see Riccardo. Determined to be ready for whatever happened tonight, she forced herself to eat a small meal, which she took in her room, and lay herself down on her bed, willing sleep, which did not come. She rose again and went to the library, her harbour and solace, but today she did not reach for the *Morte d'Arthur*. She thought that if Riccardo did not come back she would never read it again. Instead she took down her copy of Dante, bound in buckram the red of blood. She took it back to her room, lay on her bed and leafed through the pages to *Purgatory*, where the Pia of old dwelled; and where the Pia of today dwelled too. Violante suddenly needed to remind herself of the story of the first Pia of the Tolomei.

She needed to remember how Pia had died.

16
The Tower

In Dante's Purgatorio, *the poet meets a young and beautiful*
woman who had come there following her murder.

> 'Deh, quando tu sarai tornato al mondo,
> e riposato de la lunga via',
> seguitò 'l terzo spirito al secondo,
> 'Ricorditi di me, che son la Pia;
> Siena mi fé, disfecemi Maremma:
> salsi colui che 'nnanellata pria
> disposando m'avea con la sua gemma.'

'Ah, when you have returned to the world, and rested from
the long journey,' followed the third spirit after the second,
'remember me, the one who is Pia; Siena made me, Maremma
undid me: he knows it, the one who first encircled my finger
with his jewel, when he married me.'

The Palio.

A year of planning, ten men and horses, three circuits of the piazza, and all of it over in one single moment.

The Palio was the centre, the Palio was Siena. Once you knew that, you knew all.

Siena was punishingly hot that August day but, despite the heat, the numbers assembled to catch a glimpse of the Palio dell'Assunta seemed greater than ever. On other days the beauteous shell-shaped Piazza del Campo lay as serene and empty as a Saint Jacques scallop, but today it was crammed with a thousand Sienese, drumming their drums and waving their flags. Even the starlings gathered to watch in the hot blue circle of sky high over the track. They wheeled around the tower-tops, to gather in smoky clouds and break apart again, dissipating like ink in water, all the time screeching with excitement.

Everyone else had their role, their task on this day of days, from the greatest degree to the least. Pia of the Tolomei felt the lowliest of them all, but she had her role too. She was, again, merely a spectator, required to cheer for her husband and nothing more. But she had no intention of cheering for her husband, oh no. Pia of the Tolomei was going to watch her husband ride in the Palio and pray that, during the course of it, he would be killed.

It was the sixteenth day of August, the day after the feast of the Assumption, a feast she had celebrated in her cell with a crust of bread, a cup of water and a friendly Sienese rat. It was blisteringly hot but this month her bodice and stays were not tight; they hung from her loosely, and her shorn locks did not weigh down her head as her heavy coil used to. She was wearing the black-and-yellow plumage of the Eagles, for the very last time. She knew that, by the next Palio, Nello would have a new wife to wear these borrowed feathers.

Pia looked across the square to her father's benches of the Owlet *contrada*. Her father's face was obscured by a roiling tempest of waving banners and flags in the Civetta colours of red and white. But this month she did not wish herself back there with him. She gazed instead, with longing, at the benches of the Tower *contrada*, with their banners of burgundy and blue, sitting in the merciful shadow of the gnomon that was the Torre del Mangia, the tower that gave them their name. She wished with all her heart that she was sitting there, perhaps with Domenico, Riccardo's father, a man she had never met. She scanned the faces – kindly, excited, pent-up, but could not see any man who resembled Riccardo. In fact, Domenico was there, looking out for the son he loved, wearing an expression no one could name.

As they both watched, along with a thousand other pairs of eyes, the horses and riders circling the track, a lone horseman walked his mount, slowly and with complete control, through the Bocca del Casato gate, the arch of the architrave framing him like a painted angel. She did not know him a month ago; she knew him now. He led a white horse Pia also knew well (for he had become a particular pet of hers): Leocorno, the Unicorn – and he wore the colours of the Tower *contrada*. But it was not his horse or his dress that drew her gaze, nor that he was still the most beautiful living human she had ever seen. She knew that she'd thought him noble, a month ago, and to have a greatness to him. His actions, in that month, had defined him. He was kind, brave and loyal. He was the best person she'd ever met.

Pia did not know, of course, that he had the birthright to match his noble actions, the right to sit on the palace balcony above her head, in the place of the homely duchess who was his mother. All she knew was that she loved him, he loved her, and today he rode for her as her champion. But he was no character from legend for a maiden to sigh over. The stakes were very real. He wore Cleopatra's coin, not as a mere token of her favour, but as a symbol of her whole being. She felt as if her whole life hung about his neck.

∞

'The *capitani*, Duchess, and the *fantini*.'

Violante rose from her seat at once at Gretchen's whispered reminder. According to rank, it was now Gian Gastone's duty to greet the captains of the *contrade* and the jockeys that were shortly to run this Titans' race. But one glance at him, slumped on a velvet couch – for there was not a single chair in the palace that would take his bulk – told her he would not stir until he saw Dami freed.

She was happy to step into the breach, for now she would see Riccardo again. She would go down and greet her son. In the space of one short month she had become, at last, a Sienese; perhaps because she had given birth to one of the city's own – a horseman. She was grateful for the brief retreat into the cool dark palace, with its long deserted passages and high, airy salons. Her numerous household and servants had all quit the place for an hour, and she knew better than to deny them leave for this short time.

She emerged, head high, into the courtyard, where the baying, heated crowd now took note of her – so different, she thought, from last month. The acclaim reminded her of ten years before when she had entered the city, newly widowed but fêted and welcomed by all. It was a small balm to her wounded heart, but she was canny enough to know the power of comparison. Offered Gian Gastone in her stead, a drunk and a boor from the ancient enemy Florence, who would likely let the city descend into further crime and avarice, the people loved her once more. She wondered now, with a lurch of her stomach, how they would welcome Riccardo as duke, one of their own. She looked them all in the eye, those *contrade* that defied her, the little group who had cheated and lied to be here. The She-Wolf, the Goose, the Owlet. The Caterpillar, the Giraffe, the Porcupine. The Wave, the Dragon. And the Eagle.

The Nine.

They believed that in a few short moments they would rule here, not she. She feared them, and they knew that too. Beside each man stood his *fantino*, his jockey, each one eyeing her with matching insolence. All save one: Riccardo, tallest of all, the only one of the pack to fix his eyes to the ground with something akin to respect for her sex, if not for her rank. Her heart warmed a little, but chilled again when she laid eyes on her greatest adversary. Faustino Caprimulgo, captain of the Eagle *contrada*, was standing with his jockey, his younger and only son Nello. For a moment she pitied Faustino. The Medici line lived on in the flower of youth and beauty – she had succeeded in her duty to provide an heir. Ferdinando had had a son in his own image, to stand at his shoulder like a younger self, but Faustino had only this runt of the litter with his strange skin and eyes, his mop of unnatural black hair. Faustino had lost one son just as she had. But the flower of her womb had lived, not the runt.

The company waited in uneasy silence as the war chariot of the Palio drew up alongside the palace, drawn by four milk-white oxen with the banner of the Palio. Attendants folded and handed the flag to last month's victor, Faustino, who reluctantly gave up the banner in turn to Violante. And so the black-and-white banner returned to her hand once more, after a month of trial and suffering, pain and joy. She took it – custodian for a few short moments before she would give it to this year's victor.

She stole another look at Faustino. Like all the other captains he wore the colours of his *contrada* around his neck, painted on to a silken scarf, knotted loosely about his throat. Like all the other captains he stood steadfast, refusing, once again, to remove his cap for her. Violante averted her eyes, unwilling to face the hatred she saw writ in his. Instead she gazed on the bareheaded Riccardo with such fondness that she did not see Nello follow her gaze, his face a mask of frozen hatred.

Suddenly Nello's long arm shot out and tore the burgundy-and-blue scarf from Riccardo's neck. Some sort of chain fell sparkling to the floor, where it lay still, to be crushed underfoot by the ensuing scuffle. Riccardo grabbed his neckerchief and Nello's hand all at once, holding both in a crushing grip. The crowd near enough to the incident stilled and stared. All knew of the insult that had been given to Riccardo: to tear the colours of a man's *contrada* from his person – that meant death.

Violante, like the She-Wolf herself, leaped to Riccardo's side and to his defence. She gathered her guards with one glance, but they were too slow. It was Faustino who stepped forth, Faustino who held the hand and the scarf for many long heartbeats, as Nello raised his eyes and looked the older man full in the face.

He is afraid, thought Violante, her heart thudding as her guards sprang from the shadows to break the men up. Even only moments away from the completion of all he had planned, it seemed that Faustino could not forget that it was Riccardo who had sprung to help Vicenzo a month past. Around this knot of silence the two parties of the Eagle and the Tower began to shout at each other, almost climbing over the guards to assault the other *contrada*. And all the while, as their fellows dragged them clear, the two young men fixed their gaze upon each other, one promising death and the other defiance, and would not look away. The confrontation dissolved as the Eagle party claimed Nello, and the Torre citizens began to pull Riccardo away.

Momentarily alone, Violante bent down to the dust and picked up the chain that had dropped, unmarked, turning it over in her hand. It was a coin pendant on a chain, fashioned in gold with an owlet on one side and the head of a queen on the other.

An Egyptian queen. Cleopatra, of the Ptolemy.

Now, Violante understood. Now her heart thudded with fear, her palms prickled with sweat and her stomach churned. For Riccardo, the one man in the city – in the world – who meant anything to her, was surely doomed. The race was dangerous enough with just the usual rivalries, but he had worn against his skin a trinket that must belong to Pia of the Tolomei. Such a thing would not have been lost or stolen; such a thing was freely given by the wearer. Pia had given it to Riccardo, her champion, and, along with it, her heart. If Nello knew of this, Riccardo would be lucky to finish alive. Even so, Violante did not want him to ride without the favour he had been given.

'Signor Bruni.' She called the horseman back and held out her hand in a fist, thumb down, the pendant hidden within. 'I believe this is yours.'

He held out his hand and she dropped the chain and coin into it, with no more than a swift secret flash. Riccardo looked at his palm then at her. She gave a tiny nod, akin to a blessing. He closed his hand, opened his mouth to thank her, but said instead: 'Romulus rode in a carriage with crossed keys. He had a ring of the same design.'

He smiled at her once in the old way, a smile of complicity and comradeship and affection that cleaved her heart. Then he was gone, swallowed by the crowd.

Violante turned into the courtyard. As soon as she was safely back inside the palace, she picked up her skirts and ran along the passages and up the grand stair.

'Duchess?' Gretchen called far behind her.

She did not turn. As she reached the balcony, she leaned on the doorframe, gasping to regain her composure, before she emerged again and seated herself decorously. Only then did she realize she was shaking.

She searched for Riccardo in the Tower colours, among the others below at the *canapi* starting rope. The jockeys whispered to each other out of the sides of their mouths: last-minute threats or promises. She knew at this moment pacts were being made or broken, vast amounts of money changing hands. This time these bets had a special significance: to enrich nine *contrade* and beggar the rest.

The horses were circling and bumping shoulders; one reared fit to throw its rider. It was a white stallion rising out of the sea of horseflesh like a statue, the horse and rider resembling the bronzes of the mounted Cosimo the Great she had seen in Florence. For a heartbeat she could see Riccardo, on the rearing Leocorno, displaying the physical imprint of his heritage, for Cosimo was his namesake and forefather. She saw Pia of the Tolomei standing at once, hand to her mouth. Something was wrong.

As if time had slowed, she saw Riccardo fall.

∞

Zebra was in a distant quarter of the city on business of the Duchess's. He had been told where to wait and watch. Walking, as he had been instructed, from one statue of the She-Wolf to another, he had also been told what he might see: groups of men, in dark fustian cloaks, long enough to conceal swords or pistols, gathering in groups of six to a dozen. Each statue had its little band of men, men not dressed in the colours of any *contrada*, men who were not of Siena, men who looked resolutely at the ground or huddled together when someone passed. Each band was not great enough in number to excite comment on this busiest of days, but together they would number a multitude.

Disguised better by the crowds heading to the Palio than by their own art, they did not notice the little messenger boy among them and dropped their guards enough to speak with the southern dialect of Rome.

∞

Riccardo was in trouble. Leocorno, skittering and sweating, had reverted to his old tricks. He would not let Riccardo mount him. Bumped and harried by the other horses on all sides, his eyes were wide and his tail switched from side to side, his hard hooves shifting on the track.

Riccardo picked himself up, stroking Leocorno, kissing him. He looked in the horse's frightened eyes and understood. The press of the horses, the thousands of gathered men, the heat, the baying crowd. Leocorno was back in Milazzo. Back in battle. Zebra's words drifted back to Riccardo on the rumble of the gathering. *I'm not sure how he'll react to a crowd.*

Riccardo pressed his two hands to the sides of the white horse's face. He closed his eyes and rested his own forehead on the animal's scar. For a moment he was flooded with such love, such fellow feeling for this poor, damaged beast that he almost forgot Pia. He did not use his trickery, nor his whisperings; he just said over and over again, *please, please, please.* His voice a crescendo, shouting the word, so Leocorno could hear. He looked up into the horse's eyes. Whites showing all around. Fearful.

He had an inspiration. 'Run,' he shouted. 'Run away from it. Seventy-five heartbeats and you'll be away from here. You can be at peace. Just run. *Run.*'

Leocorno blinked and he tossed his head. Riccardo, sensing his moment, mounted easily, and Leocorno stood stock-still. Riccardo called down blessings on him and edged him, very very gently, to the starting ropes.

There was the customary confusion at the start, then finally, in a moment of almost unbearable tension, the horses lined and stilled as if bade by an invisible command. In a moment of eerie silence the unaccustomed tongue of the great bell Sunto sounded in the Torre del Mangia above Violante's head. Silent from one Palio to the next, the bell's song bawled out above the mêlée, to tell that the hour had come. All heads turned and all gazes swivelled up – to watch the *bandierino* weathervane on the Mangia Tower, which would turn in that last breath of wind to the quarter of the city that was to be favoured with victory. Unmoving in the heat, the weathervane did not budge, then slowly, slowly, it turned in a last-minute breath of breeze to the Tower *contrada.*

Riccardo's fingers tightened on the reins. Leocorno tossed his head high but was calmed by the silence. Time stretched, and Riccardo's neck and thumbs began to prickle with his sixth sense. He realized, in a flash, that the trap was about to be sprung. It was as if he was on a castle wall, the sappers already beneath him with their explosives, or standing in a deertrap, waiting for the iron teeth to close.

He understood at once the fiendishness of Faustino's plan. There was no way Leocorno would be able to survive what followed the silence. The ear-splitting roar of the crowd, of those thousand souls at the beginning of the Palio, the boom of the *mortaretto* cannon, would take him back to the battlefield and he would be driven to frenzy.

Riccardo almost smiled. Of course. Faustino had been so clever, so *damned* clever. It didn't matter how much Riccardo schooled Leocorno in the wide spaces of the Maremma, or the peaceful stone courts of the city. It was *this* moment, *now* that counted, and this moment would be too much for the Unicorn. Faustino had known it, known it all. Riccardo's card was marked.

In a sudden determination not to be beaten, he took the colours from his throat, tore off the very kerchief he had so lately defended from Nello, the beloved burgundy and blue of the Tower, the colours that were home to him, that were his father, that were everything he had ever known and loved. He tore the kerchief in two at the horrified gasps of the crowd. He stuffed each half firmly into each of Leocorno's ears, soothing and calming the stallion all the while.

At that moment everything happened at once. At the stroke of seven, Sunto stopped ringing, the *mortaretto* cannon sounded at the starting rope with a deafening boom, and the gold coin of Cleopatra, revealed at Riccardo's throat for all to see, caught the low evening sun and winked treacherously at Nello Caprimulgo.

∞

Zebra heard the Sunto bell high above the city begin to chime, and at the seventh stroke there was a great roar from the distant piazza as the Palio began. At this signal the Romans threw off their capes and advanced towards the palace, each in a livery of crossed keys.

But before they could muster themselves, hoofbeats sounded in the silent streets to match those in the thunderous square, and the gathered men faltered and turned in their march, to see a lone woman riding into the city seated astride a white palfrey. She was tall and patrician with a noble nose and hooded eyes, and only her silver hair gave away her age, for her figure was slim and straight. She might have been a fireside dowager, except that over her blue riding coat she wore a silver breastplate, bearing a gold shield with a ring of red balls upon it. Behind her, soldiers wearing the blue of the Palatinate rode in their hundreds.

She was the Electress Anna Maria Luisa de' Medici.

∞

Pia clasped her hands as she counted the bells, the tension mounting unbearably with each chime. At the seventh stroke, Sunto stopped ringing above the piazza, the *mortaretto* cannon sounded at the starting rope with a deafening boom, ten horses leaped forth from the *entrone*, and they were off.

Impossible for anyone who had not been here, thought Pia, to know that blood-curdling roar of the crowd, to hear the thunder of the hooves shiver your very ribs, to smell the sweat and the straw in your nose and taste the tufa dust in your mouth. The horses went by in a whirlwind, their flanks gleaming and polished with sweat, their mouths flecked with foam. Past the palazzo, thundering up the curve to Casato.

She could see the Tower colours – Riccardo was ahead, nudging shoulder to shoulder with Nello. Riccardo rode hard as if he were alone in the world, his body communing with Leocorno as if they were out in the salt and sand of the Maremma with not a soul in sight. They were together in their world, Leocorno streaking away from the crowd, pulling as far away from them and the other horses as he could, running away towards peace and freedom. Pia's nails bit into her palms, leaving red crescents, as the leaders reached the Casato. As they passed the benches of the Aquila, something moved her. A change, a final breaking away from everything she'd ever known.

Pia Tolomei got to her feet.

She cheered and yelled, she screamed and shouted. Never had she forgotten the constraints of her class before to this extent, never had she let herself go, never had she raised her voice above the softest of feminine tones. But today her voice was so loud, he could surely hear her even above the mêlée. It was the voice of someone sick of their personal purgatory, the voice of someone who had nothing more to lose, and she wanted him to hear her. She had never used his given name directly to him before, but now she screamed it: *Riccardo, Riccardo, Riccardo.*

She did not know if he heard her. But Nello did.

∞

Violante, from her balcony, saw it all. With an agonizing scream, Nello leaped from his horse, inviting death by crossing the path of the other riders. Riccardo, a heartbeat later, slid from Leocorno's back and followed, likewise dodging swiping whips and flashing hooves. Before Pia had time to run, Nello had clambered over the benches and laid hold of her, dragging her with freakish strength into the marble entrance of the Torre del Mangia. Even from her distance, Violante could hear Pia screaming Riccardo's name again but Riccardo was trapped by the crowd, hemmed in by the bobbing heads that separated him from Pia.

Violante rose at once and hurried into the palace. She prayed, as she ran through the library to the tower stair, that she would be in time. She had no clear idea of what she was going to do, but she had a crystal-clear certainty of what Nello intended. As she passed through the library, Dante's words, the words she had read earlier that day, soaked into her consciousness like water to a sponge.

How did Pia of the Tolomei die?
Her husband threw her from a tower.

∞

Blinded by the darkness as she was dragged upwards, tens, hundreds of steps, Pia wondered if the first Pia had felt this too, this dryness of her mouth so she could not even scream, this weakness in her legs so she could barely climb? Gaining, foot by foot, the height that would destroy her, climbing away from the earth step by step, to give her the momentum to fall back through all these hundreds of feet of space to her death?

Pia could hear voices echoing around the tower, but whether above or below, male or female, she did not know. They sounded like sirens mocking her last moments. But in the dreadful echoes she could hear one voice, the voice she loved above all others, calling out as if his heart would break. 'Pia!'

Riccardo. He would not be in time.

As they burst out into the light Pia was blinded again. She could not see, once in the dizzying sunlight, nor hear for the thundering toll of the Sunto bell.

As she clung to the balustrade she thought the end had come but her last moments were to be prolonged. Nello half dragged, half carried Pia up to the crenellated white crown of the tower. If he had cast her over the balustrade she would already be dead, but he clearly wanted the entire city to see this execution, to notice him for once, and this bought Pia time. She realized that he planned to take her to the very top where the golden ball of the

Medici crowned the tower. Pia looked her last on the far horizon and thought, irrelevantly, *I will never, now, see the sea.* She did not scream nor struggle any more but clung to him, as she never had before, terrified by the dizzying view, horrified by the drop. Weedy and undersized all his life, forever compared to his brother Vicenzo, Nello had assumed superhuman strength in this final act.

Through tear-blurred eyes, Pia saw Riccardo, closely followed by a figure in purple – the duchess. Pia wanted to laugh. They were too far below her. She was doomed.

Riccardo started to climb and Nello, a good deal higher, shouted down at his pursuer. 'Stay back! You will not win this time. For once, for *once*, I shall have my way.'

And Pia knew then it was down to her. She embraced Nello for the first time, and felt a sudden and wholly unwelcome pang of pity. Nello, unwanted, unmarked: included by his father only once his brother was dead, and then only to achieve the city. Below them, Riccardo was climbing. Slowly, stealthily. She had to buy him time, and the sole way to do it was to give Nello the attention he desired.

She began to speak, gently, struggling to keep her voice level, soft, her lips as near to his ear and the rough black hair as she could bear.

'Your father, he wanted you to win today. He designed the whole syndicate around you, around your skill, around his esteem for you. He gave you a wondrous horse, and the chance to win the city.'

Pia could hardly have chosen a more disastrous gambit.

Nello's mouth fell open in a terrible, jackal laugh, while his pink eyes reddened further with tears of rage.

'Don't you understand?' he said. 'I don't want to win the race. I just want the prize.'

Pia, fighting every desire to scream and struggle, looked him in his pink eyes as Riccardo edged upward. 'The city will be yours by tonight. You know it. Romulus comes.'

'The *city*?' Nello spat the word. 'The city is not the prize.'

He shook Pia until her teeth rattled, and she screamed at last at the sickening, dizzying drop below.

'*You* are the prize. And my father offered you to *him*, pandered for *him*, so you could ride and talk and . . . kiss.' His face was a ruin. 'He could not trust me to win for him, for the Eagles, or as a champion for a wife who might love me. He had to create a rival for me in *him*, but he had no need. You would have been enough. I wanted you, only you. I wanted you to look at me, just once, the way you look at him. But he shall not have you, if I cannot.'

Gazing into those maddened eyes, Pia steeled herself to say the unsayable.

'Then, come, my husband. Let us go home. For if I die tonight, I will never have had the chance to lie with you.'

And she kissed him, full on the lips.

In that dreadful moment when he held her tight, devouring her, she reached to her boot. As Nello's tongue pushed into her mouth, she thrust the horse shears through his tunic with all her desperate strength, and felt the hot flood of blood on her hands. His lips slackened against hers, his grasp loosened and she clung to the battlements. Nello looked at her for the fraction of one heartbeat, a hurt, questioning look that she would remember for ever, a red ribbon of blood falling from his mouth.

Then he fell, in the shape of a cross, down, down, plunging from purgatory to hell.

∞

Zebra marvelled at the practised speed and dispatch with which the Palatinate army followed and surrounded the papal troops. There was no bloodshed, just a calm and quiet understanding; the pope's men knew when they were outnumbered and when to cut their losses. The fellows with the crossed keys laid down their arms, and were bound and led away by the infantry. Then the Palatinate cavalry, led by the Electress herself, rode quietly and without incident to the piazza, and the palace of her brother the heir of Tuscany, whose letter she had received.

∞

Gian Gastone de' Medici was not concerned for Siena, for he knew his sister would be hard by with her cavalry. Whatever his opinion of Anna Maria Luisa, he knew that her loyalty to her family was beyond question, and that she was as jealous of the Medici dominions as he was; she would not stand by while the Nine took Siena.

He idly watched the end of the race, only because

every hoofbeat brought him closer to Dami's freedom, for the statutes stipulated that the condemned man was freed when the winner was announced. He vaguely registered that this year's winner was a handsome white horse without a rider. He ignored some sort of drama that was taking place on the tower above his head and made no note of the pointing, gasping crowd. He did not even turn his head.

No, Gian Gastone de' Medici had eyes only for his lover as he made his way across the piazza, a freed man. Giuliano Dami enjoyed perhaps a whole minute of his freedom, perhaps shared one glance and wave with his master, before a dark shadow grew around him like a stain as Nello Caprimulgo fell, with great precision, directly upon him.

∞

Riccardo stumbled into the light from the marble porticoes of the chapel at the bottom of the great tower, half carrying, half leading Pia, who clung to him as if she would never let him go. His instincts were to take her into the shadowy alleys of the Tower *contrada* to safety, but the delighted whicker of a horse halted him. Leocorno, who had valiantly won the race for him riderless, barged his way through the crowds, dodging a sea of patting hands, and trailing a collection of Torre children who were garlanding him with wreaths and ribbons of blue and burgundy.

Riccardo strode towards the horse, and as he and Pia wrapped their arms around his white neck, Leocorno stumbled, as if the weight of the garlands or the love were too much for him. His knees folded and he staggered, then fell to the ground. Pia pulled the great head into her lap, not understanding.

But Riccardo knew.

He bent to the white ear for the last time.

'You won,' he shouted above the mêlée. 'And now you are free.'

The large liquid eye regarded him, then deadened; Riccardo could see only his own reflection now and knew Leocorno was gone. The fragment of spear in the Unicorn's skull had freed him at last; the battle cries had ceased for him, and he was at peace.

Pia's tears fell on the white velvet cheek, and Violante, seeing it all from her vantage point, was visited by a memory. As she watched Pia cradle the huge white head, it was as though a virgin of old had, at last, found that creature of fable that she sought.

17

The Shell

Violante had been married for one year. She went with Ferdinando to a party at one of his father Cosimo de' Medici's summer palaces, high on the hills above Florence. The palazzo was a beautiful long white house with ornamental gardens, dark spears of cypress trees piercing the sky and the scent of myrtle in the air. Violante was as happy on that day as she had ever been in her marriage; her disillusion not quite complete, her barrenness not yet a certainty.

The heat in the gardens was fierce and she retreated inside the cool house. She wandered into a huge room and was drawn to the windows. In the gardens, musicians played and there was the tinkle of crystal and laughter drifting on the breeze that shifted the gauzy drapes. She could see Ferdinando, his head thrown back, laughing with his beloved sister Anna Maria Luisa, and her insides contracted with love. The older siblings ignored their younger brother Gian Gastone, who stood a little apart. But Violante did not mark him; she looked instead at her husband, unable to believe her luck. Almost overwhelmed by her feelings, she turned and noticed for the first time a painting on the opposite wall.

And what a painting. A huge poplar panel depicting a woman of great beauty, with flowing red hair, rising naked from a great scallop shell floating on a blue sea, the kindly winds personified to blow her to shore on an azure wave. Violante walked forward and looked that fortunate goddess right in her serene green eyes. She was so beautiful, so abundant; naked as the day she was born, with glowing skin the hue of an apricot, perfect breasts and long limbs. The other figures in the painting focused their attention entirely on the goddess, waiting, rapt, for her to speak or gesture. She was everything Violante had never been, never had. She wondered what it was like to feel the heat of everyone's attention, to succeed in your own beauty, to be desired.

She heard a step at the door and hoped it was Ferdinando, optimistic, for once, that she could borrow some of the goddess's magic. But it was her father-in-law, Grand Duke Cosimo de' Medici, a man she had always found courteous, but frightening.

He came to stand beside her.

'It's an allegory,' he said, 'about birth. The shell represents a cunt.'

He turned and fixed her with his hooded Medici eyes, giving Violante his full attention.

'And when, my dear, might you be going to conceive?'

Domenico Bruni lit a candle and stole quietly past the door of his tiny parlour. As he passed the jamb he put his head into the room, and his goodnights died on his lips. The two young people within, sitting close on the settle, were lit gold by the fire. Pia Tolomei's head lay on his son's shoulder and her dark eyes, huge in the firelight, seemed utterly at peace. His son's face wore the same expression, a completeness Domenico had never seen. Both of them looked as if they had come home.

As Domenico climbed the little stair to his room he regarded his truckle bed as he set his candle down. Ordinarily, after the Palio dell'Assunta in August, he would take to his bed with nothing but the drear cold winter to look forward to, a whole year to wait before the Palio di Provenzano in July. But this time he did not want to take to his bed; he wanted to be with Riccardo.

For the first time since Dami had visited him late at night, he felt safe. Dami could not now tell anyone that, twenty years past, he had given a royal child to Domenico; he could not tell anyone that the child Domenico had loved and raised was not his.

For the first and only time in his life, Domenico did not care who had won the Palio, or that, outside, a raucous feast was taking place under the Palio banner of black-and-white silk, which the valiant Leocorno had won for the Tower before he died. He did not even care that his son had stopped in the middle of the race to save a woman of the Owlet *contrada*. He did not even care to go down to his stable and make the arrangements for the

Lipizzaner's body, the corpse that Riccardo had insisted be brought home.

All he wanted was for Riccardo to stay.

∞

Violante de' Medici was not in the habit of walking abroad on the night of the Palio. Boisterous winners and doleful losers both could make for trouble on the streets. She took two sergeants-at-arms with her and left them outside Domenico's door, sharing a cup with the jubilant citizens who had ranged a dozen trestle tables along the streets, bedecked in burgundy and blue. Violante had no idea what she would say to the old man.

She didn't knock but went straight into the little firelit room. There she found Riccardo on the settle, with Pia's head on his knee, stroking her hair as she slept.

Riccardo did not see her until she broke the firelight with her shadow, but he raised his eyes to her unsurprised. He had known she would come for him. 'When will you tell them?'

She was glad he understood. 'Tomorrow. The Electress Palatine Anna Maria Luisa is in residence at the palace. She is a good woman and will not let her brother Gian Gastone act against you. She will see justice done. You will be invested as governor of Siena and grand duke of Tuscany.'

'Grand duke?'

'Yes. Can you not hear the bells?'

Riccardo cocked his head. Above the crackle of the sticks in the grate, above the screams and songs outside, he could hear the great bell Sunto ringing a passing bell. All he could think of was that the last time he had heard that bell he had been riding Leocorno, about to start the race. At that moment it seemed that the bell rang for that valiant, troubled horse who had ended his life in a victory, not the defeat of battle.

Violante said gently, 'Cosimo de' Medici, your name-sake, your . . . grandsire, is dead.'

She could not grieve for the grand duke, who had abandoned her when she needed him most. The only point on which she could be grateful to him was that he had needed a shoe for his favourite horse on the day the twins were born, and had called on the best farrier in Tuscany, a man who had taken Cosimo's grandson home to Siena. She smiled at that child now.

'It is your time.'

Riccardo stared again at the fire. 'Will he give up his inheritance so easily?'

'Gian Gastone?'

She thought of her sorry brother-in-law, sobbing in his bed at the palace, useless now that his paramour was gone. Justice had been well served for him and Dami – Dami had taken a child and lost his life; Gian Gastone had attempted murder for his dukedom and lost that.

'I cannot imagine that, in his current state, he will even leave his bed, let alone fight for his dukedom,' she replied.

'And the Electress Palatine? Will she not wish to inherit? For it may easily be said that your brother-in-law has not long for this world.'

She had not thought that he understood so much.

'She has no living heir. Her husband died of the syphilis, like mine. She is too old to carry a child. She will be glad that the line will carry on, otherwise the dukedom will pass to the Bourbon or Spain. She loved Ferdinando well, and will love you too.' She did not mean to lie to him but spoke with emphasis, as if her certainty would make it so.

'And my father?'

He had asked her this question before, in the Tower church, with exactly the same intonation. Then, he had sought to know more about Ferdinando. Now, she knew exactly whom he meant.

'Domenico Bruni will have my thanks, and the city's thanks. I will repay him for his service to you. But from today,' she said gently, 'he must be as one of your subjects to you.'

The irony, the cruelty of her position was not lost upon her. She, who had lost Riccardo so long ago, was now to deprive a true father of his son.

Still Riccardo said nothing but looked down at Pia. He stroked her hair and tucked a black lock of it tenderly behind her ear. 'And Pia?'

He asked the question with the air of one who knew the answer.

Violante spoke softly, but clearly, so he should be in absolutely no doubt of the truth.

'She will return to her father's house, as a widow must. Faustino has lost everything and will not act against her now. I had the horse shears brought down from the tower and disposed of – there is no need for anyone to know that Nello was dead before he fell. Pia is guiltless and free.'

'And then?'

She loved him too well to wilfully misinterpret the question. 'One day she may marry again, but she cannot marry you.'

'Cannot?'

Riccardo raised his eyes to hers. In his firelight reveries he had dreamed of being duke, of riding to Pia's house to carry her away, a man of power, a man who could not be gainsaid. In these dreams he resembled his real father better than he knew, for Ferdinando had followed his own appetites without pause. But in reality Riccardo knew that if he was to rule, he could not rule that way. He could not be a despot. He should rule in the manner of his mother, justly and well.

Violante lowered her voice still more, tender to the feelings of the sleeping girl.

'She may marry within her own class. A high-born citizen of Siena will do well for her. But not a duke. A duke must marry for alliance, for fortune, but not for love. Believe me,' she said with feeling, 'I know whereof I speak.'

'Did you not love, then, where you wed?' Riccardo was almost pleading.

'I? I did, yes. So much. Your father,' she stumbled at the word, 'he did not.'

She had loved a man and lost him. She had loved his sons and lost one of them. Now she must take from her remaining son the only father he had known and the woman he loved. She knew that the replacement of them with herself could be no consolation. She could see it writ in Riccardo's expression. He looked at her across fathoms of loss and there was no love there. He stared his duty in the face, not his mother.

'How long do I have?' It seemed to her that he hated her then.

'Till noon. Come to the palace. All will be readied there.'

She wanted to wish him to enjoy this precious night, but could not find the words to do it. She left them then to the little time that they had remaining.

∞

Violante went back across the piazza, that great scallop shell where all this had begun, where all this would end. She knew that there was no way forward for her and Riccardo. He could never, now, be her boy. They could never fill in those years, the seasons, the decades they had missed. She would be, at best, a benevolent stranger. A councillor, a dowager. Once Riccardo was installed, Gian Gastone would return to Florence, or his hated, chilly, marital castle, or wherever he would now go to eke out his existence without Dami.

And she? What would become of her? Perhaps she would go to Rome, as she had once planned to do before Ferdinando died, to the Palazzo Madama, a Medici palace where she could console herself with the balm of having done her duty, and lighten her days with the twin wonders of religion and art.

Violante stood in the middle of the *campo* and looked at the place where, yesterday, the starting line had been. Then she turned around, slowly and methodically, the ageless palaces wheeling about her, until she faced the finish line. She looked at the ground, dizzy, at the nine divisions of the scallop shell, at the place where Vicenzo had died last month, at the fountain where Egidio had lain, and at the shadow below the balcony where Nello and Dami had died. Libations of blood, given to the ground by the sacrificial sons of Siena, dark blots on the perfect shell of the *campo*. If the Palio was Siena and Siena was the Palio, she could at least, before she left, leave a framework of laws for Riccardo, in the hope that no more young men would die. A series of proclamations would do, an attempt to codify this most ancient of sports, to prevent future tragedy.

Violante quickened her steps toward the palace, her guard at her heels. She knew that tonight there would be no dreams of the twins, for she would not sleep. She climbed wearily to the library, called for paper and ink, and sat heavily at the round table. Before she lifted her pen, she laid one hand on the fine buckram of the *Morte d'Arthur*, the book she had once read to her son.

∽

Riccardo, too, spent the night awake. He cradled Pia's dear head at his lap, spent long, long moments looking down at her, her raven hair burnished by fire. He could have waked her and ravished her, claimed her. So that whoever else had her in the future, he'd had her first. But he did not want to dishonour her, to destroy her peace. She was free, for one night, from Nello, from Faustino, from her father. She was in hiding, in harbour. He loved her completely, and if this was to be their last night together, his last night as Riccardo Bruni, he did not want to spend it in sin, no matter how much he wanted her. He touched her pearly wrist with one finger where it had been rubbed raw by the shackles of her prison, and then closed his fingers around it one by one like a jailer.

She stirred, and he let go. Suddenly he knew what to do. He smiled with a complete joy that suffused his chest and warmed him more than any fire. He would not accept his heritage. He would go with her, now, before the city woke. They would go far away, together, tonight. He threw his head back and laughed, enjoying the moment, the fraction of still time before he would wake her and the world would change.

∞

Pia listened to him, smiling gently while her heart broke. Riccardo had told her an extraordinary tale of baby twins – one dead, one alive – a lost son and the heir to a dukedom. He might as well have been telling her a fairy tale by the fire, so incredible did it sound to her ears. Then he told her of the future, that they'd go now, tonight, and she'd put her hand in his as they walked through Siena at night and out of the Camollia gate, where they had oftimes ridden, this time never to return.

When he'd done she shook her head, not too much lest the tears fall from her eyes. Who knew better than she that what he'd asked was impossible? Who but Pia, who'd lived her life bound by class and obligation, knew better that he had a duty not to her, but to his mother and his state? She knew her answer, but hardly knew how to express it.

'When we rode from the Camollia gate on the day we were discovered by Nello, we saw a little pile of donkey bones. Do you recall?'

He nodded.

'They were a sign that the city was going to fall. It is no good, Riccardo.'

The city would stand or fall by his actions alone, and when weighed in the scales with the wishes of two people, Siena, with her mass of history, outweighed them. They could not take hold of this future, this fantasy.

'You must take your place in the palace, and ... marry,' she choked on the word, 'suitably.'

'*Suitably.*' He was moved to anger. '*You* can say that? You who have suffered nameless cruelties under Nello, you would have me end my days with some royal miss, who ...'

Her tears spilled then and he stopped, mortified.

'None of this is what I wished,' she whispered. 'But I do know this. You have to go.'

She stepped forward and snapped Cleopatra's coin pendant from his neck. He flinched, and she was glad; she did not have the strength to send him from her unless she used the force of his own anger. If he held her again she would be lost.

So she snatched it back, hard, hurting him, and he left the room. She turned to the fire so she would not hear him go, concentrating on something, anything, so that she should not hear the bang of the front door. She stood for a moment, numb, and stunned, the tears she had held back now flowing freely to fall and hiss on the hot stones of the hearth. The door creaked behind her and she turned. She thought he was coming back, and sprang to her feet, ready to cover him with kisses, to say she'd been wrong, to hold him and never let him go.

But it was Riccardo's father. Domenico Bruni.

She looked at him, small, squat and kindly. She did not have to wonder, now, why father and son bore no resemblance. She and he, though, shared something now. Pain and loss. She held out her hand to him.

'He's gone?' he said, a pitiful hope in his voice.

His accent: *that* was where the resemblance to his son lay. Somehow hearing it hurt the most of all.

'He's gone,' she said, sorry to be the one to kill that hope.

By tacit consent they sat down on the settle and spent the rest of the night together next to the dying fire. Loss, thought Pia, loss for everyone and for Riccardo most of all. He had gained a dukedom, but he had lost everything else.

∞

The next morning Violante had her heralds give it out around the city that she would be making a proclamation at noon. She had spent the morning in discussion with

Anna Maria Luisa de' Medici. She had sat with that redoubtable lady in the Hall of the Nine, and had caused two golden chairs to be set beneath the Lorenzetti fresco depicting good government. She hoped it was an omen.

She regarded her sister-in-law, seeing in her strong dark features echoes of Ferdinando, and Riccardo too. Anna Maria Luisa had not followed her father and brother into corpulence, but was thin almost to the point of asceticism. She regarded Violante with a guarded eye, but did not seem unfriendly. The truth was that too much time had passed, too many pains borne, for her to feel any further hostility towards her sister-in-law.

'Well, Violante, we have not been friends, I think?' began the Electress Palatine in her cultured Florentine accents. Violante inclined her head to acknowledge the honesty of this. 'But we have shared so much, in the fate of our babes, and the fate of our husbands, that we have much to ally us. And in the spirit of openness between allies, suppose you set before me the events that led to my intervention yesterday.'

Violante told the Electress the story of the Palio, of the Nine. She did not, as yet, speak of Riccardo's identity but merely included him as a player in this drama. She went on to talk of Francesco Maria Conti, and of the mysterious Romulus, who travelled in a carriage with crossed keys.

'I now know, of course, that Romulus represented Rome itself.'

She could have said a great deal at this point on the symbolism of this alias, and the personal significance of the boy twins to her own history, but she restricted herself to explanation.

'Thus the pope himself, Innocent XIII, otherwise known as Michelangelo Conti, conspired with the Nine to destabilize the duchy, with the connivance of his cousin, my chief councillor Francesco Maria Conti. Conti fixed the horse draw by way of his scientific arts, and it was to be Nello Caprimulgo's task to win the Palio for the syndicate on the horse Berio. The horse was dyed to appear black, so the Eagles could ride him to victory again in contravention of the rules. While the city was unguarded during the day of the Palio, the papal troops were to infiltrate the city in small groups by gathering at the statues of the She-Wolf, the statues of Romulus. Then, under the cover of the race when the city was deserted, they were to surround the square with all the citizens inside and take the palace, so that the Nine could be invested and I would be deposed.'

Violante felt a cold finger of dread touch her heart at what could have been.

'It was this, sister, which your Palatinate army prevented, in answer to your brother's letter. I thank you with all my heart.'

The Electress inclined her noble head but said nothing.

Violante, hesitantly, went on. 'May I assume, then, that the papal troops are the prisoners of your army – their horses sequestered, their weapons taken?'

Anna Maria Luisa leaned forward a little in her chair. 'You may assume that if you like, sister. But the bald truth is that I let them go.'

Violante sat forward abruptly. 'You let them go?'

'Yes.'

'But . . . *why?*'

'Diplomacy, my dear sister,' came the reply. 'I cannot move against the pope, or his troops. Nor would I, for I do not wish to accede the advantage I now hold.'

Violante was reminded of the chess game of her day-dream, when she had sent the black-and-white Palio banner to Faustino.

'In the War of Succession the papal states lost this part of Tuscany to the Farnese family. The Conti papacy will do anything to regain control of Siena, even through their puppet government of the Nine, rather than see a Farnese ruler here.' Violante could have sworn the Electress smiled a little. 'As you know, my dear sister-in-law, because you and I and Gian Gastone have no issue, the kingdom will most likely pass to Don Carlos of Spain, son of Elizabeth Farnese. If I censure the papacy, or even reveal this plot, we will hand the balance of power to Don Carlos as my heir apparent. It is a conclusion the Conti will do anything to prevent. I must admit, I am not too keen on it myself, but as the three of my father's children have been so remiss at providing heirs, it is one that will very likely come to pass.'

Violante smiled at the secret knowledge that she was about to reveal.

'You spoke before of our similarities,' went on the Electress. 'There is one more point in which we are even more in accord. I will not cede one inch of the duchy to renegade nobles, nor to robber popes.' She sniffed disapprovingly.

'I was hoping you would say that,' said Violante, clapping her hands to dismiss their attendants. 'And I ask you to consider this, before I tell you what I must. You say we have not been friends. Perhaps, for this at least, it is not too late?'

A brace of hours later Violante emerged from the chamber, well pleased with their conference, concluding what she had only suspected before: that a world run by women might be a world well run. Gian Gastone kept to his room, but his servants had promised to ready him to be in place for midday. Violante could not bring herself to care about his fate. He had taken from her the thing that was most precious to her. Now she would do the same to him. The dukedom had been everything to him for so long now, and it was about to vanish from his life.

She was shaking, but not for fear that Riccardo would not come. He had been in the palace since eight of the clock, and had spent the morning with servants to bathe and shave him, and outfitters to give him a suit of clothes. When she saw him, dressed and ready, tall and immaculate in a green velvet frock coat, she knew that his transformation from Riccardo Bruni to Cosimo Ferdinando IV de' Medici was complete.

The time came. Here she was again, on the balcony. Here was Gian Gastone to her left, blubbering on his couch, saying Dami's name over and over in his particular faithless litany. There on her right, Anna Maria Luisa de' Medici, sitting as far away from her hated brother as she could, tall and aquiline and resplendent in blue. And behind, in the shadows, the new duke of Tuscany leaned on the doorframe, looking, she knew, for Pia Tolomei in the crowd.

Violante cleared her throat.

'Good people,' she called, as the crowd nudged and shushed one another. 'I have something of great import to tell you. It is this.'

Something shone in her face, distracting her. She raised her palm to shade her brow and hesitated. She looked down and by some trick of the light the sun struck the golden coin of Pia's pendant, slicing through the air and shining directly in her eyes.

∞

Pia of the Tolomei was reflecting on the dreadful irony of getting what she wanted.

Nello was dead and she was free; Faustino, beset by his creditors, no longer had an interest in his daughter-in-law. Her own father, Salvatore, struggling with similar problems, apparently took the same position. And so, on the day of the proclamations of Violante Beatrix de' Medici, Pia of the Tolomei found herself standing in a crowd of Torre citizens, still cock-a-hoop from their victory of the Palio, and holding the arm of Domenico Bruni. It was not clear from the position of their linked arms whether the old man supported the girl, or the girl supported the old man.

Pia strained her eyes, looking for Riccardo in the shadow of the palace balcony, knowing he was there, wondering if he could see her, and turned the pendant, that hung once more at her neck, to catch the sun.

∞

Violante looked down at Pia, standing by Riccardo's father Domenico, both mute and pale, both faces ruined. She turned to Riccardo and on his noble face saw the same loss writ there. And to her right, Gian Gastone, huge, pitiful, ruined by greatness.

Ruined by greatness.

Why should she foist such a life on her son? Why should she fulfil the imperative of heritage at the cost to his personal happiness, and to Pia's? And Domenico Bruni, that poor good man, whose crime was no more than to raise an orphan with years of care and unspoken love. She who had lost a son once, would she wish this most hideous of fates upon him? Would she, thus, force Riccardo into princeship, and from thence to a marriage he did not want? So many Medicis had been made unhappy by their loveless marriages: Anna Maria Luisa, Gian Gastone, herself and Ferdinando. And Gian Gastone had been destroyed further by ambition and excess.

Suddenly Violante of Bavaria knew what she must do. After all, she had thought it herself: *a world run by women would be a world well run.*

She turned back to the assembly. 'Good people,' she said again. 'We have lately seen two Palios, just weeks apart. Both have ended in tragedy.'

She caught here the silver head of Faustino Caprimulgo

in the crowd, bowed under the loss of his sons and the loss of his fortune.

'Therefore,' Violante went on, 'it is my task today, as part of my continuing office as your governess, a role that I intend to fulfil for many years yet,' she was gratified to hear the scattered cheers this elicited, 'to regulate the rules of the Palio. Some are old; some are new; all will be codified here and immutable from this day. Thus we may move forward in amity and safety to the years ahead, with myself as your sole ruler and duchess. This I have done. I hereby declare that, item one: each *contrada* must sign up for the drawing. Ten and only ten will be drawn by chance to run in the Palio.'

Violante was aware of the mildly curious eyes of Anna Maria Luisa. She carried on regardless.

'Item two: the *contrada* must deposit a sum that will go to the owners of the horses. Item three: the jockeys must use only "an ordinary riding crop" and go to the starting rope after the *mortaretto* cannon is fired. Item four: no one from the ground may hit or incite the horses at the starting rope. Item five: no one may help a fallen jockey to remount a horse.'

Here she looked at Riccardo in the shadows and made a tiny, imperceptible movement with her head: *go.*

'Item six: the first horse to complete three circuits and to reach the judges' stand wins. Item seven: the Palio will be claimed by official representatives of the winning *contrada*.'

Violante went on to declare the new rules of the Palio, rules that would outlive her, and Riccardo too, and stand for the next two hundred years.

Behind her in the shadows, Riccardo Bruni began to unbutton his frock coat. He laid it gently on a golden chair and stole quietly down the stairs. No one challenged the last Medici as he walked into the sun. He was just a man now, an ordinary man, a son of Siena, and the crowd were too busy to notice when a girl, just a girl, a daughter of Siena, ran to meet him and fell into his arms.

∞

'Thank you.'

Dawn had broken on a new day: fresh, golden and full of promise, the air smelling new and innocent. Violante was in the Giraffa church of San Francesco, praying before the icon of the Madonna del Latte. This time she felt no need to sneak into the *contrada*, for she was now welcomed wherever she went: the people of Siena had finally realized how fortunate they were in her governorship. Gian Gastone's men were even now boxing up his possessions; he was to return to Florence to assume his dukedom this very day. Violante did not think he would rule long, for his heart and his health were broken.

Now, kneeling on the cold pavings before the sacred mother feeding her child, she had so much to be thankful for. And the Madonna looked on her kindly from her almond eyes, with fellow feeling. She knew what Violante was most grateful for: her son.

∞

'Thank you.'

It was noon, and the three of them, Pia, Riccardo and

Violante, had met at the Camollia gate as arranged. They stood on the very spot where a dead donkey had dried to bleached bones, to be collected piecemeal by the curs of the city. Pia and Riccardo, twined about each other like ivy, were standing in the shadow of the gate from which the donkey had fallen.

It was the first time Pia had met the duchess face to face, and she liked what she saw. She smiled at her. 'You have given us our lives.'

'Then I charge you to spend them together, my dear.'

'And we are safe?' Riccardo asked.

The duchess did not trouble to look about her. 'No one else knows your true identity beyond we three and your father,' she said soothingly, 'and he, I am sure, is happy to keep his peace.'

Pia knew this to be true. Yesterday when Riccardo had left behind his birthright and come out into the square, Pia had broken their kiss to bring him to his father. Domenico had enfolded his son in an embrace even harder and longer than the one the lovers had shared. Pia had watched as Riccardo closed his eyes and leaned into his father, his knees almost buckling under the weight of the love he felt for this man who was no blood nor kin, but far, far more.

'What of the Electress Palatine?' It was Pia who asked the question.

Her intelligence pleased the duchess even more than her beauty and she smiled on her again.

'I did not tell her the exact nature of the proclamation

I would make. I merely said that I would make an announcement about the future of the city, and asked if she would agree to stand by it and the laws of Tuscany, whatever the ramifications may be. She said she would always be found on the side of right and law and Tuscany, and that I may rely upon her. She will make a good grand duchess one day. On that day, women will rule in both Siena and Florence.'

The thought seemed pleasing to the duchess and it pleased Pia too.

'And Gian Gastone?' This from Riccardo.

'He is set to return to Florence,' replied his mother. 'He will take his father's place, but I think he will not rule long. He is not well in body. This has been so for a while. But when we are sick at heart too, we are not long for the world. I think the Electress will not have long to wait.'

Pia registered the pang of pity in the words, and knew that the duchess had freed her son so that he need not follow in the footsteps of his uncle to corruption, to excess, to decadence.

'And you?' Pia asked, filled with a sharp regret that the duchess might leave this place. 'Will you stay now?'

'I think so, there is still much to do. After all, I am still governess of Siena. The grand duke has stated that he has no wish ever to set foot in the place again.'

She could not disguise the relief she felt that Gian Gastone would soon be gone from her house, from her city.

'And you two, what will you do? Marry, I suppose?' It was said with a smile.

'Yes, we are to live with my father,' replied Riccardo.

'And *your* father, Pia? He has agreed to this?'

Pia nodded. 'He was given advice from an unexpected quarter.'

The duchess raised her pale brows.

'Faustino Caprimulgo,' said Pia, almost not believing it herself. 'He vouched for Riccardo and said he was a good man. Moreover, my father is now ruined too and cannot provide me a dowry. Riccardo will take me without one.'

She took hold of his hand and with the other she touched, briefly, the coin of Cleopatra at her throat. It did not matter that this was now all the dowry she possessed. Pia had all the riches that she could hold, not in the hand that held the coin, but in the hand that held Riccardo's.

'I will settle some money on you both to begin your life,' said the duchess.

Pia knew as she said it that Riccardo would refuse, and he did. But the duchess was ready with another suggestion.

'Then perhaps you will let me pay you for honest work,' she said. 'I'd like you to be the palace ostler, as my current man is in his dotage and in need of rest. There are rooms, in the servants' quarters, that come with the job. I have a notion,' she said, smiling, 'that you will like them much more than you would have done the duke's salon.'

'It feels wrong to take from someone who has given us so much,' said Riccardo, 'but to work with horses for a wage is something I would enjoy. Thank you.'

Pia took her cue. 'And now, I would like to give *you* a gift.'

She held out a parcel, wrapped in canvas. When the duchess parted the rough cloth she found finer threads beneath, a bale of dark-red samite, the colour of blood. The duchess shook it out. It was a dress, cut for a woman of her girth and height, the material dark and glowing like carnelians. She held it to herself, and Pia noted that she had chosen well.

Somehow Zebra had managed to rescue her mother's gowns from the Eagles' palace and had brought them to Domenico's house. There Pia had laid them out in the little parlour. In the folds of the leather garde-corps she had found her copy of the *Morte d'Arthur*, a volume she thought she would never see again, and she blessed Zebra with every saint she could remember. She had walked up and down, looking at the rainbow of gowns, considering. Before this day she would have sworn she would never part with a single one, but she had not hesitated. In this city where colour was so loaded, had such meaning, she did not let any of these considerations of heraldry and *contrade* enter her mind. She did not avoid yellow because it meant the Goose, or green because it meant the Caterpillar. She just picked a colour that she thought would warm the duchess's skin.

The duchess smiled. '*Red*,' she said, looking almost pretty.

Pia nodded, adding shyly, 'It belonged to *my* mother. I thought it would become you.'

Violante heard that stress on the word *my*, almost imperceptible. *The dress belonged to* my *mother.* You *are Riccardo's.*

It was an invitation. Pia wanted the duchess to know that even though Riccardo had not accepted his heritage, his mother should not consign their bond to the dust. The duchess folded the gown tenderly, clearly touched by the gesture. Then she took her son's hand and led them through the Camollia gate.

Outside the gateway Zebra was ready, holding Berio's leading rein. Given in bad faith under another name, he was now Pia's in the eyes of the law, as the property of her dead husband. The horse lifted his head and whickered when he saw her, the dull black beginning to grow out of his coat and the shining bay beneath revealed like a new skin. Pia had no need of Riccardo's hand to help her up to the horse in front of him. Zebra looked at the colour of the coin Riccardo gave him and bit it in delight.

∞

As Violante clutched the dress with one hand and waved with the other, the couple rode away across the plain. She looked down at Zebra, wistfully watching his friend ride away, and suddenly it all fell into place.

The child was the missing piece in a puzzle or the last counter of a game. She had not been allowed to raise her son. Here was a boy with no home or family, who had spent his nine years of life carrying water, relaying messages or holding horses for coin.

She said quickly, before she thought better of it, 'Zebra, how would you like to sleep in the same bed every night? Your *own* bed?'

The boy squinted up at her and smiled, screwing up his eyes and his freckled nose against the sun. He slotted his little hand into hers and she had her answer. She returned the squeeze.

'If you are to live in the palace with me, I cannot call you Zebra,' said she. 'What is your given name?'

'Pietro.'

Pietro, Peter, Petrus. The holder of the crossed keys. The patron saint of Rome, of Romulus, of the Rock.

Violante smiled down at him. 'Well, Pietro, let's go home.'

∞

Pia and Riccardo rode out for the rest of the day. They had two very important tasks to fulfil. Firstly, they rode into the hills to that beautiful western aspect of the city, where Leocorno had once ridden against the peerless view. Here, under the cover of night, the duchess's men had brought Leocorno's body, no boon too great for her to grant her secret son, who could not bear his valiant mount to be fed to the city's hounds. There, in the hills, the horse was rolled from the sheepcart that carried him and buried in the soft earth. No one but the duchess's most trusted guards knew that the horse's body was wrapped in the Palio banner that he'd won, and even now the Bruco silkmakers of the Caterpillar *contrada* were busily making a new one.

As the sun soared the couple stopped by the great mound of soil. Pia watched Riccardo as he laid his hand on the heaped earth and finally marked the place with a great stone so that he might find it again, when the mound had fallen in and flattened, and when Leocorno's bones were as dry as the bones of the little donkey who had been thrown over the Camollia gate six weeks ago. For an instant Pia felt a connection between the two beasts, the humble ass who had died outside the walls and was buried within, the noble horse who had died inside the walls and was buried without.

When he was done Pia paid her own respects. She took Cleopatra's coin from her neck, made a deep divot in the soft earth with her finger and dropped the pendant in. As she covered it over Riccardo caught her wrist. The green eyes of the Medici looked into the black eyes of the Tolomei.

'Are you sure?' he said.

'Yes,' she said. 'Quite sure. You see, I've been Pia of the Tolomei, I've been Pia of the Caprimulgo. But I'm not any more. I'm not Cleopatra, or the first Pia. I'm not Guinevere. I'm not Minerva. I'm not a long-dead empress, or my tragic ancestress, a faithless queen, or a goddess. I'm not even Pia of the Bruni, even when we wed.'

She held his dear face in her hands, to mitigate any hurt he might feel that she would not take his name.

'Your wife soon, a mother one day if God grants it; but whatever He brings henceforth I'm just *me*.' She leaned forward and kissed him. '*La Pia*. Just Pia.'

Riccardo nodded then, and put his arm about her, and they walked back to the horse.

They left the grave as the sun was lowering, but

Riccardo pointed Berio's head easterly, away from the city. They rode on, seemingly for hours, racing the sun as it ran ahead of them over the hills and valleys, buttered with gold. By the time they stopped on a high dune there was still just enough light for him to show her what he wanted to before they turned for home. A blue, calm line on the horizon, glittering with dying sunlight.

The sea.

The Sixteenth Day of August 1724

Riccardo gazed into the waters of the Arno from the Ponte Vecchio. It was one year later and once again the day of the Palio dell'Assunta. He did not want to be in Siena on this day, so he had come to Florence on a pilgrimage, leaving Pia in the care of his father. He had wed Pia in the Torre church, handfasting her in the incensed dark, with Domenico as their witness. He'd noticed, as he repeated the vows of the priest, two figures slipping into the church: a lady of middle years wearing a dress of deep red, and a boy who used to wear black and white every day, but now wore the velvets of a little princeling. The boy had his small hand in the lady's, and they looked, to the casual observer, like mother and son.

Riccardo looked down, deep, deep into the water, as if he could part the current and see the river bed, burn with his gaze through the silt and sacking to see the tiny bleached bones of his twin, his brother, the other half of his own heart. If he was grand duke of Tuscany he could have dragged the river with cannon and found that pathetic sack with three stones and a skeleton of a child;

now he would never meet his twin. But as he looked, intently, at his own reflection, another face transposed itself upon his own. A face just like his, but with eyes a little wiser, hair a little blonder. His heart thumped, his flesh chilled, and then he smiled at his own fear, the half-smile he had always thought unique until now. His twin smiled back at him, until a passing grain barge broke the image and his brother returned to the deep.

Riccardo lifted his hand to his throat and pulled off the kerchief of the Torre colours, burgundy and sky-blue, with the blazon of the elephant and castle. Dropping it into the water, he watched it darken, then be pulled beneath, in the same way that a weighted sack had sunk over twenty years before.

He mounted Berio and trotted into the Piazza della Signoria. He tethered the horse to a great iron ring bored into the wall of the palace where he had been born. He did not come to visit Gian Gastone, for the duke had already followed his brother to the Medici mausoleum. Gian Gastone had had little time to enjoy the dukedom he had always craved, and had died in his bed, watching the moon set over Florence, an end far more serene and poetic than his life had been.

But there was someone left. Riccardo had come to see the Last Medici. The inscription on the palace door announced that the grand duchess was holding a public audience. He had Violante to thank for improving his letters, but he no longer read the books in her library, nor sat while she read to him. He stayed away because he knew that she had another to perform this service for.

Zebra, or Pietro, adopted as her ducal ward, was growing up with all the education and privileges Riccardo had missed.

Faustino Caprimulgo had not been so lucky. Shorn of both his heirs, ruined by his betting syndicate, he might have lived a long and bitter life in his shell of a palace. But one day a gift came to the house – a new whip, wrapped in silk, with no direction or note. He left it, for some weeks, on the side table in his empty hall. Then one day, seeking diversion, he took the one broken-down nag left in his rotting stables for a trot in the hills. He sought diversion from his troubles, and no longer had his fine carriage. But the horse was dull and lazy and when the beast hesitated at a narrow gate, he thrashed it furiously and repeatedly with the new whip. The poison that had been soaked into the leather made great ugly, burning weals in the stallion's flank. Maddened with pain, the horse fled down the hillside and threw his rider. Faustino was found with his neck broken in the same place as Vicenzo's.

The shepherd who saw it all, the shepherd who had once given a little boy a jackdaw, the shepherd from the Panther *contrada* who came to tell his captain Raffaello Albani that his plan had worked, said he could have sworn that he heard an eagle crying far above Faustino's body. Raffaello Albani of the Panther *contrada*, apothecary, maker of poisons and father to Egidio Albani, merely nodded.

Today, Riccardo Bruni filed into the Palazzo Vecchio with the good citizens of Florence, noting as he did so that they were numerous, respectful and manifested a sort of muted excitement. He divined that the incumbent was well loved and respected, that her stance of repelling the foreign pretenders to the dukedom, and protecting the treasure trove of the city's art, had endeared her to the public.

In the roped-off gloom of the presence rooms he expected to be able to see her face, but as he filed into the presence chamber all he could see was silver. Everything in the chamber was of that metal or hue, from the duchess's chair to the silver awning above her head: her gown, her looking-glasses, her ornaments. If it were true that this princess of Florence protected all the artworks that her profligate father had sold for relics and her brother for pleasure, then above half of them must be in this room.

He bent to kiss a hand encased in a silver filigree glove and for a moment he met the eyes of Anna Maria Luisa de' Medici, his aunt. She nodded to him, and something, maybe the resemblance to her long-dead, much beloved brother Ferdinando, lifted the corners of her thin mouth in what Riccardo could tell was an unaccustomed smile. He felt in that tiny gesture a fraction of warmth, as if she had bestowed a little grace upon him. As he passed along the line he wished he could give her something, but then, as he descended the stone steps and walked out into the light, he chided himself. He had already given her everything – he had given her the duchy.

Riccardo untethered Berio and walked him round, stepping up on the mounting block worn by generations of Medici princes, by his father Ferdinando as he pursued his princely pastimes, and by his true father Domenico as he set off for Siena with his precious foundling.

As he vaulted on to the saddle his heart was light. Riccardo Bruni turned Berio's head and the Last of the Medici rode out into the west.

∞

La Pia waited for him, as she said she would, under the merciful shadow of the Camollia gate. The sun was setting but was still fierce, and she had to rest a little by leaning against the buttress of the gate, for she was getting heavier by the month. She was not wearing the red and white of the Civetta, nor the yellow and black of the Eagles, nor even the burgundy and blue of her new *contrada*, the Tower. She had chosen a sprigged muslin shift from her mother's wardrobe, tiny flowers on pale cloth, all colours and none. She had chosen the gown because it was loose and flowing, and when she tried it on she saw a panel of extra cloth had been let into the waist. She smoothed the panel down over her great belly, enjoying its significance. Her mother had worn the dress when she carried Pia.

Pia huffed and puffed a little as she straddled her legs to take the weight of her distended womb. She recalled, almost with a pang, how she would never have leaned on a wall a year ago, and smiled a small smile of valediction for her dignity. She had no need of it now.

Besides there was no one about to mark her. There was a hum in the distance, like a great hive of bees, and she lifted her head as the great bell Sunto struck seven. Then a cloud of frighted starlings inked the sky as a great roar of cheering almost lifted the tops off the towers. The Palio had begun.

Pia linked her hands around her stomach to cradle the weight of her enormous, precious burden. She puffed a strand of hair out of her eyes so she could better see; her hair was longer now, curlier. She scanned the horizon under the great red sun for Riccardo, anxious for his return, for she had something to tell him, a delicious secret known only to her and Sister Concetta of the hospital-church of Santa Maria Maddalena, who had visited her this morning. The nun had edged her fingers around Pia's distended belly, then cocked her ear to the bump with a little wooden trumpet, listening in one place, and then another. Listening, listening. Now, Pia pushed her fingers into the swollen bumpy flesh, trying to feel what the sister had felt. Miraculously, the bumps pushed back.

Another great cheer, and the distant race was over for another year. And as if that cheer had brought him into being, she saw a horseman resolve on to the horizon, riding far and fast towards Siena and her arms. She came out of the shadow and into the light. For the last furlong he slid from the saddle and ran to her, enfolding her in his arms. They embraced under the sun. All four of them.

The man, the woman and the twins inside her.

HISTORICAL NOTE

After a long and stable governorship in Siena, VIOLANTE DE' MEDICI retired to the Palazzo Madama in Rome where she lived peacefully for the rest of her life. Her series of proclamations to regulate the Palio are observed to this day and form the rules by which the race is still run in July and August every year.

GIAN GASTONE DE' MEDICI returned to Florence and died there. His tombstone reads 'Sic Transit Gloria Mundi': 'Here pass all the glories of this world'.

His sister ANNA MARIA LUISA, the Last Medici, made a provision in her will to state that all of Florence's great paintings and sculptures would remain in Florence. She is remembered today as the duchess who kept the Medici's greatest legacy safe.

FRANCESCO MARIA CONTI fled to Rome and the protection of his cousin the pope, to offer his services at the court of James Francis Edward Stuart, Old Pretender to the throne of England. Thus Conti embroiled himself in another unsuccessful coup.

The DUKE OF BOURBON was made Gian Gastone's heir to the grand duchy of Tuscany by statute. After all the trials and tribulations of the Medici inheritance, Gian Gastone commented that he had 'got his heir by the stroke of a pen'.

AUTHOR'S NOTE

In 2009, the year in which this book was written, the Palio dell'Assunta of 16 August was won by the Civetta, the Owlet *contrada* of Pia of the Tolomei.

ACKNOWLEDGEMENTS

I very much enjoyed entering the world of horses for this book and talking to those who ride them, own them or just love them.

First, I must mention my sister Veronica and her husband Richard Brown (the real-life Riccardo Bruni!) who own various bits of racehorses through a syndicate and were very helpful in their insights into the world of racing. For the same reason, I'm grateful to Mark Kershaw, one-time MD of both Newbury and Sandown racecourses. I'd like to thank experienced horsewoman and friend Amy Shortt for reading the manuscript for horsey errors, and her father, trainer and breeder Joe McElroy, for pointing me towards the right places for my research. I'm also indebted to Lance Bombardier Dan Richards of the King's Troop in St John's Wood for allowing me access to their barracks and stables, and for giving me invaluable information on the life of an army horse. Thanks too to the farriers of the Troop who kindly allowed me to watch a horseshoe being made. I was lucky enough to visit the stud farm of the Lipizzaners at Lipica, which celebrated its 430th anniversary in 2010. There I was very privileged to see these wonderful horses performing an unforgettable riding display. Thanks must also go to my late grandfather William Donald Hoggarth who first got me interested in horses by letting me watch the racing and placing bets for me on Grand National day!

In other arenas, thanks to Hayley Nebauer, expert film costumier, who was most helpful on the matter of corsets, riding habits and the other accoutrements that had to be tolerated by the poor daughters of Siena in the eighteenth century, and also to hair and make-up artist Lorraine Hill who filled me in on the matter of wigs and early hair dyes.

Happily my research took me to Siena, and I would like to thank both the Comune of Siena and the separate *contrade* who were most welcoming and helpful, both to me personally on my visits there and through their excellent archives and related websites, which are mines of information. My apologies to the Eagle *contrada* who never had a family as evil as the Caprimulgi to darken their history, and my apologies, too, to the true victors of the 1723 Palio, who had to be nudged into second place for the purposes of this story.

It's not often that I find myself acknowledging a film in the course of writing a novel, but the award-winning documentary *The Last Victory* (2004), directed by John Appel, which follows the residents of the Civetta *contrada* in the days before the 2003 Palio, offered me the greatest single insight into the power and the passion of this legendary race.

As always I must thank my brilliant agent Teresa Chris, and also the wonderful team at my new home John Murray, especially Kate Parkin for her editing skills, Celia Levett for helping me clamber out of a number of plot holes, and Caroline Westmore for managing the whole project so ably.

Most of all my thanks go, as ever, to Sacha for his constant support and advice, and to Conrad and Ruby who had more than a little to contribute to the character of Zebra.

And last, but not least, I would like to thank Sienna Sewell, a very inspirational little girl, whose name once gave me an idea.

THE DAUGHTER OF SIENA

by Marina Fiorato

A
Reading
Group Gold
Selection

For more reading group suggestions,
visit www.readinggroupgold.com.

ST. MARTIN'S GRIFFIN

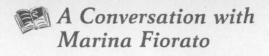
A Conversation with
Marina Fiorato

This is your third novel set in Italy. Your first, *The Glassblower of Murano*, took place in Venice; *The Botticelli Secret*, Tuscany; and this one, Siena. What led you to this city? And why did you want to write about it?

Siena is a fascinating city, which, before writing this novel, I'd only visited in passing. What's interesting about it is that when you actually stay there and get to know it, rather than visit on a day trip, you realize that it is a complete little world of its own—a microcosm of a larger society and the world outside. *The Daughter of Siena* reflects all the political and social tensions that were going on in the city, in Italy, and in society at large at the time. It deals with tensions between classes and tensions between royalty and republic, as well as love between man and woman, parent and child, horse and rider, and love for one's city. The unique way that Siena is organized—small city wards known as *contrade* with their animal symbols and fierce loyalties—means that each area behaves as a little nation, with alliances giving way to wars and then periods of peace. And all of these tensions come to a head twice a year, at the famous Palio horse race.

How, if at all, was the process of writing *The Daughter of Siena* different from your other novels? Did you do a lot of research about the Palio? And, in crafting your story, did you stick to historical fact? Or did you take artistic liberties?

I did a lot of research into the Palio in particular and horses in general. Although I visited Siena, of course, I also did a lot of research into horses in England, not in an intellectual sense, but in a hands-on way. I got to know my neighbor's ponies, went to horse races, and learned much more about these fascinating creatures. The research for this book was therefore much more practical than before: I got my hands dirty in the stable! As far as fact versus fiction goes, I always try to be historically accurate, broadly speaking. But as I'm writing a work of fiction, rather than a historical tract, sometimes I will bend the truth in the cause of a good story, or dramatize certain events.

Your depictions of the Palio horse races are heart-pounding. What about riding horses or attending horse races inspired you?

One of the things that struck me about the Palio and horse races that I attended in England was the fact that you could actually feel the thunder of the race in your chest as the runners go past. This singular sensation, that it's a physical experience for the watchers, gave me the most insight into the excitement of the race. Of course, if you add into the mix that you may have put a bet on a horse, or that you might care very deeply about one of the riders as Pia and Violante do, it becomes a financial, mental, and emotional experience too. It's completely holistic. I used to ride as a child, and still do when I get the chance. I'm drawn to it because it's so essentially historical. Whatever the modern changes in tack or saddlery, the fact is that riding—the relationship between horse and rider—has gone unchanged for thousands of years. That connection with the past is very beguiling to me.

How much—or how little—are you like Pia? Did you find inspiration for her character, or her story, anywhere in your own life?

Well, I certainly wasn't sold into an arranged marriage and I've never suffered in the ways she has! But I admire—and aspire to achieve—her spirit, and hope that I would show the same ingenuity and "gumption" in circumventing her circumstances. She can be quite impulsive though, whereas I'm a bit more calculating!

You once wrote that "when [you] open a historical novel [you're] taking a trip to a different land." Do you do a lot of traveling? Do you have any fantasy vacations in mind that you'd like to take? Or places you'd like to visit . . . and write about someday?

I do a fair bit of traveling for research that gives me the pleasure of going to Italy about twice a year. This year I also went to Zagreb for a literary conference and look forward to going back to Croatia this summer, this time to the coast. But my next book is partly set in Istanbul so I'm slowly edging to points farther east—the relationship between Byzantium and Venice has always fascinated me and I'm looking forward to discovering more about it.

Marina Fiorato

Marina with her children, Conrad and Ruby, at Venice's Palazzo del Popolo

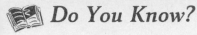 ## Do You Know?

There used to be twenty-three *contrade* instead of seventeen. In the sixteenth century, the *contrade* of the Viper, Strongsword, Cock, Oak-Tree, Lion, and Bear were suppressed for sedition and violence.

The entire Palio race takes only seventy seconds.

Horses can win the Palio without a rider. This is called riding *scosso*.

Riccardo Bruni was named after Richard Brown, Marina's brother-in-law, who's a keen horseman and racehorse owner.

The Tower *contrade* connects Riccardo with the character of Brother Guido from *The Botticelli Secret*, who was from Pisa and named della Torre.

Marina has included the "lucky totem" of a giraffe in all of her novels. In *The Daugher of Siena*, one of Siena's seventeen *contrade* is called Giraffa, and the animal is its emblem.

Behind the Novel

📖 Recommended Reading

The Flambards Trilogy, K. M. Peyton

Starting at the beginning . . . my interest in horses really began with this series. The trilogy is actually for young adults, but it is a wonderful trio of books about English heiress Christina Parsons growing up just before and during World War I. In the first book, the orphaned Christina moves to the eponymous *Flambards,* a crumbling mansion that is home to the all-male, horse-mad Russell family. The scenes where the groom, Dick, teaches Christina to ride are beautifully written and insightful. In the third book, *Flambards in Summer,* the newly widowed Christina returns to the house and makes it live again through the stables. She buys a damaged warhorse, Argus Pheasant, whom she rehabilitates, and through him, heals herself.

Airs Above the Ground, Mary Stewart

A wonderful adventure novel about the world of the peerless Lipizzaner stallions. Vanessa March travels to Austria as a chaperone for a young friend and is soon embroiled in a world of espionage that seems to somehow involve her absent husband. This novel benefits from the wonderful settings of Tyrolean villages and Gothic castles, a good dollop of romance, spies, missing jewels, a traveling circus, and, at the center of it all, a mythical horse who is not quite what he seems.

Summer's Lease, John Mortimer

No horses in this one but this is a great novel stuffed with the wit of John Mortimer. An English family take a villa near Siena for the summer holiday. While there they are forced to examine their own family relationships, thrown into sharp relief by the presence of mischievous patriarch Haverford Downs. They mix with their eccentric neighbors, battle with the intrac-

table Italian plumbing, and take a trip into Siena to watch the Palio. At the heart of this social comedy in this matchless setting is a mystery: who is their secretive landlord, and where on earth is he?

Riders, Jilly Cooper

Light as air but shamelessly engaging, Jilly Cooper's novel about the world of show jumping deals with the rivalry between orphaned Gypsy Jake Lovell and privileged sprig of nobility Rupert Campbell-Black. The two men compete for precedence on the show-jumping circuit and for the love of the same woman. Underneath the froth is some razor-sharp social commentary about England in the '80s as well as incredibly detailed knowledge of the horse world.

The Raphael Affair, Iain Pears

Art-theft officer Flavia di Stefano becomes embroiled in the mystery of a recovered painting that may or may not be a lost Raphael. In the process she becomes drawn to English art dealer Jonathan Argyll; but is he the real thing or a common thief? Including some fascinating insights into the art world, *The Raphael Affair* culminates in Siena itself, involving a nail-biting denouement on the tower of the Palazzo Pubblico.

Enquiry, Dick Francis

It's hard to single out one novel from the master of racehorse writing, but *Enquiry* is one of my favorites. Jockey Kelly Hughes is labeled a cheat by a Steward's enquiry and the racing establishment seems to be trying to shut him out. It is up to him to take matters into his own hands and clear his name, revealing a seam of corruption that is deeper and more pervasive than he could ever have imagined. Francis's novel gives great insight into the rules and regulations of the British racing scene.

Reading Group Questions

1. Siena is a small city in which local loyalties matter most above all. How easy do you think it would have been to keep secrets? You may wish to discuss your own hometowns—and/or scandals within your communities—as well.

2. Pia is valuable to her father only as a bargaining tool. How does she assert her own independence? In what ways is she a "woman ahead of her time?" What does that definition mean to you?

3. Riccardo, the son of an ostler, behaves with instinctive grace. Discuss nobility in the context of the story. How is it personified?

4. Do you think Riccardo was right to reject his inheritance? Why? And: what would *you* have done?

5. Pia wears Cleopatra's coin around her neck. What is the significance of this charm? What other important artifacts, symbols, or talismans can be found in the book—and what do they mean to the beholder?

6. Discuss the role of the church in the story. How does it influence each of the characters in terms of belief and behavior?

7. To what extent has Violante become reconciled to her husband's homosexuality by the end of the book? How would this story play out in a modern setting?

8. What changes Violante from a passive woman to a woman of bravery and determination? Again, take a moment to envision her in the world today. Would she be considered a feminist? Would *she* consider herself one?

9. How have Gian Gastone's expectations corrupted his character? Also, does this make him a more *interesting* character, in terms of your reading experience?

10. There is an absence of mothers in the story but many fathers throughout. Do we, as readers, judge the fathers' actions more or less harshly because of this gender imbalance? You may also wish to imagine the roles of some of the missing mothers in this novel. How might their offspring have turned out if they had been on the scene?

11. How does the art and architecture of the city support Violante as a ruler? How is the city of Siena a character in and of itself?

12. Discuss the equine "characters"—the donkey, Berio, Leocorno—in this novel. How does the author bring them to life for the reader? Moreover, how do they reflect the struggles of their human counterparts?